Anything
Could Happen

Lucy Diamond

Anything Could Happen

QUERCUS

First published in Great Britain in 2021 by

QUERCUS

Quercus Editions Ltd
Carmelite House
50 Victoria Embankment
London EC4Y 0DZ

An Hachette UK company

A CIP catalogue record for this book is available
from the British Library

HB ISBN 978 1 52941 960 3
TPB ISBN 978 1 52941 961 0

10 9 8 7 6 5 4 3 2 1

Typeset by CC Book Production
Printed and bound in Great Britain by Clays Ltd, Elcograf S.p.A.

MIX
Paper from
responsible sources
FSC® C104740
www.fsc.org

Papers used by Quercus Editions Ltd. are from well-managed forests and other responsible sources.

For Hannah, Tom and Holly
I hope that all the good things happen for you

Prologue

All those years ago

Even the next morning, when the two of them might both have been self-conscious and hungover, Lara still felt exactly the same as she had the night before – as if she had stepped into a new and better life. With him. Light-headed from happiness and lack of sleep, she made coffee and had just enough bread left for them to have a slice of toast each, and then they sat in bed together, bare legs entwined, sleepy and content, not saying much. Friday morning, and she was due at work before long, despite his attempts to persuade her to skive off.

'But I'm free this evening?' she suggested shyly. 'If you are too.'

'Definitely,' he said. 'Let me find us somewhere stunning to meet, so that we can celebrate a whole twenty-four hours of knowing each other.' He reached over to grab her New York guidebook from the bedside table and began flipping through its pages. 'Hey, how about Grand Central Station?' he suggested. 'We can pretend we're in a movie and run towards each other, like long-lost lovers.'

1

'I'm up for that,' she said, trying and failing to hide how pleased his words made her feel. *Long-lost lovers!* So this was going to be a thing then, the two of them; a proper, wonderful thing, she thought joyfully. It was as if every other event in her life had led up to this precise moment: the pair of them lolling on her crumpled sheets making plans for that evening, a shaft of warm June sunlight falling through the broken blind and leaving a golden splash on his bare shoulder, the smell of slightly scorched toast in the air. Each tiny decision and step and turn she'd ever taken had brought her all the way through the long, winding maze that was her previous twenty-six years to this exact time and place. She'd only just met him and already he felt like everything: a door opening to her future that was suddenly full of bright, shiny colours. Her New York experience was bursting from its tight chrysalis there and then, on the verge of shaking loose its wings into the best summer of her life. 'Although ... the station's presumably massive, right?' she pointed out. 'How will we find each other?'

'Good question,' he said, running a finger down the page. He even had nice *fingers*, she thought dreamily, wondering if he played the piano or guitar. How could you feel so sure of another person, when in reality there was so much you didn't know? 'Okay, there's a very posh oyster bar downstairs apparently,' he went on. 'How about meeting outside that? Six-thirty? Look how fancy it is,' he added, showing her a picture. 'I'm not sure I can run to actually going *inside* it, but we could pretend for a moment that we live that sort of life. Before moving on somewhere more in keeping with our pitiful budgets. What do you think?'

'Wow,' she said, leaning against his arm to see the page. His skin was honey-coloured and he smelled faintly of soap and coffee. 'Nice. Six-thirty sounds perfect. I think I can just about make it till then without you.'

He grinned at her, his cheekbones catching the soft morning light, his dark hair tousled. Had she appreciated quite how good-looking he was last night? How generous his mouth, how beautiful his eyes; how, when he smiled like that, it took her breath away? She could feel herself becoming intoxicated by him all over again from his sheer closeness, the warmth of his body, and the instinct to touch him was so strong, she found herself reaching over to brush a stray toast crumb off his cheek.

'Thank you,' he said. 'See? Yet another reason why I'm better off with you in my life.'

She laughed, knowing he was exaggerating, but somehow the words felt right nonetheless. Then she peeled herself reluctantly away. 'I wish I didn't have to go to work,' she groaned, sorting through the scant contents of her wardrobe and wondering if her flatmate Toni had any nice tops she could borrow. It felt like a day for wearing something eye-catching, for alerting the rest of the world to the fact that delight was spilling from her like an overflowing fountain.

He stood up, buttoning his shirt. 'I too wish you didn't,' he said. 'Last night was seriously one of the best nights of my life. I feel as if everything has changed, don't you?' He glanced over at her as if his tender words had left him feeling vulnerable.

'Yes,' she said. 'I know what you mean.'

'But I'll see you in ...' He screwed up his face, making calculations as he pulled on his jeans. 'Ten and a half hours? The countdown starts now.'

They kissed again, even though neither of them had brushed their teeth, and held each other close. She could feel his heart beating through his soft rumpled shirt. She liked him so much, she thought dazedly. She really, really liked him. He hadn't even left the flat, and already she could feel the ache of his potential absence starting to form; a delicious, tormented pain at the prospect of missing him. Of course, if she'd known then what was to happen later, she wouldn't have let him out the door at all, she'd have phoned in sick and led him back to bed by his shirt collar. But instead . . .

'See you later, Lara,' he said, and let himself out.

Part One
SPRING

Chapter One

Eliza was sitting on the wall, the hedge behind her prickling through her jacket, when a grubby white van slowed to a stop nearby. Right on time. A flurry of nerves whirled up inside her like a shaken snow globe on seeing the van's logo: *Steve Pickering, Painting and Decorating.* The lettering was crummy and basic-looking, like something stencilled from a cheap kit. The P of Pickering was even wonky, as if the person applying the letter had coughed in the middle, or lost concentration. She allowed herself a scornful lip curl. If she ever started up her own decorating business – or any business for that matter – you could bet she would at least put *some* effort into her branding. Eliza Spencer Magnificent Transformations, she could market herself. Or maybe ... She rummaged through every paint-inspired pun at her disposal. Brush Hour? she considered, wrinkling her nose. Fifty Shades of Great?

Whatever. Right now, she had other, more pressing items on her agenda. Number one: the puffy-faced man with a sparse thatch of reddish-brown hair and low-slung paunch currently clambering down from the van, as shambling as a bear emerging from a cave, post-hibernation.

A bold new chapter in your life begins today, Eliza's horoscope app had encouraged her that morning, and the words came back to her now. Here goes, she thought, jumping off the wall.

'Hi,' she said coolly, taking in the stain on his faded T-shirt and the ancient trainers flecked with paint. So he was a slob as well as a terrible person, she thought in disapproval. When she was a proper grown-up with a job and everything, there was no way she would ever dream of leaving the house looking so unkempt. She'd been in the Co-op the other day when a woman had walked in wearing a dressing gown, with tangled bed hair. What was wrong with people?

'I'm your two o'clock,' she said now. And then, because she couldn't help herself, she blurted out, 'Remember me?'

His pudgy face creased in a frown, then he glanced down at his phone before looking uncertainly back at her. 'Mrs Robinson?' he said. You could almost hear the cogs grinding in his brain with painful slowness. Is she even old enough? he'd be thinking. What am I missing here?

Eliza folded her arms across her chest and tapped her foot. Come on, Steve, make the connection, she thought. You can do it.

'You asked me to quote for . . .' he said, followed by another swift check of his phone, renewed doubt in his eyes. Apparently basic logic was still beyond his means. 'A kitchen redecoration?'

Eliza snorted sarcastically, louder than was necessary, in an attempt to cover up precisely how crushed his blankness had left her. Despite everything. When she should have known better. Because he clearly didn't remember her at all, unless his gormlessness was merely an act of cruelty. Her insides felt newly hollowed out; she was an avocado with the flesh scooped clean away. 'Yeah, I did, didn't I?' she replied, deadpan. Still nothing.

He hesitated, then gestured at the house. 'Er . . . Shall we go in, then?'

'No,' she said impatiently, and then her muddled feelings gave way to facetiousness because it seemed to be all she had left. 'Let's not. Because I don't live there and we probably shouldn't go breaking and entering. Not on a Thursday, anyway.' Her own home was twenty miles away in Scarborough; her journey had involved two buses and a walk up from the bus station, plus a lie to her mum that morning about a migraine, so that she could have time off school. And now here she was, standing in front of a smart semi-detached house just outside Whitby, her heart thumping while Steve Pickering gazed at her in confusion. She was starting to wish she hadn't bothered.

Dejection took hold and she sighed. Even after so many years, she'd hoped there might be at least a *flicker* of recognition. Blood calling to blood. 'I'm not Mrs Robinson,' she said through clenched teeth, because clearly she would have to spell this out to him. 'I'm Eliza. Eliza Spencer. Your daughter.'

A flash of pure astonishment crossed his face, then he blinked several times before he looked at her with a new, unreadable expression. Fondness or regret? Horror? Eliza wondered, hardly able to breathe as they stood staring at one another for an intense, heart-pounding moment.

'Eliza, hey?' he said eventually. 'Wow. Look at you. You must be – what, seventeen now?' He shook his head. 'Wow,' he said again, as if that was all he could come up with.

She rolled her eyes, fists curled so tightly that on the bus ride home, she'd find crescent-moon imprints gouged in her palms from her fingernails. For crying out loud. Was that it? He was *hopeless*. An abomination of a man. Could he make it any more obvious that he didn't care? 'Eighteen,' she replied crisply. 'An adult. And I arranged this because I want some answers. I need some answers, all right? *Dad,*' she added, for good measure.

Was it her imagination or did the name make him cringe momentarily? His wide shoulders slumped and he stared down at the pavement for a long few seconds. The wind blew in Eliza's face, cold and spiteful, and she felt her eyes begin to water. Great. Now it would look as if she was crying, she thought, furiously wiping them with her jacket sleeve. At last he lifted his head and spoke. 'Listen, we should probably talk about this inside,' he said gruffly, with another miserable glance over at the house.

'I don't live there!' Eliza repeated, throwing up her hands in annoyance. God, was he completely thick, as well? How many times did she have to tell him? Although he had a point, she conceded grudgingly in the next second. Nobody wanted to air their dirty laundry in public. 'We could sit in your van though,' she suggested after a beat of silence. 'If you're that embarrassed about talking to me out here.'

He hesitated, running a hand through his hair. It needed a cut, she noticed, feeling more and more contempt for him with every minute. He was pathetic! Mum was right, they were definitely better off without him. It was rubbish being related to someone like Steve Pickering, now that she had seen for herself exactly how weak and shabby he was.

'Look, Eliza,' he said, then stopped again. He seemed to be having some kind of internal wrestling match about what to do. 'I'm not sure there's much point us having this conversation,' he went on eventually, his voice so gentle it seemed impossible that he could be saying these horrific words aloud.

Fury burst up in Eliza, consuming her entirely. 'Well, what a fucking surprise,' she snapped, glaring at him with such hatred she almost believed she could scorch him with it, given long enough. Blow up his van too, while she was at it. Set the privet hedge alight with crackling flames. 'And there was me hoping we could both be adults about this. Start again. Attempt some kind of connection, like two human beings, but—'

'Eliza, stop,' he said, then rubbed his face, seeming exasperated. Possibly even sad, on a closer look. She could hear the bristles rasping on his chin now that the breeze had dropped. 'She hasn't told you, has she? She's never actually told you.'

That brought Eliza up short. 'Told me what?'

'That . . .' His shoulders sank again. He could barely look at her, glancing instead over at his badly painted van. 'On second thoughts, yes, let's sit in the van. Have a proper chat, rather than—'

'Just tell me,' she broke in, unable to bear stringing this out any longer. 'Please. Whatever it is.'

'Okay,' he said heavily. 'Well . . . bottom line is, I'm not your dad. That's why we broke up, me and her. All right? I'm sorry, love,' he added, his brown eyes moist all of a sudden. 'I was devastated. Because . . . you know.' His voice had become gruff. 'Because I really liked being your dad. But . . .'

She blinked because his words were hitting her belatedly. *I'm not your dad. All right?* No, she was not all right. Each word was like a sledgehammer, battering the breath from her lungs. 'You're not . . .' she croaked before breaking off. 'Well, who is, then? Who is my dad?'

There was an air of apology, even mournfulness, about his shrug. 'I'm not sure, Eliza. Sorry,' he said again. 'You'll have to ask your mum. I've got no idea.'

She scowled at him with new ferocity because what he was

saying couldn't possibly be true. It simply couldn't. 'I don't believe you,' she said. 'God! Even now you still can't be honest. You can't admit that you've been a total shit to me *and* to her.' She wheeled around on the spot, partly to avoid letting him see the hot tears that had suddenly swelled in her eyes. 'Well, sod off, then. We don't care. We don't need you anyway!'

Marching away, something seemed to crack inside her. The hopeful buoyancy that had propelled her this far crumbled abruptly to rubble, leaving a paralysing disquiet in its place. It couldn't be true, could it, what he'd said? Because who even *was* she, if not the daughter of Steve Pickering? What did this mean?

'Hey!'

His shout took her by surprise and she stopped dead on the pavement. He was back in his van and had pulled up beside her, leaning out of the window. Her heart galloped, her hands squeezing into tight knots of expectation. 'What?'

He looked cross now. 'Is it you who's been leaving me all those made-up reviews, by the way?'

Eliza rubbed her eyes, trying to dash away the tears. 'I don't know what you're talking about,' she managed to reply, nose in the air.

'I think you do,' he said. 'And I'd appreciate it if you could take them down. It's not a game, all right? I've done nothing wrong. Ask your mum if you don't believe me.'

He drove away, leaving her standing there shaken, unable to breathe momentarily, the very ground seeming to shudder and fracture beneath her feet. His van disappeared around the corner and she was alone. She felt as if she were an image on a computer screen, disintegrating into pixels before reforming in a new, unknown shape; her old self gone, invalidated. But who remained?

The wind rushed around her again, tugging at her long chestnut hair, and she shoved her hands in her pockets, bowed her head and began walking back to the bus stop. One last tear dripped from her chin on to the pavement and she gave an angry sniff. She had come here hoping for answers but had been left facing more questions than ever. So now what?

Chapter Two

While her daughter fumed tearfully on the bus back from Whitby, Lara Spencer was at work, sitting as usual in the passenger seat of her dual-control car, as one student after another stalled the engine, crunched the gears or, if she was lucky, pootled slowly and without incident around the quiet backstreets of Scarborough. When she'd initially trained to be a driving instructor, she had optimistically imagined herself jaunting about all over the place, but in truth, she tended to patrol the same old suburban estates week in, week out. Driving for a living but never actually getting anywhere, endless three-point turns in silent cul-de-sacs: that was about the sum of Lara's life, really. But look, it paid the mortgage, it meant she could keep herself and Eliza warm and fed, and that was all that mattered. Right?

On this particular Thursday afternoon, eighteen-year-old Jake Watson was having his lesson and he was always entertaining company, if sometimes eccentric. 'Have you ever, like, tried to kill someone with your eyes?' he asked, midway round a roundabout, as if to confirm Lara's private opinion of him.

'Indicate left now,' she replied. 'Next exit. That's it.' She waited until he was safely through the junction before returning to his inquiry. 'Say that again. You were asking me about, er, killing people? With my eyes?'

'Yeah,' he said, jerkily changing gear from second to third. 'You know, by really staring at them? Like this—'

'Eyes on the road, Jake,' she said automatically as he swung his head towards her, presumably to demonstrate. Christ, a death glare was the last thing you wanted when you were trying to teach a young person how to operate a heavy piece of machinery moving at thirty miles an hour. 'Concentrate on what you're doing. Check your mirror. Look – the car behind you is overtaking.'

He tutted. 'Someone's in a hurry,' he said, sounding more like a critical fifty-something than a teenager. 'Idiot's breaking the speed limit, too.'

She hid a smile at his self-righteous tone. 'Thank goodness you're far too sensible a driver to even think about doing such a thing.'

'I know, right? Anyway – have you?'

'What, tried to kill someone by staring at them? No,' she said firmly. Amusement rose in her nonetheless. This was what she knew of Jake Watson so far: he lived in a pleasant street of 50s-built bungalows where people tended their front gardens and kept their cars gleaming. His mum sometimes waved him off from the doorway and on more than one occasion had been wearing an apron, indicating a bout of pastry-making or some other domestic goddessery. So far, so pedestrian – and yet here he was now, asking her innocently, startlingly, about killing people. Despite her instinct that this could be straying into inappropriate conversational realms, she was intrigued enough that it was impossible not to ask, 'Why, have you?'

He shrugged. 'I mean, I gave my French teacher a seizure with a look, back in Year 10, so ... you know. Kind of, I guess. It was pretty bad.'

'Gosh.' Lara gently took the wheel where he was starting to drift across the central road markings. 'Stay in lane,' she said, guiding him back. 'Let's try not to kill anyone today, eh?'

He made a pleased sort of sound through his nostrils. Heavens, he was adorable, she thought to herself. She especially liked the kooky kids she came across, the ones who were so themselves, so other to the rest of the crowd. She couldn't help wondering how the saintly, apron-wearing Mrs Watson dealt with such conversations though. 'How's college going?' she asked now in order to change the subject. 'What are your plans for next year?'

This was one thing about teaching teenagers that she loved: the fact that they all had their big life hopes glittering like beacons ahead of them. They talked to her about university applications, about apprenticeships, applying for jobs and training courses. Some shyly mentioned boyfriends and girlfriends; one boy a few years ago had come out to her before he'd even told his parents. Of course, it wasn't all dreams and wishes – there were painful situations, too; she'd noticed what looked like self-inflicted cuts on more than one student's arm and had wondered with anguish what misery must lurk in the shadows of their lives. Others poured out their sadnesses to her: first relationships faltering, parents separating, exam stress and disappointments. Last year, there had also been one girl, Romilly, who'd become thinner and thinner with each passing week, until she'd eventually passed out at the wheel, weak from starving herself for so long. She'd had to stop lessons and Lara hadn't heard from her since.

For students undergoing such difficult times, she consoled

herself that she was at least teaching them a valuable life skill, one that could make a real, practical difference to their lives. On the whole, it was hard not to become very fond of most of her clients; she adored their general resilience and spirit.

Take Jake, for instance. Here he was, telling her enthusiastically of his plans to study marine biology, followed by a tub-thumping sermon on the joys of fish. 'I mean, people think that fish are just, like, *cold*, right? That they don't have any feelings or much of a brain. But they're so *interesting*,' he said, accelerating triumphantly out of a successful three-point turn.

'I'll take your word for it,' Lara replied, smiling to herself. She felt a small stab of envy though, as she often did when hearing about her students' aspirations – especially as becoming a driving instructor had definitely not been a career ambition back when she was a teenager. Her dreams then had been of escaping her quiet Cumbrian town for the bright lights of London, becoming a journalist, working in busy, gossipy offices full of interesting twenty-somethings, wearing black, having excellent hair and drinking red wine in bohemian bars. And, to be fair, for a number of years, she'd managed all of those things, and more. Until—

A siren was wailing behind them, an ambulance with its blue lights flashing. 'Okay, slow down, move over to the left, you need to give way,' she instructed Jake.

'The feds are coming for me!' he cried, forgetting to slow down in his thrill as he flung the car over.

'Foot on the brake,' she said as the ambulance loomed in her rear-view mirror, its siren in crescendo. 'Brake!' She had to stamp on her own brake pedal, jerking the car to a stop as the other vehicle hurtled past, resisting the urge to cross herself, like her mother always did whenever she saw an ambulance or funeral procession. Lara wasn't all that superstitious but she knew that life could surprise you, and not always in a good way.

'Sorry,' said Jake, chastened.

'And we call them "police" in this country anyway,' she teased as he recovered himself. 'Or actually, if it says "ambulance" across the top of the vehicle in big letters, "paramedics". Okay, straighten up and let's go again.'

They were trundling around the northern outskirts of Scarborough, the town that had been home to Lara and Eliza for the last eighteen years. She'd moved here amidst a flurry of big life changes; leaving her job and her small shared flat in North London five months' pregnant, in order to make a new, fingers-crossed start with Steve. Since then, life had taken a slower turn and she'd settled into the place, loving its big skies, sandy beaches and old-fashioned seafront. Unable to pursue her fashion journalist career here – at the time of moving, the internet was still in its infancy and the scene very much London-centric – she had trained as a driving instructor as a stop-gap role, plucking the notion pretty randomly from the air when her relationship fell apart and single motherhood demanded back-up plans. What else could she do, besides write about the season's new hemlines and trouser styles? Drive. That was about it. Okay, she'd thought, signing up for a course – she would give it a whirl as an interim measure, then return to journalism once the dust had settled. Somehow or other though, fifteen years later, here she was, still booking lessons and arranging tests, motoring up and down the same roads, as the sun went on rising and setting, and the seasons wheeled slowly around her. It was early spring now, with its heavy rain showers and fresh winds; the time of year when every student of hers familiarised themselves with the windscreen wipers pretty quickly.

'How are you ever going to meet a new man, though, teaching teenagers to drive all day?' her best friend Heidi tutted now and then, and it was true, Lara did spend most of her time with young people, the small confines of the car scented with their cheap perfumes and hair products. There was no flirty office banter when you were a driving instructor, no watercooler chat with attractive colleagues to get your pulse racing. How did other people meet their soulmates anyway? It all seemed so random. Heidi, for instance, had got chatting to her now-husband Jim purely by chance when they'd been given seats next to each other at a Violent Femmes gig twenty years ago. Lara's brother Richie had met *his* husband Jordan at a bus stop in Sheffield following a train cancellation; these days they lived in Auckland together and had recently celebrated their tenth wedding anniversary. To think that such perfect couples had only met because they had been allocated certain tickets from a concert venue or were meant to be catching a particular train . . . it blew Lara's mind, actually, to think that these paths could so easily never have crossed at all. And what if you *had* met your soulmate, only to have lost them almost immediately? Maybe it was better not to dwell on that.

She found herself thinking about Jake and his love of marine biology as she made her way home at the end of the day. He'd told her about a phenomenon called 'mouth-brooding', where certain species of fish incubated their eggs in their mouths, which often meant the parent fish not being able to eat, presumably for fear of swallowing their own offspring. The sacrifices made by parents – humans and fish alike! She wondered how it must feel when the parent fish eventually dared release their young, in the hope that they could survive alone, swim safely away. Then she

19

gave a hollow laugh, recognising her own projection. No surprises where that particular train of thought was coming from. This autumn, exam results permitting, her daughter Eliza would be heading off to university and leaving her mother behind. While Lara was excited for her that the world was about to open up so thrillingly, she couldn't deny that she also felt a stomach-turning dread at the prospect of being completely alone for the first time in years. Sometimes in the dead of the night she lay awake, the same old questions looping around her mind. What would she do to fill the evenings and weekends? How would she manage in a silent, empty house, with no one to chat to about the day, to laugh with, groan over trashy TV, nag about leaving wet towels on the bathroom floor for the millionth time? She thought again of her mum, who allotted different chores to each day of the week so that she always had 'something to look forward to'. This was not a future Lara wanted for herself. But how else should she fill the absence Eliza would leave? Who *was* she, without her child?

'Hi love,' she called, letting herself in to their small semi, a mile or so out of town. Up on the hill, there was a sea view from the bathroom window if you leaned out far enough, and a sky full of swooping gulls. Tonight she was greeted by a thud of loud music from upstairs – presumably this meant Eliza's migraine had abated. 'I'm home!' Lara shouted, but no reply came.

Ah well. She'd make a start on dinner. Eliza babysat every Thursday evening for the Partridges, three doors down, so there wasn't much time to cook anything elaborate, just some noodles and a stir-fry, she decided. She made a fuss of the cat, then washed her hands, switched on the radio and began chopping an onion. The news was being read and she frowned as she heard one story about a sinkhole in China, where a busy road junction had just cratered out of sight with no warning. Fifty metres deep, the newsreader said in sober tones. An entire bus and several other vehicles had been swallowed up, with the number of casualties unconfirmed as yet.

It gave her pause, her hand momentarily still on the knife, as she tried to imagine how it would feel to have the road suddenly collapse like that. Would you even have time to process what was happening as you plunged into the crevasse? Would you pray, scream, clutch at the person next to you on the bus seat? She visualised the terrible crash of impact, followed by the moments of stunned silence immediately afterwards, the startled cries of birds as they scattered above the scene.

Shuddering, she resumed chopping, only for Eliza to burst into the room, looking stormy. 'Hi,' Lara said, taken aback. 'Is everything okay?'

The question was met by a disdainful snort. 'Is everything okay, she says,' Eliza commented sardonically to the air around her as if a vast TV studio audience were hanging on her every word. 'Well, no, actually, everything is not okay, *Mother.* Starting with you, lying to me – that's *really* not okay.'

Lying? This didn't sound like the preamble to a standard moan about missing tights or Lara having failed to iron a top she'd promised to. 'What do you mean?' she asked, plucking a clove of garlic and peeling off its papery outer layer.

'I didn't have a migraine today,' Eliza announced. 'I had a little day trip out instead, all by myself. Want to guess where I went?'

Lara put the garlic down and stared blankly at her. She had no idea where this was heading. 'Why don't you just tell me?' she suggested.

'I went to Whitby,' the girl said, pacing across the floor, ponytail swinging behind her, fists clenched. 'I saw *Dad*. Or should I say Steve?'

Okay, so this was unexpected. And alarming too. Why was Eliza calling him Steve? Did this mean . . . ? 'What—?' she began but her daughter was already speaking over her.

'Because he's not my dad, is he? He told me, so you can drop the act now.' Eliza's voice shook with emotion, her wide grey eyes full of accusation. 'Have you any idea how embarrassing that was, by the way? That he had to tell me, in the middle of the street, that he wasn't really my dad? Can you even *imagine* how I felt at that moment?'

Lara had to put both hands down on the worktop because here was her own personal sinkhole, weakening the ground beneath her, threatening to drag her down. The secret she had buried for so long, and so carefully, now exposed to the open air for the first time in years. Her breath seemed to seize in her lungs. 'I'm sorry,' she managed to say. 'That must have been horrible.'

'Oh, you think?' Eliza's sarcasm was belied by the fact that her face was turning red, just as it always had when she was a small girl and trying not to cry. It pained Lara to register this. 'Correct! It *was* horrible. It was fucking awful, Mum!'

Lara gulped. 'I'm really sorry,' she said again, aware of how weak the words sounded, how woefully inadequate.

'Well, guess what, that's not good enough,' Eliza retaliated. She was Lara's height, five foot six, and stood opposite her, bristling with such ferocity that Lara took a step back. 'You can't apologise your way out of this one. You let me think Steve was my dad – and that he didn't care enough to have anything to do with me. You let me *think* that, even though it's not true. That's really shitty, Mum. That is just . . . *wrong*.'

Lara closed her eyes briefly, wishing there was something she could say to turn the situation round, an explanation she could produce that might make this better. But there was nothing. Because it *was* shitty. It *was* wrong. She'd always had to live with that knowledge. 'I—'

'Don't say you're sorry again because I don't want to hear it. I'm not interested in you being sorry.' Hatred was practically radiating out from Eliza's pores and it pierced Lara to her very marrow. 'I'm just so … hurt. You know? So fucking hurt that you have been lying to me all this time. I thought you were better than that!'

The words stung like a slapped face. Lara's hands trembled so violently she had to clutch them together. She didn't know what to say other than sorry, but if she dared bleat that out for a third time, her daughter's anger might become incandescent. But how could she explain? 'It didn't start as a lie,' she mumbled, her face flooding with heat.

Eliza stared at her, allowing the words to hang between them. 'It didn't *start* as a *lie*?' she repeated. 'What the hell does that even mean?'

Lara dropped her gaze to the scuffed lino floor. It meant that, all those years ago, when she'd told Steve she was pregnant and he'd assumed the baby was his, she had kept silent when a more honest person would have corrected him with a 'might be'. She had agonised over the omission, truly grappling with the ethics of the dilemma, but at the time she'd had very few choices. Steve had effectively been offering to rescue her from a difficult situation; he was a decent, steady bloke, trying to be responsible. Sure, had things been different, he'd have remained merely a drunken, consoling encounter during a bad patch and nothing more; she never would have bothered seeing him again. This was not how the dice fell though – and so she'd made a go of it with him, for better or worse. In retrospect, for worse.

'It means that I thought you were his,' Lara replied, low-voiced. The old shame surged through her, forcing her to add the muttered caveat, 'Well, probably anyway. I hoped you were.'

This was greeted by a long, sarcastic whistle. '*Probably*, she says. Probably. Jesus Christ, Mum, do you know how you sound? This is . . . I can't believe it. Poor Steve! I've spent all these years despising the man and now I actually feel sorry for him. I can't *believe*—'

Whatever it was Eliza couldn't believe remained unspoken; she let out a noise that was somewhere between a scream and a growl, and threw her hands in the air. 'So who is he, then? My real dad, who you've kept hidden from me my whole life? Were you *ever* going to tell me? Or was it more convenient for you to go on letting me think my dad hated me and wanted nothing to do with me?' She was crying by now, tears rolling down her round freckled face. 'Does everyone else know, by the way? Does Grandma know, and Uncle Richie? Is this some big family secret that you've all been keeping from clueless little Eliza?'

'No!' Lara protested, even though yes, her mum did know – having moved down from Cumbria in the aftermath of Steve's departure in an act of solidarity. And yes, okay, so Richie knew too, but that was because he was kind and wise, and a good person to talk to in a crisis. It wasn't as if she'd gone round broadcasting her secrets to the world at large though. 'Well – all right, they do know,' she conceded in the next moment, wretched at the thought of another layer of untruths, 'but it's not like we've all been talking about it behind your back. It's more that—'

24

She couldn't find the words to explain – *were* there any words good enough to explain? – but it didn't matter because Eliza was yelling now, fists clenched by her sides. 'How could you do this to me, Mum? I hate you for doing this!'

At that precise moment, Lara hated herself too. If someone else had caused that blanching anguish on her girl's face, the shocked tremor in her voice, she'd be going after them with a rolling pin, but *she* was the one to blame this time; she'd done that to her, the person she loved the most. She mentally turned the rolling pin on herself, beating herself up with her usual comparisons: that if she was any kind of proper mother, like the apron-clad Mrs Watson, this would never have happened. 'Darling, I'm so sorry,' she said again, but Eliza rounded on her before she could continue.

'Stop bloody saying that! If you were really sorry, we'd have had this conversation years ago. You wouldn't have lied to me from the day I was born!' She scrubbed at her face with a tissue, inadvertently smearing mascara around her eyes. 'You still haven't told me who he is, anyway. Or how I can find him.'

Lara's throat felt as if it were closing up and she had to force herself to swallow back the rearing tide of panic. Of course Eliza wanted to find him, to know about him. But she in turn felt so unprepared for the telling of this story, she had no idea how to begin. She steeled herself. 'Listen, you're upset, maybe this is not the time—'

'Oh, it's the time, all right. I'm not waiting another eighteen years for further updates, Mum.' Eliza perched on the table, folding her arms with a glare. 'This ends tonight. You need to tell me now. Right now.'

Lara's knees seemed soft and unreliable, as if she might sag to the floor any second. 'I don't know where he is, I'm afraid,' she said. An old film began playing in her head: starring her, running full pelt and tear-stained into Grand Central Station, before coming to a halt outside the Oyster Bar, her hands flying up to clutch her face in dismay. 'It was over before I knew it,' she said, her voice thick with regret even after so many years.

'What? So it was a one-night stand? After the times you've nagged me about being careful and respecting myself ... God, Mum!' Eliza slammed a fist down on the table, causing the salt and pepper pots to rattle nervously against one another. Then she exhaled loudly and asked in a quieter voice, 'So who was he?'

Lara bowed her head, trying to gather the pieces of herself back together. 'His name was – *is*, presumably – Ben. Ben McManus,' she replied eventually. It was like reciting an incantation, saying his name aloud after so long, and she almost expected him to materialise at the table on her command, like a storybook demon, complete with sulphurous smoke. 'And he was from Cambridge originally, although when I met him, he'd been living in Glasgow, then London,' she went on, pausing as a further wave of memories slapped against her. Him leaning over the table in that Greenwich Village bar, his handsome face animated under the too bright lights as they swapped life stories. The wide grey eyes that his daughter had inherited. 'Just to complicate things, I met him in New York,' she added.

Eliza raised an eyebrow, briefly forgetting her fury. 'What – so I was conceived in New York?' she asked, interest piqued.

'Yeah. You were conceived in New York,' Lara replied tonelessly.

Hunched over her phone, Eliza's fingers flew in a rapid burst of typing, then she held it up to show Lara the screen. 'Which of these is him, then? Any of them?'

Lara went over to see, feeling a mix of reluctance and intrigue. She had vowed never to look for him again, not to let him back into her life after what had happened. Whenever he had crossed her mind and she'd been tempted to look him up online, she had refused herself that knowledge. What was the point? It was sure to only rub salt in the wound. And yet now here she was, gaping at the sea of men's faces on her daughter's phone, arranged in a grid, like a bingo card or a digital police line-up.

'Well?' prompted Eliza, unable to wait any longer. 'So which Ben McManus do you think is my dad?'

Chapter Three

Kirsten Jensen was sitting at a packed, rowdy dinner table, having a moment of introspection. When you had as big and as noisy an extended family as she did (*three* sisters-in-law, would you believe, who came with an entire luggage carousel of accompanying baggage), being able to sit there amidst the crowd, smiling and apparently engaging with them while secretly chewing over matters of deep personal interest, was an extremely useful acquired skill. She was, by now, an expert.

Charlotte, whose birthday it was, held court at the head of the table, still red in the face after cooking and serving two massive moussakas, glassy-eyed from wine, recounting a story about accidentally putting on a stranger's bra after swimming that day, while everyone laughed along. Kirsten too, even though privately she was often horrified at Charlotte's shambolic approach to life. That said, despite finding her husband's sisters all pretty aggravating in their own ways (the dramas! The crises! The phone calls at all hours breathlessly recounting the latest saga!), she couldn't deny there was something impressive about Charlotte's apparently undampenable optimism. Look at her now, pantomiming her surprise at trying to squeeze into a bra three cup sizes too small followed by the awkwardness of being confronted by the woman whose bra it actually was. And yet this was Charlotte, who'd lost her dad as a teenager, been jilted at the altar by Alec Dunstable (the family still boycotted his butcher's shop, almost fifteen years later), had had her house repossessed five years ago when her current idiot husband (she knew how to pick 'em) ran up massive gambling debts ... Life kept throwing stuff at Charlotte and she kept gamely scrambling back on her feet, undaunted. Cheeks flushed, eyes shining, laughing uproariously as she reached the punchline of her bra anecdote.

It made Kirsten wonder why she couldn't tap into her own vein of contentment with such apparent ease. After all, compared to what Charlotte had been through, she had it made. Both her parents were still alive, she had a satisfying midwifery career and solid marriage, she lived in a nice house and had friends, hobbies and lovely holidays every year. You'd think all the ingredients would be there for life to be, if not a literal palm-tree-fringed paradise, then at least a cheering, stress-free existence. So why didn't it feel that way?

She'd been in the DIY superstore that afternoon when this thought occurred to her. In truth, it had been lurking close by for some time now, as each day ended with the usual perfunctory kisses in bed, after which she'd lie awake in the darkness with the uncomfortable nudging of the same old questions in her head. *Is this it? Is this enough?* Now, standing in front of shelves of overpriced, neutral-toned paint, the mood seemed to settle with a new heaviness on her shoulders as if her location was the very epicentre of her ennui, made real. *God, just look at you. Choosing between magnolia and vanilla, like it actually matters which bland nothingy shade you paint the downstairs loo. Like that's all your world has shrunk down to. Who cares?*

Her frustration over the limited colour palette must have shown on her face – maybe she had even groaned aloud – because a man nearby turned towards her. 'All beige, really, aren't they?' he'd said, raising an eyebrow. 'Beige with fancy names. Might as well call them "Boring Bastard" and be done with it, if you ask me.'

Kirsten wasn't usually one for striking up conversation with complete strangers in public places but she found herself laughing, because it was as if he'd read her mind. The man had a Geordie accent and looked a bit younger than her with scruffy brown hair and a trendy little beard. He'd spent longer on that crappy beard than the rest of him, she thought in amusement, taking in the knackered jeans and black sweatshirt. 'From one "Boring Bastard" to another,' she agreed, reaching out to pick up one of the tins. 'Goose Egg' it was called, which meant nothing to her. What was so special about a goose egg anyway, that you'd want its shade on your wall? She'd grown up in Milton Keynes; she was pretty sure she'd never even seen a goose egg before.

'Do you know, when I was a kid,' he went on, 'I always thought I'd paint my house red. Or striped. Or, you know, something really bright and interesting. Something fun! Why is it that when we reach adulthood, we all start choosing these dreary non-colours instead?'

Kirsten smiled in a way that she hoped was polite yet not wholly encouraging. An elderly man in a green anorak further down the aisle was looking at them disapprovingly, as if they were breaking the silence of a library or a cathedral. And yet there was no denying that the Geordie guy had a point. 'I used to love purple when I was a teenager,' she heard herself reply. 'I was a bit of a goth, mind, but all the same – my clothes were purple, my DMs were purple, even my hair was purple at one point. But now …'

'Now here we are, looking at bloody Linen White and Clotted Cream and No Personality,' he said, gesturing contemptuously at the tins in front of him. 'Sod it, I'm going retro after all. I'm too young to die a beige, middle-class death. I'm going to find some colours. Are you with me?'

This was the moment Kirsten probably should have given him another polite smile, shaken her head and turned back to the sea of uninspiring neutrals. She was pretty sure there wasn't even a shade called 'No Personality'. But despite everything, his words were ringing a bell within her, activating some part of her that had been buried too long beneath thoughts about mid-price wine and Egyptian cotton sheets and yes, endless boring dinner party conversations. Suddenly she was sick of tepid, scared-looking colour schemes. 'Yeah,' she said impulsively. 'I'm with you.'

Kirsten snapped back to the room just as Charlotte reached her latest punchline and everyone burst out laughing again. She joined in hurriedly with a fake chuckle so that nobody would notice she hadn't been paying attention. Were they still on bras, or had they moved on to something else? Had Charlotte swiped someone's knickers this time? 'Brilliant,' she said to no one in particular, and wondered how long it was before they could leave. She was on earlies this week and by now – Thursday evening – her very bones felt as if they were too tired to hold her upright much longer. She glanced across the table at her husband, trying to catch his eye, but he'd been nobbled by Annie, whose head was close to his as she spoke – asking for something, at a guess.

Charlotte pissed, Annie on the scrounge, her mother-in-law, Gwen, updating them at length on her usual ailments ... they just needed Sophie now to dredge up a childhood argument or injustice, and it would be full house.

Or maybe, Kirsten thought, struck by how mean-spirited she sounded in her own head, maybe she needed to lighten up. Get over herself. Stop seeing everything through the critical filter that seemed to have dropped before her eyes after discussing paint shades with the Geordie hipster. Because for some reason, he – Neil – had been popping up in her mind with a running commentary ever since she'd left the store and returned to her car ('Does anyone actually *yearn* to drive a Vauxhall Vectra? I mean, did you? What sort of person chooses the most boring car on the road anyway?'). She'd heard him again as she paused outside her front door ('Is that it? I'm not being rude, but does this building say Dream Home to you? Because it looks pretty dull from where I'm standing') and now she was even imagining what he would have to say about Charlotte's birthday party. ('Well, this is wild, right? That anecdote about the broken fridge-freezer is really up there in my collection of life highlights.')

Was it possible to have an epiphany in the paint aisle of a DIY superstore? It seemed unlikely but look at her now, with her tin of unopened plum paint sitting like a small act of rebellion in the utility room back home, plus her dissatisfied eye tonight, flicking to and fro around the faces of her in-laws, around Charlotte's ivory walls ('Hey, is that Goose Egg?' she felt like asking). She had washed up in a world of oatmeal carpets and double-glazed windows, with a safe husband who never surprised her any more, and suddenly all she felt like doing was running away from it all.

32

She pictured herself leaping to her feet, striding for the door. 'So sorry,' she imagined calling back over her shoulder. 'But I've realised I'm in the wrong life. I'm off to find out what happened to the real me, the Kirsten who used to have fun. Bye!'

They would be confused, the lot of them. Charlotte might try to hug her and press the number of a psychotherapist into her hand. Annie would roll her eyes and mouth 'attention-seeker' across the table. Sophie would give one of her suspicious little frowns as if worried a trick was being played on her. Gwen would claim that the exact same thing had happened to her last week, only worse, and she had put it down to allergy-related hallucinations. As for Kirsten's husband . . . would he notice? Would he try and stop her, even?

Better not think about that.

Back under the bright lights and canned elevator music of the DIY store, Neil had eventually chosen a can of bright turquoise paint for his kitchen. 'This is the one,' he'd said, hefting it down with a decisive air. 'Perfect.'

'What's your wife going to say about that?' Kirsten had asked, hearing a certain archness in her tone, only to regret it in the next moment. She didn't usually talk that way. Had she sounded too flirty?

He looked her full in the face, and all the blood rushed dizzyingly to her head. 'What wife?' he asked, deadpan.

She gulped. Clearly it *had* sounded too flirty, she thought, panic quickening inside. Way too flirty, and now his response was like a gauntlet thrown down. *Your turn.* She was too chicken to proceed any further though. The last scraps of her bravery were spent sliding the can of Iced Plum from the shelf.

'This one, I think,' she mumbled, fixating on the label – *matt emulsion interior paint* – and nodding to herself as if to say, yes, this is definitely the only thing on my mind right now.

'I don't have a wife,' he said, apparently determined to hammer his point home. 'Or a husband,' he added with another twitch of his eyebrow when she dared look at him. They were very expressive eyebrows, she noted, feeling her cheeks turn hot. He could have conducted an orchestra with them, given the slightest encouragement.

Well, she had given him enough encouragement, she decided. Perhaps too much. And now she needed to row back to the safety of shore. 'Good to have that cleared up,' she said, trying to disguise her embarrassment. 'Anyway, nice to—'

'I'm Neil, by the way,' he said, holding out a hand.

She fumbled with the paint tin, swapping it into her left hand, feeling the plastic handle dig into her palm as she reached out to shake. 'Kirsten,' she replied. Her heart was actually starting to pound now, her back prickling with a sudden sweat. Alarm or excitement? It was hard to tell. Oh God. Where was this going? What was happening? It was as if something had been awoken in her with the press of his fingers. Some animal instinct raising its head, testing the air.

'Great to meet you, Kirsten,' he said, his gaze direct, as if he could see right into her mind. His black sweatshirt had the words Landscape Legends printed on it in neon pink, she noticed distractedly, along with an illustrated pink spade (was he a gardener?), but then all she could think about was how strong and warm his hand was. Firm. Not clammy. A perfect specimen handshake, in fact.

She disentangled herself abruptly. 'You too. Thanks for the inspiration!' Then she held up the Iced Plum, hoping that this gesture said, *Our entire exchange has been about paint. Nothing more.* 'Good luck with your kitchen.'

'And you.' His smile was wide and charming, his blue eyes crinkling at the edges, a dimple in his left cheek. Then he saluted. 'Paint rebels of the world, unite!'

With that, he was gone, whistling as he went to pay. Kirsten let out her breath in a gust of relief. There, she told herself. The end. As soon as he vanished around the end of the aisle, her mind scrambled to reframe the whole sequence merely as a funny story that had happened to her. Maybe something she could confess over dinner tonight even, laugh about, then file away. *And you actually bought the paint?* she imagined Charlotte hooting. *Oh, Kirsten!*

She hesitated though, because then she was thinking about how grating she always found it, the way her sisters-in-law liked to 'Oh, Kirsten' her in that ever so slightly patronising way. Not least because Sophie was seven years younger than her, Annie couldn't do a thing for herself, and Charlotte was the dictionary definition of a flake. *Oh, Kirsten!* As if she would never quite understand the McManus family ways; their glance-exchanging refrain othering her, keeping her apart from the tribe. The three sisters with their shared history and shared jokes, all mothers who seemed to love endlessly discussing their adored children in front of her, knowing that she had no such stories of her own to contribute. *Oh, Kirsten! You'll never be one of us!* Perhaps this imagined response was why, despite her strong impulse to quietly replace the Iced Plum on its shelf and return shamefacedly to the beige selection for something more suitable, she didn't do any such thing.

Yes, Charlotte. I actually bought the sodding paint. What of it?

'Can anyone squeeze in dessert?' Charlotte asked at that moment. 'There's the most amazing-looking birthday cake out there, thanks to Kirsten.' She twinkled her eyes across the table at her, and there were a couple of smiling 'Oooh!'s from the others. Kirsten suddenly felt mean for all her bitchy thoughts that evening, because on the rare occasions when the sisters extended their collective warmth to include her, she always experienced such a wave of corresponding pleasure, as if she was part of their family after all. Despite everything, she still longed to be included. Was that the curse of being an only child? Or a sign that she was tragically insecure?

The main course over, there was a bustle of activity: plates cleared, drinks poured, Charlotte shouting unintelligibly from the kitchen about cream and ice cream. Kirsten seized the chance for a moment to herself and escaped to the downstairs loo, grabbing her phone from her handbag on the way. How was it possible that you could be in a room full of loud, jolly people and yet feel so alone?

Once locked away, she exhaled, rolling her eyes at her flush-faced reflection, already thinking yearningly of her quiet, dark bedroom, of how her weary body would sink into the mattress later. Not long now, she reassured herself.

Then, for some reason, she found herself typing *Landscape Legends* into the notes app on her phone and saving it. Just in case she ever needed it in future.

Chapter Four

Eliza's quest had begun in an A-level biology lesson on genetics a month earlier, when the teacher, Dr Khan, had started speaking about genetic conditions and disorders that were passed down through families. Sickle cell anaemia, cystic fibrosis, kidney and heart disease ... as the list increased on Dr Khan's whiteboard, Eliza had felt a new panic grip her insides. Because who could say what genes her dad had passed on to her? What nasties might be lurking in her body's cells waiting to surprise her in the future? Who even *was* she?

The relentless drumbeat of *Who am I?* had propelled her as far as Whitby, determined to get some answers, and the same *Who am I?* still looped around her head as she sat now in the Partridges' too warm living room for an evening's babysitting. Admittedly, there were worse places to be undergoing a traumatic crisis of self than this room, with its chintzy curtains, massive telly and fake-coals gas fire, plus the sofa that practically swallowed you up with its cushion mountain. (Mrs Partridge worked in a soft-furnishings shop in town and you could tell.) But even with such creature comforts, Eliza's head still jangled from the shocking revelations that had emerged earlier. She was even further from knowing her own self because she wasn't the daughter of Steve the Abandoner after all, but of Ben the Enigma. Ben McManus, a blip in her mum's life, a man she hardly knew, who, like it or not, had helped bring about Eliza's entire existence. (How was that even allowed, anyway? What kind of design fault of the human body was it when people could create a whole other person from a random sexual encounter, conducted hours after meeting? Without planning, consideration, applying for a pro-creation licence ... without so much as knowing each other's star sign, in the case of her parents!)

It had been too surreal almost for words, typing her father's name into her phone to be presented with a series of pictures of different men. Might that be him with the shock of white hair and laughing smile? Him, in the black and white shot, with an artfully posed side profile, hand to his chin? God, she hoped not. He looked a right arsehole. Please let her real dad not be an arsehole, she prayed fervently. Not on top of everything else.

'Well?' she'd demanded, as her mum scrolled through the images with infuriating slowness. There was a Ben McManus who was a chef in North Carolina. An Irish firefighter who'd raised thousands of pounds running marathons for a prostate cancer charity. A young student, a football player in a minor league. And then ...

Her mum made a gasping noise as she zoomed in on the photo of a friendly-faced man, forty-something, standing behind a shop counter with his sleeves rolled up. Was that him? His expression was one of faint awkwardness, perhaps from having his photo taken, but beyond that, Eliza could see he had grey eyes like her and a beaky sort of nose that she'd inherited too (*thanks for nothing, Dad*). She thought of Steve's pudgy face and scruffy appearance, then stared back at the man on her phone. 'Is that him?' The caption beneath the picture read *Ben McManus, owner of All Mapped Out, Cambridge*. 'Mum?' she prompted, unable to bear the silence any longer.

Lara nodded weakly. 'Yes,' she said in a strange voice. 'I'm pretty sure that's him.'

Eliza gazed anew into the eyes of the Cambridge Ben McManus, her tummy twisting a peculiar spiral inside her. *You are my dad. Hi there. This is weird, isn't it? Are we at all alike, I wonder?* Presumably he had absolutely no idea she even existed, no clue that he had an eighteen-year-old daughter who was fifty percent him walking the planet. Just as she'd had no idea he existed either, until five minutes ago.

She glanced up at Lara, desperate to know more. 'He looks nice,' she said, her mind whirling with questions. 'Was he?'

Lara paused for a moment then nodded. 'Yes,' she said. 'He was. Until . . .' Then, exasperatingly, she had clammed up. 'Look, I need to get on with dinner,' she'd muttered to the floor, no longer looking at Eliza.

Eliza groaned in disbelief. '*What?* Seriously? I'm not done yet, Mum. What are you not telling me? There must be more to the story than his face on a screen. And I deserve to know, all right?' Her voice shook. 'I'm desperate to know. This is my *father!*'

It was like finding yourself in a juicy episode of a soap opera – both thrilling and terrifying to be playing a lead role. Shouting the words *This is my father!* across the kitchen was exhilarating and also intense – because this was happening, and real. Her life, rather than a dramatic plot line of some fictional character. But her mum was closed all the way up now, a purse snapped shut.

'I don't know what else to say,' she replied, her back to Eliza, chopping garlic as if her life depended on it. 'It's been nearly twenty years. Can we leave it there for now? Please?'

Her voice cracked on the last word and Eliza's anger faltered somewhat. Partly because her mum sounded so pained, but also because, as a feisty Arian herself, Lara could be every bit as stubborn as Eliza. She knew already that this would be one of those times where fighting was pointless.

Letting out a strangled-sounding cry of impotence, she marched from the house and walked blindly down the street, adrenalin surging around her. She had eventually returned home minutes before she was due to babysit in order to grab an armful of schoolwork and her headphones, then headed straight out again, presenting a stony, fuck-you face to her mother's attempts at conversation, apology, a Tupperware box of congealing stir-fry. Whatever, she thought. Not interested.

Now in the hushed comfort of the Partridges' house down the road, she let her body go limp against a mound of velvety autumn-toned cushions. The sound of heavy breathing from four-year-old Milo Partridge over the baby monitor was strangely soothing, coupled with the steady tick of the clock on the mantelpiece. Pepper, the yellow Labrador, who was not allowed on the sofa, rested her heavy head against Eliza's knee, one liquid eye turned up towards her, as if offering comradeship.

Eliza exhaled slowly. I am here, within the sanctuary of a normal, happy family who don't lie to each other and keep terrible secrets, she thought, her heart splintering with envy. LOVE was spelled out on one wall in big gold letters. Wedding photos clustered cosily along the top of the mantelpiece. The Partridges – Ryan and Samantha – were resoundingly conventional types with their regular Thursday date night and neatly weeded front garden and their fridge stocked full of (disappointingly for Eliza) healthy food. She'd previously felt a degree of scorn towards them and their safe, vanilla lives (catch her being so boring when she was their age? No way) – but right now that vibe was exactly what she needed. Thank God she was here, she thought, away from Mum for a few hours and able to think alone for a while.

One hand absentmindedly caressing Pepper's soft ears, Eliza picked up her phone again and studied her father's handsome face. Greying a little at the temples, he had a strong jaw and the sort of smile that made his eyes seem twinkly. The type of person you could trust, she thought. Yet clearly her mother had decided otherwise at the time, else she might have stayed with him, rather than Steve. So what had happened between them? What had Ben done wrong, that he had not made the cut?

Of course, by now, Eliza had done further internet stalking, and had a few other facts to mull over. From what she could see on his various social media profiles, Ben McManus was forty-five, a Sagittarius (excellent) and a fan of Cambridge United. He went to the gym, had supported Labour in the last election, was married, and a graphic artist, who created prints of personalised maps for his customers, as well as selling all kinds of vintage ones. He had an online shop where she examined his work: largely graphic prints that he called *A Map of Us*, where clients provided him with the names of cities or towns that meant something to them, for Ben to chart on a blank map in blocky colourful lettering. He did a lot of wedding presents, by the look of previous artwork he had on display, and Eliza had to admit there was something visually appealing about the way the prints told a story. How, for instance, had Morag in Lincoln ever hooked up with Graham in

Exeter? Ditto Beth from Birmingham and Nina from Brighton, whose map had a third entry – 'Home' – in Stirling. Nice one, Ben. Good effort. This all gave him the edge over Steve already.

She found herself pondering what Ben's own map might look like, the places he had been to, other than New York. He must be well travelled, she imagined, before wondering, with a slight lurch, if she might have half-brothers and sisters around the world, given the circumstances of her own conception. According to her searches, his wife was called Kirsten and they had been married eighteen years, but presumably had been dating for a while before that. So either he'd cheated on Kirsten when he slept with her mum, Eliza figured, or Kirsten was a rebound fling. Admittedly, her internet forays weren't wholly conclusive, but as far as she could tell, Ben and Kirsten didn't have children together, which left her feeling uneasy. Had they deliberately decided against having kids because they hated the idea? Would Eliza popping up out of the blue be a source of huge dismay?

Pepper whined, fearing correctly that she was losing Eliza's attention. 'I know, darling,' Eliza told her, sliding off the sofa on to the carpet so that she could put her arm around the dog. They leaned against one another for a moment, Pepper's breath ticklish and meaty-smelling on Eliza's face. 'Good girl,' Eliza murmured, grateful for the large warm body beside her.

The big question, of course, was what she should do with her new information. How she should proceed. Because she could tell already that Mum would drag her heels about a decision – that was a given. She hadn't even wanted to talk about it earlier; she was hardly likely to be the one suggesting a day trip to Cambridge, making chatty phone calls and arranging a blind dad-and-daughter date for them. It had been left to Eliza to force the issue with Steve; clearly she would have to do the same with Ben McManus. (She felt odd calling him this, yet how else should she refer to him? 'Dad'? Too soon. 'Ben'? Too matey. 'Mr McManus'? Too teachery.)

The sound of an unfamiliar phone notification jerked her from her thoughts and she glanced round, startled to see that a black Samsung was poking out from the edge of the far sofa cushion; it must have fallen out of someone's pocket and slid deep into the squishy valley there. She picked it up gingerly and saw on the screen a text message from someone called Nikki:

Hey babe, thinking about u and touching myself. So wet right now

The phone might have been plague-infected for the speed with which Eliza dropped it again. 'Gross,' she whispered aloud. 'Ugh! And who the hell is Nikki anyway?' she asked Pepper. 'Mr P's bit on the side?'

Pepper licked her face sympathetically but Eliza was still grimacing as if she'd bitten into something sour. Yuck. What was wrong with these people? Was it too much to ask for a shred of loyalty to the person you'd married? Not ten minutes ago she had been thinking fondly of the Partridges and their safe suburban lives, but now it seemed you couldn't trust anyone. Not even boring people with a conservatory and a Volvo, and luxury pots of houmous in their fridge.

The phone buzzed a second time. Oh Jesus, it was Nikki again. *U make me feel so horny baby. I need u*

Grim. The words seemed particularly gnarly when read against the soundtrack of little Milo's slow, steady breathing from the baby monitor. Get some self-respect, Nikki, Eliza felt like saying. As for Mr P, what a pig. She considered typing a rude reply but that was probably a step too far. 'Better not, eh, Pepper?' she said, turning the TV on instead. 'Let's distract ourselves with some trash,' she decided, choosing a programme about bored housewives in a glamorous American suburb.

By the time the Partridges returned home, there had been several more phone notifications, all in a similarly unsubtle vein, from this Nikki person. She was persistent, you had to give her that, Eliza thought, switching off the TV at the sound of the front door. And maybe, had things been different, that might have been the end of it; she'd have left Mr and Mrs Partridge to their own goings-on, figuring that it was none of her business anyway. But having found herself hours earlier the unfortunate victim of years' worth of betrayal and lies – a lifetime's worth, in fact – it wasn't so easy to turn a blind eye to another person's deceit tonight. So when the two Partridges walked in, pink in the cheeks from wine and dinner, she found it hard to stomach the innocent smile on Mrs P's face, her husband's proprietorial hand resting in the small of her back. *He's lying to you! He's a dick*, a voice raged in Eliza's head. *Don't trust a word he says to you, Samantha!*

Mrs Partridge went to check on the baby and Eliza rose to her feet, giving Pepper one last fuss while Mr Partridge fumbled for his wallet. I've got your number, mate, she thought, as he eventually held out a twenty-pound note to her. I'm on to you. 'Thank you,' she said, stuffing the money in her pocket. Her heart was beating a little faster all of a sudden, words of accusation brimming on her tongue. Sod it, she thought in the next second. Time to make a stand for justice and honesty. 'By the way,' she said, before she could change her mind. 'Your phone has been buzzing a lot with new messages, Mr P. I did glance over, just in case it was anything really important and saw they were from someone called Nikki?'

His face spasmed then blanched, his weak chin bobbing with a panicked gulp. Good, she thought, completely without mercy. *Yes, you should be panicking right now, you creep.* Then, unable to stop herself from whacking one last nail into the coffin, she added, 'Something about . . . feeling wet and needing you?'

In the next moment she froze, noticing that Mrs Partridge had appeared in the doorway. Oh God. Had she overheard? 'Anyway, thank you,' she said, trying to avoid eye contact with either of them as she swiftly headed across the room. 'Bye!'

Moments later, she was out of there, through the front door and into the crisp, frost-glittering night, light-hearted with her own boldness as she hurried the short distance home. Whoa. Had that really just happened? Had she actually just *said* that? Until now, the world had been accustomed to good Eliza, the sensible, nicely brought up young woman who was a responsible daughter, student, friend, babysitter. It turned out that discovering your blood and genes were not what you'd always assumed changed a person in more ways than one. Who am I? she had been wondering for weeks on end. Well, maybe this, now, was her truest, purest self. Maybe this was who she was supposed to be: Eliza Mark Two, unafraid to call out bad behaviour, breaking any rule or social code she wanted. Hell, it felt good right now, really good. So why not?

Chapter Five

Lara must have fallen asleep on the sofa waiting for Eliza to come home, because the next thing she knew it was one in the morning and she was freezing cold, with a stiff neck where it had become uncomfortably twisted. Eliza's jacket and shoes were in the hall and the front door bolted, so she must have headed straight to bed, Lara deduced, turning the lights off and going up herself, heart heavy. Clearly she wasn't forgiven yet.

The next day was Friday and as Eliza stomped into the kitchen and began dumping cereal in a bowl, her frosty, reproachful air made it obvious that forgiveness wasn't in the offing this morning either. 'How was babysitting?' Lara asked, only for her daughter to snort with barely disguised contempt.

'Tell you what,' Eliza said, sloshing milk over her cereal, 'just talk to me when you've got something to talk about. Don't bother with chit-chat about babysitting. I only want to hear actual facts from now on. What happened with Ben and with Steve; the truth.' She slammed the fridge door with such vehemence, Lara could hear the milk bottles trembling together inside.

Staring down at her own breakfast, Lara knew full well that

she only had herself to blame for this situation. One snap decision all those years ago, and the ripples were still spreading. She had to try to explain.

'Okay,' she said quietly. 'Well, for one thing, Steve did really love you,' she began, which was true at least. 'He would strap you into a little seat on his bike and take you off for bike rides along the seafront on sunny days. You had the cutest little helmet and everything.'

Eliza's face was still pinched although Lara thought she could detect a faint softening. 'What else?'

'He spent hours playing dolls' houses with you,' Lara went on, a lump forming in her throat as she remembered Steve's big workman hands, how he'd wrestled with all the tiny dolly dresses and furniture. 'He was the kind of dad, in fact, that I wished I'd had myself, growing up,' she confessed, knowing deep down that this was one of the key reasons why she'd stuck with him in the first place. 'We thought it would be nice for you to have a brother or sister, so—'

'If you're about to start talking about your sex life, that's not the kind of truth I was asking for,' Eliza put in, waspishly.

'Well … it's sort of important actually, because that's why he ended up leaving,' Lara said. She put her spoon down, no longer able to eat. This was a conversation that needed a large glass of wine to help it along, not a bowl of granola and yogurt. 'You see, it turned out that he was infertile,' she went on, the words hard to say even now. After the two of them had been trying to conceive for a year without any luck, he'd taken himself off to a clinic to get his sperm tested, unbeknownst to her. The news had been devastating. 'He realised he couldn't be your dad after all,' she said.

Eliza's mouth dropped open. 'When you'd told him that he was? Mum, that's so shitty.'

Lara shut her eyes briefly. Like she didn't know that herself. For Steve, it was the sort of shock from which there was no coming back. Without the glue of their own child to seal up all the cracks and crevices of their relationship, the marriage had promptly imploded. 'Yes,' she acknowledged. 'I'm not proud of how I hurt him.' Her voice shook, remembering. Telling him that she'd never set out to deliberately deceive or trick him had done little to ease his anguish. He couldn't pretend he didn't know the truth, he'd said, desolate. He felt used, taken advantage of. Days later, he had moved out, and Lara had vowed to herself that she'd have to be everything for Eliza from now on because she knew full well that he wouldn't be back.

'So – that was it, was it?' Eliza asked, eyes flinty. 'You thought, "Oh well, I'll just let Eliza think that Steve never loved her enough to want to see her again"? You didn't think you should try and *tell* me any of this? Or track down my *real* dad?'

'I did try to find him,' Lara said defensively. This was back before everyone was on social media, when it wasn't so easy to hunt down a lost contact, but she'd set about it the old-school way at Scarborough Library: working through the phone books of Glasgow, Cambridge and London, three cities where she knew Ben to have lived, jotting down lists and numbers of McManuses. She had called and discounted all of the Glasgow listings before reaching a number in Cambridge that seemed to be the right one. But even then, having phoned twice and left him a message, he had never called her back.

The sting of rejection had hit her all over again as his silence stretched from a day to a week to months on end. She should have known he wouldn't bother! It wasn't as if he'd treated her very well in the first place. 'Sod him then,' her mum had said, shaking her head with contempt when Lara confided in her what had happened. 'He sounds a waste of space – not good enough for you *or* Eliza. You don't need him. Men make everything more complicated, take it from me!'

'You didn't try that hard, obviously,' Eliza said now, glowering. 'Seeing as it took me about two seconds to google him last night.' She got to her feet, pushing the chair back so roughly it wobbled on its back legs. 'I can't be bothered to listen to this any more. I'm off.'

'I'm sorry,' Lara cried, feeling wretchedly as if she was the worst mother ever. 'We'll talk tonight, yeah? I'll tell you whatever you want to know. Okay?'

The crash of the front door was her only answer and she slumped back in her chair. Whatever Eliza might think now, Lara *had* always intended to tell her the truth one day. The thing was, as the years rolled on, it had become increasingly onerous to tackle the revelation, and she'd found herself repeatedly kicking it ahead into the long grass, continuing to hide behind the lie that Steve was Eliza's father. Initially, she'd convinced herself that Eliza was too young to know about the facts of life, then too unworldly to be told of the uncertainties of love and conception, then at too awkward an age to want to hear anything relating to her mum having sex, ever. Even when Eliza had turned eighteen at the end of March, Lara had bottled it. She was scared, she could see now, in hindsight. Scared of trying to contact Ben again, scared of being rebuffed. Scared that she had made wrong decision after wrong decision, in fact. And, like it or not, it was these scared feelings that had led to her keeping men at a safe distance for all the years since. She'd proved twice over that her instincts were terrible when it came to love and romance. With Eliza as her priority now, there was no way she would willingly put herself in such a vulnerable situation again.

And so Lara had said nothing – but look how that had back-fired. Now the situation felt way worse than if she'd simply been straight about the facts from the start. Would Eliza ever forgive her? How could Lara rebuild foundations of trust between them when, in her daughter's eyes, she'd let her down so badly?

During driving lessons, Lara's phone was always switched to 'Do Not Disturb', with the only exceptions being the numbers of Eliza and her school, so when it started ringing two minutes after she'd picked up a new student, Billie, for a trial lesson, Lara's immediate reaction was one of alarm. The car was stationary at the time, parked up outside Billie's college on Filey Road, with Lara midway through her traditional opening spiel about how a car engine worked. 'I'm really sorry, could you excuse me a moment?' she said, breaking off to grab her phone. Eliza's name was on the screen: Eliza, who knew not to contact her unless it was an absolute house-burning-down emergency. What on earth could be wrong? 'I'm going to have to answer this.'

'Sure,' said Billie, shrugging her shoulders. She had a sleepy sort of expression with wide-set eyes and a soft voice, and a wrist full of clinking silver bracelets.

Lara fumbled to answer the call. 'Hello?' she said. 'Are you all right, love?'

There was a sniff from the other end but no further reply, and Lara pressed the phone hard against her ear, panic rising. 'Eliza? Can you hear me?'

'Yeah. I'm here. Er.' There was a pause, so long Lara thought the signal must have dropped out, until Eliza's voice came again, low and reluctant. 'Mum . . . can you do me a favour?' she asked. 'Don't be mad but . . . something's happened.'

Travel is well-starred today, Eliza's horoscope had read that morning. *Go for it! Your journey starts right here, right now.* Yeah, whatever, she'd thought, as she dragged herself out of bed. How was she meant to do that then? Cambridge was a lot further away than Whitby; too far to be able to hop on a couple of buses with the excuse of a fake migraine.

'I wish I could get out of here,' she sighed to her friends Bo and Saskia, during breaktime that morning, when they met as usual in their favourite corner of the common room. 'If I had a car, I'd take off in a second. I found out something pretty massive last night.'

And then out came the whole saga, punctuated by Saskia's dramatic gasps and frequent interjections (she was an Aquarius; she loved the drama). Bo, meanwhile, merely arched an eyebrow at the story's end. 'I can get you a car,' she said.

It had been that easy. Unbelievably easy. Bo's stepbrother Tyrone had a car and let Bo drive it all the time. He wouldn't mind Eliza borrowing it, she reckoned – he was out of work at the moment and spent all day on the sofa playing Xbox games; it wasn't like he needed the car to go anywhere.

'Oh my God,' Eliza said. 'Are you sure? When do you think I might be able to borrow it?'

Bo responded by getting to her feet and hitching her bag on her shoulder. 'Now?'

Bo was a really fun person to hang out with – she was a

Scorpio: daring, unpredictable and smart. In the past, the only downside Eliza had ever felt about their friendship was that Bo always had such bold, startling ideas, Eliza often felt unimaginative, and even a bit cowardly, in comparison. Last term, for instance, Bo had thought nothing of hacking into the school computer system and upgrading her friends' school reports. She'd brought in hash brownies for her unwitting politics class when it was her turn at cake week, and was confident in her sexuality, switching between boyfriends and girlfriends with apparent ease in a way that virginal, uncertain Eliza deeply envied. (*Will I ever have sex with anyone?* was one of the most perennially urgent questions in her head, second only to *Who am I?* right now.)

Today, on this, she would be as daring as Bo, she decided. 'Okay,' she said. 'Suits me. Yes!'

Twenty minutes later, Eliza was sitting behind the steering wheel of Tyrone's car, simple as that. 'You're sure he won't mind?' she asked again through the open window. Doubts were starting to edge into her head now that the initial adrenalin pump of Bo's offer was draining away. She'd already missed lessons yesterday and there was no way she'd be back in time for double biology this afternoon. More than that, she was about to drive off in her friend's brother's car without even getting his permission. This was definitely not typical Eliza behaviour. But then again, maybe her real dad was a lifelong rebel and thrill-seeker, and his genes were finally making themselves known in her. The thought gave her a fillip of renewed bravery.

'Course he won't mind,' Bo said. 'He probably won't even notice.' Tyrone had been out somewhere when they'd dropped round, the house quiet save for the frenzied barking of Frank,

Bo's annoying Jack Russell, but it had been easy enough to find her stepbrother's car keys. Bo's phone was almost out of credit, so rather than messaging him, she left a scrawled note on the bench in the hall explaining that Eliza would pay for the petrol costs and promising that the car would be back later. 'I've put "later" rather than an actual time, just in case traffic is shit,' she'd explained. 'But, like I said, he's hardly used it since he lost his job. And if he needs to go anywhere, my stepdad's got a van, he can use that. Sorted.'

She slapped the roof of the car now, as if she loaned out other people's vehicles all the time. Knowing Bo, it could be true. 'Have an amazing time,' she said. 'And don't come back until you've got all the answers, yeah?'

'You bet,' Eliza replied, trying to tamp down a quiver of apprehension as she set up the satnav on her phone. Steve yesterday, Ben today ... it was as if she was playing Dad Bingo, ticking them off one by one on her own private tour of discovery around the country. What the hell though – like Bo said, she needed answers, and she was sick of secrecy. And if her mum dared to give her any shit about this later, Eliza would throw Lara's own bad behaviour straight back in her face.

It was half ten now and according to her phone, if she put her foot down, she could be in Cambridge by mid-afternoon. Spend some time with her mysterious dad. Find out his side of the story and get to know one another a bit, then head home, arriving back in Scarborough for nine or thereabouts. Sure, it would be quite a lot of driving for one day, but how hard could that be? Other people seemed to manage it. 'Thanks, babe,' she said to Bo, in her most confident voice. Then, before she could change her mind, she started the engine, put the car in gear, checked her mirror and pulled smoothly away, just as her mum had taught her.

Exhilaration fired up inside her as she accelerated down the street. She was doing this. She was actually doing it: taking action, like with Mr Partridge the night before, like with Steve. Claiming back some agency in order to find out the truth she was owed. And nobody was going to stop her.

Or so she thought, anyway. Because it turned out that when Tyrone came home to find his car missing, he didn't think to search around for a hastily scrawled note of explanation as to its whereabouts. And even if he *had* thought to look for it, he wouldn't have found anything anyway, because when Bo had closed the door earlier, the draught from this had sent her note fluttering down to the floor – and then Frank, the psycho Jack Russell, had had a lovely time ripping it up, resulting in Bo's words scattering far and wide in a blizzard of dog confetti. But this was irrelevant, seeing as Tyrone was already on the phone to the police.

Meanwhile, Eliza was heading south, deep in thought about how cool she was going to play it when she introduced herself to Ben, how mature and charming and goddamn likeable she would be. She'd always envied her friends their dads, even the really square ones who made tragic, unfunny jokes and wore terrible cardigans. She'd only been little when Steve left, but there were photos of him throwing her up into the air and her screaming with excitement, as well as video footage of him reading her a story and pushing her on the swings, and they'd looked so happy together each time. Lies aside, Mum was pretty great, but it wasn't the same as having a dad in your life too, she was sure.

She was so lost in her own thoughts that it took her a few

moments to notice the flashing lights of the car behind her. The flashing lights of the *police* car behind her, that was. Oh God. Was that for her? Had she been going over the limit? She hadn't been paying attention.

Fumbling with the indicator, she pulled over to the roadside, coming to an uneasy halt outside the gates of a rugby training ground. Her heart galloped as the cops parked behind her. So the flashing lights *were* for her. Two officers got out, both men, and walked towards Tyrone's car. One of them knocked at her window and she opened it, fingers shaky. He had toffee-coloured hair and smelled of nasty aftershave, with a ruddy pink face like a joint of ham. 'Could you get out of the car, please?' he asked, unsmiling.

Shit. Turning off the engine, she unclipped her seatbelt and clambered out, the backs of her legs sweaty with stress. A man on a massive mower was puttering around the rugby pitch cutting the grass and she swallowed hard, feeling his eyes on her.

'I'm PC Shah and this is PC Vowles. Can I have your name, please?' the second officer asked, holding a notepad and pen. He had pockmarked skin that told of previous battles with acne as well as thick, excellently shaped eyebrows, the sort that Eliza and her friends dreamed of.

'Eliza Spencer,' she mumbled.

'Eliza . . . Spencer,' he repeated, writing it down. 'And do you know why we've stopped you today, Eliza?'

She stared down at the ground. Two fag butts and an ancient crisp packet lay in the grass nearby, the crisp packet so faded by the sun and rain that it was almost white, like a ghost packet. 'I'm not sure,' she mumbled, putting her arms round herself. Had her mum somehow found out what she was planning? *Had* she been driving too fast just now? Mum would kill her if she got any points on her licence.

'You're not sure,' the first guy repeated, his lips thin as he pressed them together. 'Well, let me give you a clue, Eliza. The car we're standing next to – that's the clue. Because it's not your car, is it?'

There was a plunging feeling in her stomach and then a pincer of dread took hold. Okay, rewind: she took it all back about Bo. *Course he won't mind*, she'd said – and look what had happened. Apparently Tyrone minded enough to call the police on her. 'Well, no, but ...' Her mouth dried, anxiety rising again. How was she going to get out of this?

'No,' the officer repeated. 'It's been reported stolen, in fact.' He was actually smacking his lips, enjoying himself, she thought, with a rush of queasy dismay.

Eliza hung her head. 'It's my friend's brother's car. She said I could borrow it.'

'Your friend said that?' PC Shah raised one of his fantastic eyebrows. 'When it's not her car? Because her brother didn't seem to know anything about this arrangement when he spoke to our colleagues.' A weighty pause followed. 'By the way, I take it you sorted out insurance for this little trip?' he asked next. 'You were at least responsible for *that* before setting off on your unauthorised journey?'

Insurance. Oh crap. She'd been in such a whirl about getting to Cambridge she hadn't even thought about insurance. *Fuck.* 'Um ...' Her face bloomed hot with embarrassment. Who was she? Someone young and stupid and way out of her depth, that was who. Why had she ever thought this was a good idea? 'No,' she mumbled, her voice barely above the level of a whisper. 'I ... I didn't think to—'

'You didn't think,' repeated PC Shah heavily. 'No. Are you aware that it's a criminal offence to drive a car without insurance?'

She nodded, eyes downcast, trying not to cry while two cars whizzed by in quick succession, a scatter of grit rattling against the kerb in their wake. *Oh God.* Her mum would totally lose her shit at Eliza for driving without insurance, for acting so impulsively that the thought had passed her completely by. But she'd had other things on her mind at the time, all right? She was having an extremely intense twenty-four hours! Meanwhile, were the police officers going to *arrest* her? she wondered, not daring to look up. What happened now?

'Can we see your driving licence?' PC Vowles asked.

'It's at home,' Eliza said, with a gulp. 'I'm sorry,' she added, feeling tears come to her eyes. 'I'm really sorry about this.'

The police officers exchanged a look and seemed to soften slightly. 'You know, we take these things very seriously,' PC Shah said. 'We could, for example, issue you a fine right now and six penalty points on your licence for the lack of insurance alone. As for the car theft ...'

'I didn't steal it,' Eliza cried, her bottom lip wobbling with the effort of not bursting into tears. 'Look, it's a misunderstanding, I promise. I'm friends with Tyrone's sister, Bo – she gave me the keys. If I ring her, she'll back me up, I swear.' Her heart was flip-flopping inside her like a fish on a line; she was starting to feel light-headed with panic. Another car roared past, making the ghostly crisp packet quiver on the ground. 'Please can I ring her? She can sort it out with Tyrone. I haven't stolen anything. I thought it was okay. And I'm really sorry about the insurance, but I can get that done right now on the phone, if you let me.'

Her voice was almost a squeak by now, tears just a breath away from spilling everywhere. 'Please?'

The coppers looked at each other again. 'Go on, then,' said PC Shah. 'Ring your friend to start with. Let's get to the bottom of this.' He was definitely the kinder one of the pair, she thought, weak with gratitude as she fumbled for her phone. 'In the meantime, I'll get in touch with Mr Sanderson and let him know that we've traced his vehicle.'

A breathless few minutes passed while phone calls were made and the outcome hung in the balance. Bo yelped an apology and promised to get everything put right, and then Eliza had to endure watching PC Shah's excellent eyebrows semaphore disapproval during his conversation with Tyrone. 'I see,' he said grimly. 'Okay. Not a problem. I'll send you the exact location in a moment, sir.'

Eliza felt sick as she waited for the verdict. PC Shah looked stern. 'The good news for you,' he began, 'is that he's not going to press charges. In fact,' he went on, as the breath escaped Eliza's lungs in a huge sigh, 'when I told him what had happened, he changed his story and said he *did* know about you borrowing the car and that it must have slipped his mind.' The sarcasm in the police officer's voice made it abundantly clear that he did not believe this for a minute, although right then Eliza could hardly think about anything other than a rush of pure thankfulness for Bo's brother.

The officer hadn't finished. 'And it really must be your lucky day, because as well as that, it turns out his particular car insurance covers all drivers of the vehicle.'

'Oh my God,' Eliza blurted out, weak with the sweet joy of relief. Bo and Tyrone's stepdad worked in insurance, she remembered now, and presumably he'd got a good discount on the best cover package. She almost felt like dropping to the ground on her knees with gratitude. 'Thank you.'

'You're not totally off the hook,' said PC Shah. 'For one thing, not unreasonably, Mr Sanderson doesn't want you to drive his car any further. What's more, he says you'll have to pay for the taxi fare for him to come out here in order to retrieve it.'

Eliza's flare of relief was promptly extinguished, giving way to despair. 'Right,' she said, wondering how much a taxi would cost from Scarborough to wherever she was now, somewhere around Driffield. Enough to completely wipe out her babysitting savings, no doubt. 'And . . . what about me?' she added, her voice a croak. 'Am I . . .' She couldn't quite bring herself to ask if she was under arrest. 'Am I in trouble?'

'Well, it's all a bit of a waste of police time, this, isn't it?' replied PC Vowles, unsmilingly.

She nodded in miserable agreement.

'But no, we're not going to charge you, if that's what you mean,' he said, his dark eyes drilling into hers. 'Just *think*, another time. Think about the consequences of what you're doing. Driving a vehicle is not a game, okay? This could all have been a lot worse.'

Eliza hung her head. This was the second time in two days she'd been told 'it's not a game' by an angry man. Even though she hadn't considered herself to be playing a game either time. 'I know. Sorry,' she muttered, contrite. Then a new thought struck her. 'So . . .' She licked her lips, embarrassed to ask, faltering over the words. 'So . . . are you going to just leave me here?'

The police officers looked at one another. 'You could walk into Driffield from here, catch a bus to wherever you're going,' said PC Vowles – a spectacularly unhelpful answer, Eliza thought.

'Otherwise you'll have to cross your fingers that Mr Sanderson is charitable enough to consider giving you a lift.'

'Do you have someone you could call?' PC Shah asked, noticing her face fall.

Eliza stared down at the ground again, eyes still hot from wanting to cry. 'Yes,' she said, already dreading the conversation that lay ahead. 'Thank you,' she remembered to add. Then, as the police officers began walking back to their car, she gritted her teeth and dialled a number on her phone. 'Mum?' she said when it was answered. Her throat felt thick and she couldn't speak for a second when she heard Lara's kind, concerned voice asking if she was still there. 'I'm here,' she said, then took a deep breath. 'Mum ... can you do me a favour? Don't be mad but ... something's happened.'

Chapter Six

Cancelling a student's lessons was not something Lara liked doing, especially when they were sitting in the car right next to you, but now and again, it was simply unavoidable. Billie was promised a full refund, a rebooking and apologised to several times over, and thankfully she took it pretty well. Sensing that this could end up being a difficult day (what on earth was her daughter *thinking?*), Lara went on to cancel the rest of Friday's lessons too, before taking a deep breath, contacting Tyrone and offering to drive him down to Driffield herself. Not only would this provide her with the chance to grovel on Eliza's behalf, but it would also circumvent an extortionate cab fare. As serendipity would have it, Lara had been the one to teach Tyrone to drive seven or eight years ago and – having seen him through the test with a pass first time – she hoped this might sway his feelings on the whole business.

He'd been a good kid, Tyrone, and – thank goodness – was still a decent young man. Mild-mannered. Whatever anger or irritation he might have felt about having his car taken seemed to have already dissipated by the time he was folding his long frame into her passenger seat. 'Hello again,' he said, then peered down at her dual control pedals with a laugh. 'Blimey, this takes me back.'

'Hi,' she said, waiting for him to fasten his seatbelt. 'How are you? I'm extremely sorry about all this, obviously. I'm planning to go full witch on my daughter just as soon as she's in my eyeline, don't you worry.'

'Ah, it's fine,' he said, waving a hand. He had eyes like a husky, the palest, iciest blue. These, coupled with a pair of excellent cheekbones and thick black hair that fell to his shoulders, gave him a striking, almost warrior-like appearance – right until he gave you one of his wide, easy smiles, that was. 'I did far worse things at that age. And if I'm annoyed with anyone, it's Bo for thinking that we live in some kind of communist state, where my car is also the people's car.' He snorted, but it seemed to be more from amusement than fury.

'If it makes you feel any better, Eliza's a good driver,' Lara told him as they set off. 'Really sensible and mature. I know she won't have been attempting any wheel skids or anything that might have damaged the car.'

He laughed. 'Course she's a good driver, she's your kid!' he said, and Lara's heart warmed at his niceness, her shoulders uncrunching just a fraction. Maybe this would actually be okay, she thought in relief. Until he asked in the next breath, 'So how come she was going to Cambridge today, then?'

'*What?*' Needless to say, this was news to Lara.

'Yeah, that's what Bo said. That she needed to drive down to Cambridge today for …' He spread his palms. 'I dunno. Something really urgent, my sister reckoned. So urgent they apparently couldn't wait around for me to get back, to ask me about borrowing the car.' There was an awkward pause. 'I'm guessing you didn't know that part of the story.'

Lara's mouth was dry. Taking off in someone's brother's car was stupid and impulsive enough, but driving to *Cambridge* on a whim, presumably to track down Ben and stir everything up . . . ? Her spine froze at the idea of Eliza being so far from home, impetuously searching for her father like a vigilante out for justice. 'No,' she conceded, blinking and forcing herself to focus on the junction ahead.

'Whoops. Sorry. Did I just land her in it?'

'No, it's okay.' It was not okay though, not at all. And however cross she might be feeling about this unexpectedly wilful plan of her daughter's, Lara knew too that the whole scenario could have been avoided. She shouldn't have closed down Eliza so abruptly last night. Of course an eighteen-year-old needed more than a scant few facts. But for her to go haring off to Cambridge in such a cavalier, headstrong manner was far stronger a reaction than Lara could have anticipated. 'Anyway,' she said, hands stiffening on the wheel. Tyrone didn't need to know any of this. 'How are things with you? What have you been up to for the last – what? Eight years?'

Tyrone launched into a potted history of his life, but Lara struggled to concentrate, her mind still taken up by Eliza, and what might have happened if the police hadn't stopped her. Eliza didn't have nearly enough motorway experience to drive all the way to *Cambridge* alone, and in an unfamiliar vehicle. What if she'd had an accident? Become tired or distracted, lost focus for a split second? These things happened. The world could change in a heartbeat.

She found herself remembering one of the most terrifying

moments of her life, back when her daughter was three. Eliza had managed to unclip the clasps fastening her into the buggy, midway along the street. The first Lara knew of it was when Eliza had tumbled straight out of the buggy and head first into the road. How long did it take Lara to dash forward and snatch her up while a Škoda Octavia screeched to a halt mere metres away? A second, maybe two? Long enough, certainly, that the world seemed to shiver and blur, Eliza's life hanging perilously in the balance, until, with a gasp and a prayer, she was back in Lara's arms, swept up from the tarmac and clutched tight, the blare of the car horn splitting the air as everything sped up once more.

Afterwards they'd both been in tears, but no real damage had been done, only a bumped head for Eliza, a sprinkling of new grey hairs for Lara and confirmation of the Octavia driver's excellent reflexes. It had never left her, though, that agonising moment where things could have see-sawed either way. What if the car hadn't been able to stop? What if Eliza had died? It haunted her, the idea that there was a parallel universe in which her little girl was no more, while Lara had been left a bereaved mother, destroyed by grief. Sometimes it seemed only a matter of chance that the two of them had made it this far together at all.

Half an hour or so later, Tyrone broke off from conversation to point ahead, where a white VW was parked up at the side of the road, with Eliza sitting rather forlornly beside it on a grassy verge. 'There she is,' he said.

Look at her, Lara thought, heart cracking a little as she indicated and slowed to pull in behind the white car, remembering all the younger incarnations of her daughter: in a pink leotard and tutu during the ballet years, wearing a princess swimming costume as she splashed about in turquoise holiday pools, her

64

first secondary school uniform, with her hair in bunches and a too large blazer . . . Now, in the blink of an eye, she was a young woman with smoky eye make-up, ripped jeans and a sulky expression. *She's leaving me*, Lara thought with a lurch, heaving on the handbrake. *Somehow or other, while my attention was elsewhere, she's grown up and wants to go her own way. And right now, that means away from me.*

Eliza scowled as they approached, although she blushed and mumbled apologies as she held the car keys out to Tyrone.

'Remember what I told you,' Lara called after him as he said goodbye and began loping towards his car. 'About training to be a driving instructor – think about it. You'd be good!'

He raised a hand in acknowledgement and left them to it. Eliza's lip promptly curled. 'What, you're trying to get him to be a driving instructor now? God, Mum, is that all you think about?'

So much for meek, repentant Eliza. That hadn't lasted long. 'Well, no, obviously,' Lara replied drily, spreading her hands wide to take in the road beside them and the fact they were both there at midday on a Friday. 'Funnily enough, my mind has been taken up with other things this morning. Like you, getting in trouble with the police, after taking someone else's car with a half-brained notion of driving to bloody *Cambridge!*'

She shouldn't have said 'half-brained'. She regretted it instantly. Because now Eliza was drawing away from her, eyes narrow with anger. 'What was I supposed to do?' she retaliated. 'When I can't trust you to tell me the truth any more? I'm not going to hang about waiting for you to drip-feed me information about my own existence. I've been doing that my whole life and I'm sick of it!'

Tyrone had turned his car around by now and waved as he drove past. Lara waved back, smiling brightly, but her face sagged as soon as he'd gone. 'Let's go home,' she said, reaching out a hand for Eliza's arm. 'We can talk more about this on the way.'

The girl jerked back to avoid being touched. 'I'm not going home,' she said. 'You go if you want. Don't let me stop you.'

'What do you mean, you're not going home? Of course we're—'

'No.' Eliza's voice was low but carried real threat. The girl in the princess swimming costume had, in fact, a core of steel. 'I'm going to Cambridge. And if you don't want to come, that's fine, I'll get a coach. Or hitch a lift, if I have to.'

'Lize, this is—' Lara stopped herself microseconds before saying 'ridiculous'. No one liked being called ridiculous, especially not a teenager in full righteous flow.

'I'm eighteen years old and I want to meet my dad. I'm going and you can't stop me.'

Lara stared down at her feet and drew a breath – and as she did so, remembered a conversation they'd had three or four years ago. She'd gone to the doctor because one of her legs had become swollen, only to be told it was a blood clot that, at any given moment, could break loose and drift aimlessly up to her lungs, possibly killing her. Treatment had swiftly followed and she was absolutely fine now, but it had shaken her, imagining that she might have suffered a stroke, or even died, due to the random travels of this rogue clot. She'd drawn up a will the same week, and forced herself to discuss with Eliza who would look after her, should the worst happen. Grandma and Heidi would be there for her, Lara had assured her, but Eliza had shaken her head. 'I'd go and find Dad,' she'd said loftily. 'Force him to do some parenting for a change.'

That should have been a red flag in itself, a warning to Lara that the idea of tracking down her father was bubbling away in the back of Eliza's mind. But instead of confronting the issue, she'd plunged her head further into the sand. And now look where they were.

A powder-blue Mini sped by just then, loud music blasting from the open windows, and the sound set her teeth on edge. 'Okay,' she said. 'I hear you. But let's get in the car at least and talk it through.'

Eliza didn't move. 'I'm not getting in the car until you say that we're going to Cambridge. Today,' she replied, folding her arms.

Lara felt thoroughly beaten. Driving down to Cambridge today, in pursuit of the elusive Ben McManus, was really the very last thing she wanted to do. She'd been quite happy for the past to stay firmly in the past, to seal up the part of her heart which had been broken, and forget the whole thing for evermore. But Eliza left her with no option. If this trip had to be made now, as her daughter was insisting, then Lara couldn't let her go alone.

'Fine,' she muttered, unable to come up with a better idea. 'You win. Get in the car. Let's go.'

'So what was he like, then? My mysterious dad?' said Eliza. 'Am I allowed to ask that yet or are you going to carry on being secretive? Because it's probably in your interest to give me your side of the story before I ask him his. Don't you reckon?'

They had been driving for about twenty minutes in a bad-tempered silence, and so far Eliza had eaten almost all of the cheesy biscuits and two of the sandwiches Lara had bought as a picnic lunch from a garage shop they'd passed. If Lara had hoped that some sustenance might take the edge off her daughter's combative mood, she'd been straight-up kidding herself.

Here goes, then. No more secrecy. Might as well get it over with, she figured. 'Well,' she began, glad that she was obliged to keep her gaze on the road, rather than cope with intense eye contact on top of everything else, 'I have to say, the night I met your dad, I thought he was pretty much the best person ever.' She attempted a neutral voice but couldn't avoid a sigh creeping in. 'I thought he was really something.'

The words might sound corny but they were true. One of the reasons she tried not to think about Ben McManus for any length of time was because of how devastated she had felt when the relationship – if you could even call it that – didn't go any-where. She had played and replayed their conversations, their connection, their passion, trying to find errors, hairline cracks, moments when she should have noticed that he wasn't into it in the way she was. But either he was an astonishingly good actor, or she was astonishingly stupid, because she had never been able to detect a single glance, a single reaction that belied the bond she'd felt. So what had gone wrong? The answer had eluded her this whole time; his memory a painful, not-to-be-prodded bruise.

But she was getting ahead of herself already. 'So, like I said, we met in New York,' she went on, keeping her voice steady as she indicated to overtake a trundling lorry. 'I was doing an internship there on a magazine, a four-month placement.'

'Whoa,' Eliza said. 'Seriously? You never told me about that! I assumed you were there on holiday.'

Lara was silent for a moment. It was hard for her – and for Eliza too, apparently – to equate the daring, independent young woman from those days with the boring old mum she felt her-self to be now. 'Yeah,' she said quietly, flashing back to the thrill of being in the city and feeling as if she were constantly on a film set; the heady impression that a filter on her life had been dialled up to a brighter, more vivid configuration. 'It was pretty exciting. I loved it.'

'Wow,' said Eliza, still digesting. 'So what about Ben? My dad?' She sounded self-conscious, as if she were trying the phrase on for size. 'Was he working there too?'

'He was travelling with some mates,' Lara replied, trying not to sigh again. 'He was between jobs; a career break, he called it, so—'

'What, from running a *map* shop?'

'No.' Lara flicked on the wipers as it started to drizzle. 'He was a full-time graphic designer then, I think, but was taking some time to work out what he wanted to do for the rest of his life.'

'Right,' said Eliza, impatiently. 'So what happened?'

Chapter Seven

Easy to say in hindsight, but on that golden summer's day when she first met Ben, Lara kept getting the feeling that the world was being particularly good to her. That everything was clicking into place, the cogs of her life turning especially smoothly, that all signs pointed towards her luck being in. Purely by chance, she'd got a seat on the packed subway train to work when usually she had to stand, crammed in with her fellow passengers, her face often ending up squished into someone's hot armpit. Then, approaching her office building, she noticed a twenty-dollar bill blowing around on the sidewalk and even though she glanced around conscientiously to see if anyone had obviously just dropped it, there was no sign of this and so she pocketed it herself. That wasn't all. At work, the temperamental coffee machine behaved itself perfectly. The printer didn't jam for once. Lara was asked to write a piece on beachwear and the editor praised her 'Girls Just Wanna Have Sun' title. And then, when she took herself off for an al fresco lunch in Madison Square Park (yes, obviously she bought herself a pastrami sandwich like a proper New Yorker), a pretty blue butterfly appeared, seemingly from out of nowhere, and landed randomly on her hand for a delightful, breath-holding moment. The hot June sun shone down and she turned her face to it like a flower, feeling as if she too might be blooming. As if everything was coming together for her, right here, right now.

Lara hadn't socialised much with her colleagues by that point, but she was feeling so upbeat that when her friend Janine suggested they go for a drink after work, she said yes at once – not least because of that extra twenty dollars in her purse. Calling Janine a 'friend' was pushing it, admittedly – she was a secretary on the magazine, ten years older than Lara and clearly trying to take her under her wing a bit. Lara had only been in the city a few weeks, and was wide-eyed and, in retrospect, pretty gauche; the proverbial goldfish out of its bowl. She was glad to have something to do in the evening for a change, other than slink back to the dismal, cramped room she was renting and write airmail letters home telling everyone what an amazing time she was having.

They walked into Stefano's, a bar on the Lower East Side, and there he was, sitting near the entrance with a couple of mates. To be strictly honest, Lara noticed one of his friends first who was wearing a Paul Smith shirt, because this was the sort of detail a fashion journalist homed in on. Then she heard their accents – British – and her ears pricked up. As she and Janine passed them, Lara's eyes met Ben's – barely for a second – only to feel an unexpected jolt in response; an almost chemical reaction.

Even now, she couldn't put her finger on how it was possible that one single glance had forged such a connection between them. It had certainly never happened to her before. He was good-looking, sure, with shaggy, dark brown hair, grey eyes and an infectious smile, and wore drainpipe jeans and a faded black

71

shirt with the sleeves rolled up. And yet in response, her pulse was going berserk, her skin tingling, as if her body was priming itself for something significant to take place. *Ah – here he is*, her heart seemed to be saying. *This is the one.*

The jukebox was playing 'The Boys of Summer', as if the whole scene had been carefully staged, and he and his friends were laughing together, beer bottles in hand. Even now, Lara couldn't hear the song without flashing back to that moment when, unknown to her, her life forked into two clear paths. *With him. Without him.*

'Who *is* that guy? Do you know him? He keeps looking at you,' Janine commented as they bought drinks and a bowl of peanuts and sat down in a quiet corner.

A hot blush coursed through Lara as she turned her head towards him and he raised his bottle at her in a kind of salute. 'I have no idea,' she said, feeling a surge of gratitude towards whichever angel up there had reminded her to put on extra lipstick and mascara in the ladies' before leaving work, and for the fact that she was wearing a pencil skirt that flattered her legs, along with a cornflower-blue crepey blouse borrowed from her flatmate Toni. Back then, her thick dark brown hair had been halfway down her back, and as the summer had heated up, she'd taken to wearing it pinned up in a messy chignon, with a few loose tendrils framing her face. Plus she'd recently had a blunt fringe chopped in, and one of the designers at work had told her she reminded him of an art-school Audrey Hepburn, a compliment that continued to thrill her whenever she repeated it to herself.

'He's good-looking though, right?' Janine said, elbowing her. 'Huh?'

'Do you think?' Lara deferred, throwing a peanut up in the air and catching it in her mouth. She and her brother had driven their mum mad doing this as teenagers – 'This is not a chimps' tea party!' she'd cry, trying to slap their hands in frustration. Which, naturally, had only encouraged them further, with Richie becoming particularly obsessed with his technique. Lara remembered him even attempting to eat an entire roast dinner that way, although, unsurprisingly, the gravy proved his downfall. Years later, the knack hadn't left Lara and she threw another peanut high, feeling the man's gaze on her across the bar as she neatly caught it. Everything really was going her way today, she congratulated herself, just as—

Oh God—

The nut—

Had stuck—

'Are you okay, honey?' she heard Janine say.

And she was—

She was coughing, and—

'Are you all right? Can I help?'

A different voice now – and oh Christ, the man himself was over at their table, how humiliating could you get? She tried to smile attractively – hey, I'm fine – but she was starting to wheeze and no doubt turning scarlet and—

He banged her on the back once, twice, and just as she was thinking that it would serve her right if she choked to death in a Lower East Side bar because she had been trying to show off in front of a stranger, wouldn't that be absolutely typical of her luck, then—

Another bang on the back, harder this time, and out it came. A glistening peanut on the table in front of them. Ha ha ha, laughed the universe, clutching its sides with hilarity. Well, that cool move totally backfired, didn't it, hey?

Feeling hot all over, her back throbbing between the shoulder blades from his thump, Lara caught her breath, grateful that such a thing was possible once more. Then she grabbed a coaster and put it on top of the saliva-coated peanut so that nobody had to look at it for a second longer. 'Thank you,' she croaked, mortified that she had utterly wrecked the breezy image she'd attempted to project. What a klutz, honestly. This could only happen to her. 'Sorry about that.'

'Have a drink,' urged Janine, pushing her beer bottle over towards her. 'Are you okay now?'

'I'm fine,' Lara said, turning her eyes on the man. 'Just embarrassed. Thank you for ... well, saving me from an untimely peanut-related death. It's not really the way I thought I would go.'

He smiled at her. 'You're welcome. I knew there was a reason I did that first aid course.'

'You're a Brit too!' Janine cried in delight. 'So's Lara here. And you are ... ?'

'Ben,' he replied. He had a southern accent, Lara registered, but not posh. 'Hi Lara.'

'Hi Ben,' she said shyly, and automatically put her hand out.

Janine hooted with mirth. 'You two!' she cried, slapping her palms against the table as the two of them shook. 'You're so *British*! Shaking hands in a *bar*! That is the most British thing I ever *saw*!'

Ben laughed. 'You can always count on the Brits for an awkward formal interaction.'

'Yeah, next time you're saving my life, maybe it would be polite to tell me your name *first*?' Lara joked. 'I'm kidding. Thank you. Can I get you a drink or something?'

'Allow me,' said Janine, rising to her feet with the swiftness of a born matchmaker. 'Was that Budweiser you were drinking? I'll be right back.'

Now it was just the two of them left at the table. Ben sat down and they smiled at one another rather self-consciously. 'So ... is this a hobby of yours?' Lara said, for want of a better conversation starter. 'Sprinting to the rescue of choking strangers?'

'You're my first,' he said. 'I hope you feel special. Although, just saying, you could have gone on for a bit longer, so that I got to try out an actual Heimlich manoeuvre on you. I've never done one of those before.'

She laughed. 'Sorry about that. Pretty inconsiderate of me. Next time I'll try harder.'

'If you wouldn't mind,' he replied. 'I was just gearing up for it as well. Quite excited, to be honest. Although the one I've really been looking forward to having a go at is stopping a kid from choking. You know you have to dangle them upside down by their ankles?'

She wasn't sure whether to believe him or not, especially because she knew very little about kids. 'You don't,' she replied, sensing he was teasing her.

'You do! Hang them upside down and whack them on the back. Let gravity do its thing.'

Janine came back just then, plonking a bottle of Bud on the table. 'Is this a private first aid lesson or can anyone join in?' she asked. 'Cheers, anyway,' she went on, clinking her bottle against Lara's and Ben's. 'To surprise encounters.'

'To surprise encounters,' they echoed. She *liked* him, she thought, as the three of them began chatting. Properly *liked* him, in a warm fluttery way she hadn't experienced in so long. He was funny and friendly and interested in her, plus she was delighted to come across another British person, having spent the last few weeks feeling pretty friendless and alone. Conversation flowed easily, along with the drinks. He was a designer, taking some time out to 'find himself', he told her, making air quotes with his fingers as if the phrase embarrassed him, only to laugh when she grabbed his arm and said, 'Here you are. I found you!' They talked about living in London; how he'd been renting a flat in Stoke Newington while she shared a house with a few girlfriends in Camberwell ('What's that great pub in Camberwell? The Sun – do you ever go there?' he asked, only for her to exclaim, 'All the time! That's my local!'). They talked about each other's families – he had more sisters than was good for any man, he'd groaned, while Lara made him laugh describing a particularly disastrous camping holiday she and Richie had suffered with their mum, Frances, one summer in Morecambe – and then he'd told her about his trip, and all the sights he and his friends, Sam and Charlie, were due to take in over the next month. Sam and Charlie came over themselves when it became obvious that Ben wasn't about to return to his former seat, and the five of them shared bowls of salty chips, along with several other beers.

Janine left after a while – 'Time to get back to the ranch,' she said apologetically, winking at Lara as she sashayed out of there. She had two little children, as well as a husband who apparently broke out in a cold sweat if he was left alone with them for too long. Soon afterwards, Sam and Charlie also made their exits, saying they were going to get pizza, which left only Lara and Ben at the table.

The bar had filled up by now. It was a laid-back sort of place, all dark wood and dim lighting, with a soundtrack of easy-listening music and occasional clicks and clacks from the pool table behind them. A ceiling fan stirred the muggy air above their heads and outside Lara could see the sky darkening from rose gold to violet. They had just worked out that they'd been at the same Glastonbury festival the year before, seeing almost exactly the same bands. 'We might have been dancing right next to each other,' Lara said, laughing. 'How weird is that?'

'We could have met a whole year earlier!' he cried, slapping a hand to his head as if he regretted the intervening twelve months as lost time.

'Or before that, if we'd got chatting in The Sun,' she said, playing along. 'Small world.'

They both fell silent momentarily, looking at each other as if uncertain where they went from here. She felt such chemistry between them, such an easy, flirty rapport, but at the end of the day, they were only a couple of strangers in a bar, right? Two people who'd enjoyed a few drinks and a chat, and maybe that would have to be enough. He was heading off to Boston in a week, whereas she ... wasn't. And this was all part of being away from home, wasn't it? Striking up conversations with people along the way, meeting one another tangentially, temporarily, before moving on to the next place, the next person. Lara, who was a realist at heart, was already preparing a line about how nice it was to have met him and wishing him well on his trip. 'Well ...' she began — with some regret, admittedly, because he was by far the most fun and interesting person she'd had a drink with for ages, and if they were back in the UK, she would certainly be wondering if the evening might lead to anything more substantial.

Before she could finish her sentence though, he asked, 'Do you want to get anything else to eat? Or we could go for a walk?'

★

Lara hadn't seen much of the city by night, at that point. Toni was often out with friends or back at her parents' place in Brooklyn for family dinners, and Lara had felt apprehensive about venturing out very far on her own once the sun went down. Shy, almost, as if she were tiptoeing around this relationship with her new city, afraid to dive right in. But with Ben, she felt differently – bolder, more adventurous. Having already explored the Lower East Side a little by day, she was able to point out Katz's Deli – 'You know, from *When Harry Met Sally*?' – and the tenement buildings from the guidebook reading she'd done, but then, as they progressed towards Greenwich Village, she found herself in new territory and enjoyed that they could marvel over everything together: the jostle of bars and restaurants and arty shops, music spilling from open windows, the humidity and smells of the city as it eased from evening into night. Couples kissed on the corners of the streets. Taxis honked, their drivers' elbows angled through the windows as they waited at the lights, drumming their fingers.

'This is amazing,' he said, gazing around. 'I feel as if I've escaped everything back home and plunged straight into a proper adventure, do you know what I mean?'

'Totally,' she replied. They were walking past a cellar jazz bar just then and glimpsed a couple dancing together, her in a red dress that spun out around her knees, him in a sharp suit, his shirt open at the neck. She almost wanted to laugh at how cinematic everything seemed. 'It's like being part of a film,' she went on, before blurting out, 'Thank you.'

'What for?' he asked, bemused.

'For . . . turning up. For appearing just when I needed you to,' she said, then laughed, bashful at her own words. 'Now *I* sound like I'm in a film. A really terrible one.'

'I'm glad to be in your terrible film,' he said, taking her hand and squeezing it. 'I'm having a good night too. The sort of night you don't want to end.' He wrinkled his nose. 'My turn for the cheesy dialogue. Who wrote this thing?' he cried, shaking a fist jokily. 'I demand to see my agent. And a script editor!'

They continued along the street, still talking. At some point she remembered there was an apple in her bag, leftover from lunch, and she took it out, polished it on her skirt and crunched into it, then passed it on to him. Was there anything more companionable than sharing an apple with a delightful stranger? she thought happily, the two of them so easy with one another that their sentences overlapped frequently, punctuated with bursts of laughter.

'I was feeling a bit of a fraud before tonight,' she admitted. Maybe it was the beer making her talk so freely, or perhaps the fact that they were walking so close to one another now that their shoulders kept brushing against each other, the connection between them becoming physically, deliciously tactile.

'In what way? Oh Christ, don't say you're a spy or something. Is your name even Lara?' He stopped, eyeing her teasingly. 'Is this the moment when you tell me you're working undercover and you're really a sixty-eight-year-old bloke from Dundee called Malcolm?'

She laughed again. She was starting to feel giddy. Untethered in the best possible way. 'Ah shite. Rumbled,' she said in a gravelly Scottish accent. Now he was laughing too and the sound almost lifted her off her feet. She liked him more with every passing moment. Did he like her too? It felt dizzyingly as if he might.

The apple was finished now and she paused by a large street

planter to fish out a pip and poke it into the warm earth there. 'What are you . . . ? Is this some stealth gardening?' Ben asked.

She blushed. 'Oh. It's just a habit,' she confessed. 'I always plant the pips wherever I finish eating an apple. I like imagining trees springing up in my wake, everywhere I go. You never know.'

'Like you're a tree princess, with a legacy of mighty orchards around the world.'

'Something like that,' she replied, hoping he didn't think she was too much of a weirdo. She'd become so used to doing this with apple pips, cherry stones, tomato seeds, that it no longer seemed a big deal to her, but she could see that it might appear strange to outsiders.

'I love it,' he told her, smiling, and then they began walking again, ignoring the man selling cellophane-wrapped roses who tried to press one on them. 'Anyway, you were telling me about feeling like a fraud,' he remembered, elbowing her gently. 'How so?'

'I meant . . .' She tried to marshal her thoughts into sentences. 'Well, I've been here nearly three weeks now, and keep telling everyone back home what a wild time I'm having, how much I love New York and all that – except . . .' She hesitated, feeling as if she were peeling away the top layer of her skin, exposing her weakness. 'Except it's all been kind of exaggerated,' she admitted. 'I've felt quite lonely a lot of the time. I mean, I've been to Times Square and the Empire State Building like a tourist, but I haven't really got under the surface of the city. Not properly. But this . . .' She gestured around her, at the neon signs lighting the pizzerias and kebab places, the bars and restaurants, the zigzag of fire escapes on every building, the hum of people and traffic. She felt as if her outer edges were blurring with her surroundings suddenly, her body filling up with the evening on a cellular level, New York pouring into her veins with a heady thrill. 'This, right here, is *it*. And I feel so happy, to be here, experiencing – where are we? MacDougal Street,' she read from a nearby street sign. 'So happy to be walking down MacDougal Street for the very first time, because I finally made it. I finally got my New York. So thank you.'

His eyes were soft beneath the glow of a streetlight. 'Well, it doesn't have to end yet,' he said. 'I say we just keep going and make a proper night of it. I could walk for hours, couldn't you? Although . . . Wait a minute.' They'd reached a crossroads and he peered diagonally over at a bar, his body suddenly taut with a new energy. 'No way. There it is! Cafe Wha? – it's on my list of places to go. Jimi Hendrix and Bob Dylan used to hang out there. Oh wow. Shall we? Would you mind?'

'Absolutely!' she replied, loving his boyish enthusiasm and immediacy, delighted that he didn't feel he had to act cool in front of her. 'Let's do it.'

Inside, Cafe Wha? was grungy and dark, with framed photos of musicians on the walls and booth seating. Lightbulbs dangled from the low ceiling and a band on stage hit the last few notes of a song to a rowdy round of applause. The place was crammed with hip people in Stooges and Ramones T-shirts, snaky tattoos and great eye make-up, and for a few uncertain moments Lara wished she was dressed in something edgier than office clothes before deciding that, actually, she didn't care. Ben bought them a pitcher of beer to share and they squeezed into the last seats of a booth, having to lean their heads together in order to hear above the music as a new song started up.

The evening progressed from talking to dancing, and then,

once back in their booth to catch their breath, their eyes met, and in the next moment, they were both instinctively leaning towards the other and kissing across the table. Her lips against his, her eyes closed, her body overwhelmed by sensation. *Oh my goodness.* He was an amazing kisser. Before that night, she'd thought of kissing as a fairly boring and unhygienic part of foreplay. She'd put up with the thrusting tongues of previous boyfriends, her head pushed back so hard that her neck hurt, and the unpleasant taste of someone else's mouth – none of it good in her opinion. But with Ben, wow, she finally got it. At last, the idea – and the practice – of kissing made total, giddying sense.

'Whew,' she murmured thickly when they eventually broke apart. His pupils were massive as they gazed at one another, colourful lights strobing across their faces. The ground beneath their feet throbbed to the bass. She felt bewitched, as if she were under an enchantment from a fairy tale.

'This is ... amazing,' he shouted above the music. 'Tonight, I mean. You. What have you done to me?'

She felt the same way. Hadn't she known it, from that very first moment? 'Oh, I've barely started,' she replied, with the cockiness that came from her complete certainty about him. About them. 'Let's go back to my apartment,' she added in the next breath.

Once there, they tumbled into bed with a new urgency. 'Wait, I've got a condom somewhere,' she said, scurrying naked from the sheets after a while to rummage through the so far unused '*Sex in the City* care package' her friend Jodie had given her as a leaving present.

'Look at you,' he said huskily, propping himself up on one elbow in the bed and gazing at her. The bedroom blind was broken and an orange glow seeped through from the streetlight outside, illuminating their outlines. 'You're so beautiful.'

Nobody had ever said that word to Lara before. Nobody had looked at her that way either, as if he was seeing her, really seeing her, and he liked everything he saw. Her body flooded with heat at the compliment but she couldn't relax fully into his words. She felt disbelieving, if anything, as if he couldn't possibly mean it. The room wasn't even brightly lit, after all. 'I bet you say that to all the girls,' she mumbled, sliding quickly back under the sheet.

'I don't,' he said, putting his arms around her again. 'I promise you I don't.'

Underneath his clothes, he was lean and muscled, his hard chest pale in the dim light, his bare bottom peachy. 'Is this okay?' he asked a few minutes later. 'I don't want you to think that this is just about sex. Because it isn't, Lara.'

'Don't stop,' she groaned. She didn't want any of it to stop — the kissing, the sex, the whole evening and night. But she knew what he meant: that this had none of the hallmarks of 'random casual encounter'. There was no doubt in her mind that tonight was definitely the start of something.

The next morning, they'd woken up and the connection between them still felt right and immediate and *good*. Lara could hardly believe her luck. All of a sudden, the whole summer seemed to be stretching before her, bathed in a golden new light, full of joy and discovery. He was already talking about rearranging his itinerary so that he could spend more time with her. She was thinking about places around the city that they could explore that weekend. This is it, she kept marvelling inside her head. This is the one. She might not have met him at The Sun, or indeed at

Glastonbury, but at last, third time lucky, Fate had succeeded in flinging them together and boy, was she ever glad. Everything was stacking up perfectly; it was meant to be. Before saying goodbye, they agreed to meet that evening at a fancy oyster bar inside Grand Central Station, and she'd spent the entire day fizzing with the thrilled anticipation of seeing him again.

Only ... that was the sting in the tail. The surprise ending she hadn't anticipated. Because she *hadn't* seen him again, not once, not ever. It had been the biggest disappointment of her entire life, bar none.

Chapter Eight

'Why do you always *act* like that?' Kirsten had said to Ben the
night before. 'With your sisters, I mean. Why do you let them
push you around?'

They'd been getting ready for bed when this conversation took
place, the two of them in the lamp-lit bedroom, him standing
on one leg to remove a sock (he'd heard that it was the first
sign of old age, sitting down to take socks on and off, and was
determined not to be defeated, a mere five years into his forties).
'What?' he asked, so surprised he inadvertently wobbled and put
his foot down. 'They don't push me around.'

Kirsten snorted. She had a whole range of snorts, graded
according to mood. He reckoned he'd just been awarded one
from the category he thought of as Derision. 'Ben, you're too
kind to them, they walk all over you! *Will you move this for me?
Could you pick that up for me? Do this, do that, mend this, lend me
that* ... Honestly, I can't bear it. For your sake, I can't bear it.
They take advantage of you; you have to tell them.'

Ben said nothing at first. There had been similar outbursts
over the years, with Kirsten apparently not able to bear all sorts of

85

issues related to his family. You'd think his sisters were queuing up to antagonise her personally, the way she got so up in arms about them. 'They don't push me around,' he repeated mildly, peeling off his socks one, two and chucking them into the laundry basket. Both hit their target; still got it, he congratulated himself. 'I'm their brother, they ask me for help now and then. What's wrong with that? I don't mind.'

She was sitting at the vanity table taking off her make-up, peering at her reflection as she swooshed a cotton-wool pad across one eyelid and then the other. As a boy, he'd been fascinated by the sight of his mum transforming herself with her various powders and pastes into a sparkly, dewy-eyed, newly delineated version of herself, but had always been relieved to see her return to her softer-faced natural self again the next morning. It was the same with Kirsten; she looked so cute and vulnerable at the end of the day, he thought, stripped of her going-out warpaint, clean and scrubbed. Her small blinking face reminded him of a baby hedgehog, although he'd never dare tell her so. He wasn't a complete idiot.

'Of course you don't mind,' she was saying, sarcasm lacing her voice. 'Good old Ben, he won't mind. That's what they say about you. They treat you like a mug though. When did any of them do one nice thing for you?'

'It's not about that,' he said, undoing his jeans and hanging them over the back of the chair. Nobody ever sat in the chair that lived in their bedroom; it was a clothes horse and nothing more. He briefly considered saying to her 'You wouldn't understand', but Kirsten, an only child, had occasionally railed drunkenly about how only children got this unfair rep for being spoiled and bad sharers, and her theory was that it stemmed from basic jealousy, reckoning that everyone secretly hated their siblings. He didn't want to get into all of that again. 'And they're my *sisters*. I can't exactly say no to them.'

She exhaled noisily and he knew he'd said the wrong thing. 'That is *precisely* my point,' she said, patting night cream on to her cheeks. 'Because you *can* say no, Ben. It's very easy. No, Charlotte, I'm not going to have a look at your starter motor for you, because I'm not a mechanic, okay? No, Annie, you can't borrow our lawnmower because you still haven't given us back the power drill. Where *is* that, by the way? Has she broken it, do you think? And no, Sophie, I don't have time to go and help empty your hoarder's-paradise garage because – newsflash: you have two strapping teenage sons who should get off their idle arses and do that for you, rather than loafing around playing computer games all day.' Her jaw clenched as she smoothed in the cream. 'See? It's not hard.'

'I know,' he said because he was too tired to argue. He'd had a busy day at work and spending the evening with his extended family was always exhausting, however much he loved them all. Plus, even though he had no intention of refusing his sisters so brutally (their faces! They would be so shocked and hurt! His ears already burned to imagine the storm of follow-up phone calls that would ensue), there were times when he knew that conceding points now meant he could at least get to sleep faster once they were in bed. This was not perhaps the most healthy way to view a marital disagreement, but never mind.

'So you'll tell them that, will you?'

He pulled his shirt over his head, not wanting to meet her eye. Wishing that Kirsten didn't make him feel so weak at moments like this. He was not a weak person, all right? There was nothing wrong with wanting an easy life.

'Annie, especially,' she went on, when he didn't reply. 'Just because she's single now, she seems to think she's incapable of tackling perfectly ordinary household tasks herself. And that you are the only man in the world who can fix things for her. When, you know, there are plenty of handymen out there. And YouTube videos!'

He sighed. Kirsten and Annie had never got along; they were too similar, Ben thought privately, both unequivocal in their opinions and prone to making blunt remarks without thinking first. He rubbed his chest, feeling a sudden stab of indigestion. 'She's had a rough time,' he said, escaping through to the en suite in his boxers to brush his teeth.

'Yeah, but they're not little girls any more, are they?' she managed to get in just before he started his electric toothbrush buzzing. Mercifully he missed the rest of whatever else she wanted to say, and stared glumly at his reflection, hoping that an interval of dental care might draw a line under the conversation.

They were not little girls, his sisters, true, but he had always looked out for them. Since their dad had had a massive heart attack at the wheel of his cab, aged fifty-nine, then died days later, Ben, as the oldest sibling, had stepped in to pick up the pieces of the family as best he could. The newly appointed man of the house, as his mum kept telling him. The one they all leaned on too regularly, according to Kirsten.

The years had passed but old habits die hard, and it turned out that some habits were more difficult to shake off. The four siblings had moved individually around the country at various times but they'd all gravitated home to Cambridge eventually, and Ben had made it his business to keep an eye on his sisters. Not least because there was plenty to keep an eye on, what with their poor romantic choices, financial dramas and children galore, which meant oh-so many favours from their long-suffering big brother. 'What would we do without you?' Gwen, his mum, was always exclaiming with grateful fondness, and he secretly rather enjoyed his long-established position as golden boy of the family, never putting a foot wrong. That was the way the rest of them liked it too, as far as he could tell. Apart from his wife, apparently.

Tooth-brushing complete, he rinsed his mouth then turned off the tap with a certain amount of trepidation, as if he might discover that Kirsten was still bad-mouthing his family. Thankfully he heard nothing. Was he safe to return?

Back in the bedroom, he found her looking at her phone. She stopped and glanced up at him with a strange expression, and he eyed her warily, wondering what it meant as he got into bed.

'Oh, by the way,' she said in a casual, almost offhand tone he didn't recognise. 'I bought some paint for the downstairs loo earlier.'

Okay, he thought, recalibrating. The discussion had moved on, it seemed. 'Right,' he said neutrally. 'Great.' Then, just to show willing, added, 'I'll get on to that at the weekend.'

'Yeah,' she said, as if she wasn't really listening. 'So I went for a plum-coloured shade in the end. Something a bit different.'

'Plum?' Now he was baffled. Where had this come from? 'For the loo? I assumed we'd paint it cream again.'

'Actually ...' She was acting very cagey, he thought, surprised. No longer looking at him. 'I got chatting to—' She hesitated. Only a microsecond but he caught it. His ears were well and truly pricking up now – 'someone in the paint aisle in B&Q, and I thought, why do we always go for such boring shades for our walls?'

'So you bought some purple paint, is that what you're telling me? For our downstairs loo?'

She attached her phone to the charger and put it face down on the bedside table. 'Yeah, basically,' she said. 'Because I'm sick of everything being boring.' You could practically hear the defensiveness crackling around her like a force field. *Back off*, it said. *Don't push it.*

'Right,' he said, startled, as she marched to the en suite and shut the door. Boring, eh? He imagined how, if another person was in the room at that moment, he'd look at them in disbelief. *That was weird, right?* Ben's eyes would say. *What do you think's going on there?*

The conversation came back to him now as he sat behind the shop counter the following day, jotting answers into a crossword in the newspaper during a quiet spell. Friday afternoons were often pretty uneventful in the shop, the yawning lull before the weekend got underway. People had other things on their minds at that point in the week: plans for a night out, the prospect of a lie-in and some free time, or indeed mulling over the mystery surrounding who their wife might have been talking to in the paint aisle of B&Q. This unnamed person who may or may not have gone putting ideas in her head about her so-called boring existence.

When he got up for breakfast that morning, he'd glimpsed said paint, left pointedly on the kitchen table. Kirsten worked as a midwife and was on earlies this week, another reason for her bad temper the night before, he assured himself. Making tea, bleary-eyed and regretting the late round of whisky coffees Charlotte had served up, he had eyed the paint tin with suspicion before going over for a closer look. Iced Plum, the label said, and he'd pulled a face at the rich red-purple shade, already certain that the downstairs loo would look small and dark when painted that colour, like being inside a womb. Or a wound even. Neither seemed a relaxing option for a private moment.

Ben's shop was on a quiet, not particularly picturesque, street and from where he was sitting, he could see a couple drifting by outside, hand in hand. Despite the closed door, he caught the sound of their laughter floating behind them, and experienced a twist of sadness inside. *Was* Kirsten bored? he wondered again. Bored of him, their life together? He tried to remember when they had last held hands like the pair outside and couldn't put his finger on a single instance all year. When had they stopped holding hands?

The bell on the shop door tinkled and in came the couple. They were in their twenties, he guessed, both with golden tans and sun-streaked hair. Australian, Ben predicted. Working in retail in Cambridge gave you an eye for identifying tourists. 'Hi,' said the guy, who had a shark's tooth on a leather string around his neck and bright blue eyes. 'We love the maps you've got in the window – the personalised ones?' Yes, definitely Australian, Ben thought, his mind conjuring up images of huge surfing waves and red desert. 'Would you be able to do one for us?'

'Sure,' Ben said, jotting down some details from the man – Jonathan from Perth, Cate from Melbourne – while the woman (Cate, presumably) wandered around the small shop interior, eyeing the Cambridge prints and postcards he'd designed, before standing in front of Ben's favourite piece in the entire shop: the steel-plate-engraved, hand-coloured Cambridgeshire map, from the mid seventeenth century. It was on sale for a cool eight hundred quid and Ben loved it so much he knew he'd be gutted if anyone ever actually bought it. He also knew that if he brought it home and hung it on their wall, Kirsten would raise an eyebrow in her most long-suffering manner and demand that it go straight back for someone else to buy. 'It's a shop, it's not your spare bedroom,' she was fond of saying.

Ben had owned the shop for twelve years now and business was pretty good. When he'd returned to Cambridge following his father's death, he'd initially taken on his dad's cab round for want of anything else to do with himself, ferrying passengers to and from the airport, the station, the hospital, the city centre, picking up the elderly and infirm, drunk club-goers and jet-lagged tourists alike. The money was decent and the work was steady, plus there was some comfort to be had from being in his dad's cab, doing his dad's job for him – especially since his father had disapproved of Ben's decision to give up his lucrative corporate design job to go travelling. *There comes a time in a man's life when he has to grow up and settle down*, he'd said, more than once, puffing out his chest as he liked to do when delivering one of his Dad Homilies. It had seemed to Ben as if the time to grow up had finally arrived.

The problem was that after a year's taxi-driving, Ben began to feel lodged in a rut. A rut that was deepening with every week. He and Kirsten were married by then, and he felt a quiet premonition of horror at the thought of spending the rest of his years trapped in the driver's seat of a cab while life happened on the other side of the windscreen. All he was doing was taking people to places and never going anywhere himself. His creativity felt like a wilting plant with no means of nourishment. He needed more, before the last of his leaves shrivelled to a crisp and fell right off. It really came home to him one afternoon when he was dropping a middle-aged couple at the crematorium for, as it turned out, their nephew's funeral. This nephew had died unexpectedly, falling down a flight of stone steps and breaking his neck. Only twenty-seven, the same age as Ben. 'You never know, do you?' the man said grimly. 'What's in store for you. All we can do is try and live our best lives, every single day.'

'And not put things off,' his wife had added, dabbing her eyes. 'Do everything you can before it's too late.'

It had sowed a seed deep inside Ben – the feeling that he *wasn't* living his best life, that he wasn't making the most of his opportunities. That he had shelved pretty much all his ambitions without even trying. Didn't he owe it to the couple's nephew, and every other young person who'd died too soon, to try harder, to seize every chance that came his way?

As if some higher power heard him, a new business idea sent up a little green shoot the very next day. He'd been chatting to a passenger who told him her husband was from Leeds, and that the early years of their relationship had been conducted up and down the M1. This brought to mind dots on a satellite map, moving towards one another, and then Ben thought about all the many similar journeys travelled between other couples. Could you plot a relationship on a map? It turned out that, with bold colours on a clear background, you could tell a visual story, clearly and effectively. He started small, designing prints as gifts for friends and family, before building himself a website and getting on to an independent shopping platform. Suddenly he was receiving orders from around the country – around the world, occasionally – and after six months or so, he decided to take the plunge, give up the cab-driving and throw himself into his own business.

He diversified into Cambridge souvenirs, designing prints and postcards, tote bags and mugs, which he sold to several tourist sites in town, and then, when the old vintage maps shop went up for sale five or so years later, the idea of having an actual storefront and a presence within the city was too appealing to ignore. Since then, he'd taken on two part-time members of staff to help run the shop while he produced the personalised maps, and his profit margins were gratifyingly robust year on year.

'You must have been to so many places, I'm guessing,' said the Australian woman now, pausing in front of an antique map of Patagonia. 'Even looking at these maps, I'm getting itchy feet again. Hey, Jon, when are we going to make it to South America? There's so much world to see, right?'

Ben smiled politely but felt something of an impostor, as he always did whenever people asked him about his own travels. He was glad that his assistant, Nick, was in the back room, parcelling up prints to send out to customers, and couldn't see the awkward expression on Ben's face. Because in truth, although he loved maps and thought they were beautiful, fascinating objects, he was embarrassed to admit that he'd hardly been to any of the places displayed in frames around the walls of his shop. He hadn't been to Greece or Rome; he hadn't been to China or Indonesia or Australia. He definitely hadn't been to Patagonia. Did it matter? Did it make him a fake?

'Your dad didn't die because you went to New York,' Kirsten had gently reminded him a few years ago, when she mooted the idea of going somewhere far-flung on holiday (Thailand? Bali?) only for him to mumble reasons about why he didn't want to. Environmental concerns, he'd said. Long flights. Tropical diseases. And then she'd said that, about his dad, and it was as if she'd seen right through him. Of course Ben's aborted trip to the States hadn't caused Stewart McManus's heart attack. He knew that, obviously, as a rational human being. Yet it was hard to shake off the superstition that still gripped him – that if he took his eye off the family circle, if he went too far away again, then something else bad would happen, and it would be all his fault.

Did that make him an idiot? Or merely the punchline to a joke – a man selling maps who never travelled anywhere himself? It was almost as ridiculous as a man driving a cab and never going anywhere. 'We need an adventure,' Kirsten had said to him at the time and the words echoed in his head now, as he thanked the young Australians for their custom, promised he'd have their print ready within a few days, and they left the shop. He and Kirsten could have had more adventures together, he thought ruefully, watching the couple resume their hand-holding outside with easy intimacy. But he'd never come good on delivering one, had he? Somehow the spontaneity had silently departed their relationship. On impulse, he picked up his phone and dialled her number, suddenly needing to prove that he could still surprise her.

Chapter Nine

Rain began to patter against the windscreen as Lara and Eliza approached Peterborough, one of the wipers screeching and juddering each time it moved, where the rubber trim needed replacing. Once Lara finished describing how she'd met Ben, only for him to vanish completely after one single, glorious night, Eliza loudly professed her outrage.

'What, so he stood you up? And you were hanging around waiting for him?' cried Eliza. 'How could he *do* that?'

'Well—' Lara hesitated, but Eliza was still in full flow. 'What do you think *happened*? Why didn't he meet you?'

'I don't know,' Lara sighed. 'I went to his hostel the morning after, but was told he'd checked out the previous afternoon – before we were even due to meet.'

'What the hell?' Eliza looked incensed now. 'What a complete and utter shithead.'

'My thoughts exactly,' Lara replied grimly. And yet she still didn't know if it was quite as straightforward as all that. Had he *really* been a straight-up con man, a so-called shithead, only out for sex? He'd been incredibly convincing if so. But who wanted a relationship with someone like that? Not her. So good riddance, frankly.

Had she been too full-on, maybe? Too keen? The morning after, she'd jokingly asked how the two of them were going to spend the rest of their lives together – but it *had* been a joke. If anything, he'd been more overtly enthusiastic about a relationship, telling her that he'd changed his mind about moving back to Scotland following his trip. 'I hear Camberwell's a great place to live,' he'd said, arching an eyebrow at her that made her tummy flip over. Yes, please, she'd thought, smiling at the idea.

Maybe, though, he'd woken up and decided he didn't fancy her any more without his beer goggles. Perhaps her chunky thighs had put him off, the sight of her bare bum or terrible bed hair the next morning. Maybe she had farted in her sleep all night. Maybe he actually had a secret wife and kids. Good riddance in that case, too.

Whatever the reason, she'd go as far as to say that the experience had tarnished every encounter she'd had with a man from that day on. What an idiot she'd been to believe in love, like it was some kind of fairy tale. And how stupid of her to imagine that anyone might fall head over heels in love with *her*!

Men, it seemed, always left in the end. Her dad. Ben. Steve. Even Richie her brother had moved halfway round the world to live with Jordan, his Kiwi boyfriend – now husband – and he might as well have died for all the grieving she and her mum had done following his departure. They stalked him on Facebook like a pair of jealous exes, pouncing on every new detail as it appeared: sighing over the pictures of Richie and Jordan's elegant house, their Labradoodle Daisy, their social lives, Jordan's large, beautiful family ... Lara was glad for them, truly, but their happiness came at the cost of her own bereft feelings and those of her mum, Frances, whose living room now resembled a shrine to her son. What was it about these men, that they kept on going elsewhere?

'This morning, you told me you tried to get in touch with him again,' Eliza said now, 'once you were sure I was his daughter. So what happened? Didn't he want to know me?'

'It wasn't like that,' Lara replied. Having photocopied the relevant pages of the library's phone books, she had methodically called every McManus listed, eventually ringing a Cambridge number, marked 'G McManus', which was answered by a young woman.

'Hi,' Lara had said with the usual jolt of trepidation that these calls evoked. 'I'm looking for Ben McManus. Is he there?'

She had asked the question so many times by now, to be met with countless replies of 'wrong number', that she was surprised when the woman answered, 'No, thank God. You've just missed him.'

It took her a moment to recover from the shock. Could she have found him at last? She had to make sure, she realised. 'Oh,' she said. 'Okay. And this Ben – he's around thirty now, right? Went to uni in Glasgow?'

'Yeah, but like I said, he's not here, all right? He doesn't even live here,' came the impatient response. 'Yes, in a MINUTE!' she yelled in the next second, over the sound of a muffled shout. 'I've got to go. Bye.'

'Wait!' Lara cried, reeling. He was back in Cambridge then, she thought, her heart pounding. He existed. 'Could I leave a message for him, please?'

'No, you bloody can't,' the retort had been. 'I'm not his answering service. I'm not even speaking to him right now!'

Before Lara could say another word, the woman hung up on her. Which was odd. So he was alive but still pissing off other women. Perhaps she shouldn't be all that surprised, she told herself wryly. Had she just spoken to Ben's wife? Girlfriend? One of the sisters he'd told her about? What, exactly, was going on?

Eliza made an annoyed clicking sound with her tongue on hearing this. 'Rude,' she said. 'So what did you do?'

'Well, I tried again,' Lara replied. 'About a week later, I rang back one evening to see if I could find out anything else.'

It had been different that time. A young woman had answered once more – the same one? Lara couldn't tell – but she'd been more agreeable at least. 'He's not here,' she'd replied. 'Is that you, Kirsten?'

'No,' Lara had said, wondering who Kirsten might be. The angry woman she'd spoken to previously? How many women were *in* Ben McManus's life, anyway? 'It's . . . it's Lara,' she'd said. 'Would you be able to give him a message for me, please? It's really important. Would you ask him to call Lara Spencer as soon as possible? I'll give you my number.'

'Sure,' the woman said. 'Hang on a second while I find a pen . . . Okay, go for it.'

'Let me guess,' Eliza put in. 'He never called you back.'

'He never called me back,' Lara confirmed. 'And – do you know what? By this point, I was sick of him being so crap and unreliable. I didn't want that for you. I never want anyone to treat you that way!' Her voice rose with passion. 'There's only so many times you can keep trying with a person. You deserved better. We both did.'

Silence fell in the car and Lara couldn't tell what Eliza was thinking. Did she blame her for giving up too easily? *Had* she given up too easily? There was more she could have done, sure – she could have written a letter to the address in the phone book, she could have phoned more times until she eventually got through to him, she could have gone to the house and knocked on the door, even. But she hadn't, in the end, done any of those things. She had closed the chapter on Ben McManus and moved on. And frankly, after the way he'd behaved, he didn't deserve any more chances.

'Let's stop here for a cup of tea,' she suggested now, seeing a sign for a service station and flicking on her indicator. She was getting a headache from frowning, she realised, and could do with some fresh air. Maybe a swift pep talk to herself in the loos, too. Now that she'd relinquished the truth to Eliza – most of it, anyway – she felt vulnerable, as if her armour had slipped, revealing a wound that had never quite healed over.

She reversed into a space, watched the entire time by a German shepherd with a cocked head in the neighbouring Volkswagen, and tried to imagine what it would be like to meet Ben again. He'd probably done loads of exciting things in his life, she predicted. If he ran a map shop now, it was almost certainly because he'd been all over the world, clocking up thrilling life experiences across every continent. She just hoped his expression wouldn't be too mortifyingly blank when they eventually came face to face once more. *Lara who? When?* It would make it even more cringey if he'd forgotten her, so that she'd then have to mumble, *Okay, never mind, we did sleep together in New York though, and by the way, this is our eighteen-year-old daughter.* Still, it would be an ice-breaker at least, she supposed.

Outside the car, the air was cool and breezy, the rain now reduced to drizzle, soft and wet on her face. It was the exact sort of dampening weather that completely wrecked your hair, Lara thought, pulling up her hood. Call her vain, but she didn't want to see Ben again for the first time in years, and for her hair to be one gigantic frizzball.

Eliza was already walking away. 'Won't be long,' she yelled over her shoulder.

Lara bought herself a coffee and paced around the muddy stretch of grass where dogs could be exercised. The sky was marbled with clouds that felt low and oppressive, as if it might go on raining for ever. What am I doing? she thought for the hundredth time, then jumped as a rotund, sandy-coloured Labrador lolloped over and bumped against her jeaned leg with its quivering wet nose.

'Sorry,' yelled its owner, a tall man with designer stubble. He was holding hands with a woman in a red coat, while two little girls skipped and twirled nearby. A proper family, dog and all, Lara thought enviously, as she always did when confronted with the perfect nuclear set-up. Some people not only managed it but made it look easy. It was one of her biggest regrets, that she'd failed to give Eliza this cosy sort of upbringing herself. 'He's too friendly for his own good,' the man was saying, like anyone could think that was a fault. 'Albert, come here. Here!'

Lara reached down to pat Albert's warm flank before he bundled back to his owner, tail whirring. The contact made her think of Bruce, the large black rescue cat they'd rehomed five years ago, who was always deeply offended if his dinner was late for any reason. When she'd adopted Bruce, she'd been advised by the rescue centre that he had been abandoned, had picked up some bad habits and didn't trust men. You and me both, mate, Lara had thought, feeling an immediate kinship with his suspicious yellow glare. But today, in all of the palaver, she hadn't spared a thought to who'd be giving him dinner that evening. She pictured his tail-stiffened indignation as the house grew dark and cold and his plate remained empty and then, because she was a soft-hearted idiot, started worrying about him feeling walked out on all over again. Who would feed him? Her mum and her best friend, Heidi, both had spare keys to her house but she wasn't sure she wanted to tell her mum the reason for their absence. Frances was the dictionary definition of pessimist, especially when it came to men; a person for whom there was never any light at the end of the tunnel, only a dumpster aflame with burning toxic waste. Heidi, meanwhile, was the polar opposite – and on balance, Lara needed optimism today.

Retrieving her phone, she noticed that Heidi had actually just sent a message to their book group thread.

Everyone still on for tonight? Have emptied Tesco's wine shelves in readiness. Thought the book was shite, mind, but looking forward to an argument about it!!

Lara smiled to herself. Heidi thought a lot of the books they read at book group were 'shite'. 'I guessed the murderer in, like, chapter two or something,' she'd claim whenever they discussed a thriller. 'Is this author up themselves or *what*?' she'd mutter if they tackled something Booker-shortlisted. 'Not as good as *The Hobbit*' was her perennial verdict on any novel that turned out to be vaguely fantastical. Natalie, another book group member, had even ordered Heidi a T-shirt with this last slogan printed on the chest, because it had become such a catchphrase among them.

Lara pressed 'Call' and swigged more coffee while she waited for her friend to reply.

'No, you're not,' was Heidi's opening gambit on picking up.

'Don't you dare bail on me, Spenno. I didn't want to spoil the surprise on WhatsApp, but I've made a coffee and walnut cake and everything and it took me bloody ages. Do not give me your *I'm really tired* crap and stay home, otherwise we're going to seriously fall out.'

Lara laughed. She and Heidi had met on their children's first day at primary school, bonding instantly when Eliza emerged holding hands with Heidi's son Ned, announcing that they were going to get married. 'Well, hello there, mother of the bride,' Heidi had said to Lara, eyes twinkling. 'You and my new daughter-in-law will have to come round for tea one day. Start planning the wedding.' If she'd been less friendly, Heidi might have intimidated Lara: she was one of those women who apparently had everything – the husband, three children, guinea pigs in hutches, a successful career as a wedding photographer; another perfect family right there – but she was so warm and funny, it was impossible to dislike her. Plus she had a wild streak to her that Lara discovered the first time they went out together when, hammered on tequila, Heidi had started demonstrating high kicks at the bar before flirting outrageously with Mr Hawkins, the nervous-looking peripatetic violin teacher from school. 'Get out of this friendship while the going's good, Lara,' Heidi had slurred on the way home, stumbling against a parked car and setting off a shrieking alarm. 'I am a terrible person, I warn you now.'

'Are you kidding me? This is the most fun I've had in years,' Lara had told her, hauling her upright again. 'I'm not going anywhere.'

Since then, their friendship had become strong and sisterly. Heidi and her husband, Jim, were the sort who always had extra chairs at their dinner table, and while Lara still secretly envied them their solid, cheerful marriage and rumbustious family life, she was glad to have been welcomed into it – or to feel she had an honorary place on the sidelines at least.

'I'm not bailing because I'm tired,' she began now, only to be interrupted by a loud huffing sound.

'I knew it! I bloody knew it! And there's me, slaving over my effing buttercream icing and for what? For—'

'I'm on my way to Cambridge,' Lara put in quickly, before her friend could blow a gasket. She had a sudden yearning to be in Heidi's cosy living room instead, cackling with her book group while they tucked in to wine and cake, setting the world to rights before belatedly remembering, several hours in, that they were meant to be discussing a novel. 'And I won't be back until late tonight. Possibly not even till tomorrow, realistically,' she said, thinking aloud as she checked her watch and did some calculations. Shit. Where would they sleep? 'Even with the temptations of your baking. Sorry.'

'What? *Cambridge?* Since when? What's going on?' Never one to ask a single question when you could get four in, Heidi rattled them out like gunfire.

'Remember me telling you about that guy I met in New York?' Lara asked.

'The gorgeous, enigmatic one-night stand who ruined your love life for evermore by setting the bar impossibly high and also being a bastard? Yes, of course. Why?' A gasp rushed out of the phone in the next second. 'No! Seriously? You've found him? You're back in touch?'

'Well ...' The rain was pattering down on her hood and shoulders and she headed back to find shelter. She didn't want to be sitting in the car for the next hour with wet trousers. 'It's a long story. Basically, Eliza found out about him being her dad. She's really angry. And we're on our way to see him – impulse road trip. Well, her impulse, not mine, to be fair. I've kind of been strong-armed into the whole thing. Anyway,' she went on, aware that she was veering away from the favour she needed to ask, 'I was wondering – you've still got a spare key, haven't you? Would you be able to pop round and feed the cat? We'll be back tomorrow, so if you just give him two scoops of food tonight, that should be—'

But Heidi didn't want to be deflected by cat talk. 'Oh my God, Lara. I can't believe this. You're going to see him again. The one who got away. Fuck!'

'I'm not sure *that* will be on the cards for today,' Lara joked, deadpan. 'He's married apparently. But yeah, I'm going to see him again. I'm bricking it, actually.'

'Don't! This could be the turning point of your life! A romantic reunion after, what, nearly twenty years? Whoa. This is major. How are you feeling? What are you going to say? What are you *wearing*?'

Lara glanced down at the pair of very ordinary mum jeans and the rather bobbly navy blue jumper she was wearing, neither of which screamed 'romantic heroine'. When you sat in a car all day long for a living, you dressed for comfort rather than glamour; you barely thought about what outfit you threw on, as long as it was presentable. 'I don't think it will be like that,' she replied.

'Why not? It sounded amazing, your night in New York. Imagine, if you look at one another and there's that zap of connection again, sheer chemical attraction. The years will melt away as your eyes lock. You'll run into each other's arms, an orchestra will start up . . .'

'More like one of those sad trombones, knowing my luck,' Lara scoffed. Her eye fell on a couple hurrying towards the service station entrance, him holding his jacket above both of their heads, and she had to look away because she couldn't remember the last time anyone had done something like that for her. 'Anyway, I can't chat for long. Sorry about book group, but if you could just pop in and feed the cat, that would be brilliant, thanks.'

'Sure, no problem. Just . . . keep me posted, yeah? And good luck.'

'Thanks.'

Lara hung up, already wondering if she'd said too much to her friend. Wondering also if she might have been better asking the favour of her mother after all, who'd have reframed the trip in the cold hard colours of reality. Because Heidi's exuberant optimism was surely misguided, and now Lara couldn't help dreading Eliza being rejected by Ben, just like she had been.

Oh God, please let him not be a complete shit, she prayed, draining her coffee cup and throwing it into the nearest bin. Well, not actually *into* the nearest bin, in fact, because her aim was off and the cup bounced off the side and landed on the ground, earning her a dirty look from a woman wearing a plastic head-scarf who clearly thought she was littering. Growling under her breath, Lara stooped down to retrieve the cup, rammed it into the bin, then headed back into the service station in search of some emergency chocolate. It definitely felt as if she would need it.

Chapter Ten

Back in the car, they set off once more. Less than an hour to go now. It was shallow of her, but following Heidi's question about what she was wearing, the nearer their approach to Cambridge, the more pressing it felt for Lara to change her clothes to something more flattering. When Ben had met her, she'd been young and cared far more about her appearance than she did nowadays: she'd rocked that cool Audrey fringe for starters, and worn make-up and jewellery as standard, rather than a belated afterthought, sometimes spending hours choosing the right outfit for an occasion. Fast-forward to the present day and her look had degenerated from Girl About Town to Woman Putting the Bins Out. Whatever the outcome might be today, Lara still had some remaining shreds of pride, and definitely didn't want Ben's first impression of her to be one of dreariness: dressed in plain old work clothes with frizz-bomb hair, straight off the back of a long drive. Far better for him to experience a stab of loss at what might have been. To register, even on a subconscious level, that she had aged well over the years, and had managed perfectly fine without him. She thought back to the dishevelled reflection she'd seen in the service station loos and mentally added mascara, lipstick and a hairbrush to her shopping list.

By the time they reached the Cambridge road, the butterflies in Lara's stomach were beating their wings a little faster. Keep breathing, she reminded herself. Keep your cool. However awkward things might be with Ben, she would survive the day. One way or another.

Her thoughts turned back to the aftermath of the night she'd spent with him; how dismal and lonely the following fortnight had seemed, how it had felt as if everyone in New York City was having a blast except for her. Still, days later, she'd been distracted at least by the arrival of Richie and a load of his mates, who had come over on someone's stag do for a long messy weekend. Lara forced herself to put on a spangly top and a face full of make-up to go out with them, feelings of dejection temporarily shelved. 'This is Danno, this is Sarge, this is Mick, this is Steve,' said Richie, greeting her when she turned up at the bar, followed by introductions to all the other lads present, the names of whom she'd now forgotten. The stags were collectively on a mission to party hard and get hammered, and their buoyant moods proved infectious. Exactly what she needed.

Which was why she bought a round of shots, and gave herself up to a long night.

Which was why she found herself involved with shouty drinking games and competitively funny stories, with teasing and jokes and banter.

Which was why she didn't bail out and go home when they moved on to a grimy nightclub just off Times Square, and why, several drinks later, she ended up drunkenly grinding against best-man-to-be Steve on the dance floor. And then snogging his face off at the end of the night and inviting him back to her place, because why not? She didn't care what happened any more, and you know what everyone said about getting straight back on a horse after you fell off.

If she'd been hoping to break the enchantment Ben had cast upon her, it didn't work. Instead of waking the next morning feeling free and unburdened, she woke with the worst hangover of her life, wishing that there wasn't this large snoring man in her bed. A large snoring naked man with whom, it quickly transpired, she had little in common. If anything, their pairing only served to leave her feeling worse than ever. Cheap. Seedy. As if she needed a red-hot shower and a month-long detox afterwards.

He'd been nice though, taking her out for breakfast in her nearest café rather than bolting at the first opportunity as other men might have done. He'd even suggested they meet up again while he was in New York – or, given that she was returning to the UK in the autumn, perhaps they could see one another once she was home? Okay, she said, although she didn't really mean it. However decent and uncomplicated he appeared, he wasn't Ben; there wasn't the same spark or easy intimacy, and she was pretty sure she'd never see him again.

Except that three months later, back in London, she discovered to her horror that she was pregnant. Life had been so chaotic, what with the move home and the whirl of catching up with her British friends, that by the time she realised what was happening, it was pretty much too late to do anything about it. 'That bloke Steve's been asking after you, by the way,' her brother said, when he phoned for a chat soon afterwards. Richie and Steve weren't friends as such, but moved in overlapping circles. 'He's going to be down in London next weekend for Adam's wedding. Want me to pass on your number?'

It had felt like one of those see-saw moments where a person's future can tilt either up or down. Poised in the middle, Lara was scarcely able to balance for a few heady seconds in an agony of hesitation. Was the baby Steve's or Ben's? They'd both used condoms and Lara had never been one to keep on top of her cycle dates – she genuinely had no idea. But did that matter right now? Ever since she'd seen the pregnancy test stick, she'd been obsessing about how much she'd hated growing up without a dad (he'd walked out weeks after she was born; she had tried not to take it personally but, you know, it did make her wonder if there was something repellent about her even then). Conscious of the ache that came from a parent's absence, shouldn't she at least *try* and nobble a father for her unborn child?

The see-saw tipped as she realised that a practical option might be right there in front of her. It felt as if the universe, having chucked her overboard into a stormy sea, had belatedly thought to toss her a life raft. And so, after a shaky breath, she replied, 'Sure,' in the hope this would take her to a better place.

'Did you ever really love him though?' Heidi had tentatively asked Lara, years later, during an alcohol-fuelled heart-to-heart about relationships gone by. 'Like, "throw yourself in front of a bus to save him" love? Did you ever rip his clothes off with lust? Did he make you laugh every single day you were together?'

Sadly, Lara didn't even need to think about her answer. 'Not really,' she had confessed, eyes down. 'No. It wasn't like that.'

You couldn't fault the man for his reaction to hearing that Lara was pregnant, though. Sure, settling down with a kid had not been high on his list of priorities when he turned up for a second date with her, following Richie's intervention, but he didn't leap up and run screaming from the premises when she broke the news. He'd blanched, admittedly, and stared into his pint glass for several long seconds, probably seeing his future dwindling to a small cramped semi with a sensible family car, rather than the glorious wild-oat-sowing expanse he'd had the luxury of five minutes earlier. But then he'd looked up again, laughed nervously and said, 'Wow. That was an unexpected plot twist.'

'I know, right?' Lara replied, her heart pounding. She would have understood if he'd tried to fob her off with excuses and a few quid, she really would. Even if he'd bolted, she'd have understood, because panic and denial had been her initial reactions too.

Perhaps his friend's wedding had given him ideas about settling down himself though, because then Steve was clearing his throat as if he were about to make a speech. 'Well,' he began. 'I mean, it's not the most conventional start to a relationship but I ... I do really like you, Lara. That night in New York – I haven't been able to stop thinking about it.'

Oh help. She wasn't sure she could bear the guilt when he said this. Because of course, of the two New York nights she'd spent with different men, there was only one which kept returning to her mind, and it wasn't the drunken fumblings with Steve.

'So,' he went on, apparently not having noticed her flinch, 'we could ... try making a go of things?'

Poor Steve. He was so trusting – some would say naïve – that he didn't even think to ask, 'By the way, is the baby definitely mine?' And okay, so the baby wasn't *definitely* his, but he didn't need to know that, Lara thought with a squirm of guilt, as she nodded and smiled, and tried to squash down her feelings of apprehension.

'I thought he would be a good dad for Eliza though,' she told Heidi. 'That was what it was all about – so that she'd have two parents to love her. And he did love her. He *was* a good dad.'

'But you can't stay with a man because of their dad qualities,' Heidi had gently reminded her. Not that Lara needed telling by then. 'Brilliant, if they make your kids feel great and that all works out too – but the starting point should be about *you* feeling great with him. And vice versa. Jim and I drive each other mad half the time but I still fancy the pants off him. He still makes me laugh like no one else can.' She topped up Lara's wine glass and pressed it into her hand. 'Lara, you're the loveliest woman I've ever met but I've got to tell you, you and Steve got together for all the wrong reasons. And there's someone better out there for you, I just know it.'

These words had come back to Lara at intervals over the years and she knew that Heidi was right. Yes, Steve was solid and reliable but life with him had been quite . . . well, boring, if that wasn't too unkind, like porridge or a duffel coat. With every day that passed, Lara had felt herself become smaller and duller too, trapped in their box together while the rest of the world around them had passionate affairs, went on adventures, and challenged themselves in exciting ways. She stopped caring about the things that had once made her happy – a fabulous top or a gorgeous coat. She grew out her fringe because she didn't have time to keep getting regular trims. She couldn't be bothered to faff about with make-up and jewellery unless they were going on a rare date night, because what was the point? She was too busy and the effort didn't seem worth it any more.

Anyway, that was all in the past and there was no use crying over spilt relationships. Especially as they were currently approaching the centre of Cambridge, following directions to the cheap hotel Eliza had picked out, and Lara was possibly on the verge of coming full circle at last. Completing a puzzle that had mystified her for too long. Buckle up, kid, she told herself, as her arms prickled with sudden goosebumps. Things are about to get a whole lot rockier.

Chapter Eleven

Kirsten gently pressed the Doppler device against the woman's belly and an anxious hush cloaked the room. It was her antenatal clinic at one of the city's health centres and lying on the white-sheeted bed, hands clenched into tense fists, was Alice Weatherly, a woman who had so far endured the misery of three pregnancies ending in miscarriage. This was pregnancy number four and she had already shut her eyes as if braced for further bad news.

The device was used to listen to a baby's heartbeat, but so far Kirsten hadn't been able to detect a sound. She moved it gingerly along the soft swell of Alice's belly, willing the baby's tiny heart to still be pumping. *Come on, little one. Please be okay.* It was the worst part of the job, having to break this sort of bad news, seeing a woman's face collapse with sheer grief, then hearing their wrenching sobs, knowing that there was very little you could say to make the pain any less agonising. She didn't know how women like Alice put themselves through it again and again. It astonished her, the resilience and courage of some people, how strong and determined they could prove themselves. By comparison, she was left feeling weak and inadequate, fully aware that she had her limits. Did that make her a bad person? Or merely practical?

People tended to assume that, being a midwife, she must have borne a whole brood of healthy tots herself, but in truth, although she and Ben had tried for a while, including two rounds of IVF, it hadn't happened for them, and do you know what? She was okay with that. She was absolutely fine.

Yes, all right, so every now and then she would find herself glancing at her friends' children or their nieces and nephews, and marvelling that wow, they were five now, they were ten, they were at secondary school, they were getting piercings and drinking in the park and answering back, they were choosing A-level subjects, they were leaving home. She thought: that could have been me with our child. We could have been having those conversations too if life had taken an alternative route. It wasn't so much devastating regret as a mild curiosity, a fleeting disappointment, but nothing that developed into outright sadness.

Ben, however, felt differently. Kirsten knew that he had been broken-hearted once they'd agreed that a third round of IVF was not for them, either emotionally or financially, and that it was time to close the door on the whole endeavour. Give up. He had sunk into quite a depression for months afterwards, been listless and subdued, as if the hope that had been sucked out of him had caused an emptiness inside, a hollow space that nothing could fill. In turn, she'd had to grapple with her own feelings of guilt that she didn't grieve more about them being childless, the self-criticism that she wasn't similarly mourning the family they could have been. Was something wrong with her on a fundamental level? Friends had rallied round them, consoling and sympathetic, while even Ben's sisters tactfully talked less of their own babies and children for a time, leaving Kirsten with the uncomfortable impression that she must be a fraud, who hadn't earned such compassionate responses. She'd hated going through IVF, the injections and the hormones; she was a private person and found the lack of control and dignity humiliating, however nice the nurses and staff. In some ways – yes, it was a relief when they decided not to go through that again. Did that make her a bad person to admit as much?

'We're enough,' she kept telling Ben, trying to shoulder his pain, supporting him as if he were an invalid. And he'd come out through the other side eventually; their marriage had survived the ordeal, and that, she thought, had been the end of it.

But now look at her, with the deep, uncomfortable sense that something was missing in her life, that a hole lay beneath the surface. That maybe the two of them *weren't* enough for one another as things stood. He'd rung her earlier and sounded very pleased with himself as he suggested meeting for a drink that evening, saying that he'd booked them a table for dinner at the tapas place she liked on Green Street. After she'd been on earlies all week and was knackered. When they'd just been out to Charlotte's the night before, and she was desperate for an early night.

She'd hesitated before saying yes, great, because she knew he was making an effort, but she still felt numb. Could this be the belated bereavement her female friends had warned her about, finally making itself known? Or was her mum right, that married life always bumped along the bottom of a few long troughs during its course? Whichever, the fact that she'd had more of a thrill tracking down the phone number of a man she'd met briefly when shopping for paint, than at the prospect of going for a lovely dinner with her husband, was not exactly a healthy response to the midlife blues.

116

The other night, she had lain awake for hours while Ben slept beside her, snoring gently into the pillow. I need something else, she'd thought, gazing up through the darkness. I am ripe for something to happen – some drama, a challenge, for my heart to thump with excitement once more.

Talking of a heart thumping . . . She moved the Doppler and there it was, the fast drumming sound of the foetal heartbeat, like tiny galloping hooves. A smile broke across Alice's face and she opened her eyes.

'There's your baby,' Kirsten said, smiling back. She must have been getting soft or something because as a tear broke free from Alice's eye and went spilling down the side of her cheek, Kirsten felt a lump in her own throat, as if she too was on the verge of a sob. 'Perfect!' she said instead, squeezing Alice's hand.

Somehow it was already five o'clock in the afternoon and Lara felt as if the day was slipping away from them. Having arrived at their budget hotel, they had made an emergency dash to the high street where she'd bought a denim skirt and a short-sleeved zebra-print blouse that was flattering and not too try-hard. She'd also shelled out on a few toiletries for the night, some cheap cotton pyjamas and clean underwear for them both and a lipstick because, sod it, she needed every little boost she could get. 'Can I have this perfume?' Eliza had asked, trying her luck at the counter. 'It *is* a special occasion, after all.'

'Yes, yes, all right,' Lara had replied, so flustered that she hadn't noticed, until the cashier rang their items through the till, that the scent cost way more than she'd ordinarily spend on an impulse treat.

Having now spruced up in their bland bedroom, Lara procrastinated further by bagging up the remains of their garage-bought lunch that she'd carried in from the car – the empty sandwich wrappers and crisp packets and the punnet of half-eaten grapes. Grapes, she thought, her hand on the plastic carton, and then a memory returned to her suddenly: of Eliza, aged three, choking on a grape one Saturday lunchtime, her small face startled and then frightened as she gasped for air. Lara's first thought had been that she would kill Steve for giving their little girl a whole grape without cutting it in half – hadn't she told him a million times already that grapes were a choking hazard otherwise? But her next thought was of a voice in her head telling her what to do with a choking child: *Hang them upside down and whack them on the back. Let gravity do its thing* – and then she was leaping up from her chair, swift and decisive. Grabbing Eliza and turning her upside down, slapping her back once, twice. *Please God, please let this work.* She brought her hand away to go in for a third slap – just as Eliza let out a cry and a shining green grape tumbled down on to the lino.

'Oh my God,' she murmured to herself now, finally making the connection. She hadn't thought about it at the time – too busy with comforting Eliza and glowering at Steve – but the voice in her head had been *Ben's*. He'd said those words to her in Stefano's and they must have lodged deep in a part of her brain marked 'Useful Stuff'. 'I've just thought of something,' she said, and went on to recount the story to Eliza. 'Don't you see how weird that is? Your dad saved your life – without even knowing he had *given* you life in the first place.'

'Eww, gross, don't say "given you life" like that,' Eliza scolded her, pretending to vomit. 'But yeah, I guess that is kind of spooky,' she added grudgingly. Then she hopped off the bed. 'We should get going, anyway. Head over to meet Grape-Defeater McManus himself.' She checked her phone. 'Like now, Mum. The shop closes at six.'

Lara pushed the bag of rubbish into the small hotel room bin, simultaneously trying to dump her own reluctant feelings. 'Okay,' she said. They were going to turn up at his shop unannounced, having figured that the end of the day might be an opportune time to chat. 'I hope he's there after all this,' she fretted, as the possibility occurred to her. 'We have to prepare ourselves for the fact that he might be on holiday or—'

'He's not on holiday,' Eliza said, walking across the room. 'I phoned from the service station when I was waiting for you and hung up when he answered. He's definitely there, flogging his crumbly old maps across town. So shall we go and say hello?'

Setting off through the narrow streets, Lara and Eliza had to dodge between tourists, cyclists and shoppers. The sky was darkening and the bright shop windows cast gleaming splashes of light on to the wet pavements. The city had a buzzy, Friday-evening feel but after a few minutes, they turned off into Hobson Street, leaving the crowds behind. The sudden quiet heightened Lara's nerves. Nearly there.

'There it is. Oh God.' Eliza stopped dead halfway along the street, pointing ahead to a shop sign that read All Mapped Out. She bit her lip, all previous bravado gone. 'Do you think I look like him?'

'Yes,' Lara replied, studying the beloved contours of her daughter's face, the full rosy lips, the skewering grey eyes, the small delicate ears. Admittedly, Ben's features had faded in her mind over the years but she thought she detected a similarity between the set of their eyes, the fullness of their mouths. 'I think you do, actually. I can see a resemblance from how he was back then, anyway.'

Eliza gave a nervous laugh. 'What, so you don't think I look like the pictures we saw of him as a middle-aged man? Well, that's a relief.'

It felt like a dream, walking towards the shop. As if at any moment their surroundings were about to break into fragments and disperse, as if Lara would wake up and find herself back home in her own bed. The ground didn't feel quite steady beneath her feet; the air was clammy in her lungs. Her heart was really pounding now, to a fast rhythm of *Fuck fuck fuck fuck fuck*.

A bell on the door jingled as they went in – the sort of old-fashioned detail that would normally charm Lara, but on this occasion, her system was so overloaded with adrenalin as she scanned the inside of the shop that it was hard to process any niceties. Two customers were browsing: a red-haired woman slowly turning a postcard carousel, an elderly man looking at a Bridge of Sighs print. Noodling jazz rippled through the air and a bearded man of dual heritage behind the counter bobbed his head to the beat. So where was Ben?

'Maybe he's in a back room,' Lara muttered, noticing a half-open door beyond the main shop area, through which they could just see a large filing cabinet and sash window. At that moment, the bearded man looked up and caught her eye, and she realised how odd they must look, standing there frozen in the doorway.

'Can I help you?' he asked.

This was it. Now or never. 'We're looking for Ben,' she said, her voice sounding strangely high-pitched, even to her own ears. 'Ben McManus?'

'Ah,' said the man. 'You've just missed him, I'm afraid. Can I help at all?'

Chapter Twelve

A pint of lager and a corner table in the Salamander; this was a pretty good start to Ben's Friday evening, he thought to himself, taking the first cold mouthful and feeling as if an elixir was sinking through his veins. And relax. Nick had offered to close up the shop so that he could get away early, and now the weekend had begun, with Kirsten on her way to meet him for a spontaneous date night – and who knew, she might even be so pleased and charmed by Ben for organising this that he'd be able to persuade her into having sex later once they were back home. If she wasn't too knackered, that was. Shit, she probably would be, he realised, having just finished a week of early shifts. He'd managed to forget about that, so caught up had he been in his flush of doing something impulsive for once.

His phone rang just then and he picked it up from the table, only for it to stop ringing in the next second. A number he didn't recognise was on the screen – some scammer, he guessed, rolling his eyes. But then, as he was raising his pint glass to his lips once more, he spotted two women approaching – one middle-aged and anxious-looking, one much younger with an unfathomably direct gaze. They were making for his table, he registered – which was odd, and kind of annoying, actually, when there were plenty of other empty seats around. And why was the younger one staring at him like that? Were they peeved customers that Nick had sent his way? Or zealous religious types with an agenda to convert him, maybe?

They'd arrived at his table by now and stood shoulder to shoulder before him. What *was* this? Some kind of delegation? 'Ben?' the older woman said, and he distractedly noticed her taking the younger woman's hand as if in solidarity. 'I'm Lara. We met in New York?'

It took his brain a second to catch up – Lara? New York? – but in the meantime her face had already collapsed as if his delayed reaction was enough to crush her. 'Nineteen years ago,' she went on, sounding miserable. 'In a bar, on the Lower East Side. I was—'

'You were choking on a peanut,' he blurted out. 'Yes. I remember.' His head filled with images suddenly – vibrant with colour as if it had been yesterday. The two of them walking through the city streets at night. Yellow cabs, music drifting up from cellar bars, neon lights. Tenement buildings and iconic green street signs. Dancing in a bar. Going back to her place. How her skin had felt against his. He swallowed, hardly able to believe that this slice of his own past history, perfect and pure in his memory, had collided with the present day, overlapping like an architect's acetates. A Venn diagram of people and places. 'Of *course* I remember,' he added, gazing at her anew, trying to match the woman before him with the beautiful girl who'd enchanted him that night. 'Wow. *Lara*. God. I can't believe—'

'And I'm Eliza,' said the younger woman – girl, really, she couldn't be more than twenty, he thought, blinking as he turned in her direction. She had long chestnut hair and wide grey eyes fringed with thick mascara, and in the brief pause that followed, she removed her hand from Lara's in order to fold her arms across her chest, fingers curling into tight knots. There was something very tense about her, he saw; she was still looking at him in that diamond-hard way as she added, 'Lara's daughter.'

'Oh,' he said politely. 'Hi.'

'And yours too, apparently,' she said in the next breath. Then a nervous laugh jumped from her and she spread her palms wide. 'Surprise,' she said.

He stared at her, uncomprehending, his eyes travelling from the girl – Eliza, had she said? – back to middle-aged Lara. *Yours too.* What – his *daughter*? 'But—' he began, expecting there to be some kind of punchline. Some explanation. None came. The room seemed to be holding its breath, waiting for his reaction. 'Is this a joke?' he asked, uncertainly.

Eliza scowled, her eyes hooded. 'Wow, great response. That really makes me feel special.'

'No,' said Lara quietly, because Ben was no longer able to speak – he had a *daughter*? This was his *daughter*? 'It's not a joke.'

'But—' he bleated again before coming to another stop. His mouth dropped open, there was a new band of tightness across his chest. This couldn't be true, could it? How on earth could it be true? 'I don't understand,' he said. 'How ...' He broke off once more, eyes flicking desperately from one to the other, hardly able to comprehend what he was hearing. Lara and Eliza. The girl who had bewitched him all those years ago, reappearing in his life as if by magic – that alone was enough of a headfuck. But to then be told that the sulky-looking, scruffy young woman glaring at him from beside her was his *daughter*, his *child* ... He felt as if the world was spinning too fast all of a sudden. As if it had spun him right into a different universe where nothing quite made sense any more. 'Wait,' he said, 'but we used a condom, didn't we? Sorry,' he added, as Eliza pulled a face and theatrically put her hands over her ears.

'Yes,' Lara said, glancing apologetically at Eliza. 'But – you know. These things happen sometimes, regardless.'

These things happen, he repeated to himself in a daze. What a coy way to describe such a bolt from the blue: a real-life daughter happening, right before his eyes. *His* daughter.

And then a surge of injustice broke through his incredulity, hot and sour, as a whole new question occurred to him. 'Why are you only telling me this now?' he asked. He'd had a child all this time and nobody had thought to *tell* him? 'How come this is the first I've heard of it?'

'I did try!' Lara burst out defensively. Her chin jerked upwards, flashing him straight back to a late-night, summer Manhattan street; remembering her feistiness, how he'd teased her for it, how he'd been so completely drawn to her from the very first moment. It seemed impossible to reconcile how she'd been back then with who she was now. 'I called you. Several times. But—'

The memories were flooding back, thick and fast. 'I'm sorry I never turned up for our date,' he said, as she broke off. 'But I did leave a message for you. Didn't you get it?'

Her face changed. She looked aghast momentarily, then guarded. 'No,' she said after a moment. 'I didn't get any message. Although I did track down your hostel, only to be told you'd left, before we were even supposed to meet!'

He couldn't keep up with this. He couldn't think straight. They seemed to have veered away from the main headline – that hello, he had a daughter! – to instead be nitpicking about messages and phone calls. Plus, more pertinently, he realised, *Kirsten* was due to walk in at any moment and he wasn't remotely prepared for how *that* conversation might play out. Jesus Christ. 'I . . .' Words failed him. The two women were still standing there, looming over him, and he sought refuge in basic manners so as to buy himself a moment's breathing space. 'Um. Do you want to sit down?'

They sat down. 'This must be a bit of a shock,' Lara mumbled; such a ludicrous understatement that he almost wanted to laugh. 'Us coming here today was . . .' She shot a look at Eliza. 'Something of an impulse trip to find you.'

'An *impulse* trip?' he repeated with an edge of anger in his voice. He couldn't help it bubbling up through him: the sheer wrongness of his apparently having had a daughter all this time, who he was only now meeting. How could anyone think that was right or fair? 'What, after eighteen, nineteen years?'

Eliza was looking at him from under her thick black lashes. 'I only found out myself yesterday,' she said. 'That you even existed, I mean. I've spent this whole time thinking my dad was a painter and decorator in Whitby who didn't want to know me. When instead . . .'

'I had no idea,' he told her, desperate for her not to think badly of him, to lump him in with the Whitby painter. If Lara hadn't got his message, she must have assumed he hadn't bothered turning up for their date. God knows how she might have bad-mouthed him to Eliza. 'If I'd known – if I'd had even a hint that you had been born, that you were my . . .' He struggled to say it. 'That you were my girl, I would have come to find you. I promise.' He rubbed the side of his face, feeling completely ill-equipped for the emotional vocabulary required for this intense, startling conversation. He could still hardly believe it was happening. And now, of all times, five minutes before Kirsten was due to walk in for their marriage-reviving date. He knew she wanted things spicing up, but not this much, surely. 'I don't know what to say,' he confessed. 'I'm a bit overwhelmed, to be honest.' He glanced over at the pub door as it opened, his heart pounding in the horror of it being his wife, but thankfully it was a group of lads, rowdy and jubilant in anticipation of wetting the weekend's head.

'So how come you stood her up anyway?' Eliza's tone was accusatory, her expression judgemental. A pin badge on her jacket read 'Fuck the Tories'; another was of a black cat with a speech bubble that said 'MEOW'. Everything about her was utterly fascinating to Ben, as if she was a book he wanted to read cover to cover. Okay, so my daughter is left-wing and likes cats, he noted, before realising Eliza was still talking.

'Mum, I mean. How come you just went off and never contacted her again? She probably would have tried a bit harder to get hold of you if you hadn't gone and ditched her like that. Or if you'd bothered to call her back. We could have done this years ago.' She eyeballed him, her gaze measuring and not particularly friendly. 'So what was all that about?'

He flinched, not appreciating being cast as the villain of the piece – how could that be fair, when he'd been kept in the dark the whole time? If this was anyone's fault, it was Lara's! But he didn't want to christen his new-found father-daughter relationship with an argument, either with Eliza or her mum. 'Listen – I do really want to talk about this properly and explain what happened – on my side at least,' he said, 'but my wife's about to walk in at any moment, so—'

'Fine,' said Lara quickly, as if glad of a reason to leave.

'Not really,' countered Eliza, 'seeing as we've come all the way from Scarborough to meet you.'

'If you'd let me know beforehand though,' he began helplessly, before losing his cool once more and adding, 'say, in the last eighteen years or so, we could have arranged a more convenient time to—'

'Like I said, I tried that!' Lara retaliated, eyes blazing. 'And, unlike you, I did turn up at the Oyster Bar that evening but—'

'Oh shit,' he interrupted, no longer listening because the door had opened again and there was Kirsten walking in, her blonde hair shining bright around her shoulders as she looked around the pub and saw him. It was like being in a bad dream, except he was wide awake and pumped full of adrenalin. 'You need to go,' he blurted out shakily. 'I can't – I can't do this now. Can we—?' But he didn't know what to suggest because Kirsten was weaving her way through the tables towards them, and his mind had become utterly, paralysingly blank. Bloody hell, here she was. Two worlds colliding. How was he going to navigate his way out of this? 'Hi!' he said with false cheer, standing up so abruptly the table shuddered and he had to make a grab for his pint glass. He went to kiss her cheek, resisting the sudden urge to hang on to her tight and stay there, eyes shut, until the world returned to normal once more.

'Hi,' she said, disentangling herself and eyeing Lara and Eliza with a quizzical air. 'Making friends, are we?'

'Oh! No. Just . . . um . . . just giving these two directions,' he blustered, hoping to God they wouldn't contradict him – or worse, reveal the truth. 'Um. Yeah. So . . . it's probably easier if I show you from the doorway,' he improvised to them, 'and then I can point out the road you need.' He was barely aware of the words coming from his mouth in his desperation to break up the party but thankfully, after a split second's hesitation, Lara and Eliza rose from their seats. 'Back in a minute, Kirst,' he said, ushering them towards the exit, his heart hammering so frenziedly he half expected it to come through his chest. 'I'm sorry about this,' he mumbled, shoulders collapsing as they went out the door. 'That's my wife. I can't— I need to— Sorry.'

'Right,' said Lara. Her face was rounder since they'd first met, and her hair was different too, but there was no disguising the hurt wobble of her mouth. He'd forgotten how expressive her face was, how she wore her emotions for everyone to see. 'That's it, then, is it? That's all we get?'

'No! Well – yes, for now, obviously, because I'm here with my wife and she has no idea that—'

'That we exist? That you slept with me in New York? Okay. Yep. I kind of got that impression anyway when you couldn't even remember who I was just now.' She grabbed Eliza's hand again. 'Come on, Lize, let's go.'

'Wait!' he protested. 'It's not—' He didn't seem able to finish a sentence any more, his mind stuck in free fall, thoughts coming too fast to process. 'I do want to talk to you both – I promise! – but can't you see, it's not possible right now?' He exhaled with frustration, aware that his question sounded accusing rather than placatory. That he just did not have a clue how to handle this situation. Try again, he told himself. 'Can we meet tomorrow or something instead? Please?'

Lara and Eliza looked at one another. 'Sure,' Lara said after a moment, but her eyes remained wary. Eliza, now staring down at the ground, lifted one shoulder in a shrug. He couldn't tell what she was thinking. His own daughter, his flesh and blood, and he

128

barely knew a thing about her, he realised, feeling agonisingly torn – between his wife, innocently waiting for him back inside the pub, and these two: Lara, the woman he'd fallen for in New York, and his own mysterious daughter. But he had to put Kirsten first on this occasion. He simply had to.

'Okay, so should we swap numbers, or—?'

'You've already got mine,' Eliza told him before he could finish. 'I called you as we were coming into the pub so that we knew who you were. Mine will be the last number called.' She shrugged again, offhand as if she didn't care, although the fact that she was twisting her hands together gave away the clue that she probably did. 'Text me. If you want.'

'I *do* want,' he assured her. 'I will. Sorry this is all so . . .' There was no single word to describe the tumult of the last five min-utes; he was forced to abandon yet another sentence unfinished. 'I'm a bit overwhelmed. I thought I'd never see you again,' he said to Lara. 'As for you . . .' He felt a new rush of emotion as he looked at Eliza, really looked closely at her, and thought he could detect in her features his sister's nose, his own eyes, his dad's blunt chin. It was real. This was all real. 'God. I can't believe it,' he stuttered, a tidal wave of feelings threatening to drown him all of a sudden. 'I'm desperate to get to know you, okay? I can't tell you what this means to me. I'll text you, all right? We'll sort something out.'

Eliza, he said to himself, walking dazedly back into the pub. He had to lean against the wall out of sight of Kirsten for a moment in an attempt to pull himself together, but already it felt as if everything had changed, irreversibly. Eliza was his *daughter*. Hadn't he wanted a child of his own, someone to love and dote on? They had tried for a baby for years and years, he and Kirsten, suffering the silent pain of countless well-meaning 'your turn next!' remarks as his sisters produced armfuls of infants each, only to then endure the dreadful rounds of sorrowful looks and sympathetic 'it must be so hard' comments when the IVF failed both times.

Coming to terms with the fact that it wasn't going to happen for them had taken a while, the heartbreak eventually dulling to an ache of disappointment over time, for what might have been. It had been the hardest thing, trying to squash back down all the fatherhood dreams he'd entertained: of teaching his children how to ride their bikes, for instance, lying on a living room floor to build Lego creations and marble runs together, noisy penalty shoot-outs in the garden, seeing their little faces light up on Christmas Day. Being an uncle was brilliant and he'd thrown himself into the job anew with each niece and nephew, but it wasn't the same. It just wasn't.

And yet now ... in the space of an awkward few minutes' conversation, it turned out he was a dad after all. An extra layer, new colours, had been added to his previously ordinary-looking life. A whole new *person*. And ...

'Everything all right?' Kirsten asked as he rejoined her and his heart juddered again, wondering wildly if he looked different somehow, if she could guess from his face that the world had just changed so astonishingly.

'Yeah, sure,' he lied. 'Let me get you a drink,' he added, because he didn't quite trust himself to act normally while his head was still whirling at such alarming speed. Whenever he'd imagined parenthood, he hadn't ever dreamed it could be quite so ... well, so *stressful*. So complicated. And how on earth was he going to break the news to his wife?

★

'Here we are, ladies,' said the waitress, who had black hair in a millimetre-perfect bob and a pierced nose. 'Half a Peroni and a gin and tonic. Enjoy!'

Eliza and Lara had retreated to a nearby pizza restaurant for sustenance and a debrief, and normally Eliza would have smirked to herself at this point, knowing that it was one of her mum's pet peeves, the way that every bar and waiting staff said, 'Enjoy!' in that perky, insincere manner these days. Lara was allergic to being told what to do by anyone, couldn't even bear to have the voice on when using a satnav because it made her feel 'bossed around'. 'I'll be the one to decide, thank you, if I enjoy it or not,' she'd grumbled under her breath more than once in the past as the unfortunate *Enjoy!*-wisher had departed the table.

Today though, Eliza merely gave the waitress a wan smile, too shell-shocked to make a comment or goad her mum, who was looking as pale and stunned as Eliza herself felt. They'd hardly spoken as they walked away from the pub – and from *him* – both of them reeling and unable to mutter much more than a 'bloody hell' and an 'I *know*' after the encounter. It wasn't as if she'd expected her dad to take one look at her and be mad with joy at the news but, you know, she could have done without that expression of utter shock – even *horror* – on his face, not to mention the fact that he could hardly get rid of them fast enough. She had wanted him to like her at least, she acknowledged privately, dismay skewering her. On a very primitive level, this whole trip had come from her feelings of uncertainty about herself, the sense that she couldn't find out who she was without this missing jigsaw piece. She'd hoped for validation; to feel that she was good enough, deserving of a father. Instead she felt vulnerable and more unsure than ever.

What was more, her mum seemed pretty shaken too – her face when she'd seen him there across the pub! She'd looked so disappointed, as if the current version of Ben McManus didn't come anywhere close to the rose-tinted glow of her faded memories. *Am I doing the right thing?* Eliza had wondered in a sudden burst of panic, glancing between them, but by then it was too late to stop.

She must have been cringing all over again, there in the res-taurant, because Lara reached over and squeezed her hand, as if reading her mind. 'Don't worry,' she said. 'That wasn't great but at least it's done – he knows about you, and has a bit of time to get his head together before we see him again.'

'*If* we see him again,' Eliza corrected her glumly. 'I bet he won't get in touch after that. He's probably running for the hills as we speak, throwing his phone in the nearest skip.' She felt like crying all of a sudden, her last shred of positivity deserting her as his incredulous face flashed up in her mind once more. 'I don't even know if I like him,' she said miserably. 'I wish we had never come here in the first place!'

Chapter Thirteen

Ben had almost but not quite forgotten his trip to New York because it had been snatched from his hands barely before it began. He'd flown over with Sam and Charlie, two uni mates from Glasgow, for a month-long spree travelling around the US. Aged twenty-six, he felt he'd reached the point in life where he wasn't sure what he was supposed to be doing with the rest of it, where doors seemed to be closing rather than opening. Since graduating, he'd tried on a few careers for size – work experience for a photographic agency, a temporary post with a marketing firm, a spot of moonlighting for various Scottish festivals – none of which had ever become anything solid and full-time. Then had come the job with a global finance firm, designing their brochures and advertising campaigns, which rewarded him with a sizable income, a private health plan and a plush office in Bishopsgate. For the first three months of employment there, he thought he'd made it – success at last! – only for the shine to quickly tarnish as he discovered some of the company's more dubious investment practices, and started to wonder if he'd sold out on his principles.

'For heaven's sake, son, you can't keep chopping and changing like this,' his dad said, exasperated, when Ben voiced his concerns over the phone. 'They're paying you enough, aren't they? So what's the problem? You need to stick to something for once, settle down.' Easy for him to say though; Stewart McManus had been a cab driver for almost thirty years and wasn't about to hang up his car keys any time soon. Or at least that's what they all thought.

A year into the job, there was a company cost-cutting exercise and Ben had opted for voluntary redundancy, with the distinct feeling that he'd wriggled out of a difficult decision he might never have had the guts to make otherwise. The trip to the US was intended to be one last hurrah: thinking time in order to plot out his next move, as well as a laugh with mates, a chance to see a bit of the world. A final taste of freedom in the land of the free, before he had to grow up and make some sensible decisions. And then, on the very first day, mere hours after stepping on to American soil, he'd met Lara and fallen for her completely. Maybe, he pondered (young fool that he was), he'd been looking at his future from the wrong angle. Perhaps it wasn't so much the job you did that mattered, it was who you spent your time with outside work that was key. One evening with this funny, sweet northern girl, a self-confessed fish out of water in New York, and he was forced to do some rapid rethinking. Maybe meeting the right person and falling in love was the real answer to all those big questions? He had woken up in her bed that morning and thought, with more certainty than he'd thought about pretty much anything else before: this is the woman I'm going to spend the rest of my life with.

Until life itself got in the way of his plans, that was; until bad luck or bad timing – or Fate, if you wanted to call it that – cast a mocking glance at his lovestruck face and said, *I don't think so, pal.*

He had put Lara reluctantly from his thoughts since then – he'd had to, like it or not – but she'd remained a flicker at the back of his mind for this whole time: a bright, warm memory of a happy, giddy night when anything had seemed possible, when his whole life appeared to be one endless horizon, glittering with opportunity. And yet, unbeknownst to him, for the last – what? eighteen years? – she'd been raising her daughter – raising *their* daughter – when he'd had absolutely no idea. No idea whatsoever.

It was impossible to have an ordinary evening when such a seismic bombshell had blown apart everything he thought he knew. He bought Kirsten's glass of wine, frantically testing out possible lines of explanation in his head at the bar, but nothing worked; there was no sentence in the world he could say describing what he had just learned that wouldn't leave her open-mouthed with shock or anger. Normal conversation seemed similarly beyond him though, because his thoughts kept looping back to the sight of Lara and Eliza beside his table saying those startling, mind-bending things. Later, when Kirsten went to buy another round, he sent a hurried text to Eliza – *Sorry about earlier. Can we meet tomorrow? 11am at the Corpus Clock?* – vowing that when his wife returned, he would just have to make a good fist of things and be honest. Cards on the table, his own astonishment expressed, a plea for her to believe and forgive him. Unfortunately, at the very second he was gearing up for his opening line – *So, about those two women I was talking to when you came in* – Kirsten let out a cry of surprise and rushed over to hug a couple of friends she'd seen walking in, before bringing them back over to the table. 'Look who I bumped into!'

There was no chance of any explaining then. Zero chance of a story about the wild, thrilling night he'd spent in New York and the repercussions that had only now rippled out to him. Instead, Ben became progressively drunker and drunker as their friends, Molly and Rob, joined them for tapas and further rounds of beer, and then poky Irish coffees to end the night. His secret remained locked inside him, a heavy weight on his conscience, a tangle of confused feelings: excitement and wonder and intrigue, but also a creeping anger towards Lara, a rising pain for his own missed opportunities. Memories of her kept bubbling to the surface: how she had laughed, her endearingly uncoordinated dance moves in that grungy bar they'd ended up in, and the morning after, the two of them sharing a plate of toast in her small bedroom. For some reason, this was what he kept coming back to: how happy he'd felt to be there beside her, a sheaf of her hickory-brown hair falling over the smooth curve of her shoulder. He had a lump in his throat, remembering how he'd rested his cheek against her cool bare shoulder then kissed it, as if introducing himself to this particular part of her. He remembered too how pleased he'd felt at the prospect of getting to know the rest of her body in intimate detail over the years and years together that were sure to come. But for there to be a *child*, an eighteen-year-old young woman, as a result of that night was a twist in the story he absolutely had not seen coming.

A second twist, technically, because the first had come less than two hours after he'd said goodbye to Lara and walked out of her apartment block. He'd returned to the grimy hostel where he and his friends had checked in, light-headed with happiness, only to find a note on his unused bed, saying 'URGENT – CALL HOME ASAP'. It had been the initial domino in a tumbling series of events: the shattering news that his dad had had a massive heart attack, the emergency flight home that same day, a sod-the-cost taxi all the way from the airport to the hospital – 'Fast as you can, please, mate' – followed by a gruelling three-day bedside marathon while his dad clung to life in the intensive care unit.

Caught up in a panic, it wasn't until Ben was waiting to board the plane to London that he remembered the plan he and Lara had made to meet that evening. Here, in the sterile, airless confines of the airport terminal, her smiling face seemed like a fragment from a dream, something that had happened to a different version of himself, back before life had constricted to his current windowless surroundings, this heart-galloping journey homeward, the fear that he might already be too late. Lara, he thought, and her very name was a pang, a physical ache for what might have been. He had to let her know that everything had changed; that in the blink of an eye, the space of a transatlantic phone call, his path had taken a wholly unexpected turn.

He rushed back out to the corridor in search of a payphone, digging his hands into his pockets for coins, just as there came a tannoy announcement stating that the Heathrow departure was now boarding, and could all passengers have their tickets and passports ready. Sprinting down the corridor, he had to dodge and swerve through the approaching tide of passengers wheeling cases along towards their boarding gates. The first phone he spotted was already in use by a woman leaning comfortably against it, in full conversational flow. 'Oh, I *know*,' she was saying with the relish of one bedded in for a long, enjoyable gossip. He couldn't wait. She might yet be hours on the call, if his mother and sisters were anything to go by.

He ran further, faster; past toilets and a snack bar, avoiding a large shrieking group of women in pink cowboy hats. Sweat prickled between his shoulder blades because whatever happened, he must not miss the flight. He must not squander the chance to say goodbye to his father, to hold his hand and hope for some last words, a last embrace, any final shreds of fatherly wisdom that might be dispensed. Because there was no 'if' about his dad dying, his mum had said between sobs on the phone. No 'if', only a matter of 'when'. Please let him get there before that happened. *Please.*

At last – another phone, just as he was becoming breathless. He snatched up the receiver, hands clammy. Dialling tone – good. Connection to the operator – successful. Transfer to the Oyster Bar – yes. The phone was ringing. He crammed further coins into the slot, adrenalin jagging through his system as he heard his flight being called once more. *Yes, yes, I'll be there in a minute. Don't go without me.* They wouldn't, would they?

A pre-recorded message about opening times began in his ear, followed by a long beep as the answerphone system kicked in. 'Um. Hi. My name's Ben,' he stuttered, almost lost for words now that he had the opportunity to speak. 'I'm meant to be meeting someone outside your restaurant tonight, six-thirty. Her name's Lara. She's got long brown hair.' His voice trembled as the events of the last twenty-four hours caught up with him. 'She's . . . she's beautiful. She's really lovely. If you see her waiting for me, please could you pass on a message? It's Ben. I've had to go home, family emergency. But—' He came to a stop because he couldn't think beyond this. What now? What next? 'Um . . . tell her I'll find her,' he improvised, just as his last coin dropped with a clunk and the display flashed, warning that cut-off was imminent. 'Tell her I'll find her!' he repeated frantically, before he was disconnected.

Okay. It wasn't perfect, but hopefully whoever listened to his garbled nonsense would hear his urgency and pass on his words so that she wouldn't be left hanging around pointlessly for him later. He'd spared her that much at least. Afterwards . . . Well, he'd come up with something when he had time to think straight. Now, though – he had a plane to catch. He turned and ran back towards the boarding gate, and Lara slipped clean out of his mind.

Seventy-two long, gritty-eyed hours later, Stewart McManus finally lost his fingertip grip on life, the last breath sighing out of him with what felt like regret. The monitors around him beeped in unison, like a lamenting chorus, echoed by his mother's wail. Ben had hugged her and his sisters, all of them weeping and distraught. *I'm very sorry*, the nurse had said, over their cries of sorrow.

Anyway. That was all a long time ago – although by the sound of things, Lara had never been given his message. Nor had he come good on his promise to find her again, he acknowledged dully. Whatever. More pressingly, today was Saturday, he was due to meet his daughter for the second time, and Lara for the third, while suffering the mother of all hangovers. Worse, he still hadn't been able to unburden himself to his wife about the news. By the time he'd showered and seen off a strong coffee and was feeling vaguely human again, he'd just plucked up the courage to ask if they could have a chat, only to notice, too late, that she was dressed in Lycra and zipping her yoga mat into its carry-bag. 'What about?' she'd asked and then, without pausing for his answer, 'Can it wait till later? Only I've got my ashtanga class in twenty minutes, so I need to get a move on.'

Yes, he'd said, feeling like a rubbish human being for the surge of guilty relief that accompanied her words. No problem. Later was fine.

The Corpus Clock – or the Grasshopper Clock as it was sometimes known – was one of Cambridge's oddities: a round, gold-plated timepiece consisting of concentric circles, with a mechanical beast on top that 'ate' each passing minute. Built into the wall on the end of Bene't Street, it was a popular tourist attraction and, on arriving there at two minutes to eleven that morning, his pulse quickened as he spotted Eliza taking a photograph of it, while Lara gazed warily around. Their eyes met and he tried to smile, although he still couldn't quite believe that this middle-aged woman was the same girl he'd fallen for miles and miles from home. He thought again of her youthful, animated face back then, the way her hair had smelled when it brushed against him. The intoxicating hum of the city around them as they walked through the night together, hand in hand.

Lara of Manhattan, hey? He had fancied her straightaway, as she walked into that bar with her shy smile. Their eyes had met and he'd felt a thud of instant attraction, unable to concentrate on his friends' conversation any more because he was watching her, the nape of her neck pale and sexy beneath the bundled-up hair atop her head. He remembered how he'd said something early on about coming to the States in order to find himself, and how she'd put a small freckled hand on his arm, smiled up at him and said, 'Here you are. I found you.'

Yes, he'd thought, gripped by how pretty she was, how sweet her smile. He couldn't stop looking at her. *You found me.*

Since then, he'd thought about her now and then, wondering with some regret what she was doing with her life. They had both mentioned different cities and countries they wanted to visit; she'd told him about the promotion she'd got her eye on at work, how she'd love to become an editor one day. Whenever he'd

140

thought of her, he'd imagined her in Melbourne, Toronto, Paris, at fashion shows and editorial meetings. She'd represented hope to him, he realised now. Hope and freedom and independence. The sense of possibility.

'Morning,' he said coolly, then smiled at Eliza as she turned around and saw him. 'Hi there,' he added, a lump in his throat. 'So it's true. I didn't just imagine meeting you yesterday.'

She smiled back. 'Afraid not,' she replied. 'Sorry about last night, by the way. It was my idea to go and find you like that.' She bit her lip. 'I just couldn't wait any more.'

'Fair enough. I think we've both waited long enough to meet each other,' he said, unable to help the tart edge to his voice aimed at Lara. 'Shall we get a coffee or something?' He gestured down Trumpington Street. 'We could go to Fitzbillies, it's one of Cambridge's landmarks. Nearly a hundred years old, you know! They're famous for their Chelsea buns. The buns aren't old, though, obviously.' Was he babbling? He was definitely babbling, but maybe the others felt as nervous as he did, because thankfully they merely nodded and agreed.

Fitzbillies seemed like a safe place to have a difficult conversation, Ben assured himself as they walked in a few minutes later. He remembered coming here as a boy for an occasional special treat, his mum buying cakes for him and his sisters to break up the monotony of school uniform shopping, and it had always felt warm and welcoming, as if nothing bad could happen within its walls. Having nabbed a window table, and decided, after some deliberation, on drinks and buns, the three of them fell momentarily silent as if nobody quite knew how to steer the difficult conversation that awaited. Keen to set the record straight on his own behalf, Ben took a deep breath and launched in.

'So. I need to tell you what happened after we said goodbye,' he began stiffly to Lara.

She was stirring sugar into her mug of tea but then looked up and met his gaze. 'Yes,' she said. 'That would be a good start.'

'Basically . . . well, my dad had a massive heart attack,' he said. Even now, it was horrible to say the words out loud. Stewart McManus had always been such a big solid bloke, so full of life, it still felt wrong that he wasn't having an opinion or telling an outrageous story from the driver's seat of his cab. 'I had to fly straight home to be with him. Then he died three days later.' Needless to say, there had been no option of flying back to the States after his dad's death; it would have felt like an insult to his memory. There was the funeral to arrange, his mum and sisters to comfort and then, because Stewart's car was standing there in the driveway and his mum kept sobbing that it was what his dad would have wanted, the cab round to take on, for eighteen mind-numbing months before Ben had finally cracked.

'Oh gosh, I'm so sorry,' Lara said, and he jerked back to the here and now. 'How awful.'

'Yeah,' he agreed. 'But I'm sorry too, that you had to wait around for me at the Oyster Bar. I swear I called them from the airport and asked them to look out for you waiting there at six-thirty, to pass on my message.'

She was silent for a moment, her cheeks flaring with sudden colour. 'Nobody told me that,' she said in a strained voice, then sighed, still not making eye contact. 'Okay, my turn. So I realised I was pregnant quite late on but didn't know if . . .' She was blushing even harder now. 'To cut a long story short, there was another guy,' she mumbled.

Oh, thought Ben, wrong-footed. Despite everything, he found

142

himself experiencing what felt like a stab of jealousy at this news. She hadn't mentioned any other guy at the time; he would have remembered. And there he'd been thinking that they'd shared something really special together.

'After you,' she added, as if reading his mind. 'Another meaningless one-night stand, you could say.'

Ben flinched at both her frosty tone and choice of words – *meaningless?* Was that how it had been for her? – but then Eliza broke in, her voice indistinct from where she was clutching her head in her hands. 'Er, FYI, I'm not really enjoying this chat,' she announced. 'Do we have to go into specifics here, Mum?'

Lara's eyes glittered, her mouth tight. 'Well, yes, I think we do, because your dad seems quite angry and cold with me, so I'm trying to explain,' she replied.

'Don't say "your dad" like that, he *is* sitting right next to us,' Eliza said, pulling a face. 'Ugh! Maybe you two should have this conversation without me.'

Ben clenched his jaw. 'It's fine, I'm more interested in talking about you anyway,' he told her. 'I want to know everything about you just as soon as we've cleared this up. Because even if I do seem angry or cold, it's only because I would have liked to have met you years ago.' Emotion rose in him. 'I've always wanted to be a dad.'

'I've always wanted to *have* a dad,' Eliza replied in the next breath. 'I mean, I had one for a while but then he found out that he couldn't have kids, and realised I couldn't be his, so he left us.' She pressed her lips together for a moment as if this was still hurtful, years later. 'Which was all news to me until two days ago, by the way. I thought he just didn't care about Mum *or* me.'

'He did care!' Lara put in. 'He loved you. Him leaving was my fault, not yours, Lize.'

'This is the painter and decorator from Whitby?' asked Ben. 'Sounds like a total idiot if he could walk out on you like that.'

He meant the words for Eliza, not Lara, and was gratified to see her small smile in return. But then Lara spoke up again.

'He wasn't an idiot,' she said snappishly. 'He was good to us, at least at first. And I thought Eliza was his child,' she went on. 'I hoped she was, anyway. And do you know what? In hindsight, I wish she *was* his child. It would have made all of our lives a lot easier.'

'Mum! Don't say that when Ben's right here!'

'But it's true. And what else was I supposed to do? Steve was there, he was kind, he offered to make a go of things.' She turned towards Ben, eyes narrowed. 'Which – you know, circumstances aside – was more than you had done.'

Ben stared at her, incredulous. Was she for real? 'What did you expect me to do when I didn't even know you were pregnant in the first place?' he asked, trying and failing to keep his cool. Honestly, she was the limit. How dare she try to make him feel bad when it was her fault he'd been kept completely in the dark this whole time?

Eliza had her hand on his arm suddenly. 'Hey, wait,' she said, peering through the window. 'Is that your *wife* out there?'

The irony of it all – one of the many ironies, for that matter – was that Kirsten had been feeling particularly mellow that morning as she left her yoga class: aching but glowing after an hour of energetic stretches. She loved the rhythm of ashtanga, of feeling as if she was working every muscle as they proceeded through the familiar sequences, her mind calmed, her body invigorated. It was the weekend, the sun was breaking through the clouds;

she felt on top of everything. For about ten minutes anyway – because then, on her way across town, her eye was caught by the sight of her husband in Fitzbillies with two women – the two women he'd been talking to the night before, in fact. Tourists needing directions, he'd said at the time. But Kirsten was not born yesterday. Nobody fooled her twice.

He looked panic-stricken when he saw her through the window, there was no other word for it. *Something* was definitely up, that was for sure, and there was no way Kirsten was about to keep on walking by without finding out what, exactly, this was about.

She went into the café, adrenalin spiking through her post-yoga chill. They *all* looked aghast to see her, she registered: the middle-aged woman, the younger one, and Ben most of all. He got to his feet, his chair scraping across the floor with a horrible squawk. 'Kirsten,' he said, flustered. 'Hi. Um, how was yoga?'

His inane question was almost enough to make her snort in disbelief. Did he seriously think she'd come in here to discuss her vinyasas with him? 'What's going on?' she asked, her eyes flicking from Ben, to the women – these so-called tourists – then back to her husband. 'Didn't I see you three together yesterday as well? Is there something I should know about?'

He shut his eyes briefly, his whole face sagging, and she felt her nerve crumble at the guilt written all over him. Oh Christ. What *was* this?

'I was going to tell you last night, I swear,' he mumbled. 'And I tried to this morning, but ...' He broke off, gesturing to the table. 'Sit down,' he said, dragging another stool over. He looked as if he were on the verge of vomiting. It was big, whatever this was about. He seemed totally rattled. 'Please. There's something I need to tell you.'

'Do you want us to go?' Lara put in nervously.

'This is all very dramatic,' Kirsten commented, trying to disguise the twinge of dread she felt as she sat down. He wasn't going to tell her he was dying or something, was he?

'I . . . God, this is such a shock to me, you've got to believe me,' he began unhappily, passing a hand across his face. 'I had no idea until yesterday. No idea at all.'

'No idea about what?' She had never liked surprises. 'Just say it, Ben, whatever it is.' Her mind was already spinning ahead – she was planning which of the oncology team at the hospital she'd want for him if it was cancer, imagining rearranging her rota around his appointments, his care. But then he spoke again.

'I've got a daughter,' he said baldly. 'Eliza.' And then he was gesturing miserably at the young woman alongside him. 'This is her,' he said.

The girl – Eliza – looked mortified, her cheeks turning cherry red. 'Hi,' she said in a tiny voice.

The room seemed to tilt. Kirsten half-expected the table to tip over, for the mugs and teapots to fall smashing to the floor. '*What?*' Was he joking? He must be. But one look at Ben's face told Kirsten that he really, really wasn't.

He nodded. 'Yeah. It's true. I literally just found out myself. I'm pretty overwhelmed too.' He indicated the woman sitting there, clutching her mug as if her hands were glued tight to it. 'This is Lara. Um, Eliza's mum.'

Kirsten blinked but it wasn't a dream. He was still there, saying this crazy stuff, his mouth opening and closing as the madness spilled forth. 'But how?' she managed to get out. 'I mean – *when?*' This Eliza girl couldn't be much more than a teenager, but Kirsten and Ben had been together for nearly twenty years, married for

146

eighteen of those. This didn't add up. This didn't add up at all. 'When did this happen?'

'Last night in the pub,' Ben said, agitated. 'I swear, I never knew, I never—'

'I didn't mean that,' Kirsten interrupted. 'I wasn't asking when you *met* her. I meant, when was she conceived? When did you sleep with – with Lara, here?' Her voice cracked on the other woman's name as the full implications of what Ben was saying burned through her like the hot blue roar of a welder's flame. He had betrayed her. He had gone behind her back. There was a daughter to prove it, a flesh and blood young woman sitting right there, looking terrified. It was almost more than she could bear. 'What the hell, Ben?' she cried, gripping on to the table edge as the room spun once more. On second thoughts, she preferred it when he'd been boring and predictable, she thought, amidst a rising tide of hysteria. 'How could you *do* this?'

He hung his head, looking thoroughly wretched, as well he bloody should. 'It was when I was in New York,' he muttered. 'You and I had agreed . . . We weren't actually a couple then, if you remember, so . . .'

He trailed off, possibly at the way her eyes had become stabbing daggers at his naff 'if you remember' line. If you remember, indeed! Oh, she remembered all right. He'd gone off for his big adventure, saying to her that he thought they should cool things for a while; that she'd always be his best friend, but he didn't know how long he'd be away so he didn't want to keep her dangling. Shorthand for: he was off with the lads and wanted to get his leg over without any guilt cramping his style. Then he'd come back almost immediately when his dad had been taken into hospital and, sucker that she was, Kirsten had rushed to his side, comforting and consoling him through the tragedy. Even getting a new job and moving to bloody Cambridge within six weeks! As far as she'd been concerned, the gap in their relationship had been minimal: mere days. But apparently he hadn't needed long.

She could feel herself shaking with shock, rage and injury. 'Ben, you were in New York for less than *forty-eight hours*,' she reminded him, voice trembling. People were looking over at them but she didn't care, their glances bouncing off her as if she were Teflon. She remembered how she'd turned her face wistfully to the sky at the time his plane was due to take off back then, silently wishing him well; how she'd missed him from the very first minute. He, on the other hand . . . 'Are you seriously telling me that was all it took for you to shag someone else? And get her *pregnant*? Sorry,' she mumbled to Lara, out of some weird automatic politeness. (Why? She didn't owe this woman anything, let alone manners!)

But now Lara was rounding accusingly on Ben. 'You had a *girlfriend*? When we met, you already had a girlfriend?' she asked, horrified. 'I didn't know,' she told Kirsten, eyes wide. 'I swear I wouldn't have gone near him if I'd known. He never said anything about having a girlfriend!'

'Mum, let's go,' Eliza pleaded, getting to her feet. She was still red in the face and looked completely distraught. 'I'm sorry,' she said to the table at large and then burst into tears. 'This is all my fault. I'm really, really sorry!'

'Wait!' Lara cried, but the girl was already rushing out of the coffee shop, tears spilling down her face. Lara jumped up and followed her, the door banging behind her. Then, just as Kirsten turned back to Ben, trembling with hurt and anger, and with a million questions brimming on her lips, she heard a yell from outside, a screech of brakes and then a piercing shriek.

'Oh my God,' said Ben, and then it was his turn to leap up from the table and sprint away because there in the middle of the road was a shocked-looking cyclist, shakily dismounting from his bike – while on the tarmac below lay Lara, motionless, a splash of scarlet blood bright on her forehead.

Chapter Fourteen

It was all so awful. Definitely the worst few seconds of Eliza's whole life, those terrible moments where everything went into slow-motion and she thought Lara might be dead. Mum had made such a horrible sound hitting the tarmac and there was blood everywhere and she wasn't opening her eyes. Eliza felt so frightened, she forgot all the first aid she'd ever learned and didn't know what to do.

'I couldn't stop! She just ran out in front of me!' the cyclist kept saying, which only left Eliza feeling worse than ever because Lara had been running after *her,* which made her entirely to blame. Then Ben and Kirsten had appeared, Ben calling an ambulance on his phone while Kirsten knelt down and checked Mum's pulse before peeling off her own hoody and covering Mum with it to keep her warm, even getting blood on it in the process. Meanwhile, Eliza couldn't stop crying. 'Is she going to be okay?' she wailed to Kirsten, kneeling beside her. 'Mum! Please open your eyes. I'm so sorry, Mum!'

It turned out that furious, shouting Kirsten was actually a midwife and really calm in a crisis, thank God, because Eliza certainly wasn't. She told Eliza that Lara was concussed, and definitely not dead, and that although it looked as if there was tons of blood, her head wound appeared superficial rather than anything life-threatening, and not to worry, she knew pretty much all the A&E doctors in Cambridge and they were all completely brilliant. Which was bloody nice of her, frankly, when Eliza had basically just blown up her marriage by existing.

That said, once the paramedics arrived, she cleared off pretty quickly, refusing to let Ben hug her or apologise, saying, 'This isn't over yet,' before walking angrily away down the road. Ben watched her go, looking helpless for a moment, before switching his attention back to the matter in hand, putting his arm around Eliza while he talked to the paramedics, finding a grubby tissue from his pocket for her so that she could wipe her eyes and reassuring her that he would stay with her. Then, once Lara had been manoeuvred on to a stretcher and into the ambulance, he flagged down a taxi for the two of them so that they could follow on to the hospital.

'I'm so sorry about all of this,' Eliza said for the millionth time, teeth chattering with shock, but he merely hugged her and said that none of it was her fault and she had nothing to be sorry about. And even amidst all her worry about Mum, and the conviction that whatever anyone might say, this *was* most definitely her fault, every bit, she felt a warm feeling in her belly nevertheless because do you know what, her dad seemed like a pretty decent person, on the whole. She was glad of him, put it that way – although, given what had just kicked off between him and his wife, she couldn't be certain that he felt remotely the same about *her* right now.

Once they arrived at the hospital, they found Lara on a trolley bed, awaiting an X-ray for a suspected broken wrist. The wounds on her face and hands had already been dressed and bandaged, and the nurse with her told them that although she'd come round, the painkillers she'd been given were making her very groggy so not to expect too much in the way of conversation. 'Mum, you scared me, are you okay?' Eliza cried, gently stroking the side of her face, but Lara merely groaned, a thick noise from her throat, her eyes only open to slits.

The X-ray showed that yes, her wrist was broken and although she wouldn't need any surgery, she'd have to wear a cast for around six weeks. 'We'll get her plastered – so to speak – and once she's feeling a bit more like herself, the doctor will make a decision about when she can go home. But obviously someone will need to keep an eye on her for the twenty-four hours afterwards, what with the bump on her head. Would you be able to do that, Mr – sorry, I didn't catch your name?'

Eliza's face burned. Oh my God, no, she thought, agonised, because surely this was asking way too much, surely this was one step too far – five hundred million steps too far – especially after everything that had just happened with Kirsten? 'It's fine, I can do that,' she put in quickly. 'I'm eighteen, I'm her daughter, so—'

Meanwhile Ben was already speaking. 'Yes, of course,' he said, with a quick nod at Eliza. 'You can both stay at our place until she's okay to go home. We can keep an eye on her together, yeah?'

'But—'

'Honestly, it's fine. We'll sort it out. Don't worry,' he told her. Was this what it meant, to have a dad? she thought, weak with gratitude for his arm still around her, his steady presence. Someone stepping up and taking care of things on your behalf?

In which case, how was it possible that she had managed without one for so long?

Lara was floating in a sea of calm. It was like being suspended in soothing black waters, merely existing rather than doing or thinking anything, and so she was surprised, whenever she opened her eyes, to remember that she was actually lying on the crisp starched sheets of a bed rather than the liquid surroundings of her imagination. Experimentally she moved a finger across the sheet and its texture reminded her, of all things, of the bed linen in the hotel where she and Ben had stayed for their honeymoon. Where was it, again? She couldn't put her finger on the exact name of the place, but she remembered clutching a fold of said sheet during their love-making, and even at the height of passion, she'd found herself thinking, *Nice quality linen, that.*

There had been that lovely view from the balcony over the sea, too. Such a beautiful spot! They liked to sit there and drink cocktails in the evening – sundowners, he'd called them – and she distinctly recalled feeling the warmth of the day's sun tingling on her skin, as if she were glowing. (She *had* been glowing, needless to say, with sheer happiness. Married to Ben McManus, the love of her life! Was there a luckier woman alive? She thought not.)

Wherever it was, the days had been hot, that was for sure. He'd burned his nose on the first afternoon, while her shoulders had turned pink where they'd both been slapdash with the sun cream; you could chart the changing shades of their skin through the photos they took, from pasty white to pink to bronze over the course of the fortnight's holiday. She remembered how the floor of the shower became gritty with sand underfoot each evening after they'd scrubbed the sea salt from their bodies following another day at the beach. Oh, it had been the most joyful time of her life, a perfect slice of paradise, theirs to enjoy for two wonderful weeks. Even now, she could bring to mind the sweet fragrance of the pink flowers that had bloomed everywhere on the resort; Ben had tucked one behind her ear that first evening, and she'd laughed, but left it there all the same. She'd felt like a princess.

Of course, everything changed when the kids came along, she reflected, but with each new member of the family, they'd been surprised by just how much love they had to give. Eliza first, of course, and then ... Lara frowned to herself, adrift in her dark sea. What were the other children called? For the life of her she couldn't remember. Panicking, she tried to find their faces in her mind – birthday celebrations, quirks of personality – but her head started to hurt with the effort. Heavens, she couldn't even recall whether her other children were girls or boys, she realised. This was ridiculous. Dreadful! What kind of a mother was she?

There was a voice speaking nearby. 'Mum? Can you hear me? We're just going to get a sandwich but we'll be right back, okay?' but she had no idea who was saying this or where they were. Was it one of her mysterious children? Were they angry with her? She shifted her position and opened her mouth to reply but the words felt too heavy to push out from between her lips, her eyelids lead weights that she couldn't lift. As a black wave of nothingness overtook her once more, she let herself sink into the embrace of its comforting depths, the volume turning lower on her thoughts until all that remained was a blissful void of silence.

Eliza seemed so wobbly and upset that Ben decided food was required, urgently, not least because neither of them had taken more than a few bites of their Chelsea buns before Kirsten had arrived and everyone had promptly lost their appetites. (Poor Kirsten, he thought with a wrench of guilt. He had tried texting her a couple of times to explain and apologise but so far she hadn't replied. But she'd come round, surely? She'd understand in time, because ... Well, because he'd make her understand. He had to put this right somehow.)

'Come on, let's find a sandwich and get some fresh air while they plaster your mum's wrist,' he suggested to Eliza now. 'She'll be fine for twenty minutes while we pop out – and they've got our phone numbers if they need to get hold of us for any reason.' He could see her turning it over in her mind as if checking the idea from all angles but then she nodded agreement and he led the way towards the exit. 'You know, this is not exactly what I'd envisaged for my first day with a new daughter,' he said ruefully as they walked. 'I'd thought we might rent a bike for you and cycle out to Grantchester together – it's really lovely out there.' He was waffling, trying to distract her, but his efforts were rewarded by a small, brief smile, at least.

'Sounds good,' she said. Then her lower lip trembled again. 'Thank you for all of this, by the way. I don't know what I'd have done if it had been just me on my own with her. I'd probably still be crying in the middle of the road back there.'

'It's fine,' he said. 'No problem at all. Hey, and what are dads for? I'm making up for lost time, at least, right?' He repeated the words in his head with a sort of dazed wonder as they followed signs for the café. *What are dads for?* He still could hardly believe he could use that phrase about himself. I'm her dad, he marvelled. I'm looking after her, sorting stuff out, buying her a sandwich. Because this is what dads do. God, it felt good, he realised. Really, astonishingly good.

Once he'd bought up half the contents of the snack bar – they were both ravenous, they agreed – they found a courtyard garden with some shrubs in planters and an apple tree just coming into blossom. 'Here we are,' he said, spreading their makeshift picnic between them on the bench. 'Tuck in. Let's pretend we're not at a hospital for a little while. You can tell me all about yourself instead. Every single thing, please.'

She laughed, tearing open a packet of tuna sandwiches. 'It's weird, isn't it, this? I mean – there's, like, absolutely loads to say but also – where do you begin?' She bit into her sandwich, a thoughtful frown creasing her forehead. 'I'm quite an okay sort of person on the whole, I suppose,' she replied, somewhat bashfully. 'Don't worry, I haven't been in a borstal or anything, I don't have a criminal record – or at least . . .'

She broke off for some reason and he wondered why but decided he probably shouldn't ask. Had he ever had a more surreal conversation? he reflected as she took another bite of her sandwich. The initial shock of discovering his own fatherhood was starting to ease its tight pinch and he was left feeling oddly calm. Fascinated, but at the same time detached, as if it wasn't quite real. *I have a daughter. She's apparently quite an okay sort of person.* It was a good start.

'Um, what else?' she went on. 'I'm an Aries, like Mum. I've got some really nice friends and a cat called Bruce. I'm doing A levels and hoping to go to Edinburgh University to study psychology.'

'Edinburgh? Oh, nice,' he said. 'I went to uni in Glasgow, funnily enough – had some great nights out in Edinburgh too. I love Scotland.' They smiled at each other, both acknowledging this tiny new connection; he was startled by how delighted he felt. 'I'll definitely come and visit you if you end up there,' he went on. 'Well – if that's all right, of course. If you'd like that.'

She had such sweet round apple cheeks whenever she smiled, he noticed. 'I'd like that,' she said shyly, nodding.

'Great,' he said. 'Me too.'

There was a moment's silence while they ate their sandwiches and he wondered which of the many questions for her he should ask next, before she beat him to it with one of her own.

'How about you?' she asked. 'I know you're a designer and like football – I did some internet stalking,' she confessed. 'But what about family? Do I have any aunts and uncles? Or cousins?'

'Shed–loads of them,' he told her. 'I have three sisters – so you have three aunts and lots of cousins.' He counted quickly on his fingers. 'Eight cousins plus a new grandma. They all live here in Cambridge and are pretty great. Loud, mind you, especially my sisters. Nosy, too, but fun, you know – a good laugh. I can already imagine the screams of excitement when they find out about you.'

'Brilliant!' she said, her face lighting up. 'We don't have a big family. Gran's up the road from us – she moved from Keswick when my d— when Steve left, and then my one and only uncle lives in New Zealand. No cousins until now. No aunts either.' Then she bit her lip. 'Talking of family stuff – what about … I hope this doesn't sound weird, but am I in for any horrible genetic problems? Are you healthy?'

He thought she was joking for a moment but her gaze was serious and it gave him an inkling of how strange and uncertain it must make you feel, not knowing your own biological inheritance, not having a clear sense of self and family. 'Well—'

'Sorry, is that too personal?' She looked stricken now. 'We were studying genetics in biology recently and it really brought it home to me, how little I know of what might be in store for me. It made me wonder who I really was. And because of that, who you might be.'

He nodded, understanding. 'Well, I don't think there's anything huge to worry about, health-wise,' he replied. 'Let me think. My sister Sophie has type 1 diabetes but manages it okay. My sister Charlotte has asthma and her kids do too. Um . . . as for me, I mean, I had all the childhood illnesses, and broke my arm twice, but I think I've got away pretty lightly in terms of my health.'

'What about your dad, though? Didn't you say he had a heart attack? I thought heart disease was a hereditary thing.'

He banged his chest rather self-consciously. 'I've never had any problems with mine,' he told her. 'Dad smoked forty a day and spent his life driving a taxi. I'm fit, I cycle everywhere, I don't smoke . . . I look after myself, don't worry.'

'Cool,' she said, then attempted a joke. 'That's lucky because it turns out I'm not that great when parents end up in hospital.'

'Hey, don't give yourself a hard time,' he said. 'I'll tell you a secret – nobody likes it when their parents end up in hospital. But your mum's going to be right as rain by the sound of it. Absolutely fine, you wait.'

She gave him a quick sideways glance. 'Can I ask you some-thing else? Did she mean anything to you? When you met in New York, I mean.' She grimaced as if already regretting her question, but ploughed on regardless. 'Because the way she told the story, you two were, like, really into each other.' She frowned. 'Did you at least like her? I reckon she was gutted when you didn't show up later on.'

'I did like her, yes,' he assured her, still smarting from Lara's description of them being a meaningless one-night stand, and keen to make it clear that he was not that sort of person. 'I really liked her,' he added for good measure. 'We clicked straightaway. She seemed so funny and smart and cool.'

Eliza appeared to find that amusing. 'Let's not get carried away,' she scoffed. 'I'm pretty sure my mum has never been *cool*. She's completely uncool, in fact. I thought she was going to cry when I told her I was planning to get a tattoo this summer.'

'What's wrong with tattoos?' he asked, before he could stop and consider whether this was an ideal parental response.

Too late. Eliza was already throwing her hands up and crying, '*Exactly!* That's what I said.' She smiled to herself. 'Great – that's two against one, then.'

'Well—' he said helplessly but she was already moving on as if the tattoo was now a done deal. *Shit.*

'Talking of Mum, guess what she does for a job these days,' she said. 'Here's a clue: it's literally the least cool job on the planet.'

'Wow.' Ben was thrown by the challenge. Presumably that meant she wasn't a high-flying editor as he'd previously imagined, then. 'I don't know ... er ... Is she one of those people who stand around city centres with a clipboard and collection bucket trying to get you to sign up for charities no one's ever heard of?'

'No, but five points for a good guess,' came the reply. 'I'll tell you. She's a driving instructor. I mean ...' She slapped a hand to her head. 'It's pretty tragic. Very, very boring. Don't you think?'

'Well ...' He hesitated because he wasn't sure his own job would score that highly against Eliza's criteria for a desirable career either. 'It's solid work, though, right? And she makes people's lives better by teaching them a very useful skill, so ...'

Eliza gave him a full-on side-eye and he found himself laughing, even if he then felt a twist of disloyalty. He was pretty

sure one of the parenting golden rules – aside from not encouraging an impulsive teenager to have a tattoo – was that you
weren't supposed to be unkind about the other parent in the
equation. At least not out loud.

'Anyway,' she went on, 'my next question is, if you liked each
other that much, why didn't you bother getting in touch with
her again, later on? Why didn't you try and find her?'

The smile vanished from his face immediately. It was a good
question and more pertinent than she could know, given the
promise he'd made into the Oyster Bar answerphone, about
finding Lara again. Not that she or Eliza *knew* this, at least, he
realised. 'Well,' he said, and suddenly he was back there, at his
father's bedside, holding his hand and bargaining desperately for
his dad's heart to keep on pumping. *I'll do anything*, he'd promised
whichever god might be listening. *I'll settle down, like he wants
me to, I'll give it my best shot.* 'After my dad died,' he continued
haltingly, 'things were pretty rough for a while.'

That was putting it mildly. He had been all over the place;
the whole family had. His mum had been catatonic for weeks,
his sisters in bits. The carefree, optimistic young man who had
met Lara no longer existed; he'd dematerialised on the flight
home, replaced instead with this numb depleted shell of himself
who had to keep it together in order to organise the funeral,
take care of everyone, and drive his dad's sodding cab. It seemed
easier to put his dreams to one side, file them in the nearest bin,
than pursue a romantic vision. And of course Kirsten had been
there anyway, his on-off girlfriend for the last year in London
and, even though they'd broken things off shortly before he
went travelling (and they *had,* however scathing she'd been
earlier in the café), it was easy to slip back into the comfort of

160

a relationship when she came calling, all kind eyes and sympathetic touches.

In hindsight, he had been pretty passive at the time, leaning hard on her for support and grateful for her calm, practical compassion. If he was honest, he probably wasn't in the right frame of mind for a relationship at all and should have allowed himself grieving space rather than clinging to the woman who had become his rescuer. This wasn't to say he didn't love her. He did, one hundred percent. But he had wondered since then if they had rushed things, under the circumstances – if, had events played out differently, she would have offered to move to Cambridge so soon. If maybe they had got married too quickly, for the wrong reasons.

He was still driving that cab, and running round after his sisters and mum, while his dreams slid ever further out of reach until they vanished completely from sight. So no, he hadn't really thought to look up Lara or attempt to track her down. Because the fun, life-seizing, spontaneous Ben she had met no longer existed. What did he have to offer her any more? Nothing.

Eliza was looking at him through narrowed eyes as if his heavily abridged response wasn't to her liking. 'I mean – of course, if I'd had the slightest idea about you, I would have done everything,' he felt compelled to add. 'But at the time, I was . . .' He swallowed, trying to find the words. 'It felt as if there was too much water under the bridge. I didn't think she would be interested in me after so long.' He thought back to the chasm that had opened up between New York Ben and grieving, exhausted, cab-driving Ben. He'd been depressed, he saw now. Flattened by life. 'I didn't feel worthy of her, I guess.'

He opened a packet of crisps, wondering how to dig himself

out of this hole, but Eliza's next words were an olive branch of sorts. 'Well, if it makes you feel any better, you *were* worthy of her and me, because you actually kind of saved my life, you know.'

'I did?'

She nodded and went on to tell a story of a grape-choking incident and how Lara had remembered his first aid advice from when they'd met. 'Thanks, by the way,' Eliza finished, nonchalantly. 'You probably didn't realise it at the time but I reckon you had a premonition that night, about this amazing daughter you were going to have, and how you had to impart one crucial bit of advice to Mum so that I would survive this far, until I was old enough to finally meet you.'

She was smiling and he found that he was too. He was exhilarated, he realised. 'That does make me feel better,' he told her, astonished by the way that an off-the-cuff remark made in a bar could resonate with real consequences years later. That he had already done something pretty huge for her without even being aware of it. 'Wow. Thank you for telling me that.'

'Thank *you*,' she said. 'And, you know, if there's any massive life-changing advice you've got to give *me*, then I'm totally up for hearing it.' She put her hands behind her ears and waggled them back and forth. 'All ears, me.'

He smiled again. She was *great,* he thought happily. She was really, startlingly great. A breeze stirred the branches of the apple tree nearby and in the next moment a memory came to him from out of the blue, something he hadn't thought about in years. A beautiful dark-eyed girl, smiling at him from under her fringe, having planted an apple pip in central New York. 'By the way, does your mum still plant apple trees everywhere?' he blurted out.

Eliza looked puzzled. 'What?'

'Nothing,' he said, feeling foolish and deciding to change the subject. 'Anyway, so my first bit of life-changing advice is to warn you that a massive blob of tuna mayo is about to drop out of your sandwich on to your jeans and you should really do something about it.'

'Argh.' She turned the sandwich over in the nick of time to eat the blob in question, then grinned at him, wiping a smear of mayonnaise from her lip. 'Thank you. Good work. Okay, I'm pleased to tell you, you've passed the test. You can stay.'

She was kidding, obviously, but it was ridiculous how full his heart seemed at that moment. How brilliant he felt about himself, about her, about all the other conversations they might have together, all the important dad stuff he should pass on to her. He was definitely going to think hard about this responsibility, possibly even make a list. Until he remembered Kirsten's face, that was, as she'd stalked away from him clutching her bloodied hoody. She would forgive him, wouldn't she? There had to be a way to add Eliza into his life without wrecking everything else – right?

Chapter Fifteen

'What's happening?' Lara asked, blinking in alarm when she came to shortly afterwards to discover that there was a weighty, gleaming plaster cast on her right wrist that definitely hadn't been there before. She looked around wildly. 'Where did everyone go?' She fell silent because the room was whirling drunkenly about her, nonsensical images jumbling in her head. Sun cream, she thought, feeling dazed. A pink flower in her hair. Where *was* she?

'Hello,' said a woman who was dressed in a nurse's uniform for some reason. 'I'm Rebecca, I'm looking after you today. You're in hospital – you were knocked over by a cyclist and you've fractured your wrist. Bit of a bump on the head too. You've had some strong painkillers, which might be why things seem a little strange.' She had a kind face, Lara registered woozily, with really amazing dark eyelashes. Were they real? Was anything real? 'Your husband and daughter are here but they've just gone for something to eat,' Rebecca went on. 'They'll be back soon, I'm sure.'

'My husband?' Lara repeated, trying to take everything in. Something wasn't quite right about this. She'd been somewhere else altogether a few minutes ago, she was sure. Floating in the sea. A white sand beach. Cocktails in tall glasses. But that world had inexplicably splintered and broken up, replaced with this hospital ward, with faded curtains around the bed and the strong smell of disinfectant in the air.

'Mr McManus, is it? They shouldn't be long. Now, can I get you a cup of tea or coffee? Are you hungry at all?'

'No, thanks,' Lara mumbled, shutting her eyes again because she was too befuddled to look at the world any more. Also because she'd preferred things when she was by the sea, with Ben in his short-sleeved white shirt and tanned arms, the sound of the waves rushing in the background. Her limbs felt heavy as sleep stole up on her and then, thank goodness, she was drifting away from everything again.

Kirsten had managed not to cry the entire way home but as soon as she was through the front door, she broke down – crumpling to the hall floor with her hands over her eyes and weeping as if she couldn't stop. Never in a million years had she expected this. Ben – unfaithful? Ben – having a child with someone else? She wouldn't have believed it had she not heard the words from his own lips just now. The irony – another one – that she had been wishing only recently that he would be more dynamic, more surprising, was not lost on her. Maybe there was something to be said for a person being predictable, after all. Why couldn't he have been *more* predictable, in fact?

Her phone rang and it was him again, but she ignored it. How were they supposed to find the words for a conversation now? What did you even say in this situation? The discovery of his daughter, of his betrayal, made a complete mockery of their

marriage. It changed everything. This Lara woman had unwittingly been able to award Kirsten's husband the exact thing he'd
always longed for, the child that Kirsten hadn't been able to give
him herself. Oh God! She couldn't bear it. Was this her pun-
ishment for something, her comeuppance for not trying a third
round of IVF as he'd begged her to?

She leaned her head against the door, with the bleak sensation
that the world was having a good old laugh at her. At the time,
she and Ben had both tried their best to deal with not being
able to have children, but now it felt as if she alone had been
the one to fail them. Nothing wrong with *his* reproductive kit,
was there? One shag with someone else and he'd been potent
enough to create this whole other person, no problem. Kirsten
hadn't been able to give him that, and she felt horrible about it.
As if everyone would know now that she was the one to blame.

Her hands trembled in her lap at her own poor choice of
language, fresh tears spilling down her cheeks. Blame was a toxic,
deeply unhelpful word to use when it came to a couple's inability
to conceive a child. How could something like that ever be seen
as somebody's fault? She never, ever used that word when talking
to one of her mums at work, yet somehow she thought it was
okay to apply it to herself. As for the thought of Ben's sisters
whispering behind her back and labelling her that way too, it
only made her cry even harder. She'd tried, all right? She'd tried
to give him a baby, damn it!

'The baby's room', they'd called the box room of their house,
jokingly, lovingly, back when they moved in. This was when they
were still young and carefree, before they'd even had a conversation about trying for a child of their own, when it was all a game,
playing at being proper grown-ups. The words had haunted her

for a long time after their failed rounds of IVF, when it became clear that no baby of theirs would be joining them, needing a bedroom of his or her own. They stopped calling it 'the baby's room' to one another, eventually painting it white and installing a desk and a filing cabinet, to create a home office. But the room still held a trace of sadness within its walls that was detectable even to a practical-minded person like Kirsten.

Ben had pissed all over that now though. Whether it was twenty minutes or twenty years ago that he'd gone behind her back, it was equally as bad. The thought of him carrying his dirty little secret for so long made her feel sick. Him and that other woman, on his first day in New York – what did that say about his feelings for Kirsten, that he could have dismissed her so easily from his mind? What a bastard, she raged. What an absolute pig!

Wait a minute. Something had occurred to her. Hanging on their living room wall was a black and gold print of a Manhattan map that Ben had bought from an art fair years earlier, and decided to keep rather than sell on in the shop. The penny dropped, as did her jaw. Is that why he'd chosen it? Did he reflect fondly on his betrayal each time he looked at it, experience a throb of yearning for that super-fertile woman Kirsten had just met, last seen being stretchered into an ambulance?

A fiery blast of rage coursed through her veins as the pieces fitted together, and without another word, she was up on her feet and running through to the living room where the print mocked her from the wall. Ha ha, Ben's little secret. Well, not any more. In a single fluid movement, she wrenched it from its hook and hurled it forcefully at the fireplace. The glass shattered as the picture crashed against the tiled hearth, glinting shards flying everywhere. 'Fuck you, Ben, you liar,' she shouted at the top of her voice. It might have felt cathartic if her heart hadn't been simultaneously shattering.

A sob in her throat, wild with adrenalin, she ran upstairs to pack a bag of things. Let Ben deal with the mess. She was out of here.

'Mum!' Sometime later, Lara was woken by the curtain around her cubicle swishing and then Eliza was standing beside her. 'Are you waking up? How are you feeling?'

Lara's eyes cracked open and the scene assembled itself before her. Hospital bed. Wrist in plaster. Head aching. Face feeling as if someone had taken a cheese grater to it. Oh Lord, and there was her girl, so pale and anxious too. They were in Cambridge, she remembered, fragments of the trip piecing together in her mind, and – yes. They had come to find Ben. Shit. *Ben*. He was there too, at the end of the bed, hatchet-faced like some kind of Grim Reaper.

'I'm fine, love,' she said, heroically if not entirely truthfully, but closed her eyes in the next moment because everything felt too much, too intense all of a sudden, her head muddled with images. It had been a dream, hadn't it, that Ben was her husband? The two of them on holiday together? Yes, it must be because now she was remembering sitting in that café with him and a plate of Chelsea buns, his face so cold and forbidding. And then what had happened? 'I don't know,' she murmured under her breath in answer to her own question.

'You were hit by a bike, do you remember? You've got a broken wrist and concussion. You were running to catch me up outside the café. Sorry about that, by the way.'

Lara opened her eyes again at Eliza's doleful tone. 'It's fine,' she said, the fog clearing a little to reveal new flashes of memory: Eliza crying and rushing out into the street. Lara sprinting after her, racked with guilt, so intent on comforting her that she didn't stop to check for traffic. A shout from nearby, the squeal of bike brakes, an alarmed pink face looming close to hers. Then … this. Here.

'Bloody cyclists,' she joked feebly. 'Why can't they drive cars like sensible people?'

'Hey, no slagging off cyclists, thank you very much,' Ben said with rather forced jollity, but Lara's brain had already moved on.

Wait. *Drive cars*, she was repeating to herself with a bolt of panic. They still had to get home, back to Scarborough. But how would she be able to drive with her wrist like this?

'Anyway, you're not to worry about anything,' Eliza was saying before Lara could work out the answer. 'Ben – Dad – argh, sorry, I don't know what to call you,' she said, glancing over at him, 'has been great, he's sorted everything out. We're going to stay at his place tonight; he said it's no problem.'

'Absolutely,' Ben put in. 'If you let me know where your car is and give me the keys, I can pick it up and collect you both.'

'The doctor thinks you'll be fine to go later today but someone needs to keep an eye on you for twenty-four hours,' Eliza added, as if they were some kind of tag team, taking it in turns to order her around. 'Oh, and by the way, Ben agrees with me about tattoos. Just saying.'

'What? No!' Lara cried weakly. She snapped her head round to glare at Ben – what on *earth* had he said? – but the sharp movement made her feel dizzy. Was this a nightmare? It must be because Eliza had said they would be staying at Ben's place that night. No way, she thought grimly. He had made it all too clear he was furious with her, he hated her, and thus he was the last person on earth she wanted to spend any more time with. She did not want to stay in his house. She did not want him driving her car. She wanted to go home and block this whole awful Cambridge trip out of her head as fast as possible. Preferably without Eliza getting herself inked in the meantime.

'I didn't actually say I thought she should get a tattoo—' Ben began awkwardly.

'We'll stay in a hotel,' she announced, speaking over him, hardly able to look at his stupid, apologetic face. 'I'm pretty sure your wife would have something to say about that, otherwise. We've caused enough upheaval.'

Ben looked downcast momentarily – God, he must be in *so* much trouble with his wife, Lara thought to herself – but then shook his head. 'I can't get hold of Kirsten, but if she has a problem with it, there are other options. You could stay at my mum's, for instance.'

'Ooh, my new grandma!' Eliza said, eyes lighting up at once. 'Do you think she'd mind?'

'*No,*' said Lara again, desperation in her voice. 'Thank you, but no.' Christ, there was absolutely no way she was going to stay at Ben's mother's house after all this. She would rather sleep in her car. She would rather sleep in the *street,* actually, if it came down to it.

'And then tomorrow, Ben-slash-Dad is going to drive us up to Scarborough in your car, so that I won't miss school on Monday – and then he'll get the train back down to Cambridge again,' Eliza went on, as if Lara hadn't spoken. She grimaced. 'Sorry, Mum, I did think about driving us back myself but I wasn't sure I'd be able to manage the whole journey on my own,' she confessed in a rush. 'And I was stressed about it being just me and you, in case you're still really concussed tomorrow, and something happens and I don't know what to do.' She bit her lip. 'You don't mind, do you?'

She looked so anguished that Lara felt her heart crack. 'No,' she mumbled, but yes, of course she minded. She minded horribly that their trip had turned out so badly. If she couldn't drive, she couldn't work, for one thing. Plus Ben wasn't who she thought he was, now that she knew he'd had a girlfriend, Kirsten, that night in New York. He might hate her for not telling him about Eliza sooner, but do you know what, she didn't feel exactly enamoured of *him* any more, after this new bombshell.

Ben and Eliza began making plans in low voices and Lara's chin wobbled as fresh anguish swept through her. Why had she allowed herself to feel even the faintest flutter of hope that anything good might come of this ill-thought-through venture? It was foolish of her to have hung on to – to have *treasured* – her memories of that night in New York with such romantic fondness for so long. How often she had replayed that night to herself! Held up Ben as the one that got away, the only man with whom she'd ever felt such an intense, immediate connection, such a powerful spark. What a total mug she felt, finding out that he hadn't even been single at the time. Clearly he hadn't meant anything he'd said to her. Wasn't that utterly typical of her luck?

And yet he *had* tried to get a message to her, at least, she reflected miserably. Everything might have been different, if—Well, there was no point getting into that now, was there? She certainly wasn't about to let on to Ben what had really happened that night. What was the point? Earlier, she'd had a whole barrage of texts from Heidi, wanting to know how it had gone with him, and Lara had been forced to reply that actually there was no longer any spark, and definitely no connection, and she'd been kidding herself pointlessly, for nineteen years, that they'd shared something special. And *still,* despite everything, her subconscious was trolling her, she realised with a sob, what with the ridiculous dream she'd just had, of the two of them being married and on holiday. *Look what you could have had in a different universe, where you both lived happily ever after together,* it seemed to be taunting her. For heaven's sake, hadn't her stupid brain learned anything yet?

'Oh Mum, don't cry,' Eliza said, sounding wretched. 'It's going to be okay, honestly. I was joking about the tattoo anyway. Kind of.'

'I can't do this,' Lara burst out, overcome by everything. Why hadn't she insisted she and Eliza return to Scarborough when she'd picked her up from the roadside yesterday? Why had she allowed this trip to happen at all?

'Nonsense,' the nurse said briskly, coming into the cubicle just then. 'Six to eight weeks, and it'll be good as new.'

Lara didn't have the heart to say that she hadn't been talking about her wrist. If only that was all she had to worry about. She shut her eyes again because it seemed to be the only refuge she had left.

Chapter Sixteen

On Sunday morning, Ben and his unlikely clutch of passengers set out for Scarborough in Lara's car, with a pungent air of trepidation hanging between them, as if a car freshener marked 'Doom' was dangling from the rear-view mirror. Eliza was in the passenger seat beside him while Lara spread out across the back, weary and crumpled. He had the feeling that the journey would seem a lot longer than the three hours thirty-eight minutes that the satnav currently predicted. *Give me strength,* he remembered his father saying when he was at the end of his tether, and he sent up the same words in a silent prayer now before turning the key in the ignition.

The night before had been ... well, the words 'thoroughly awkward' didn't even begin to describe it. Once Lara had been given the all-clear to leave the hospital late yesterday afternoon, he'd taken them both back to his place, having warned Kirsten in advance with an apologetic text that this was his plan. *It doesn't mean anything,* he had written. *I'm only doing this for Eliza. I've said I'll take them back to Scarborough, but then you're my priority. Our marriage is my priority. Please ring me?*

He hadn't heard back from her – but in some ways, he didn't need to, because as soon as he'd walked into the house that evening, her feelings towards him had been starkly clear. Her half of the wardrobe had been emptied, and the Manhattan map he'd had framed on the living room wall had been hurled against the fireplace, leaving broken glass glittering across the carpet like a scatter of frost. For the final touch, she must have thrown the tin of horrible damson-coloured paint against the wall because it had sprayed absolutely everywhere. The sofa, the TV, the wedding photos, the curtains – all of them were splattered with streaks of livid paint. It looked like a crime scene – but he knew that the real crime had been his.

'Oh my God,' Eliza had said, looking devastated as she came in behind him and saw what had happened. 'Listen, we'll go. I can drive us back, I'll manage. You need to talk to her—'

'No,' he'd replied, tired but resolute. What kind of dad would he be if he let that happen when Eliza had already admitted that she felt apprehensive about making such a long journey alone? When he'd already put his foot in it with the tattoo issue, and when Lara still seemed so fragile and out of it, eyes red from crying? Besides, Kirsten had taken her toothbrush and clothes; she was probably camping out with a friend and almost certainly wouldn't be back here tonight. 'You're not going anywhere now, you look exhausted,' he'd told Eliza. 'I'll clear this lot up and then we can sort out the spare room for you two, and get in a takeaway or something.'

The evening had been pretty subdued. Lara had gone up to bed as soon as it was ready, and he thought he'd heard her crying again. The nursing staff at the hospital had been adamant that she needed to rest, and to have a close eye kept on her in terms of the concussion worsening, but Eliza had put herself firmly forward for that job, leaving Ben feeling useless. At least it gave him time to try ringing Kirsten again, if only to end up leaving further pleading messages on her voicemail.

And now they were on their way to Scarborough, the house still smelling faintly of paint despite his best efforts, but he could deal with that properly once he was back. He still hadn't heard anything from Kirsten and he wondered how long it would be before she spoke to him again. Nothing like this had ever happened between them before. Sure, they'd had their ups and downs like every couple: petty arguments and resentments, irritations that sometimes blew out of proportion. But her smashing stuff up, throwing paint everywhere, packing a case full of clothes and leaving in anger ... this was a first. He had no idea what he was meant to do, other than keep trying to say sorry.

He understood why she was so upset, of course. For one thing, there was the huge shock of Eliza's existence, but there was also the fact that, dress it up however he wanted, he had betrayed her. Yes, he could argue that, technically, they had agreed to cool the relationship before he went travelling, but there was no denying that it was fairly shitty of him to have slept with another woman mere hours after saying goodbye to her. *The thing was, I was absolutely mad about her from the first moment*, was something he couldn't exactly say. *For one wonderful evening, I thought I had met my soulmate.* No, he definitely wouldn't be saying that either.

He glanced in the rear-view mirror at Lara, who had fallen asleep in the back, and his heart gave an unexpected twist. Even in her current state, injured and emotionally turbulent, there was something about her that drew him to her. Something intriguing. *I didn't have anything to offer her*, he'd explained to Eliza the day before, but a memory had returned to him since, of being in London for a friend's thirtieth birthday, how he'd been driving through Camberwell on his way to the party, when he'd thought about her again. It must have been two or three years after he'd returned from New York, but suddenly, pausing at the traffic lights on Coldharbour Lane, he was flung back to that Lower East Side bar, talking to Lara about going to The Sun, which had turned out to be her local pub. His heart sped up as he sat there, waiting at the red light. Should he drop in at the pub on the off-chance? He had time to spare, traffic had been light – and hadn't he promised, in the garbled message he'd left at the Oyster Bar, that he would find her again? Plus, he was on his own, Kirsten working a weekend shift and unable to join him. The night was his, he told himself as the light turned green and then, before he could change his mind, he'd flicked on his indicator and was driving down a side street to find a parking place.

It was foolish of him, of course, to imagine that she'd have stayed put. A momentary dream to think he could walk into a pub and discover her there. What would he even have said? He was married to Kirsten by then; he had made vows of love and fidelity to her. What was he thinking, following an impulse so recklessly? Anyway, that turned out to be wholly beside the point, because of course she wasn't there. Nobody at the bar knew of her or recognised her description. The Lara who'd bewitched him in New York would be long gone, he figured: in Berlin or Helsinki or Madrid. Somewhere cool and exciting, seizing life by the horns.

Or not, as it now transpired. How was it that you could get such a clear, strong impression of a person, only for them to turn into someone completely different? How, for example, had that quirky, gorgeous, fascinating woman in her mid-twenties become this harassed-looking middle-aged driving instructor? Beneath the layers of respectability and experience that had settled on her over the passing years, was there anything left of the person he had fallen for so giddily, in a strange city far from home? Despite everything, he realised he was curious to find out.

'So this is the beach,' Eliza said unnecessarily, as she gestured to the wide sweep of golden sand before them. It was late afternoon and they were finally back in Scarborough. Her mum was still a bit out of it and not really saying much, other than some apologetic fussing over the cat, and so it had fallen to Eliza to be something of a conduit between her parents. (*Parents*, plural! It was a word that had only ever belonged to other people before now.) They'd left Lara at home to rest, while Eliza suggested showing Ben a bit of her town. The beach seemed a good place to begin.

South Bay was the one you saw on all the postcards, a vast sandy crescent bookended by the towering Grand Hotel and the ruined castle up on the hill, and edged by a bustling promenade. In summer, this stretch of sand was alive with holidaymakers, the sea bobbing with tourist boats and yachts, the old donkeys trudging up and down the sand with their squealing infant cargo. In April, however, it was empty, save for a few dog walkers and a scattering of seagulls poking their long beaks into the wet sand, leaving tiny arrow-shaped footprints as they went.

'Wow,' said Ben, as they descended from the prom. A determined breeze tugged at their hair and jackets as the sea crashed into the shore, waves ruffling like frills on a prom dress. 'It's wonderful. Lucky you, having this on your doorstep all year round. What a beach!'

Eliza smiled, gratified to have impressed him. 'It's best when it's like this,' she said. 'Empty, I mean. We never come down here in the summer when it's heaving.'

'The sky looks massive, doesn't it? That big old horizon,' he said, swivelling his head to take it in. 'Puts everything in perspective. Makes all those problems seem somehow less important.'

Eliza didn't mean to laugh quite so sarcastically but it fell out of her nevertheless. 'Um . . .' she replied, raising an eyebrow. 'Not sure Mum would agree with you there – or your wife, for that matter – but nice theory.'

As soon as she'd said the words, she wondered if it had been too critical, too personal, but he gave her a wry smile in return, wrinkling his nose. Luckily for her, he didn't seem the precious sort to take offence at everything, at least. 'Fair enough,' he said. 'But . . . I dunno, there's something about the sea and sky that always make me feel insignificant. Like – whatever's happening, the world's going to keep on turning, the tide's going to keep on rushing in and rushing out. It's a reminder that we're all only tiny, tiny dots in the great soup of humanity.'

'Croutons, maybe,' Eliza said. 'In the soup.'

'Croutons, exactly!' He laughed and she experienced a brief flare of pleasure at the sound. 'Sometimes it's good to be a crouton and remember your place.'

'Speak for yourself,' she retorted. 'I have aspirations to be . . . a noodle. Or maybe a really big chunk of tomato.'

He laughed again. 'Good for you,' he said. 'The world needs ambitious people. A tomato, eh? Now that *would* make a dad proud.'

She smiled, faintly self-conscious at the notion of him ever being proud of her, possibly for something less silly than her being a tomato. Despite all her cynicism, there was a part of her that

178

longed for him to feel that way about her, for real. To introduce her as 'my amazing daughter, Eliza', his eyes shining with pride. Unless he realised how weird and neurotic she was, mind you, and felt crashing disappointment instead. Anyway, in the meantime, it was easier than she'd expected, talking to him about daft stuff. And genuinely nice too, when there had been so much intense, crazy drama going on, that they could both waffle on about soup. Had it really only been three days since she'd accosted Steve in Whitby and set them on this collision course together?

A tendril of guilt uncurled inside her as she remembered Steve's parting shot to her, regarding the fake one-star reviews of his decorating services that she'd spread liberally around on various trade websites. Yes, okay, he'd rumbled her. *Steve Pickering walked out on this job*, she'd written, or variations on that theme. *He doesn't seem to be able to commit to anything. Don't trust him!* She'd created multiple aliases for herself to cover her tracks – ordinary names like Alison Smith and Robert Winter, as well as the occasional flourish of a Colonel G Maddingley or Venetia Peacock, for her own amusement. She should probably delete them all now, she supposed. Now that she knew he'd had a reason to leave her mum behind, even if she wished he hadn't been able to turn his back on her, his nearly daughter, so easily.

'It must have been brilliant, growing up here,' Ben said, and Eliza snapped back to the present.

'It was all right, I suppose,' she said, not having lived anywhere else as a comparison. When she'd gone to visit universities in big cities, to look round on open days – Birmingham and Newcastle and Edinburgh – she'd felt exhilarated by the pace and atmosphere in those places, the size of the buildings, the rush of traffic. Scarborough had seemed small and quiet on her return. Boring, said her friends who couldn't wait to escape to places with better shops, cooler bars, more opportunities to have fun. But was it as straightforward as all that? She felt conflicted, already.

They had almost reached the water's edge by now and Ben picked up a flat stone, then crooked his wrist and sent it bouncing across the dimpling sea: one, two, three, four times. 'That's not fair,' Eliza said. 'You don't even live here and you can do that. I've never been able to.'

'It's all in the flick of the wrist,' he said, looking for another stone. 'Here, have a go with this one.'

He handed her a blue-grey pebble, smooth and flat, and demonstrated how to hold it, with the thumb and first finger slightly sticking out, so that the stone rested on her second finger. 'Crouch down a bit, so that you're more on a level with the water,' he instructed, 'then snap back your wrist and release.' He sent his stone skimming effortlessly across the water, bounce-bounce-bounce-plop. 'Your turn,' he said.

It was nice, standing there skimming stones together – or rather, trying to, as even with some individual coaching, she could still only manage one or two bounces each time. He was patient and encouraging with every attempt and she couldn't help becoming aware of a parallel life that could have been hers glimmering in her peripheral vision, of standing here as a much smaller girl, learning this precise skill, years earlier.

Maybe it was the confusing emotions the image prompted that made her eventually pull away. It was probably best not to think too hard about what might have been. What was the point? 'I'll keep trying,' she said, laughing as she held up her hands in defeat.

'Next time I'm here, I'll be expecting a massive improvement,' he warned. 'Ten bounces, at least.'

She smiled. 'So you're coming back, then, are you?' she asked. 'We haven't put you off?'

'Oh, I'm definitely coming back,' he said at once. 'If that's all right with you, obviously? But God, yeah, absolutely – I really want to be part of your life from now on.'

Eliza couldn't speak for a moment because she felt so pleased at his words. So happy at what he was saying. Back in the hospital, she'd joked about him passing a test but now it felt as if she had passed one herself. 'I'd like that too,' she said shyly.

'Great,' he said, smiling. 'Fantastic. I'm already thinking there's loads of stuff we could do together, either up here or, if I sort out train tickets, for you to come and stay in Cambridge. And maybe even ...' He hesitated, seeming shy himself, momentarily, before continuing. 'We could go on a trip somewhere, just me and you.' His expression was uncertain as if he anticipated rejection. 'Just a thought, no pressure.'

Eliza's instinct was not one of rejection though – quite the contrary. She felt sheer jubilation at his suggestion. *Oh my God. Yes!* Wasn't this the sort of thing she'd always wished for? Whenever she'd indulged in *Dad Returns!*-type fantasies as a kid, these had universally involved Steve coming back saying how sorry he was to have been gone for so long and offering all kinds of breathtaking gifts by way of apology – a pony, a princess bed, scuba-diving lessons, a mega shopping trip ('Choose whatever you like'), a holiday somewhere hot with white sands and palm trees ... This wasn't the *sole* reason she'd gone seeking out first Steve, and now Ben, of course, but all the same, the prospect of a bonus trip somewhere glamorous definitely ticked a box.

'Yes, please,' she said shyly, her imagination leaping to Paris, Copenhagen, Prague. Culture-crammed, beautiful cities to explore, just the two of them, with him paying for everything (and hopefully not fussing and budgeting like Mum always did). Maybe he'd want to make a grand gesture, go all-out on a proper adventure: Tokyo or Sydney. A road trip through California! Let's face it, they had missed a lot of precious time. Getting up to speed on stone-skimming was just the start. 'I'd be up for anything,' she said, hoping that her subtext – *Be as generous as you like!* – came through loud and clear.

'Maybe we could go on a cycling trip together,' he said, a sequence of words which instantly swept away the panoramic vistas of Eliza's imagination, only to replace them with visions of aching legs under iron-grey skies. 'Take a couple of tents and head off for an adventure?'

Camping, even worse. As a little girl, she'd had to come home early from a Brownies' camping trip because Imogen Farrington had told such terrifying ghost stories that Eliza had become hysterical with fear. Sure, since then, she'd broken the curse by going to a couple of festivals with mates, and camping out for her Duke of Edinburgh bronze award on the Yorkshire Dales, all of which had been a laugh, but Eliza wasn't sure she was the outdoorsy type who yearned to sleep beneath the stars. She'd rather have four walls, a bed that wasn't on the actual ground, a flushing toilet and a decent shower, thanks.

Still, she didn't want her new dad to think she was wet behind the ears or ungrateful, so she managed to put on an enthusiastic smile for his benefit. 'Cool! I'd love that,' she said.

He looked thrilled, so the lie was worth it at least. 'Brilliant,' he said, with one of his goofy grins. 'Kirsten never wants to go out on the bike. She'd rather stay in a posh hotel but ... well, I don't know about you, but I find that sort of place really soulless. Give me a tent and a bit of wilderness any day.'

Eliza's smile was becoming more rigid by the second, especially as she was firmly with Kirsten on the posh-hotel front, but thankfully she was saved from having to make an insincere reply because she heard her name bellowed down from the prom just then. Turning, she saw Bo, Saskia and six or seven other friends clustered around one of the benches, some of the boys with bottles of WKD, and what looked like a joint in Joel's hand.

She waved at them but made no move to go and say hello in person. Although she'd kept Bo in particular updated with her trip to the Fatherland (as Bo now called Cambridge), she felt shy about bringing the two worlds together. For one thing, she wasn't sure how disapproving or otherwise Ben was about people smoking weed. Also because she was suddenly aware that he was wearing quite a naff khaki jacket and she wasn't sure she could bear to have her mates making any jokey remarks about it at school tomorrow. She'd only known him two days, all right? She wasn't yet able to tease him about his dress sense or work on improving it, like her friends were able to with their dads. What with that and her somehow having agreed to go on a camping/cycling trip with him, this having-a-dad business was turning out to be more of a minefield than she'd anticipated.

'Why don't we head up to the castle?' she suggested quickly, seeing him glancing over at her friends and wanting to pre-empt any comments or questions he might have. She was pretty sure that it was an established rule that all dads loved castles.

'Excellent plan,' he said with pleasing eagerness, and she hustled him on, trying to unravel the tangle of emotions within her. Perhaps she'd been naïve before now, but she really hoped that having a dad would get easier in time. Wouldn't it?

Chapter Seventeen

'I should probably head off,' said Ben the next morning. It was ten o'clock and normally Lara would be taking a student for a driving lesson right now, but frustratingly, she'd had to reassign all her learners to other local driving instructors for the next six weeks or so, until she was able to get behind the wheel again. At least she would finally get something out of the expensive career insurance policy she'd been shelling out for over the years, she supposed.

Was it unkind to say she'd been counting down the minutes until Ben left? Well, she had. Staying at his place and enduring the long journey north had been trials in themselves. Then last night she'd managed to remain polite through an awkwardly stilted dinner conversation, followed by an evening where Eliza showed Ben countless family photos and old videos, their heads close as they leaned over the albums.

Lara was glad they were getting on. No, really. Coming round in the hospital, she had frightened herself with images of what might have been: if she'd been hit by a car rather than a bike, if her head had smashed a fraction harder against the road, if she'd ended up in a coma – or worse, the morgue. Anything could have happened. Of course Eliza needed another parent, of course it was only right that the two of them forged their new connection together. It didn't matter what Ben thought of her – and vice versa – as long as he was there for Eliza. Lara would overlook her difficult feelings for him, step back and let them get on with it.

And this she had done, so far with impressive self-restraint. Eliza was at school now and Ben was about to go back to Cambridge, and Lara wouldn't have to see him again for a long, long time. She'd left it as late as possible to get up herself, so that they'd only overlap for a short time in the house together, and then she would close the door behind him with a sigh of relief and curl up with Bruce for a day of rest. She was already imagining the air inside the house rearranging its particles in Ben's absence, the week settling back to its usual rhythm of schooldays and mealtimes. With a bit of luck, it would soon feel as if he'd never been there at all.

But wait – he'd sat down again at the kitchen table, fiddling with his phone, a shifty expression on his face. Saying something about his train being delayed and could he make himself another coffee? *Oh, for goodness' sake!* Lara was desperate to get rid of him by now but said a grudging yes, through clenched teeth, because she supposed she probably shouldn't throw her daughter's father out on the street. How could he stand it though, hanging around to make coffee, as if this wasn't the weirdest, most stressful situation ever? How long would they have to spend together without Eliza there to defuse the tension?

'Oh,' he said, peering into the tin marked 'Coffee' with a puzzled expression. 'There are tea bags in here.'

'Yep,' she said shortly.

'So ... where do you keep the coffee?'

'See that tin with "Tea" on?' she replied. 'In there.'

'Right,' he said, taking it down from the shelf. 'Any reason for this arrangement?'

Was he taking the piss out of her? Her hackles immediately went up. 'I'm not going to be told what to do by a couple of *tins*,' she said, as if it were obvious. 'I can make that sort of decision myself.'

He stared at her, apparently unsure if she were serious or not. 'They're not telling you what to do,' he pointed out. 'Merely existing as helpfully labelled receptacles.'

Pompous prat, she thought. Whatever. She wasn't going to admit that she'd actually mistakenly put the coffee and tea in the wrong tins initially, and then been too pig-headed – or perhaps just too lazy – ever to switch them over again. Let him think what he wanted though. 'Well, I prefer to make my own decisions about these things,' she said.

'Okaaaay,' he replied, in a voice which left her in no doubt whatsoever as to his opinion. Not that she cared. Frankly she couldn't have cared less even if she'd burst a blood vessel trying.

Silence fell, save for the low rumble of the fridge and the occasional carolling from a blackbird on the fence. A pair of blackbirds had been building a nest in the hawthorn recently and she'd found herself admiring their teamwork. 'Any news from your wife?' she asked after a while. That woman you conveniently forgot to tell me about when we were snogging on the dance floor in Cafe Wha?, she added waspishly in her head, but managed not to say aloud. Men, honestly. She was so done with them. All of them. She was going to end up like her mother, curdled with bitterness, judging every man by her bad experiences. Life seemed a lot simpler that way, for sure.

He was pouring milk into a mug, his back to her, but she noticed a new tightness in his shoulders at her question. 'No,' he replied. 'She's not answering my calls.'

Perhaps she should have left the subject there, taken the higher ground and enjoyed its lofty altitude. But there was only so much self-control a person could muster at the end of the day. 'I'm not sure who was more surprised to find out about each other, her or me,' she found herself saying, as lightly and brightly as if they'd been discussing the weather.

She thought she detected a sigh in his breath. 'Mmm,' he said non-committally. 'It wasn't exactly . . .' He turned as if he wanted to make a long explanation but faltered at her expression. 'Well, everything's out in the open now, I guess,' was all he said.

'Certainly is,' she agreed. To be fair, she'd never told Steve about him either, but there was a difference, she was sure: Ben had forgotten her instantly; she'd bet anything on it. Her name, her face, everything she'd said about herself – it had vanished with a click of his fingers the moment he left the US. Whereas for her . . . stupidly, despite the bruises left by his rejection, she had held up that night ever since, like a glowing lantern, her own private beacon of happiness. She now knew her precious memories had been nothing more than a fantasy: rose-tinted spectacles and soft-soaping. He'd walked away without a backward glance and in hindsight, she wished that she'd had the cynicism – or perhaps wisdom – to do the same.

Paths not taken – why were they so powerful in the imagination? So tantalising in their mysteries? Why were you always left with the impression that you could have done everything so much better given a second chance? It had come back to her by now, the vision she'd had in the hospital: her make-believe marriage to Ben (their honeymoon!), and their imaginary children, and she forced herself to examine, wincingly, this strange delusion. Was it a glimpse of what could have been, had the dice landed differently? If Ben's dad's heart had merely juddered a little that day, given him a scare, rather than spasming into irreversible catastrophe? If they had met as planned at the Oyster Bar, become a proper couple? Oh, but what was the point in considering alternatives, she reminded herself furiously, when the past had already happened?

'Changing the subject: Eliza's great,' he said now, sitting down at the kitchen table opposite her. His sudden warm smile was disarming and her instinct was one of immediate mistrust. If he dared muck her daughter around, then God help her, she might actually kill the man.

'Yes,' she said guardedly. 'She is.'

'If it's okay with you, I suggested that I take her for a bit of a holiday this summer, once her exams are over,' he went on, all bashful enthusiasm. 'I thought we could pack up a couple of tents and head off on bikes, maybe into Suffolk. She seemed pretty keen when we talked about it.'

Lara couldn't help a disparaging scoffing noise. 'It's fine by me, but really you should be double-checking it's all right with her,' she replied. 'Seeing as she hates camping, for one thing.'

She must be a thoroughly unpleasant person because when his face fell (as she'd fully intended it to), she felt a frisson of triumph. Glee, even. *Yeah, fuck you, Ben. You know nothing.* The glee only lasted for a fleeting moment though, before she recognised her own schadenfreude and felt ashamed. So much for being civil; that hadn't lasted long.

'Oh,' he said, crestfallen. 'She didn't give me that impression but . . .' He gazed down at his coffee. 'Maybe I'll suggest some-thing else.'

She examined her fingernails, as if it was no skin off her nose what he did, simultaneously feeling like a total cow for crushing him, while not being in any great hurry to repair the damage. God, it was complicated, all of this. She'd dug herself a hole and wasn't sure how to get out of it.

'I guess I might have known that about Eliza,' he went on, in barbed tones, 'if I'd been given the chance to meet her earlier.'

She raised an eyebrow at him, expression stony. Oh, here we go. 'Yes, you would have done,' she said, hoping that she sounded bored and sarcastic, and definitely not as if it mattered to her what he thought. And then anger needled under her attempt at nonchalance and she blew right on up. Let him have it. 'Although if you'd bothered to look me up once you got back to the UK, you know, just as a courtesy in case I didn't get your message – which I *didn't*—' She faltered momentarily, guilt rushing in before continuing. 'Then we could have kept in touch, I would have been able to tell you I was pregnant, we could have made some decisions together about that.' Her voice shook. I wouldn't have slept with Steve if I'd got the message, she thought bitterly. There wouldn't have been any doubt in my mind about who Eliza's father was. Her hands trembled and she clutched them in her lap, wrestling with her feelings, not wanting to give him the satisfac-tion of knowing how she had struggled. 'You would have known her from day one, in fact, if you'd wanted that,' she reminded him. 'So don't try and pin your guilt on me, okay, because I'm not having it.' She jabbed a finger at the table, furious all of a sudden. 'I am not having that for one second.'

He seemed unmoved by her tirade. 'My dad was *dying*,' he

said coldly. 'My family was falling apart. So forgive me if I didn't prioritise trying to track you down to apologise for why I hadn't turned up for a date. After less than twenty-four hours' knowing you. When, as far as I was concerned, I'd sent word to you that I couldn't make it. And—' He broke off for some reason, and Lara seized the chance to wade right back in.

'Oh right, but you still expected me to bother tracking *you* down to say I was pregnant and the baby might be yours, when, as far as *I* was concerned, you'd used me for a one-night stand and then fucked off?'

'But I didn't! It wasn't like that.' His jaw clenched. 'Not for me, anyway.'

'How was I supposed to know that? Because it really looked that way from where I was sitting,' she retaliated. 'You certainly didn't bother telling me you had a girlfriend either! And— '

She had more to say (so much more) but he had dived in, looking exasperated, before she could continue. 'We had split up! Just before I left to go travelling, we split up!' he retaliated. 'I was single, okay? And yes, things started back up with Kirsten after Dad died but when I met you, we were not together. I was not cheating on anyone.'

Lara pursed her lips. She wasn't convinced Kirsten saw it that way but whatever, she thought. 'Anyway,' she went on, 'as I've already told you, I *did* try to find you. When Steve left, and I realised Eliza could only be your daughter, I rang every bloody McManus in the Glasgow and Cambridge phone books until I found your number, then called you twice. Left a message with my details. And you couldn't even be arsed to get back to me.'

'I never got your message!' he protested. 'We're not even listed under my name, we're under Jensen, for Kirsten. Are you sure you had the right number?'

'Yes! I'm not a complete halfwit!' she snapped. 'And it must have been your number – or someone related to you – because the second time I rang, the person asked if I was Kirsten.' She glared at him. 'The first time, the woman who answered was so pissy, she sounded as if she hated you. Refused to talk to me and hung up. So if you're looking for someone to blame, you could stop picking fights with me and consider blaming whoever that was – or the second one, who took my message but didn't bother passing it on to you.'

She was almost out of breath from shouting; the two of them like sparring boxers, trying to stare the other out, neither willing to budge. Her pulse was thumping. Now we're getting to it, she thought. No more covering up with fake politeness. Cards-on-the-table time.

But then, before they could delve any further into the missed phone calls, they heard the sound of a key in the front door. Eliza? No – a different voice was calling through. 'Only me, don't get up!' It was Heidi, Lara realised, feeling flustered to be interrupted in the middle of a deeply personal argument, as if her friend was walking in on her half dressed. 'Thought I'd come round, check out that bump on your head, make sure you haven't totally lost the plot on your own.'

'I'm in the kitchen,' Lara called tonelessly, flicking a glance at Ben which said, *Bugger off now, please.* 'And—' But Heidi was still in full flow.

'Also to hear all about this absolute tosser you've been stuck with. What a nightmare!' her friend said cheerfully, breezing into the room. At which point, she saw Ben and her jaw dropped so quickly she was lucky not to dislocate it, while her eyes flashed weapons-grade panic. 'Oh. Shit. I didn't realise that—'

Lara cringed. Yes, she'd texted her friend an angry rant about him, and yes, she might have called Ben a rude name, but she'd never thought her actual words would be hurled into conversation while he was still present. Ground, open up and swallow me, she pleaded in her head, but the kitchen floor remained resolutely intact underfoot. 'This is Ben,' she mumbled, if only to break the horrified silence that now gaped between them all.

'Hi,' said Ben grimly. 'The tosser himself.'

Lara shut her eyes briefly, wishing she was somewhere else, far away. Could this get any worse? Then he rose to his feet, leaving his coffee mostly undrunk. 'Well, I wish I could say it's been a pleasure seeing you again,' he said to Lara. 'But that would be stretching the truth.'

Water off a duck's back, thought Lara, hardening herself. 'The feeling's entirely mutual, needless to say,' she retorted, not bothering to move as he walked across the room. Let him flounce out, she didn't care. She was done with this whole encounter.

He stopped in the doorway and looked back at her. 'What happened to you, Lara?' he asked, his face contemptuous. 'When did you get so nasty?'

He left without waiting for a reply which was just as well because Lara's throat was suddenly thick and tight with hurt. Nasty? She wasn't nasty. How could he say that to her? She gasped, trying not to broadcast her feelings too freely on her face and then, as they heard the front door crash behind him seconds later, she put her head in her hands and groaned, the sound coming from deep within. 'Fuck,' she said. 'Fuuuuuuuccckkkk.'

Heidi rushed over in a fluster. 'Oh my God, I am so, so sorry,' she wailed. 'I could kick myself. I had no idea he was still here! Are you okay? Do you hate me? Lara, I'm appalled at myself. I'm so sorry.'

Lara made a noise that was half laugh, half sob. 'I'm such an idiot,' she groaned.

'*You* are? What does that make me?' Heidi cried.

'Building him up like that in my head,' Lara went on. She could hardly look at Heidi, she felt so stupid. So angry with her own dumb self. 'Like some kind of myth. A legend! When all the time – I mean, you saw him. He's just a man. An ordinary, shitty man who—' She felt like crying all of a sudden, a lump the size of an egg in her throat. 'Who thinks I'm *nasty.*'

'Oh lovey.' Heidi put an arm around her, their heads close together. Her short blonde hair smelled sweet, like honey. 'I could punch him for saying that. Because you are the last person on earth I would ever dream of calling nasty, okay? You can dismiss that right now, because he's wrong. If anyone's nasty, it's him. You were right, he *is* a tosser.' She squeezed Lara with a sudden fierceness and kissed the top of her head. 'And don't you be hard on yourself for the way you felt about him. You were hopeful, that's all. Optimistic. And those are good qualities! You had a dream – and everyone needs dreams.'

'Yeah, except mine didn't come true, did it? My dream fell apart when it came to a second look.' She scrubbed at her eyes with her good hand, the plaster cast on her wrist feeling hot and itchy and heavier than ever.

'Well, stuff him, then,' Heidi replied. 'He's not good enough for you anyway. You were generous with your memories, it's not your fault he didn't live up to them.'

Lara said nothing for a moment, fully immersed in despair.

193

Heidi didn't get it. Lara had allowed herself to get caught up in romantic notions on the flimsiest of pretexts. She'd welcomed in hope, deluded herself with it. And now, without that hope, what was left for her? Would it ever be her turn to feel love again, or was her last chance already used up?

'It doesn't matter,' she said eventually. The worst was done, she reminded herself, as if that was any kind of reassurance. It was obvious Ben didn't like her – and now he knew that she didn't like him either. At least they were finally being honest with each other, she supposed. 'Good riddance to him, frankly. Good bloody riddance!'

Part Two
SUMMER

Chapter Eighteen

It was early June and Scarborough was enjoying a welcome blast of sunshine, the sea full of swimmers and small boats, the beaches adorned with deckchairs and newly constructed sandcastles every day. Souvenir shops were refreshing their stock, seafront restaurants were updating their menus, and in all the hotels and guesthouses, sheets were being laundered, windows cleaned and last-minute repairs undertaken, in preparation for the annual summer influx of holidaymakers. Lara loved this time of year, with the optimism of bright mornings and long, light evenings, when the entire town seemed to have a new bounce in its step, a cheerful whistle under its breath.

Almost the entire town, anyway. Because seasons might come and go, people aged and moods changed, but Lara could always rely on one constant in life: that her mother, Frances, would have a singularly dour take on events. On this particular day, for example – when the sun was streaming in through the windows, the summer air was soft and warm, and Lara had surprised her mum by turning up with a bunch of heavenly smelling white roses and some home-made shortbread – Frances only had one thing on her mind: how much she despised her new neighbour.

'I couldn't believe it. I mean, I just couldn't believe it. What on *earth*, I said, do you think you are *doing*? Get that thing away from my hedge immediately! And do you know what he said? Have a guess what he said, the miserable old goat.'

Lara spread her hands wide, having long since given up trying to predict the latest indignity inflicted upon her mother. They were sitting in Frances's stuffy living room despite the glorious weather and the fact that there was a perfectly nice garden outside. She caught the eye of her brother up on the mantelpiece, frozen in time as a gap-toothed lad in school uniform, and wished he was there too so that they could pull long-suffering faces at each other for real. 'I've no idea, Mum.'

'He said it was *his* hedge – he'd checked the boundaries on the council records, and it was his!' Frances was turning red with outrage, although perhaps that was in part due to the semi-tropical temperature of the room. 'I said to him, excuse me, but that was planted by *me*, twelve years ago, thank you very much. And you can take that spade of yours and shove it, because my hedge is staying right where it is.'

'Good for you,' Lara said, shifting the bunch of roses on her lap. 'Should I put these in water now? Make us both a drink?'

'But do you know what he did next? He said, "Well, I'm sorry, love" – yes, he actually called me that, "love", like we're friends, like we even *know* each other, the cheeky so-and-so – he said, "I'm sorry, love, but I can't stand laurel hedging. And it's completely overgrown. And it's on my land."' She paused for breath, knotting her hands furiously in her lap, her eyes glittering with the thrill of combat. 'Well! I was not about to take *that* lying down, I can tell you. I said, "Over my dead body, Mr Granger. Over my cold, dead, *rigid* body."'

Lara rose to her feet, feeling a pang of sympathy for Mr Granger. He clearly had no idea what he was up against. 'I'll put these in water,' she said, heading towards the kitchen. 'It's lovely out, you know,' she called over her shoulder as she filled a vase with water and sprinkled in the flower food. 'Shall we go and sit in the garden when I've done this?'

'What and have *him* eavesdropping on our conversation? He would, you know. Horrible man. Awful man!'

Out of sight, Lara rolled her eyes. At a guess, Mr Granger was nothing of the sort. They never were, as a rule. 'And talking of men,' she heard next, 'what's all this about Eliza meeting up with her dad again? She said she was going off to Manchester with him and all sorts. Let's see how long *this* lasts then. I hope for her sake he'll make a better fist of fatherhood than *your* dad, that's all I can say.'

'It's a pretty low bar, to be honest,' Lara replied, drily. She didn't know much about her dad, Eric, although she'd been told the story of how he and Frances had first met in a park, because their dogs got into a fight. It sounded as if this had set the tone for the entire relationship ('I should have known he was a bad lot from the way his dog behaved,' Frances had commented darkly more than once) although Lara had been more perturbed by the fact that she might very well not have existed, had it not been for Eric's aggressive Staffie.

'Well, he'd better not be rotten to Eliza or he'll have me to deal with,' Frances said as Lara returned with the vase of flowers. 'Then he'll be sorry.'

'Lucky for him, I don't think that's going to be a problem,' Lara replied. Indeed, whatever Ben might think of *her*, he'd been pretty great to Eliza so far – calling her often to chat, and messaging her after each exam for a debrief of how it had gone. Last month, when they met in Manchester, he'd taken her to see a manga exhibition that they'd both been interested in, as well as surprising her by having booked them in for an indoor sky-diving session in a wind tunnel ('Mum, it was just the best thing ever!'). He'd also treated her to dinner in a hipster Japanese restaurant, where they'd eaten dishes that Lara had never even heard of.

Frances seemed unimpressed on hearing the details. 'Anyone can shower money on a child,' she commented. 'But has he got what it takes to be a proper dad? He'll have to do better than that, if he's to convince me he's up to the job.'

Privately, Lara agreed but it was complicated. She felt torn between wanting Ben to screw up and make mistakes so that she could pour scorn on him ('Not as easy as you think, parenthood, is it?') – while simultaneously being desperate for him *not* to screw up, for Eliza's sake. Of course the latter was more important, she reminded herself now. (Did it, in fact, prove Ben's point and make her a nasty person for even thinking otherwise?)

Anyway, the main thing was that Eliza had come home absolutely radiant and beaming after seeing him; the man was clearly getting something right. What was more, Eliza seemed to have forgiven *her* to some degree for keeping Ben under wraps for so long, becoming noticeably sunnier again. The two of them had settled back into a comfortable routine together of favourite TV shows and Monday afternoon Victoria sponges, as well as their 'Sunday night salon' which saw them putting on face packs and doing each other's nails each week. 'Grooming each other like monkeys,' as Eliza liked to say.

'It pains me to admit it but he's actually doing all right,' Lara told her mum now. 'She seems to really like him. So I'm letting them get on with it, to be honest, and you can stand down from Vengeful Grandma duty for the time being, okay?'

'Hmph,' said Frances. 'Well, he's got one thing in his favour, I suppose. If it hadn't been for him, we'd never have Eliza at all. Imagine that!'

Down in Cambridge, the sun was spreading its syrupy golden light across the old stone buildings, the city falling under its annual summer hush as the student population prepared to face their exams. Libraries and study rooms hummed with the feverish concentration of those cramming. Pages turned in whispery rustlings, while highlighters picked out key lines, dates and formulae with decisive, colourful sweeps. And at single-spaced desks in echoing halls, nervous energy pinballed around those sitting there as they feverishly wrote, calculated, argued and summarised data on to scrawled pages, while the clock ticked relentlessly down. Within days there would be a relieved outpouring on to the streets, with music and revelry and bad behaviour throughout the colleges, as the last paper was finished and handed in, but in the meantime, the city held its breath, drummed its fingers and waited.

For Kirsten too, time seemed suspended. Of course, as a midwife, the workload never stopped and she was as busy as ever, running her clinic, delivering babies, looking after her mums and their tiny ones as best she could. But in terms of her personal life, everything felt stuck, in a holding pattern. Following the weekend when her marriage had fallen apart, Ben had turned up to meet her outside her antenatal clinic and begged her to come home. 'It's you I want,' he'd said, tears in his eyes. 'You, Kirsten. Please, can't we talk about this?'

She'd felt too broken to talk, though. Too wounded. How had she even ended up in this position? she found herself thinking, with a burst of hurt pride. The two of them had met over twenty years ago, following a bomb scare and evacuation at Liverpool Street Station. A chance encounter between two complete strangers; a sparked-up conversation with the funny, nice-looking man standing beside her on a cold January evening that had led to the impulsive swapping of numbers, a drink, a kiss, love, holidays, marriage ... and then on, through days and nights, weeks and years, all the way up to this point now, where she looked at him and thought, I don't even know who you are any more. Did I ever?

'Do you think maybe this girl could actually bring about some ... healing?' her friend Vick had tentatively suggested, while Kirsten was staying there. 'I know it's a shock now but she might even add something to you guys? She could be the making of a new family dynamic, three rather than two. It could work, you know, given time.'

It was rare for Vick to get something so wrong. Parents never understood how it felt to be a non-parent, end of story. 'But it's a family dynamic I'm not part of,' Kirsten pointed out, grimacing.

'But you could be. That's what I'm saying, Kirst. You could be part of it if you tried?'

It was hard to know *what* to try or do. Following a fortnight camped out in Vick's spare room, she'd struggled to pinpoint her next move. It felt impossible to return home to Ben and pick up where they'd left off when so many unstarted, unimaginable conversations still stretched between them, and therefore Kirsten had taken a week's annual leave and gone to hunker down with her parents in the hope of clearing her head. Back in her old childhood bedroom with all its familiar comforts, she'd felt relaxed for the first time in ages, sleeping deeply and enjoying spending time with her mum and dad, as well as visiting old school friends in nearby Stony Stratford. Cambridge was lovely but it did often feel like living in a theme park, with the constant hordes of tourists and students thronging the streets. This – middle England – was more real to her. A place to think, and be fussed over, a place pre-Ben where she'd always felt she belonged.

But she couldn't run away for ever. On returning, she'd taken a short-term flat rental near the hospital to afford herself further thinking time. That had been a month ago, and she was still no closer to making any decisions. Being married to Ben, their lives comfortably mingled, waking up every morning next to him . . . already it seemed as if a canyon had hollowed out between now and then. Well, most of the time.

'Kirsten, how *are* you?' Charlotte had said, practically grabbing hold of her when they'd bumped into one another on Sidney Street the other week. 'We miss you. Are you okay?'

We miss you, like they were a committee, her and Ben's other sisters, making group decisions; none of them able to speak for themselves. It was an accurate description, actually. They'd each left her practically identical voicemails saying they hoped she was okay, as if they'd collectively prepared a statement on the matter.

Kirsten had taken a step back, maintaining a neutral expression. 'I'm fine, thanks,' she'd replied, although the description was completely inadequate. It didn't, for instance, come close to conveying the tranquil feminine cosiness of her small flat, how she had taken to buying herself fresh flowers every week, and other small treats: a block of her favourite Marseille soap (lime), fruit by the punnetful, a potted sunflower to lift her spirits. Nor did it properly describe the conflicted times when she lay in bed, fully appreciating the absence of a snoring husband while simultaneously longing for the warmth of a human body beside her. Arms holding her tight.

She wouldn't try articulating any of that to Ben's sister though. 'How are you?' she asked, deftly switching the attention back to the other woman. No, she thought, as Charlotte rattled on, she would not give anything away in the street, knowing full well that any morsel she tossed to her sister-in-law would be squirrelled straight back to the rest of the pack for the others to gnaw over.

Charlotte broke off, looking uncharacteristically uncertain. 'It's not my place to say anything, I know, but I must tell you, I'm so sorry that . . .' She stumbled over the wording, her green eyes anxious behind her glasses. 'We're all so sorry that you and Ben . . . you know.'

Kirsten helped her out. 'What, that he went behind my back and got another woman pregnant?' She'd just come off a twelve-hour shift on this particular day and was not in the mood for any pussy-footing about.

Charlotte's face dropped. A receptionist at one of the city hotels, she looked overdressed for the humid day, in a raspberry-pink suit and nude tights, her name badge still pinned to her lapel. *Charlotte Pringle, Here to Help.* Not right now, she wasn't, Kirsten thought, tight-lipped. She wasn't helping at all.

'Well . . . he's very sorry,' her sister-in-law said after a moment.

'I know he is,' Kirsten said because Ben must have told her a hundred times by now that he was sorry. She was sick of hearing how sorry he was, frankly; the word had become meaningless. 'But being sorry doesn't change anything, does it?'

There was no answer to that, as they both knew, and they'd

gone their separate ways soon afterwards, no doubt Charlotte breathing a sigh of relief every bit as gusty as Kirsten's. At least she had bothered to acknowledge the situation though, which was more than Annie had done two days later, when their paths had crossed outside Marks & Spencer. Ben's middle sister had stiffened in obvious panic, before pretending not to have seen Kirsten and walking quickly in the opposite direction, head down. Pathetic. As for Sophie, the youngest of the trio, Kirsten was just glad to have an excuse to avoid her birthday party next week, especially as it was fancy dress. Sophie took it very personally when she felt people weren't trying hard enough on her behalf. Silver linings, Kirsten reminded herself with a shudder.

Anyway, that was then. Today was her day off, and she was meeting Vick for lunch at La Mimosa, an Italian restaurant by the river. Despite the ongoing situation with Ben, Kirsten was in a good mood, having savoured a lie-in that morning, and a long pleasurable faff about getting ready. Her blonde hair was freshly blow-dried and bouncy, the sun was shining, and she was wearing a strappy sun dress – cream with navy polka dots – the skirt of which swished very satisfyingly as she walked along.

Vick had nabbed them a table outside and after the two of them had kissed hello, and Vick had complimented her new dress, Kirsten sat down feeling a welcome moment of serenity. She could do this, she told herself. She had friends, a job she loved, her own place, and she was about to enjoy a long gossipy lunch here in dappled sunshine, amidst the sound of twittering bird song, the soft clink of cutlery and the slow pop of wine corks being pulled. If this was how life without Ben was to be, then she had absolutely no problem with that. 'This is *nice*,' she said.

'Isn't it? I've ordered us a jug of iced water but I was thinking

I might be debauched and go for a fruity cocktail too. Do you fancy one? It just feels like that kind of a day to me, do you know what I mean?'

Kirsten knew exactly what she meant. 'I'm so on board for that,' she assured her friend. 'Let's make an afternoon of it.'

After some careful deliberations of the cocktail list and menu, they ordered food and drink and settled into conversation. But barely had Kirsten started telling Vick a story about the twins she'd delivered yesterday, than she heard a male voice she recognised, speaking with a Geordie accent. A frisson rippled right through her, as if her body was alerting her to something significant. She stopped mid-sentence and peered across to the river path where a man was walking along, talking into his phone. He paused to lean against a railing nearby and she realised in the next second who he was: the man she'd met in the DIY store back in April, who'd flirted with her about paint shades. Cambridge was a small place but even so, she felt the finger of Fate giving her a sharp and meaningful prod. *Hello again, you.*

'Go on, so what happened next?' Vick prompted at that moment, then swung her head back to see who Kirsten was looking at. 'Why are you staring at that man?'

Kirsten's face bloomed with sudden heat. Neil, that was it. He was called Neil and he was a gardener, and she'd ended up buying that tin of horrible purple paint just because he'd given her the eye and egged her on. Paint that had ended up splattered across her living room as her parting shot, in fact, she remembered. The last time she'd been over to pick something up from the house, she'd noticed that Ben had redecorated, as if the tin of Iced Plum had never been there at all. 'Nobody,' she replied, before amending with slightly more truth, 'Just ... somebody.'

Vick gave her the same look she used on her children when they were trying to pull a fast one. 'Nobody. Just somebody,' she repeated deadpan, head rearing back on her neck. 'That makes perfect sense. Come on, Kirst. There's a story here, I can smell it. Get talking.'

Kirsten could feel herself turning redder. Neil was taller than she remembered, and looked undeniably sexy in a pale blue T-shirt and jeans, his body lean and long. She felt a hollowing sensation in her knickers and tried to pull herself together, just as he hung up, shoved the phone in his pocket and glanced her way. There were railings between them and a fair amount of greenery, but all the same, Kirsten gave a muffled squawk and pretended to be diving to get something out of her bag. Oh Lord. Had he caught her staring?

Vick was enjoying all of this very much, needless to say. 'What the hell is going on?' she hissed, poking Kirsten under the table with her toe. 'If I didn't know you better, I'd be highly suspicious by now. He's good-looking, I'll give you that. Oh – and he's leaving. Quick, get up while you can still glimpse his bum.'

Kirsten sat up – *not* in order to see his bum, whatever her friend might think – and fanned herself with the menu. 'Sorry,' she said, feeling weak and giggly, as if she was fifteen again and eyeing up the sixth-form boys with her school friends.

'Um . . . yes? *And?* Who is that man to you, anyway? What have you been doing?' Vick demanded, slit-eyed.

'Well . . .' Kirsten wrinkled her nose, almost embarrassed that she was acting this way when there was so little to confess. There was *nothing* to confess, she amended herself, bar a few tragic middle-aged fantasies. Nothing had happened, other than in the wild flights of her imagination. 'Honestly, it's . . . You're going to be so disappointed,' she warned, 'but—'

'I'll be the judge of that,' said Vick. 'Keep talking.'

Kirsten raked a hand through her hair, feeling hot and bothered – and grateful that the waiter arrived just then, bearing their cocktails. She took a sip of her mango bellini, trying to compose herself. 'Okay,' she began, once they were left alone again. 'So I met him months ago, choosing paint of all things, in B&Q.'

'That well-known romantic hotspot,' Vick put in drily.

'You'd be surprised,' Kirsten parried. 'Anyway, so he was flirty and . . . well, I suppose I quite fancied him. Not that I *did* anything, obviously!' she added hastily, seeing Vick's eyebrows rising higher and higher. 'Cheating might be part of my husband's remit but not mine. I just looked and enjoyed.'

'You just looked and enjoyed,' repeated Vick. 'Mm-hmm. I hear you.' She pursed her lips. 'Although now . . . Well, technically, I suppose, there's no need to leave things at *just looking* any more, right? Seeing as you're so determined not to go back to that poor lonely husband of yours, and all?'

Her friend was pushing her buttons – Vick had long been encouraging her to try again with Ben, to book couples' counselling sessions, to accept his apology and ultimately move on from the betrayal. However her words might sound, Vick was absolutely not urging her to do anything rash with a handsome man who'd happened to pass their way. All the same, Kirsten couldn't resist calling her bluff. 'You're right,' she said innocently. 'What's stopping me from getting in touch with him? Maybe a summer fling is exactly what I need.'

Vick spluttered on her iced Pimm's. 'Are you serious?'

Was she? Kirsten wondered. She'd only been winding Vick up, but all of a sudden, she felt an inexplicable reluctance to immediately laugh and demur. It was summer and she was single, she figured, plus the man in question had an air of danger about him which she found deeply attractive. When had she last done anything exciting or hedonistic? When had she last embarked on an adventure? Buying posh soap and summer berries was all very well, but neither gave her half the thrill that Neil had just done, walking past, leaving a cloud of head-turning pheromones in his wake. This could be a little treat, solely for her.

She smiled, feeling her nerve endings awakening, her pleasure centres yawning and stretching deliciously after what seemed like a very long winter's hibernation. 'I'm serious,' she replied. 'Watch this space.'

Chapter Nineteen

Later that day, Lara floated in the sea beside Heidi, the sunset colours of the sky streaking the water rose-pink and orange around them. It was too early in the season for many tourists to have descended on the town and the beach was largely empty, save for a cluster of teenagers on a picnic blanket at the far end of the sand. The two women had come for a spontaneous evening dip after a hot sticky summer's afternoon, and it felt absolutely heavenly.

'There's something so relaxing about being in the sea,' Lara commented dreamily, pedalling slowly in the cool water to keep herself afloat. 'Like being held by a giant hand. Being supported. God, it's nice. We should do this more often.'

'Agreed,' said Heidi. 'We should join one of those sea swimming clubs, Lara. My neighbour goes every day of the year, rain or shine. Even when it's snowing, the maniac.' She turned a watery pirouette. 'I've always fancied myself in neoprene, actually. Especially those socks. And a big woolly bobble hat, too – what's not to love?'

'It's a look,' Lara said, smiling at her friend. She moved her arms gingerly beneath the water in parallel figures of eight, still conscious of her newly mended wrist. It was wonderful to be out of plaster and back to her old life once more: able to work, drive, cook and dress herself with the ease of two working hands formerly taken for granted. Not that she'd been sitting around idly watching the clock tick while she'd been off work. Admittedly, it had taken her a couple of weeks to drag herself out of the dark hole of despair she'd initially plunged into, following the Cambridge trip, but she had managed it eventually. Managed it, and then had a good hard look at herself. With Ben's words ringing in her ears – *What happened to you? When did you get so NASTY?* – she'd found herself making comparisons between her old self and her current one: the Lara she'd been in New York and the Lara of today, seeing the changes in her as he must have seen them. It had been a sobering exercise, to say the least.

Getting pregnant, she realised, had forked the path she was taking in life, sending her off in a completely different direction. All the socialising fun of her twenties – her wardrobe stuffed full of sequins and party dresses; career hopes and ambitions gleaming in her eyeline – had pretty much vanished once she'd seen the two blue lines on a test stick. No more nights dancing in bars, no more fevered typing over a deadline, just a panicked latching on to Steve, swiftly followed by the move north to take a chance on cohabitation and motherhood. *What happened to you?* The question kept echoing around her head because Ben had a point. She wouldn't have changed being Eliza's mum for a minute – her daughter was the best thing that had ever happened to her – but she had let so many other aspects of herself go. She had shrunk as a person, become passive. *Life* had happened to her, in other words.

The scary thing was that she hadn't noticed herself changing along the way. Year after year, she had accrued these layers of self-doubt and narrowness, her world quietly minimising to a small circle of people, streets and houses. After the Cambridge trip, Lara had dug out a box of old photos and pored over them, noting how much better her hair had looked in her twenties (why had she ever grown out that fringe?) and how much more adventurous she'd been, clothes-wise. That fabulous damson-coloured velvet coat she'd worn everywhere! Those amazing oxblood-leather boots! Her favourite mustard shift dress with the pockets that had always made her feel such a girl about town. It was as if she'd given up on herself, as if she no longer deserved such outfits of joy. Was it too late to change back? Maybe it was time to *make* things happen again, rather than meekly accepting whatever came her way.

Out for daily walks along the seafront while recuperating, she'd pause to gaze at the wide indigo band of horizon, her mind churning like the waves. What will make me happy and fulfilled? she wondered. How can I reconnect with the old Lara who once had the world at her feet? She wasn't doing this for Ben, she told herself, whenever his scornful expression flitted through her mind. She definitely wasn't doing this because she wanted him to like her again, or even for him to alter his opinion of her. All the same, it had taken his rudely flung question and this wrist-inflicted hiatus for her to hold the words up to herself and warily eye the reflection.

'Yeah, I'd be up for a sea swimming club,' she told Heidi, realising that here was an opportunity to weave in an extra thread to her life. Often, if one of her learner's lessons took them along the prom, she'd see swimmers out there, year-round, their rubber-capped heads bobbing in the waves like colourful seals. She had always admired their fortitude, albeit with a slight shiver at

212

the prospect of immersing her own goose-pimpled limbs in the icy water. Yet now that she considered it, she loved the vision of herself as one of those hardy souls, emerging vigorous, tingle-skinned and energised. Possibly quite smug too. Oh yes, she'd be one of the worst sorts, she recognised with a smile – taking the chance to drop her own toughness into a conversation whenever possible. She'd be *unbearable.*

'Great. I'm going to hold you to that, so don't even pretend we didn't have this conversation,' said Heidi, with a knowing look.

'No need to say it like that!' Lara protested. 'I told you – I'm changing my ways. I'm throwing myself back into life. This is the new me, who's up for anything. Making shit happen again.'

'Controversial suggestion here but the old you was pretty great anyway, you know,' Heidi said, as they began a slow companionable backstroke alongside one another. 'You don't have to prove anything to anyone, Lara, least of all El Tosser.'

Lara wrinkled her nose because El Tosser himself had texted earlier, when she'd got back from her mum's, asking if there was anything he could do to help around Eliza's revision. He'd already offered Eliza his assistance several times, he said, but so far she hadn't taken him up on it. He'd also sent a couple of photos from their Manchester day, which was nice, admittedly, but the whole thing smacked of virtue-signalling to Lara. As if he was trying to prove what a great person he was, compared to her, the so-called nasty one. She'd been tempted to retaliate by sending photos of the washing machine stuffed with Eliza's clothes, of Eliza's messy bedroom floor before and after she tidied it, of the cupboards full of food that Lara would be cooking for Eliza, day in, day out. *Good parent right here, thank you very much,* the subtext would have been. *Caring for our wonderful daughter for eighteen years now, actually!* But she'd decided in the end that she was perhaps being a bit petty about the whole situation. *Thanks,* she'd replied coolly instead. *I'll mention it to her.*

'I'm doing this for me,' she told her friend now, 'not him.' It was different for Heidi – she'd never seen the former Lara who liked lipstick and pints and cigarettes; she'd only known this single mum version who got her kicks doing a really big supermarket shop and whitening the grout between the shower tiles. 'Don't you ever feel sick of doing the same old thing every week?'

'I do the same old thing every week because those are the things I like doing,' Heidi pointed out mildly. 'But I'm here for your midlife-crisis ride, don't worry. I'm totally on side to enable any extravagant purchases you might be considering. Although a red sports car is just plain tacky, by the way. And I'm not sure they come with dual control pedals anyway.'

Lara laughed. Was this a midlife crisis? It felt more like a do-over. Something positive. On impulse she'd gone into her local charity shop yesterday and snapped up a pair of amazing shoes, as scarlet and glossy as pomegranate seeds, having spotted them in the window. She'd also successfully bid for the most beautiful shearling coat on eBay, worth ten times what she paid for it, which she was saving for autumn, as well as a couple of pretty short-sleeved blouses, one with a pink flamingo print, one with leaping silver hares. It was extraordinary how uplifting it was to put on something that made her feel good every day, rather than slinging on the nearest clean top and jeans. She *liked* being a person who wore red shoes and bright patterns for the hell of it. How had she managed to forget this?

Fired up with enthusiasm, she'd also dusted down her laptop a fortnight ago, opened a brand new document and secretly started typing a speculative piece about falling back in love with joy-bringing clothes. The words seemed to fall out of her, as easy as breathing, as if she'd never been away from her byline, and she felt her confidence growing with every paragraph. She'd reluctantly shelved her career when moving up here because back then, it would have meant working for a small regional newspaper – and although there was nothing wrong with that, it was a far cry from the glossy magazines she'd written for in London, and their accompanying glitzy circles. But the world had changed a great deal since those days, not least with the internet, and journalists could work from anywhere now, she figured. So what was stopping her?

Since then she'd been mulling over other feature ideas, and trying to put a few pitches together. She'd begun a blog called *Scenes from the Passenger Seat*, a series of amusing, fictionalised episodes of life as a driving instructor, and was also working on a column idea provisionally titled 'Ask a Friend's Mum', an agony series aimed at teens, that she planned to punt round all the weekend newspapers for their family sections. It had occurred to her that her years teaching young people to drive had given her a unique insight into teenage lives – the car often acted like a confessional booth; a space for her clients to air any problems. She'd also frequently served as an informal agony aunt to Eliza's friends when they came over, to the extent that occasionally Eliza would jokingly complain that she wasn't sure who her mates had turned up for: her or Lara. The next step would be to make a few phone calls to features editors to see if any of them were interested in her ideas. If she had the bottle to take the plunge, that was.

'Don't worry, I'm not buying a red sports car,' she told Heidi now. 'Chance would be a fine thing, anyway. But I might get myself a new hairdo. Be honest – do you think a fringe would suit me?'

Chapter Twenty

Ben emerged from the framer's shop with the welcome satisfaction of having ticked off a task that had been languishing too long on a list. The black and gold print of the Manhattan street map that Kirsten had ripped off the wall and smashed to the ground in a fit of rage in spring was now safely back within a frame, and tightly mummified in bubble wrap and brown paper. Good as new.

It had been strange the way that Kirsten had seized upon the map as proof of Ben's treachery. Understandable, sure – she must have looked at it and imagined him fondly harking back to his time there, interpreting that as a still-throbbing yearning for Lara and freedom – but in truth, Ben had never consciously connected the two in that way. In recent weeks, however, he'd found himself wondering if maybe there had been some long-buried feelings after all, quietly glowing like embers in the depths of his subconscious. Why *had* he bought a street map of Manhattan when he'd barely scratched the surface of the place? He'd spent far more time in other cities – Cambridge and Glasgow and London – yet you didn't see him framing prints of their street maps on his wall.

Could it be the grid aesthetic of Manhattan that had appealed to his sense of design? Or merely a slightly lame attempt to present himself (falsely) as a sophisticated, well-travelled person who spent a lot of time in New York?

He wasn't sure, but whatever the case, he would not be hanging up the print back in its previous place at home. Kirsten would take it as an act of antagonism and he wanted to avoid making any stupid mistakes if he could help it, having spent weeks trying to win her back – with promises and flowers, suggestions of dinner and drinks, even a new map he'd made for her showing the places they'd both lived, and how their paths had woven together first in London, then Cambridge. (Was it telling, he wondered with a lurch, that it was only recently he had thought to make a map for the two of them at all? Especially when, as far as she was concerned, their journey as a couple might already be over?) Anyway, that aside, the print would be hung up in the back room of his shop, where Kirsten never went. And whatever she might think, it *was* only a print, at the end of the day. Surely the fact that he'd been married to her for eighteen years more than outweighed the framed map of a city he'd spent less than two days in?

It was all very baffling, frankly. For someone who had always prided himself on being a good person, and doing the right thing whenever possible, he'd found himself wondering with an uneasy frequency, if he might in fact be one of the bad guys. A tosser, as Lara had apparently called him to her friend. He tried not to dwell on this but the question kept floating up through his mind, tormenting him. *Was* he a bad guy? The sort who was disparagingly discussed by women in resentful tones? Whenever the doubt re-emerged and jabbed at him, he had taken to mentally listing all the kind things he'd ever done for his sisters, his mum, his friends, Kirsten, as if presenting a case for defence in court – the favours, the mending, the caring, the listening, the driving. Even so, the worry never quite went away. He was doing his best to prove himself as a good dad, at least, by arranging a fun day out with Eliza and making a huge effort to get to know her, although it still felt as if she was holding him slightly at arm's length. He was the one making all the phone calls, suggesting all the plans, whereas she was yet to call him Dad (she didn't seem to know *what* to call him yet) or take him up on any of his offers of help. Did she even like him? Did she have as low an opinion of him as her mother seemed to?

'You can't expect to magic a relationship out of nowhere,' his friend Rob had told him when he'd mentioned his concerns during a long cycle ride to Ely. Rob had two stepdaughters and had therefore experienced the novice-dad situation himself. 'She needs to trust you first – and you've got to spend time in the trenches, putting in the hours and doing some of the boring, everyday stuff too. None of that will happen overnight.'

It seemed good, logical advice – and Ben appreciated being able to talk to a friend about it too. Normally he might have turned to his sisters for counsel but he was fed up with the lot of them. He'd asked them and his mum round to his place for a family meeting in order to break the news that he had a daughter, and once they'd all finished shrieking and demanding to see pictures and pumping him for the whole story, he'd adopted a more serious tone. Having heard the details of Lara's attempts to contact him, he was determined to get to the bottom of who had answered the phone each time. Ben had worked out that Lara must have dialled his mum's number when searching for him, and reasoned that it could have been any of them who'd taken the calls. Sophie had been living there at the time with her two little boys, following her divorce, but Charlotte and Annie had been in and out of Mum's house frequently in those days, as had he.

When he'd brought up the subject of the phone calls, it hadn't been surprising that none of them had put their hands up to it. It was thirteen or fourteen years ago, after all, and nobody could remember every message or conversation from so long ago. Nonetheless, it rankled with Ben that both of Lara's attempts to get hold of him had resulted in failure. One time she had been rudely hung up on, according to her version of events, another time someone had promised to pass on her message yet hadn't bothered. She was the only Lara he'd ever met; he definitely would have remembered being told that she'd called. The more he thought about his sisters' blank faces during his interrogation of them, the more his annoyance grew. Because this was typical, wasn't it? He gave and gave and gave to them, yet they never really did anything for him in return. They couldn't even manage to deal with the phone calls that might have led him to his daughter years earlier. Yes, he resented them for it. He felt angry that he had lost out on this precious time, because they couldn't do one single thing for him.

He was glumly reflecting on this as he reached his shop, at which point his phone rang. Eliza's name was on the screen, he saw with a surprised smile. Had she ever called him before? This was a real breakthrough! Unless, of course, something terrible had happened. He panicked, his finger skidding on the phone screen in his haste to find out. 'Hi there,' he said anxiously, entering the shop with a wave at Nick, who was behind the counter, then hurrying into the back room and shutting the door. 'Everything all right?'

She made a groaning sound that was initially alarming (was she having some kind of stroke? Seizure?), until he recognised it as being merely one of standard teenage melodrama. Okay, perhaps things weren't *that* harrowing. 'I can't do it any more,' she moaned. 'I'm just . . . I give up!'

'On what? The exams? Life? Ever knowing your left and right?' This last was a joke between them – of course she *did* know her left from her right, but despite growing up as the daughter of a driving instructor, she was a hopeless navigator who had got them thoroughly lost several times around Manchester.

'Ha ha,' she said sarcastically although he thought he could detect a smile. 'No, I'm giving up on biology. I don't know if I'm going to bother going in for my last exam at all on Friday. I just don't get it. I'm trying and trying but the facts aren't sticking. I'm stupid.'

'You are so *not* stupid,' he told her, serious now. Having set the brown-paper-wrapped frame down on the counter, he began opening it as she poured out her grievances: that she kept getting muddled up with the Krebs cycle and still couldn't even spell pyruvate, that she was wasting her time when she wasn't going to get a good enough grade anyway, that some of her friends had just finished their final exam and she was tempted to go and get hammered on the beach with them instead.

'Whoa, whoa, whoa,' he begged when she paused for breath. 'Don't give up now when you're so close.' He ran his finger under the masking tape holding the bubble wrap together and eased it loose. 'Have you got your revision guide there? Why don't you read some of it aloud to me – the bits you don't understand – and we can see if we can work it out together.' He had offered this kind of help to her before, both directly as well as via Lara, but she was yet to take him up on it so he didn't hold out much hope that anything would have changed. But then she asked in a meek voice, 'Is that okay? Have you got time? I'm sorry, I know it's really boring, but—'

'Not boring at all,' he told her, trying to disguise the delight that jumped inside him. 'And yes, absolutely, I've got all the time for you, Lize. Want me to ring you back, to save your bill?'

He could practically hear her shoulders descending – or at least he liked to imagine they were. Dad to the rescue, he thought, imagining a superhero cape rippling on his shoulders following a flex of his muscles. 'Thanks,' she said. 'That would be great, if you don't mind.'

'Give me five minutes to make a coffee, then I'm all yours,' he told her, before hanging up and filling the kettle with a new self-importance in his stride. Maybe even a small swagger. There – *not* a tosser, actually, Lara, he thought to himself, calling through to Nick to see if he wanted a drink. He didn't see *her* rushing to discuss anaerobic respiration and glycolysis with Eliza, unlike him. To be fair, this was no doubt because Lara was at the beck and call of her driving students, and was probably patiently explaining the technique needed for a three-point turn in a suburban street at this very moment, but anyway. It wasn't a competition, he reminded himself. He was simply glad to help.

Coffee made, he finished unpacking the framed print, gave it a wistful look, if only because he wondered if he'd ever go there again, then dialled his daughter's number. 'So,' he said. 'Thrill me with tales of pyruvate oxidation and the pyruvate dehydrogenase complex. I'm down for it.'

She gurgled a laugh. 'You totally just looked that up.'

'I totally did. But go on. Talk me through it and let's thrash it out together. We've got this.'

221

She began to read, falteringly at first, and they discussed the concepts between them, gradually making sense of the process as best they could. It was a long time since he'd studied the subject himself but he was logical and patient enough that he could eventually grasp the ideas pretty well, and by the end of an hour or so's conversation, he felt that she got them too. Was this what Rob had meant about the trenches of parenthood? Spending time unpicking science modules as well as the skydiving and sushi? It was sobering to realise how much of this Lara must have done single-handedly over the years. What a bloody good job she'd made of it too.

'I'm really impressed, you know, that you're putting in so much effort,' he said to her warmly once they'd gone over everything. 'Well done.'

She laughed. 'I'm impressed with you too, that you've actually had the stamina to listen to me boring on about enzymes and shit. You've definitely earned a dad badge for that alone.'

Kirsten would no doubt have called him a pushover but he felt an instant warmth at his daughter's words. She had said the word 'dad'. She had actually said it. He was practically radioactive with joy. 'A dad badge? What does that entail?'

'You know ... building up points for good dad work.' She sounded slightly self-conscious, as if she was trying the idea on for size, only to depersonalise the situation almost immediately. 'There should be some kind of reward scheme – like a badge and certificate and stuff,' she went on, before improvising an elaborate points system for his benefit.

He listened, smiling, but his thoughts kept circling back to the same key phrases. I *am* a good guy, he told himself. She thinks I'm a good dad. Nothing else mattered by comparison. 'What, and so I've qualified for a badge now?' he asked at the end. 'Brilliant. I will wear it with pride, believe you me.' Oh, he so wanted to wear an actual badge that had the words 'Good Dad' printed on it, he realised. Like the validation he'd always longed for.

'Hey, and it's Father's Day coming up, isn't it?' she added suddenly. 'I've never had a proper one of those before.'

'Nor me,' he said.

'Maybe I could ... come and see you?' she suggested, sounding shy. 'My exams will be over then. If you're not busy, that is.'

He felt as if his heart was overflowing, bursting open inside his chest. 'If I *am* busy, then I'm cancelling whatever plans I might have immediately,' he assured her. 'That would be great. I'll sort you out train tickets if you send me some times.' At last, he thought, suddenly overwhelmed. Here's a relationship where we're both giving and making an effort for each other. Where we both want to make it work. The rest of his family had taken him for granted for such a long time, it felt a novelty to have someone give back to him.

He realised that he was tracing a finger along the grid of streets on the map before him as he spoke, turning a corner at the end of Central Park, and found himself thinking about all the many roads and turnings and junctions that had brought them to this moment, this conversation. 'Hey, and maybe while you're here we can plan our little holiday together, like we talked about before?' he suggested.

'Yeah,' she said, sounding not altogether enthusiastic. Her hesitancy prompted the unpleasant exchange he'd had with Lara to rush back into his head: the jeering expression on her face as she'd told him that Eliza hated camping.

'It doesn't have to be camping if you're not keen,' he said

quickly. 'We could do something more exciting, like ...' His finger was still tracing the outline of Central Park, and before he knew it, the words had slipped from his lips. 'Like go to New York, maybe?'

He heard a shocked gasp. 'New York? Are you serious? Like, actual New York? Not just ... York?'

He was already half regretting his impetuosity – this was hardly trenches parenting, was it? He had leapt straight back to his old patterns of trying to woo her with his generosity, as if one measly hour of biology revision had earned him that right. And what would Lara think about his offer? What would *Kirsten* say? If he was suggesting taking anyone away, shouldn't it be his wife? Eliza's obvious and infectious delight was enough to overrule any misgivings in a heartbeat though. And hell, he did really want to take a trip with his funny, outspoken, interesting, wonderful daughter. So why not? 'Sure,' he said lavishly. 'I'm serious: not just York, actual New York. Call it my treat, for all the hard work you've put in towards these exams. All the torture of getting your head around pyruvate decarboxylation, or whatever it was. We both deserve a treat for that, I reckon, so yeah. Let's do it. Let's go to New York.'

'Oh my actual God. I can't believe it. I'm so happy! This is insane!' she cried. 'Thank you so much. This is amazing. Thank you *so much*! I'm going to try so, so hard for this last exam, you wait. Whoaaa, New *York*!'

It never failed to amaze him how her delight correlated so precisely with his own levels of happiness. Right now he was brimming over with it. Smiling from ear to ear as he stood there alone in the back room of his shop, with her voice in his ear rising ever higher in pitch. 'You are very welcome,' he said. He felt like a king. A hero, dispensing joy. He was not going to feel bad about splashing out on his own kid, no way. 'I'm excited too. It's going to be great!'

'Is this a good time to call?' Kirsten asked, her heart pounding as she stood in a sheltered spot outside the hospital, lukewarm coffee in hand. She had just finished her shift, having delivered a nine-pound baby boy to beaming parents an hour or so ago. Even after all her years of experience, it still felt like the most incredible privilege to be present, playing your part, as a tiny new person emerged wet and blinking into the world. To share that moment with elated parents, to see their faces alight with wonder as you placed the clean and checked-over infant into their waiting arms. Perhaps it was the heady mix of job satisfaction and other people's joy that had propelled her to dialling this particular number and inhaling a short, tense breath. *Why not?* said Vick in her head and she steadied her nerve. Why not, indeed. She deserved a treat. If he was up for it too.

'Absolutely,' she heard him reply. 'How can I help?'

It was definitely him. She recognised his husky Geordie accent as if she knew its cadences intimately, and her entire body reacted accordingly, synapses fizzing with anticipation. I need this, she told herself. I need some fun. Is that so wrong? Yesterday she had held the hand of a weeping woman who was labouring through the tragedy of a stillbirth, and it was as if the universe had cleared its throat and given her a shove. *Life is short. Make your move. We're all just flesh and blood at the end of the day, right?*

'Hi,' she said into the phone, feeling simultaneously self-conscious and feverish at her own daring. 'You won't remember me, but we met in the paint aisle of B&Q a few months ago and—'

'Oh, I remember you,' he interrupted, and the warm June afternoon suddenly felt as if it were rich with promise; a fruit ripening on the vine, the petals of a flower bursting open beneath the sun. 'How did your choice of paint turn out?'

He remembered her too. So precisely he could flash back to that moment straightaway, the two of them under the unflattering strip lighting of the store, making silly quips about paint. Wow. That was an ego boost in itself. She rocked backwards on her feet before steadying herself against a nearby wall. 'It turned out very badly,' she confessed honestly, remembering the mingled satisfaction and horror she'd felt as she hurled the tin at the living room wall. Not that she was about to go into details of *that* now. He laughed and it gave her a jolt, like an electric charge. 'How about yours?'

'Similarly appallingly,' he replied. 'Already painted over with something boringly tasteful, in fact. That'll teach us, eh? Lesson learned: impulse decisions are good *unless* you are making home decorating purchases. Anyway.' He cleared his throat. 'How can I help you today? Don't tell me you're turning to me for wall-paper advice now?'

'No,' she said, laughing. Her hand was still on the wall and the brick felt hot beneath her fingers. Impulse decisions, he'd said, as if reading her mind. 'Although, now that you mention it . . .' She wasn't imagining the current that was pulsing between them, was she? The easy chat masking the deeper, more urgent connection she could feel, despite them not being together in person. 'I'm joking,' she added. 'No, I was looking to get a quote for some work on my garden and came across your company name online. I remembered seeing your name on your hoody that day, so . . .'

God, it sounded lame. Like she was totally stalking him and

making up an imaginary reason to get in touch. Which, admittedly, was true, seeing as her rented flat was on the first floor and didn't have any kind of garden whatsoever. Not even a window box. Even the sunflower had keeled over and dried to a crisp last week when she'd forgotten to water it. 'So I thought I'd see if you were free,' she said, hunching over the phone as she spotted a couple of nurses she knew walking towards her. Then she straightened up, refusing to act like a guilty person. She was asking a gardener for a quote, that was all. Nothing wrong with that, was there? Well, apart from the bit about her not having a garden, she supposed.

'Sure,' he replied. 'Can I take a few details first? What sort of work do you need doing?'

She smiled and put her hand up in a wave as the nurses noticed her on their way past. Louise and Mark, both of whom worked in intensive care and, if the gossips were right, were enjoying a juicy affair on the side. The thought emboldened her. 'Actually,' she said, in a burst of sudden recklessness, 'I should come clean. I don't want to mess you around. I'm looking for something a bit ... different.'

There was a pause and she winced. Telephone conversations were all very well but you missed out on so many important visual cues – the body language, the facial expressions, the eye contact. Had she been wrong about their connection? Maybe she should start backtracking. 'Um ...' she floundered, but then he was speaking over her.

'Intriguing,' he said, his voice a slow drawl. 'I like different. Tell me more.'

'Okay. Well ... I don't have a garden,' she said baldly. 'That was just an excuse.' Her heart was pumping in such a frenzy, she put a hand to it, half expecting to collapse under the exertion. There were worse places to have heart failure than right outside a hospital, at least. 'When I said I was looking for something different, what I really meant was whether you fancied a drink one night?'

She held her breath. Now or never, she thought, her pulse galloping, the sun too hot on her hair. Now or never.

'Sure,' he said. 'How about Thursday?'

Chapter Twenty-One

Lara was having a difficult Monday. Used to the sound of Eliza's clumping footsteps serving as a wake-up call if she ever slept through her own alarm, she had woken with a start that morning, twenty minutes before she was due to begin her first lesson of the day. Eliza was in Cambridge, following a Father's Day weekend trip there and not due home until the evening. The house felt abnormally quiet without her.

It sounded as if she was having a great time – she'd booked lunch at a gastropub for Ben and herself on Sunday as a surprise treat for him, and he had taken her to meet his three sisters the day before, all of whom had apparently made a colossal fuss of Eliza. ('I have *aunties*, it's so weird!' she had laughed down the phone last night.) This was all positive, Lara kept telling herself. Good for Eliza. Even if her daughter had never done anything quite so extravagant or thoughtful on previous Mother's Days for *Lara*, mind you. And yet, despite her best efforts to talk herself up, she had been feeling unmoored ever since she'd dropped Eliza at the station on Saturday morning. One small boat out on the ocean, facing choppy waters alone.

Her mood was not soothed by that afternoon's driving lesson with Judy, her oldest client at sixty-three. Judy had recently split up with her bullying husband ('Best thing I ever did!') and, in a new spirit of liberation and independence, was changing her life in myriad admirable ways, including learning to drive. While such gutsiness was only to be applauded, and Judy was, in general, delightful company, she was also somewhat eccentric and today had insisted on bringing her corgi, Rufus, along for the lesson, because – wait for it – she'd had a dream about him dying alone, and was very anxious about this becoming a reality.

Lara liked dogs – she was only on this earth at all because of a bad-tempered Staffie, let's face it – and so she'd acquiesced, with a 'just this once'. It turned out, however, that Rufus had a few issues with his owner's driving, particularly when it came to roundabouts. There had already been two vomiting episodes, and the back of the car now smelled strongly of regurgitated dog food. Thankfully this was Lara's final lesson of the day, although she dreaded to think how long it would take her to clean up afterwards.

'And how's your daughter? Did her last exam go okay?' asked Judy. She'd been a maths teacher until retiring two years ago, and had charted the progress of Eliza's A levels almost as keenly as Lara.

'She was pretty happy with it in the end, I think,' said Lara. 'Start to brake now, Judy, can you see the crossroads coming up? We're going to turn left here, so use your indicator. That's it. Yes, she's all done and is looking forward to a lovely long summer.'

'Smashing,' said Judy, negotiating the turn smoothly with only one small nervous whine from Rufus in the back. 'And how are you? Has everything settled down with the Cambridge chap?'

'Well . . .' Lara smiled faintly. Judy must have been one of those sharp-as-a-tack teachers who never missed anything. Even now, with her eyes glued to the road ahead, it was obvious that she wasn't about to be fobbed off with a nothingy answer. 'Actually, we've been getting on a bit better recently,' she admitted.

'Is that so?' Judy replied. 'Well, I'm very pleased to hear it.'

Lara was pleased to say it, too. She couldn't put a finger on when the thaw had begun between Ben and herself, but the ice was definitely starting to melt, drip by drip. There was the fact that he'd been able to talk Eliza out of a revision wobble, for instance, and the very nice bottle of champagne he'd sent her the following day to celebrate her finishing her final exam. But this New York trip he'd proposed was a complete bolt from the blue. Are you KIDDING? Lara had thought, incredulous, when Eliza, delirious with excitement, broke the news to her. There, of all places. With her daughter – okay, *their* daughter – whom he still barely knew. It seemed a bit much, frankly. Too much, and too soon. The last Lara had heard, he'd been thinking of taking her *camping*. That was, until she'd poured cold water all over his suggestion, she supposed.

As if sensing her discomfort, an email had arrived that evening from him.

Dear Lara, he'd written.

I hope this is all right with you but earlier today I impulsively suggested a trip to New York with Eliza. I said it without really thinking things through properly. Would you be okay with me taking her there?

I know you don't think very much of me right now but I promise this is not about me trying to curry favour with either of you, or being one of those weekend dads who shower their kids with gifts out of guilt.

It's more that I love spending time with her and wanted to give her a treat. Also because you were pretty clear that a camping holiday wouldn't be her number one choice!

Let me know what you think.

Ben

'So how did you reply?' Judy indicated and neatly pulled over, even though Lara hadn't asked her to. She leaned back in her seat, one elbow propped against the steering wheel as if settling in for a session at the bar. 'I must say, I think that's pretty decent of him, explaining himself like that. Although it did sound rather as if he was blaming you, for whatever you said about camping holidays. What's wrong with a camping holiday, anyway?'

Before Lara could say anything, they were distracted by Rufus, who was on his hind legs, scrabbling at the window and barking at a passing cocker spaniel. 'Get down, you silly dog,' Judy told him, a command that was completely ignored as Rufus proceeded to bark even louder. 'RUFUS!' she roared and the dog subsided, slinking back down in the seat. 'Sorry. What were we talking about? Ah yes, camping holidays.'

Lara smiled weakly. 'Nothing's wrong with a camping holiday,' she replied. She had wondered herself if Ben's final comment had been something of a dig at her but it was hard to gauge a person's tone in an email. 'You can tell he's not used to having a kid though,' she couldn't help snarking. 'Because they don't forget broken promises, and you can't just go around randomly offering massive treats on a whim without being completely sure you can actually fulfil them. That said,' she added grudgingly, 'yes, it was nice of him to email me. Thoughtful. I just hope he won't let her down, that's all.'

'Well, quite.' Judy nodded knowingly. 'And how do you feel

about this trip? And him, more generally?' Her china-blue eyes were so steadfastly fixed on Lara that it was impossible to look away, let alone attempt to dissemble. That said, calm, wise Judy was probably a far better person to discuss this with than Heidi or Frances, both of whom she loved dearly but who had their own strong opinions about Lara's situation.

How *did* she feel? That was the big question. Mollified, for one thing, that Ben was taking her feelings into consideration. Hopeful too, that this might mean they could inch forward on to friendlier terms. Slightly perplexed, though, that he was taking Eliza to *New York*, of all the cities in the world. Should she be reading any significance into this, or was it just a cool place that Ben had picked out? Maybe he went there all the time, and it carried no association with Lara whatsoever. And yes, okay, she was big enough to admit it: she was a tiny bit jealous too. Because New York was pretty much the last place that she'd felt truly alive; where it had seemed to her that anything might happen.

'All right, I guess,' she said eventually. She'd written back; just a polite, friendly reply saying that the trip sounded fantastic and Eliza was really excited. Thanking him too for being so kind to her.

The pleasure's all mine, he'd replied. *She's great. You've done a brilliant job of bringing her up.*

Which was also nice, wasn't it? Even if it did leave her with a sense of melancholy as she reflected once more on the path not taken, the message not received, the phone calls that had never quite reconnected them, way back when. Alternative outcomes that could have been. What if she'd listened to her heart, rather than her boss, the night she was supposed to meet him at the Oyster Bar? What if she'd phoned that Cambridge number a third time, rather than giving up in a huff? The three of them might be going to New York together, had she lived that life instead. They'd be grossing Eliza out about her conception there, causing her to groan and pull disgusted faces. *Please! You two!* she would be bellowing in response, hands over her ears, pantomiming horror. *I'm going to be left with PTSD after this trip.*

Rufus let out another whine at that moment, possibly of boredom, then started trying to dig in the back seat. Lara's brief reverie came to an abrupt end as Judy whirled round and began telling him off again in her sternest tones. 'I'm starting to wish I'd left you at home, dying or not,' she scolded.

Get a grip, Lara told herself. She'd bet any amount of money that Ben wasn't mooning about alternative outcomes with *her* so pointlessly. 'Right! Where were we?' she said, as Rufus lay down once more with a weary sigh, ears flattened. 'Okay, Judy. Whenever you're ready, check your mirror, indicate, one last look over your shoulder and pull away, please.'

Kirsten was finding it hard to concentrate. She was running her weekly antenatal clinic and yet on a different plane of her mind, her thoughts were circling again and again on the same loop: Neil. His voice in her ear, low and sexy. His skin against hers, cool and smooth. How natural and simple it had felt to drink a bottle of wine together at her place and then fall into bed, tearing one another's clothes off in a frenzy of passion. God, he was delicious. And God, it felt great. A no-strings fling for the summer while she got her head around what to do with her marriage. What harm was it doing? Did it matter anyway, when he'd made her feel electrified with lust, for the first time in years?

She blinked back to attention to see Alice Weatherly across the desk from her, looking faintly quizzical and also amused. 'Sorry,' Kirsten said, hoping she hadn't just given away her own diverting daydreams with an inappropriately blissed-out expression. 'How are you feeling? Any aches or pains?'

Alice was twenty-eight weeks pregnant now, experiencing some back niggles and tiredness, but otherwise doing well. Following her long, painful history of miscarriages, she had finally started to believe that she was going to be a mum this time, and although Kirsten knew from experience that there were no guarantees to be had in any woman's pregnancy, the signs were unanimously positive, and Alice had every reason to be hopeful. You could see the happiness and excitement radiating from her face as she confessed to having begun looking at cots and tiny baby outfits – just *looking*, still, not tempting Fate by actually *buying* anything – but nevertheless, this felt like a new confidence. Faith that she was at last about to move into a different chapter of her life, one she had been longing for so desperately.

Kirsten was glad for her, and Alice seemed wreathed in contentment as she sat there, hands resting on her belly. 'All the other women I talk to at pregnancy yoga or the antenatal classes are moaning about being big and hot and tired ... I don't feel like that at all,' she said as Kirsten went on to measure her bump (perfect) and listened to her baby's heartbeat (also perfect). 'I'm so ridiculously *happy* to be big and hot and tired if it means my baby is growing healthy and strong. Bring it on, I can take it!'

'That's brilliant,' Kirsten said warmly, jotting down a few notes. 'And how are you feeling about the birth itself?' *Bring it on*, she echoed in her head, as Alice started talking about birthing pools and hypnotherapy. She was already wondering when she could see Neil again for more.

Chapter Twenty-Two

A few weeks sweltered by, as June turned into July and the days stretched out long and sticky, with occasional drenching thunderstorms to surprise the crowds on Scarborough's beaches. Lara encouraged several of her students through their driving tests, including Jake, the future marine biologist, who'd been so happy to pass that he'd hugged Lara as well as his dad on returning to the test centre.

Continuing her determination to make things happen, she had lavished some attention on herself for a change, taking the plunge with a new haircut: a choppy, shoulder-length bob with a blunt fringe, and she loved it. Pretty much all her female students had complimented her on it, Heidi told her she looked ten years younger, and Eliza had given an ear-splitting wolf-whistle when she'd first seen her mum's new look. Mind you, she did then spoil the moment by saying what a lot of money Lara would save on Botox, now that her wrinkled old forehead was covered by the fringe, which earned her a mock backhander and reprimand for cheek. As well as the haircut, Lara had added to her colourful new wardrobe, pouncing on further charity shop bargains with the zeal of a recent convert. A suede patchwork skirt with a broken zip (easily fixed) for two pounds. A vintage turquoise clutch bag with a fabulous silver snap clasp that had a small tear in the lining – a fiver. An over-the-top fake jet statement necklace that she hadn't quite dared wear in public yet, but planned to launch for Heidi's birthday next week – three pounds fifty. Whatever Ben might think, she was worth spending three pounds fifty on, so there.

'Look at you! Goodness! Are you in love, or something?' Frances had cried when she'd seen Lara with her new haircut and clothes. 'You look gorgeous, Lara. All young and dynamic!' Of course, she'd then moved almost immediately on to her preferred hot topic: the latest crimes and misdemeanours of her luckless neighbour (having his grandchildren over for a barbecue when her clean washing was hanging on the line; she'd had to wash everything again because it still smelled of sausages and charcoal. Talk about thoughtless!) Still, the compliments were nice while they lasted.

Lara had continued her writing, and although her piece about clothes-joy hadn't been picked up by any of the magazine or web editors she'd shyly offered it to, a couple of them had asked to see other work by her, which had given her a shot of pride. Not quite back in the game yet, but she felt as if she might be edging her way in the right direction at least.

Meanwhile, Eliza was working long, foot-aching days in a souvenir shop in town as well as babysitting frequently for the newly separated Mrs Partridge along the road. (The cheating Mr Partridge had been booted out of the family home, according to the street gossip.) With all that on her plate, you'd have thought she would be looking forward to getting away from everything, but to Lara's surprise, she seemed to be having second thoughts about the New York trip, now that Ben was trying to firm up dates and itineraries.

'It's not that I'm not *grateful*,' she said one evening. Eliza had picked up takeaway fish and chips on her way back from work, and Lara had walked down to meet her in the park. They were sitting on a bench by the boating lake with the warm paper packets unwrapped on their laps, spearing salty chips and doing their best to ignore the hopeful-looking seagulls that kept alighting nearby, heads cocked, eyes beady.

'Don't you want to go?' Lara asked, puzzled. Until now, the vibes she'd been picking up from her daughter about the trip had been nothing short of delight and dazzlement. Now Eliza was hanging her head over her dinner, her eyes faraway. 'What's wrong?' Then she stamped her foot at a particularly brazen seagull that shuffled rather too close for her liking. 'Get out of it!' she said, as it retreated with a clattering of wings. 'Sorry, love, carry on.'

'It's just . . . I do really want to go and everything,' Eliza began, her face contorting in an effort to unpack her feelings. 'But it's *five days* together, me and him. And I really like him, it's not that I *don't* like him, but . . .' She tried to break off a piece of fish with her plastic fork and failed, then sighed, possibly at how difficult absolutely everything was. 'Like, even the plane journey over there is eight hours. Eight *hours* sitting next to him! That's going to be so awkward! What if he thinks I'm boring? Or goes off me?'

'Oh, love,' said Lara sympathetically. Hadn't she thought herself that this whole trip was too much, too soon? At least Ben was coming good on his offer, but what had possessed him to go from a cycling weekend in the UK straight to a long-haul mega-trip, when he could have taken the middle option of an easier hop, like Paris? He hadn't thought this through at all. 'Number one, you are absolutely not boring and two, he really, really likes you,' she said. 'Also, three, you won't have to talk for the whole eight hours. You'll be watching films and reading and you'll get food brought to you now and then. You can sleep, even. There won't be any expectation for you to have deep and meaningful conversation for the entire duration of the flight, I promise.'

'I know, but . . .' Eliza shrugged, looking unconvinced. A tendril of hair had escaped her ponytail and hung loose around her face, swinging out as she exhaled. 'I sound like a spoiled brat, don't I?' she muttered. 'A total diva. Maybe I should have been more enthusiastic about going camping.'

Lara elbowed her, trying to jolly her out of her gloom. 'Now steady on,' she said. 'Let's not get carried away. You in a tent, in the middle of nowhere? Without any kind of phone signal? At least New York will have Wi-Fi, right?' Eliza's face didn't change so Lara switched tack. 'Look, try not to worry. Focus on the good things.' She popped another chip in her mouth and chewed. 'And the good things are *really* good, don't forget. The hotel he's suggesting looks fab. Lucky you! I wish I could stay somewhere like that, in the best city I've ever been to. You'll have an amazing time. Far better than any holiday you've had with me. Certainly way more exciting than the rainy cycling and camping trip he might otherwise have taken you on. And it'll be well worth any small amount of awkwardness on the plane, I guarantee it.'

She had a lump in her throat suddenly, envisaging herself embarking from the airport bus in downtown Manhattan all those years earlier. How she'd stood and gazed up at the skyscrapers around her with unparalleled awe, her mouth opening in a silent wow. The contrast with the limited journeys she took now – where the biggest thrill of the week had been discovering that her favourite shampoo was on special offer in Tesco – was almost laughable. So struck was she by the thought that it took her a moment to register what her daughter was saying.

'Why don't you come with us, Mum?'

Lara nearly choked on the piece of fish she'd just forked into her mouth. 'Don't be daft,' she said. 'I can't. This is your special trip with your dad.'

'He wouldn't mind!'

Lara snorted. 'Of course he would,' she replied darkly, remembering their last text exchange which had, unfortunately, been on a day when she felt particularly premenstrual. *I said I'd pay for Eliza's prom dress, hope that's okay*, he'd written and she'd rolled her eyes with irritation. Wow, well done. What a legend. Was he expecting a medal or something? *Cool. I've bought her a ticket for Leeds festival, hope that's okay*, she'd sent back sarcastically before she could stop herself. Maybe he was a better person than her, after all, because he'd merely replied, *Great idea!* and nothing else. Well, whatever. 'Me barge into something really lovely he's doing for you?' she went on now. 'No chance. He won't want me there.'

'Why do you say that? He likes you!' Eliza protested, to which Lara could only pull a *Oh you think so?* face of disbelief. 'Anyway, what if *I* want you there?'

'You might think you want me there now, but trust me, you wouldn't,' Lara said. 'This is for you and him to get to know one another; three's a crowd, remember.' There was a short pause as a young woman in pink cycling shorts jogged past, breathing heavily, and then curiosity got the better of her. 'What do you mean, he likes me?'

'Exactly that! He's always asking about you. And he says things like "quite right too" when I tell him your opinion, or something

240

you've said.' Eliza shot her a side-eye. 'Look, I can just tell, all right? And he's single, by the way. Did you know that? He and his wife are still living in separate places, so . . .' She sawed at her fish once more, this time with more success. 'What about you, do you like him? You never really talk about him.'

Lara swallowed. Oh Lord. This was a conversational turn she hadn't anticipated. 'Well . . . he's all right,' she said warily, concentrating hard on squeezing out some ketchup. Ben and Kirsten hadn't made up? she thought in surprise. She hadn't realised things were still so bad between them. Did he blame her for their split? Kirsten probably did. And fair enough, she thought guiltily. But if Eliza was suggesting this had any relevance to Lara, she was sadly mistaken.

'Only "all right"?' Eliza prompted.

'I mean . . . I don't really know the guy any more, but he seems okay.' Lara was floundering. Her feelings about Ben were way more complicated than 'okay' but she hadn't been able to articulate them coherently to herself yet, let alone her daughter.

Eliza wrinkled her nose at this lukewarm description. 'Will you think about it, at least?' she asked after a moment.

'What? About going to New York with you? No, love. I've already said – it's not my place to—'

'He wants you to come too,' Eliza blurted out. 'He told me.'

'Did he?' Lara's arm jerked in surprise and the chip on her fork flew off, to be snapped up instantly by a waiting gull. Her mind reeled. This was unexpected. What did it mean? How should she feel? 'Right,' she said uncertainly after a few seconds of inner turbulence. 'What did he say?'

'Just that, really,' Eliza replied. 'How it would be nice to take a family trip together, basically.'

The word 'family' was like a shot in Lara's arm because wasn't that exactly what she'd always wanted for Eliza, for her to have a proper family? She hesitated, trying to weigh everything up. If her being there would alleviate Eliza's stress, then that was a pretty strong reason for saying yes, she figured. But all this about Ben saying he liked her and suggesting she come along too . . . that was a whole other matter altogether. What was she supposed to think about *that*?

'So . . . is that a yes?'

Lara was still staring into her fish and chips as if the answer might lie within. 'Let me think about it,' she said weakly in the end.

'Oh my *God*!' cried Heidi, when Lara relayed this exchange later that evening. The two of them were peeling off their clothes down on the beach and Heidi paused with one leg in her shorts and one leg out, in order to fully take in the news. 'This is turning into an amazing rom-com. The two of you, back in New York where it all began – but nearly twenty years on, with your daughter too. A-may-zing. I love it!'

'Yeah, well.' Lara folded her skirt and put it in a neat pile with her top and towel. 'It would be amazing, maybe, if I was going. But obviously I'm not.'

'What?' Heidi's shorts dropped to the ground as she swung round. 'Lara, come *on*! Why not?'

'Because . . . I feel totally weird about it,' Lara confessed, fiddling with the strap of her swimming costume. It was a 50s-style plunging purple one that she'd found for a fiver in a seconds outlet, and made her feel like some kind of starlet. (A middle-aged starlet, admittedly, but she was a firm believer that you had to

242

take these things and appreciate them whenever possible.) 'Eliza will be fine without me.'

'That's not what I was talking about, and you know it,' Heidi said, giving her a look. 'I'm hearing Ben saying he likes you, and Eliza telling you, rather pointedly by the sound of it, that he's single. For you to not go with them, when they've both asked you – when there's a chance that you and Ben could get to know each other all over again . . . The main thing I'm hearing is that you're wussing out.'

'I'm not! It's not about that.' They had been here before, Lara thought, exasperated, with Heidi pressing romantic notions on to her, only for Lara to end up feeling foolish with her own disappointment. This time she refused to be swept along. 'Anyway, *hello*, need I remind you, I don't even *know* the man,' she went on. 'I never did. So—'

'Exactly! You don't know him very well – and yet you had one of the best nights of your life with him all those years ago. A night that, despite everything, you've treasured.' Heidi snapped on her goggles with typical briskness. 'Aren't you at least curious to see if there's that same spark, that same tingle? You thought he was the one, back then. You said to me, it was as if you'd met your soulmate, that you knew the two of you had something special.'

Lara threw up her hands, feeling exasperated. 'I was twenty-six and an idealist! Things have changed since then – *I've* changed. I've grown up, for one thing, and no longer believe in fairy tales.' She rubbed her arms as a breeze feathered her skin. 'Come on, let's get in before I lose my nerve.'

Heidi didn't seem in such a hurry, folding up her clothes, still keen to make her point. 'Maybe the timing was all off when you first met,' she went on. 'But maybe now is your moment.

This summer, this year, that city. I think it's utterly romantic and you should go. You still like him, don't you? Come on, admit it. There's a little flame burning away for him somewhere deep in your heart. You must be tempted to see if anything comes of it.'

'You were calling him a tosser not so long ago,' Lara felt obliged to remind her.

'Yeah, because you said he was! But I got the feeling you'd changed your mind lately, what with him being so nice to Eliza. Am I right?'

'Not really,' said Lara non-committally as they began walking towards the sea, the sand cool and firm beneath their feet. The two of them had come down to join the local sea swimming group for the first time, and Lara could see a cluster of people already in the water, some with matching red bathing caps. It had been another sultry day and the sea twinkled with splashes of golden sunlight as the waves rippled coaxingly towards them. 'I think he's a bit of a sanctimonious prat, to be honest,' she added, only to feel slightly mean in the next second. Because to be fair, sometimes when Eliza told her about conversations she'd had with Ben, or things he'd done, Lara had felt a grudging respect for him. A tiny glimmer of respect, admittedly, that never lasted long, but there all the same.

'Do it for me, then,' Heidi urged as they reached the shallows, the water frothing around her ankles. 'Let me have some vicarious thrills from your far more interesting life. Distract me from the fact that I caught Ned watching some really grim porn last night, and haven't been able to look him in the eye all day today.'

'Oh God,' Lara said sympathetically. This seemed to be a common theme among all her friends with teenage sons.

'Plus the only romance I'm getting is via my job, because Jim's sleep apnoea is so bad I feel like killing him every night. And my mother-in-law's coming to stay for a week in two days' time and the house is a tip. Oh yeah, and Danny lost his summer job because he got caught snogging the owner's daughter. I mean . . . I'm sick of the lot of them, frankly. My life is a disaster right now.' Braver than Lara, she was already in up to her knees, barely flinching as a wave slapped at her thighs. 'So basically what I'm saying is, I'll go to New York with them, if you won't.'

Lara was starting to wish she'd never brought up the subject, especially as she was about to meet a load of fellow swimmers and this felt completely the wrong time to be conducting a loud, personal conversation in the vicinity. 'It's not as simple as that,' she protested feebly, only for Heidi to make an impatient noise.

'It bloody is, you know,' she said. 'It's really simple. Go to New York, spend some proper time together and see what happens. Either you fall madly in love all over again, in which case, great – or you can confirm that actually he's not the amazing, perfect man of your dreams after all. In which case, also great, because you can finally let go and move on. It's win–win, Lara. At least this way you'll get to know for definite. Surely it's worth going for that, alone? We haven't even talked about the shopping opportunities!'

Admittedly the shopping opportunities had been twinkling temptingly in Lara's mind too, but thankfully she didn't have to reply because in the next moment, a couple of other people splashed into the water behind them, shouting hellos. 'Hi Rachel, hi Ollie,' Heidi called back, waving. Working as a wedding photographer, she seemed to have met everyone in Scarborough at one time or other. 'We're here for the club, are you members?'

'Yes, we are – welcome!' said the woman, who had auburn

hair tied up in a loop on her head and an amethyst stud twinkling in one nostril.

Lara, who had always been less forthcoming than her friend, smiled at them both, recognising the dark-haired man – Ollie, presumably – from somewhere but not able to pinpoint exactly where. 'Hi,' she said shyly. 'I'm Lara. Nice to meet you both.'

And then, because she didn't know what to say next, as well as really needing to clear her head, she plunged into the cool water and began a steady breaststroke across the bay. She was out of practice with social events, she thought to herself, feeling flustered and gauche, as if she were an awkward teenager rather than a forty-five-year-old woman who ought to know better.

'Hey, slow down, Rebecca Adlington,' she heard Heidi calling after her. 'Trying to make the rest of us look lazy or something?'

It transpired that after swimming sessions, there was a tradition amidst the group to stay and chat for a while, with flasks of hot drinks, the occasional nip of something stronger, and – as Lara was pleased to discover – an impressive amount of cake. The swimming itself had been lovely enough but the social aspect of the club looked as if it might be even better. Everyone had a contented glow once they'd come out of the water and warmed up, and the atmosphere was buzzy and convivial.

Tonight there were about twenty of them gathered up on the sand, drinks in hand, and as the twilight thickened and the harbour lights spangled the shadows, Lara felt a deep contentment at being with these friendly people, eating a delicious brownie and feeling the ache of tired muscles in a post-exercise endorphin high. Forget curling up in front of the TV, she thought. This is proper living again.

'Hi,' said a voice nearby at that moment. 'Lara, is it? Ollie. We met briefly earlier on. I just wanted to ask – you're not Driving Instructor Lara, are you?'

Lara laughed at the label. 'That's me,' she said. 'It's actually my full name on my passport. Who told you?'

He smiled back at her. He was good-looking, she noticed, trying not to let it distract her. 'My son. Jake? Just passed his test. I've no idea what kind of miracle you worked on him, but bloody well done. We nearly came to blows when I tried to teach him in my own car. You must have the patience of a saint.'

Ah! Of course. That was where she'd seen him – at the test centre earlier that week. 'Small world,' Lara said. She wouldn't have matched him as Jake's dad, she found herself thinking – he was much taller and broader than his lanky adolescent son, although now she looked closer, he had the same wide smile. 'I really enjoyed teaching Jake,' she went on. 'What a lovely lad he is – so interesting and funny and smart. The things I learned during our lessons together – I'm going to miss him.' She took another sip of the tea one of the club organisers had poured her, thinking back to Jake's delight on the day of the test. 'I was chuffed that he passed first time.'

'Me too!' Ollie replied. 'Especially as he's got a summer job up in Robin Hood's Bay. And now – thanks to you – he can actually drive himself there and back, rather than relying on Old Taxi Dad here all the time.'

'Oh, that's great,' said Lara. 'For both of you, I mean. Isn't it brilliant, when you can step down from the chauffeuring? My daughter's the same sort of age as Jake, and it's liberating all round.' Apart from when they decide to jaunt off to Cambridge on a whim, that is, she thought, but didn't say aloud. Instead, she found herself blurting out, 'Especially when you're a single parent like me and have done all the ferrying about so far.'

She was just wondering what had possessed her to say something so personal so quickly when Ollie answered with a heartfelt 'same', which took her aback. 'Oh,' she said, frowning at the memory of the apron-clad domestic goddess she'd sometimes seen waving Jake off before his lessons. 'I thought— I mean ...' Maybe the two of them had separated, she realised, which would explain why he'd turned up at the club with the auburn-haired woman she'd seen earlier. Rachel, was it? 'Does your wife – or ex-wife – not drive herself?' she ventured, interested in finding out more.

He shook his head. 'Chrissie? She's my ex,' he confirmed. 'And no, she's ...' He hesitated as if wondering how much to tell her. 'Well, she's agoraphobic, actually. Hasn't left the house for a long time. Caused a few problems with our marriage, sadly, so ...' He spread his hands wide and broke off momentarily. 'So yeah, I've been giving Jake lifts everywhere all this time. Which is fine, obviously – Chrissie does loads of other things, and can't help what she's going through.'

'Of course,' Lara said, who was now having to adjust all the preconceptions she'd had about Jake's mum. That would teach her to make assumptions about people. 'Absolutely. Gosh, that must be tough for her.'

'Yeah. She was always quite anxious but then there was this freak accident – must have been ten years ago – where a house collapsed on the next street to us. A gas pipe explosion, completely random. Chrissie was right there when it happened – she wasn't hurt, but the friend she was with got hit by falling masonry and died. It just completely threw her. She couldn't walk down that street any more. And then gradually she stopped going out altogether.'

'Oh my God, poor woman, that's awful,' said Lara, remembering again the news story she'd heard about the sinkhole; how the ground could literally fall from under your feet. She could well imagine how seeing a friend die before your eyes in fluke circumstances could utterly shake you. How nothing would ever seem safe again.

'Yeah,' said Ollie, then rubbed his face, looking rueful. 'Sorry, I don't know why I told you all that. Tell me more about you. You said you had a daughter?'

They chatted for a while – about kids and how strange, but also good, it felt for them to be growing up and going their own ways, and then about Ollie's line of work (he was a bespoke furniture maker) and then the conversation turned to the swimming club itself, and how they'd both stumbled upon it that year, and what a great group it seemed to be. He was so amiable and funny that Lara couldn't help feeling a tiny bit disappointed when Rachel appeared by Ollie's elbow and asked him, 'Mind if we get going soon?' before turning her friendly green eyes on Lara and saying, 'Sorry to drag him away.'

'Not at all!' Lara replied, flustered again. She'd been enjoying herself so much she'd forgotten about Rachel, she realised. Ollie was the first man she'd talked to like that for . . . Gosh. She didn't want to calculate how long, actually, because the answer would probably be quite depressing.

'Nice to meet you,' she said quickly, taking a step away from him so that Rachel wouldn't get the wrong idea. Not that there was anything for her to get the wrong idea *about*, obviously. *Don't worry*, she wanted to say. *I might be going to New York with Ben anyway, my daughter's dad who I once thought was the love of my life, so, you know, it's not as if I'm looking for things to get even more complicated right now!* She didn't say any of that though. She smiled politely, said goodbye and went to find Heidi. It was silly but her heart was stuttering a bit, and her cheeks felt very red. It was probably only that she wasn't used to talking to nice men, that was all, she told herself, and because her endorphins were still going berserk around her bloodstream from the exercise.

Accepting another brownie, she joined Heidi and a couple of other women who were discussing the new Channel 4 thriller they'd been watching. Look at you, Lara, out of your comfort zone, she congratulated herself: talking to new people on the beach and go on then, yes, moving on to a plastic cup of white wine, while the sea wrapped blueberry-coloured streaks around the headland and long shadows gathered on the sand. It felt good, she thought, laughing helplessly as one of the women did a witty impression of the series detective. She was enjoying herself. She would definitely be coming back for more.

Chapter Twenty-Three

Charlotte Pringle, née McManus, walked along the street, laden with a large bunch of candy-floss-pink peonies and frothy gypsophilia, as well as a bag containing wine and a box of posh chocolates. She checked the house numbers as she went along: thirty-seven, thirty-nine, forty-one ... Nearly there. Her mouth felt sandpaper-dry as her destination loomed. Forget wars in far-flung places and international strife, this was her own personal peace-keeping mission and she was determined to make a decent fist of it today. As her conscience kept reminding her, it was the least she could do.

In general, Charlotte had always considered herself a pretty good human being. She gave money to charity; she helped out in her children's school and was always nice to her neighbours, even the annoying ones. So it had been with a horrible lurch that she'd listened to Ben's angry interrogation of her, her sisters and their mum regarding two phone calls that this woman, Lara, had tried to make to him years ago, in order to tell him that he was a father. The one thing he'd always longed for. It had been blindingly obvious to everyone present that Ben had been sorely let down – that he'd effectively been denied the chance to be a dad for all these years.

Charlotte had felt a particular, piercing stab of shame as Ben angrily outlined what had happened, because she couldn't escape the uneasy feeling that she'd been the one to take down Lara's name and number on that second fateful call. That she'd been the one blithely promising to pass Lara's details on to her brother, but that somehow or other, it had bypassed her mind. This whole thing had Charlotte written all over it and she was certain the others were thinking the same. Throughout her entire life, friends and family had teased her for her flakiness, her forgetful, distracted air, and she'd always played up to it, rather fond of this ditzy image of herself. When you were flaky, you didn't have to be a proper grown-up, after all. Nobody relied on you, nobody handed you any real responsibility because they knew you would only muck it up. Deep down, she wasn't exactly proud of this reality-avoidance tactic but nevertheless, it had always quietly suited her to some degree. Let the others take charge. Let someone more competent handle the problem.

Maybe she needed to think again, though. Maybe her old laid-back style wasn't, in fact, the best strategy; not for anyone. Because if the crucial, life-altering gap in communication that had resulted in Ben not meeting his own child until she was eighteen – if that came down to Charlotte's personal negligence – then all of a sudden she could see, with brutal clarity, that there was actually nothing good about such airheadedness. Nothing good whatsoever.

What made it worse was the fact that Ben had always done so much for her, for all of them, and that she knew they'd each taken advantage of his generous nature, on many occasions. And then, the one time when it really mattered, Charlotte had failed him badly. Not just him, either: his daughter, and this Lara woman too. Her self-blame felt like a rock in her stomach, heavy and uncomfortable.

She hadn't confessed her guilty worries to Ben there and then – none of them had, other than defensively stating they were sure *they* weren't the ones at fault, and how were they to have known it was so important anyway? – but the doubts had plagued Charlotte's conscience for the days that followed. 'Look, you don't know for sure that it was you,' her husband, Gary, said wearily one night in bed when she was fretting about the matter again. 'There is such a thing as false memory syndrome, isn't there? Maybe you're leaping to the wrong conclusion entirely because you feel bad for him.'

'Maybe,' she mumbled, because she could tell that his patience was wearing thin.

Later that same week, she arranged to meet Sophie and Annie in The Mill, a riverside pub in town, in the hope of being able to thrash the matter out with them. 'Listen, I need to tell you something: I think it was me who spoke to Lara that second time,' was how she'd opened the conversation, followed immediately by a nervous gulp of her gin and tonic. 'The more I think about it, the more I can imagine myself doing that – taking down an important message and losing it five minutes later. Forgetting all about it. I mean, it sounds like me, doesn't it? I feel terrible. Absolutely sick!'

Annie nodded, eyes down. 'I hear you,' she said. 'Because I'm pretty sure it was me who hung up on her the first time around. You know what a temper I used to have back then.'

Used to have back then? Charlotte and Sophie couldn't quite make eye contact in response because they both knew full well that Annie's temper was still very much fiery and in frequent use.

'Well, thank God you both think you're to blame,' Sophie cried, with somewhat tactless relief, throwing her head back in an exaggerated exhalation. 'Because I did the sums and worked out that I'd have been living with Mum at the time, with the boys – it would have been after Jason had buggered off to Spain and I was in a mess. So I was assuming the phone cock-ups had been me, twice over.'

'Well, they still might have been,' Annie quickly put in, perking up, but Sophie was shaking her head.

'Nope,' she said firmly. 'Now that you've both confessed, I agree that it definitely sounds more like you two. Definitely. Which leaves me in the clear. Phew!'

Charlotte frowned as Sophie pretended to wipe sweat from her brow. Her sisters seemed to be missing the point. 'This isn't a game,' she reminded them. 'Whoever it was really mucked things up for Ben, and I feel terrible for him, even if you don't. Kirsten still hasn't come home and he's starting to lose hope that they can patch things up. And do you know what he said to me about that, by the way? That he wished we three could have been friendlier towards her. More inclusive. That she always felt left out.'

Annie made an exasperated-sounding click of her tongue. 'We *were* friendly! Nobody left her out! Christ, the number of times she was invited places and never showed up . . . What else were we supposed to do?'

'She was never all that friendly to *us*,' Sophie put in, leaping on the counter-attack. 'If she felt left out, it's her own fault.'

Charlotte took another mouthful of her drink, discomfited to notice she'd almost finished it already. 'It can't have been easy for her though,' she reasoned. 'Dealing with so many gobby in-laws, when she's an only child, used to a more peaceful way of life. Look – I'm not having a go at you two; I didn't make the effort either,' she added, noticing her sisters exchanging sullen glances. 'I just wonder if we can do anything to make it up to Ben.'

'Like what?' had come the unwilling response.

Like this, was the answer. Like Charlotte walking up the street where Kirsten was renting a flat, bearing gifts in the hope of making amends. If she could just encourage her sister-in-law back into the bosom of the family for Ben's sake, reassure her that they *did* all love her and miss her and want her back, then he'd see that she was trying to help. That she wasn't merely a flake who took-took-took all the time. That she cared about him and would be there for him from now on.

Fifty-three – this was it. Charlotte walked up to the front door, her knees a little wobbly. Here we go. She'd checked that it was Kirsten's day off and with a bit of luck, the two women could sit down and talk, then Charlotte would be able to put forward Ben's case, reminding Kirsten about all the kindness, loyalty and decency that her brother possessed. Setting down the bag of goodies on the doorstep, she raised her hand, finger outstretched towards the bell – just as a noise reached her from above. A sort of gasping sound. Then a high-pitched moan. 'Oh God, yes,' cried a woman's voice. A woman that sounded very much like Kirsten.

Charlotte gazed upwards to see an open window on the first floor, through which floated a further groan of pleasure. Gosh, she thought, goggling in surprise. If she wasn't very much mistaken, it sounded as if Kirsten was in the throes of absolute ecstasy up there. Oh wow! So she and Ben were back together? They must be! In which case, this definitely wasn't the time to drop round with flowers and kindness. A passionate reunion between Kirsten and Ben was the last thing she wanted to interrupt.

It was the last thing she wanted to *hear* as well, come to that, and the thought of becoming familiar with her brother's sex noises was enough to get her snatching up the bag again, turning abruptly and heading back along the street towards where she'd parked, before her ears could be assaulted. Once at a safe distance, she set down her undelivered gifts on a convenient wall then whipped out her phone, unable to resist a cheeky side-swipe at him. This was good news! This was really, really good news. If Ben and Kirsten were already back together then he'd be so much happier, and Charlotte would no longer feel she had to try and broker a reconciliation, as planned. Oh, thank goodness for second chances! Thank goodness Kirsten had finally accepted Ben's apologies!

So happy for you guys!! she texted her brother. *Even if my ears are still practically bleeding from the sounds I just heard. Next time, do your neighbours a favour and shut the window!* She added a string of winky emojis to show that she was only kidding. *Glad things are back on – fab news*, she finished, before pressing 'Send' and carrying on along the road. Ooh, did this mean she got to keep the flowers? she thought, brightening at the idea. She had a vase that would be perfect for them – and besides, Kirsten might think it a bit over the top for Charlotte to appear with peonies, if she and Ben were already back together. Maybe she wouldn't need to hand over the wine and chocolates either – even better. The day was looking up by the minute, she thought, reaching the car and unlocking it with a cheerful flourish of her key.

Settling herself in the driver's seat, she placed the flowers carefully in the passenger footwell, and was about to start the car when her phone rang. It was Ben.

'I just got your text,' he began. 'What are you talking about?'

Charlotte frowned in confusion. 'Well – you and Kirsten,' she replied, taken aback. A numb horror arose in her in the next second. Wait – had she misunderstood? It had certainly sounded like Kirsten's voice up there. But surely she hadn't just—?

'What do you mean, me and Kirsten?'

Charlotte bit her lip, aghast. Oh no. Please let this not be happening. 'I ... I just went over to her flat,' she blurted out because she was too stunned to think up any kind of convincing lie. 'And I thought I heard you two there. Together.'

'Not me,' he said. 'I'm at the shop. I haven't seen her for days.' There was a horrible silence for a few agonising moments where Charlotte shut her eyes, cursing her own naïve stupidity. If it wasn't Ben up there with Kirsten, making her gasp and moan, who was it?

'So what exactly did you hear?' he went on, sounding suspicious.

'Um ...' Charlotte spun into an immediate panic. Think of a lie! Make up a story! she urged her brain. Quick! Anything! But her imagination refused to cooperate, her mind remained hopelessly empty and then, because he was waiting and she felt under enormous pressure to say something, anything, she found herself bleating, 'Sex noises,' in a small, unhappy voice.

'Oh,' he said with terrible quietness. 'I see.'

'Ben, I'm so sorry,' Charlotte wailed, cursing her decision to take matters into her own hands and visit Kirsten in the first place, as well as her foolish lack of thought in hurrying to text Ben. Now she'd made things worse than ever. A million times worse! She'd shattered his heart in one single misguided message. 'I'm so, so sorry! I thought that—'

'Don't worry about it,' he said with a curt finality and hung up.

Charlotte gave a howl of anguish, so loud it made a child on the opposite pavement spin round to stare at her with interest. In a fit of impotent rage, she threw her phone down at the bunch of peonies, where it bounced off the cellophane wrapping and vanished under the passenger seat. Then she put her head in her hands and leaned against the steering wheel, groaning despairingly under her breath. What had she done? What had she *done*?

Ben had always been an optimist, hopeful all along that he and Kirsten could overcome their temporary split, that their marriage was strong enough to survive such an earthquake, but after Charlotte's phone call, the last shred of hope he'd been nurturing promptly shrivelled and expired within him. His pleas and flowers, the map he'd made her, had all been for nothing because surely it was over now. Surely, if she'd moved on to another man, their marriage was dead in a ditch and he was the last idiot to notice. And Christ, how good did the sex have to be, that someone down in the street below could hear you? Had *he* ever whipped Kirsten up into such a noisy state himself? He feared that the answer was no. In which case, she'd probably never come back to him now.

A queasy few days passed where it was an effort to slog through each hour at work, each quiet evening at home, possessed as he was by images of his wife having wild passionate afternoon sex with someone else. Someone who was surely better and funnier and more handsome than Ben, with whom she was already madly in love. The thought made him insane with jealousy, enough that he found himself punching the sofa in an attempt to get out his frustration. Work didn't help, with orders coming in from couples who'd managed to conduct relationships in places as far-flung as Liverpool and Truro, Norwich and Inverness. It felt as if they were trolling him, adding to his own torment. How come other people managed to keep romance flowering at such distances, when he himself couldn't repair one within the same small city?

He forced himself to catch up with friends for a pint, get his hair cut, put his trainers on and go for a run – small things that helped him endure the days. But even then, the weight of loss and despair remained pressing down on him, so much so that he ended up having to stop halfway through his run and breathlessly hang over his legs, panting and wheezing because his heart was pounding so hard. A niggle appeared at the back of his mind – the memory of Eliza saying that heart disease was often inherited between generations – and he wondered, straightening up and setting off once more, if he would end up the same way as his dad. If, maybe, he should get himself checked out just in case.

But no, he was being negative and doom-mongering, he decided. He had enough stress in his life right now without having to worry about that on top of everything. Anyway, he was fine! His dad had been a smoker and drank heavily; he'd loved his saturated fats and hardly did any exercise. Ben was a paragon of virtue by comparison, end of story.

And then, thank goodness, it was the weekend at last and Eliza was coming to stay again, which was a double mood boost right there. After the wonderful Father's Day they'd enjoyed together, including a ceremonial presentation of the 'Great Dad' badge she'd designed and had made up via a local merchandising company (surely no dad had ever received such a heart-warming gift before?), he refused to allow the bombshell of Kirsten's love life to spoil anything between him and his daughter. Eliza had requested that the two of them do some tourist things together around Cambridge and he threw himself willingly into planning the perfect line-up of activities.

The moment he saw her at the train station, he felt instantly better. Here she was, pretty much his favourite person in the world, and as long as he had her, he could cope with anything else, he told himself.

'Check you out, and your new barnet,' she said, hands on her hips with a nod of approval. 'Looking sharp there, Father. I didn't like to say before, but it was getting a bit tufty, that do of yours.'

'Is that a compliment? Okay, good,' he said, smiling to himself as he stowed her overnight bag in the boot of his car. *Father,* he noted, as if she still couldn't quite go there with a proper, natural 'Dad', but it was a start, he supposed. Plus, it was just so lovely to see her again. His grandma had always called Ben and his sisters a 'tonic' and he'd never really understood her meaning until now, when he had Eliza, a tonic of his own. 'Right – so are you ready for our tourist day? First stop: a punting tour along the Cam.'

'Yay!' she cheered with endearing enthusiasm and slipped an arm through his. 'I'll totally give that a punt.' She laughed at her own witticism. 'Get it? I said—'

He laughed too, and tousled her hair. 'Hey, leave the dad jokes to the actual dad here, if you don't mind. Come on, you muppet. This way.'

'So,' said Eliza in a low voice as their tour guide, ponytailed Josh, pushed the laden punt away from the riverbank an hour or so later. It was a sunny day, the city full of day-trippers, and it turned out that a lot of them were keen to take the same watery tour as Eliza and Ben. At last, following a lengthy queue at the punting station, they were now seated in the flat wooden boat, along with a noisy family of six. 'I've been thinking.'

'Well done,' teased Ben, nudging her foot with his. 'That's a great achievement for a Saturday afternoon. I'm proud of you.'

'Ha ha,' she said, rolling her eyes, while secretly quite enjoying the teasing. She was glad to hear him joking around, she realised, as he'd seemed unusually quiet so far that day. As if something was on his mind. She hoped she wasn't about to make him even quieter by what she had to say. 'No – I've been thinking about New York,' she went on after a deep breath.

'Good! Me too!' He grinned at her and she felt warm inside; she loved it when his whole face lit up like this. 'Did you get that link I sent you to the hotel I found?' he went on. 'It sounds perfect, I thought – right in the middle of everything. And I asked a friend of mine who knows the city well what he thought and he said, yeah, it's a great spot.'

'Brilliant,' Eliza said, remembering the pictures of the cool, bohemian hotel that he'd suggested, how she'd pored over the website so thoroughly she already knew what she was going to order for breakfast on her first morning there. 'Yeah, it looks amazing. Um ...' She hesitated, trying to find the right words, only to be distracted by the two little boys at the far end of the punt chanting 'wee-wee' at each other and laughing uproariously, collapsing against one another as if they were puppies. Their mum, who had a small baby strapped to her in a sling, smiled at them affectionately, and then over at the dad, who had a flaxen-haired toddler on his knee. There, Eliza thought, feeling a rueful twang inside: one happy family. Just like Mum always wanted us to be. Siblings. Two parents. A cute rabbit in a hutch at home, no doubt. Barbecues in the garden all the time, with car-loads of friends and relatives round. A big tree with presents underneath at Christmas. But she could still try for her own version of that even now, she reminded herself. Wasn't it worth a go?

'The thing is,' she began again, just as the tour guide cleared his throat and started speaking.

'We're now approaching the Mathematical Bridge,' he informed them. 'A brilliant piece of engineering, the bridge consists entirely of straight timbers and was built by James Essex in 1749.'

'Built by wee-wee,' gurgled one of the little boys.

'*You're* built by wee-wee,' gasped his brother, the two of them helpless with hysterics all over again.

'That's enough,' said their mum with a warning eyebrow.

Eliza gave a dutiful glance at the wooden spokes and tangents of the bridge – admittedly quite impressive if you were into that sort of thing – then turned back to Ben. Spit it out, she told herself. 'As I was saying,' she started, taking a deep breath.

'Oh God, this isn't about the tattoo again, is it?' he put in, one eyebrow raised. 'Don't tell me – you want to sneakily get one in New York? Or a piercing, or some other bodily mutilation that your mum will flay me alive for?'

'No,' she said, 'although now you mention it ...' She was stalling again, she realised, and forced herself back on track before she lost her nerve. 'Um ... so: New York. The thing is, I kind of want to ask Mum along too. Would that be okay?'

There was a pause, broken only by the slow swish of water against the punt and the clicking of the dad's camera as he took photos of the mathematical bridge and his giggling, pink-faced sons. When she dared look at Ben, she saw a small frown corrugating his forehead as if he didn't know what to say. 'Oh,' he mumbled. Oh no, was that hurt in his voice? Had she pissed him off?

'I know it sounds weird,' she went on, grimacing. At the front of the boat, the boys had started wrestling and one of them gave a yell as he was shoved too hard and banged an elbow. 'But it might be nice for us to go together? As a sort of family trip?'

As if to undermine the idea that a family trip could ever be wholly 'nice', the boy with the banged elbow let out an indignant yell and punched his brother hard on the arm. Ben flinched and didn't reply immediately, and Eliza crossed her fingers down by her side. *Come on,* she urged silently. *Please say yes.* She reckoned she'd pretty much wheedled her mum into the idea by now, even though this had meant a slight stretching of the truth (okay, lying), but she needed to get Ben on board too. 'Imagine if they fall in love,' she, Bo and Saskia had sighed, when Eliza had outlined her plan to them. It could happen, right? They weren't *that* old that a reunion in New York couldn't weave its magic spell on them, surely?

'I'm not sure if I should say this but ... I think she really wants to get to know you again,' Eliza went on, rushing to fill the silence Ben had left. The fingers she was crossing had turned white and bloodless by now, so tight was her grip, but the lie was worth it for the greater good, she reassured herself. Lara never had to find out. 'And when I suggested that I ask you about her coming too, she was really excited. I mean – she'll pay for herself, obviously. I'm totally not asking *that.*'

'Right,' he replied uncertainly, before Josh took up his spiel once more. Damn it, maybe Eliza had picked the wrong place to broach this subject after all. She remembered, too late, how she'd come out of work the other evening, only to be accosted by a red-faced drunk man bawling at her that she'd ruined his life. It was Mr Partridge, the creepy man she'd babysat for once upon a time, before his wife chucked him out on his ear. 'Thanks to you interfering, I've lost *everything*,' he'd yelled, before her boss had come out of the shop and told him to get lost. Eliza had tried to shrug it off but all the same, prickles of guilt had lodged under her skin. It wasn't that she wanted to ruin people's lives, she told herself now, least of all her parents'. But there was no harm in nudging things along a bit to make them better, surely?

'We're now coming up to the famous King's College lawn,' Josh said, gesturing at the wide grassy expanse at the back of the magnificent building as he punted them forward with the pole.

Eliza risked another glance at Ben, who was staring down at the bottom of the punt, oblivious to Josh's recited list of all the prestigious people who had studied at King's. Had she asked too much? Pushed her luck? *You've got to make the most of this time, he's not going to refuse you anything right now*, Saskia had advised, with the wisdom of one who had divorced parents and now extra step-parents, whom she had already milked extensively and played off against one another like a total pro.

One last try, she thought. 'Please?' she begged. 'I know it was meant to be just us on the trip, which was really generous of you, and it's not that I'm not grateful at all, because I really, really am—'

'I know you are, don't worry,' he said, smiling.

'And Mum would feel a bit awkward about coming with us, but at the same time, I know she's had this massive guilt complex about not being able to give me a so-called proper family, so I think it would make her really happy. But if that's a problem for you, then we can go back to plan A, for sure.' Her face flooded with colour. 'It was just a thought,' she finished.

264

'Right. I see,' Ben said, and Eliza had to wedge both her hands between her knees to stop herself fidgeting. They were so well-suited, her parents, that was the thing – Mum was an Aries, like her, while Ben was a Sagittarius; two fire signs, so they'd be perfect together, given the chance. And yet they were both stubborn as well – so stubborn that it was apparently down to Eliza to force them together in this way.

After another long pause, Ben nodded. He didn't look entirely convinced – in fact, he looked pretty sad for a moment, defeated even, before seeming to rally himself. 'Well ... sure. Why not? Will she book her flight separately, do you think, or should I organise the whole thing?'

'I'll talk to her,' Eliza said immediately, hugging herself inside with glee. 'Thanks,' she added and leaned against him, feeling a rush of excitement that her plan had come together, as well as a flutter of apprehension about what might become of them. 'Thanks so much. We'll have the best time, I know it!'

Chapter Twenty-Four

Dear Lara,

Hope you've had a good weekend. Eliza's on the train now, due into Scarborough 18.51. She said she'd text you if there are any delays.

We talked about making the New York trip a family one – of course you are welcome to come too. I'll look into flights and get back to you.

Ben

Lara had to read the email through several times before the words finally sank in. So it was true, then. Since the unexpected conversation with Eliza about the three of them going to New York together, she'd started to wonder if her daughter had been exaggerating, but perhaps not, because here was Ben, inviting her along with them. Admittedly, sounding stilted and a bit formal, but that didn't change the facts. So what should she do? She imagined Heidi clapping her hands with hearts in her eyes – followed swiftly by her mum's reaction of head-shaking pessimism, and mutters of leopards never changing their spots. The two of them were like the devil and angel on her shoulders, she thought ruefully. But what did *she* want?

She opened a new tab on her browser and typed the words

New York into the search engine. Up came images of glittering skyscrapers, Central Park, the Statue of Liberty, Manhattan street maps. Her blood seemed to leap as her gaze lingered on each sight, her pulse quickening with a rush of excitement. Fuck it, she thought. She'd always wanted to go back there. And if he was offering, then why the hell not?

Dear Ben,

That's incredibly nice of you, thank you. Obviously I will pay for my share of everything. We could go halves on the whole trip if that's easier?

Lara

Dear Lara,

If it's all right with you, I'd like to treat Eliza. I have some catching up to do on that front!

B

'Suit yourself,' muttered Lara, reading the latest email. Then she read his words over again, this time without the paranoia. He's being kind, dingbat, she told herself firmly, stroking Bruce who'd leapt up on to the table for attention. Besides, this was good news, seeing as even paying for herself to go on the trip would be something of a financial stretch. *Thank you*, she typed, then hesitated, wondering how he was feeling about going back to New York, wondering if she dared ask. Nope. She didn't. She should probably quit now before they could start arguing again, in fact. *Best wishes, Lara*, she finished, then pressed 'Send'.

There. Polite, civil, appreciative, she thought, exhaling rather nervously. God, she really hoped this trip was going to be all right.

Kirsten lay back in bed, panting, and Neil collapsed beside her. His skin was damp from exertion, golden brown with a white line where his trousers started, and she imagined him topless in his garden with a pleasant sort of shudder. This was the third time he'd been round in ten days and she was smitten. Dazzled. Being with him was all about bodily pleasure, touch and sensation. It felt fantastic to get out of her brain and let her animal side take over for a change.

'Whew,' said Neil sleepily, draping an arm across her body. 'That was awesome. You're spectacular.'

Kirsten snuggled against him, smiling. Had anyone ever called her that before? *Spectacular*. She could get used to it. 'You too,' she said, feeling her heart slow from its frantic pace, the heat of her skin cooling as a breeze blew in from the open window. It was four in the afternoon and she had finished her shift an hour earlier, texted him to say that she was free, and he'd appeared at her door in twenty minutes flat. They were getting to know each other's bodies and she liked his very much: leaner and more muscular than Ben's. He was athletic and lithe, his chest hard, not an ounce of fat to spare.

Sex on a Monday afternoon, how hedonistic. It made her feel young and attractive again, decadent, as if she still had something to offer. Plus it reminded her that she was independent, had agency, wasn't stuck in a long-term marriage any more. Wasn't this exactly what she'd been craving – some excitement, some thrills?

Yes, she told herself firmly, remembering the years of quiet evenings with Ben at home in front of the TV, the two of them on the sofa feeling more passion about the Scandi thriller they'd been watching than each other. Being with Neil had reminded her how to live in the moment. How to live, full stop.

And why should she suffer any guilt? It wasn't as if Ben was hanging around, pining after her. She'd gone back to the house yesterday to pick up some post and various other bits and bobs, and while there, it felt as if the ground had shifted beneath her feet. It was Sunday evening and apparently Eliza had been to stay for the weekend – whatever, thought Kirsten, hardening herself as she always did when he mentioned his daughter. Ben was in the kitchen at the time, looking distracted as he stared at his laptop screen. Previously when they'd seen one another, he'd fallen over himself to be nice to her, to reassure her how much he loved her and wanted her back. But today he didn't so much as ask about her week, let alone say anything flattering or friendly. Was she imagining it, or was he not even really looking her in the eye this evening? That was odd. Unexpected.

'Won't be long,' she said, collecting her griddle pan from the cupboard so that she could cook Neil a steak one night next week maybe, vaguely wondering if Ben had the hump with her for something. Then, as she walked around behind him, she noticed that the laptop screen he was peering at showed an airline booking page. Aha! Intriguing. Was he trying to win her back with a romantic holiday? Was that why he was acting so secretively?

'Off somewhere nice?' she'd asked blandly, like a hairdresser making chit-chat; as if she'd never been married to him at all. Come to mention it, he'd had his hair cut, she noticed. And was that a new shirt he was wearing? It gave her a strange feeling to register these differences, to have him appear unfamiliar to her. Unfamiliar but good, she acknowledged. He'd gone for a shorter cut than usual and it suited him. Made him look boyish.

His shoulders appeared to tense at her question and it took him a moment to respond. 'Um ... New York,' he said, without turning round.

It felt as if the air had vanished from the room. 'Oh,' she said, her mouth dry, certain before she even had to ask that this would not be a trip intended for her after all. Her fingers trembled as she set the pan carefully into the cardboard box she'd brought along, her breath coming hard and fast. Then she sat at the table alongside him, needing to know what was going on. 'With ... with Eliza?'

'Um, yeah,' he said, then muttered something she didn't quite catch.

'What was that?' she asked, because for a ridiculous moment she thought he'd actually said the name of Eliza's mother.

'I said, Lara's going to come too,' he mumbled, staring fixedly at his laptop screen.

The walls seemed to close in around them; this kitchen where they'd cooked and eaten together for years and years suddenly a strange, alien space in which she no longer belonged. Lara was going too. Right. Like that, was it? Say no more.

A shocked sob rose in her throat and she forced it violently back down. 'Oh,' she said again, hands gripping one another in her lap. 'I see.'

'It's not like that,' he said, swinging round. 'It—'

She stood up because she couldn't bear to hear his excuses, whatever flimsy reasoning he was about to trot out; she didn't want to know another single detail because each one would be a tiny spear in her heart, it would all hurt too much. She felt her nostrils flare as she snatched up her box of possessions. *Get out, get out.* 'Do what you want, Ben,' she said tartly. 'It's no skin off my nose. I don't care who you go with.'

She did care, obviously. She cared so much, it was as if he'd punched her in the face. What an idiot she was to care though.

When he could go from begging her to come back to him one week, to booking a transatlantic jaunt with his ex and daughter the next. Unbelievable. What kind of bastard did that? Anger calcified inside her as she recalled the occasions she'd suggested the two of them travel more adventurously, only to have him put her off each time. Yet apparently this girl only had to snap her fingers for him to sort out a lavish trip away. How was that fair?

'But I thought you weren't that bothered about him,' Vick pointed out when Kirsten rang to bitch about Ben's treachery. 'I thought you were enjoying your fling?'

'I am, I'm loving it, but—' She'd run out of words, unsure how to articulate the confused overlap of feelings inside her. It wasn't simply the case that she wasn't *bothered* about Ben, she reasoned. During their separation she'd missed him frequently – so much so that a couple of times, she'd almost packed her bags and slunk back home, unable to bear the solitude any more. But pride had always stopped her. That, plus the sense that returning might actually be a backward step rather than one taken for positive reasons. She'd felt more at home staying with her parents than she'd felt walking into the Cambridge house. And maybe now she'd left it too late anyway, if he was jetting off with this Lara woman and their kid.

She shut her eyes now, trying to stop thinking about the image of Ben's face, lit by the laptop screen, how his haircut really did flatter his features. Instead she leaned against Neil for comfort. Live in the moment, she reminded herself. Savour the here and now. 'Are you hungry? I could cook us something,' she murmured, running a finger down his bronzed chest. On her way home, she'd bought bacon, eggs, a crusty loaf of bread, a couple of steaks; anything to tempt him into staying with her a while longer, she'd thought.

But her words seemed to break the spell because in the next second, he had extricated himself from underneath her arm and sat up, scratching his head then pulling on the T-shirt he'd earlier thrown to the floor. 'I'd better head off,' he said, hauling up his boxers and jeans. 'My van's on double yellows out there.'

The bed felt empty without him, the warmth of his body noticeably absent. 'Fine,' she said, trying to sound as if it really was fine. Because that was the deal with a fling, wasn't it, that you weren't supposed to be needy or put demands on one another. You enjoyed it for what it was, then afterwards you carried on with real life again. She was cool with that. Completely cool.

'Cheers, darling,' he said, then came over, gently brushed her hair off her face and gave her a lingering kiss. 'I'm enjoying this. I'm really glad you called me.'

'Me too,' she said. 'See you soon.'

She heard the door of the flat close and sat up in bed, already mentally reframing the event from a more favourable angle, ready to relay to Vick. *He was barely through the front door before we were ripping each other's clothes off*, she would say. *I've never had sex like it. I feel so alive!*

Let Ben go to New York with that woman and their daughter, Kirsten didn't care. She would be far too busy having her own fun to even notice he'd gone.

Chapter Twenty-Five

'In front of you, you can now see the Empire State Building,' the tour guide said as the bus rumbled along Fifth Avenue. 'At 102 storeys high, with its iconic Art Deco design, this skyscraper was built between 1930 and 1931, and stands a mighty 1,454 feet tall. That's if you include the antenna, which I most certainly do.'

A few weeks had passed. It was August and Lara, Eliza and Ben were sitting on the top deck of a hop-on, hop-off double-decker bus as it toured around downtown Manhattan, with Lara experiencing what felt very much like a head rush of exhilaration. Sure, she and Eliza had taken holidays before – to Mallorca and Mykonos, as well as weeks in the Lake District and the Scottish islands – but it was a long time since she could remember feeling such a visceral thrill at being so far from home. Here she was, right now, in this busy, noisy, beautiful, exciting city and she felt simultaneously overwhelmed with sensory overload and wide-eyed for yet more. She could hardly believe she was here at all. Whoever could have predicted that Ben would turn out to be so generous-spirited as to invite her along?

In the seat behind her, her travel companions seemed to have fallen under a similar spell – their faces alight with wonder as they eagerly photographed and filmed their surroundings, pointing out classic New York sights and oddities to one another with barely suppressed enthusiasm. After the strained politeness of their transatlantic flight together, Manhattan had shaken up their little trio, wowing them with its glorious jumble of old and new, its vibrancy and hustle. It had proved impossible to be shy or awkward when you found yourself in this enthralling new world.

She hadn't expected to feel quite such joy herself at being back here, to have her synapses flicker and rattle with electric bursts of long-buried memories. It was astonishing that you could be away from a place for almost twenty years and still have vivid associations with a street corner deli, a subway sign, the shape of a skyline. A lump formed in her throat as they passed leafy Madison Square Park and she had a flash of memory, of eating her first ever pastrami sandwich there beneath the trees during a lunch break, her bare legs warm in the sunshine. Hey there, young, idealistic Lara, open to everything, giving life and all its opportunities a go whenever possible – meet your grown-up, cynical self who knows better, she thought with a rueful smile.

But in the next moment, she corrected herself, because she *hadn't* fully given up on life's opportunities, had she? Not quite. Maybe for a time she'd become bogged down in her own routine, seeking safety in the familiar, but in the last few weeks it had seemed as if she was unfurling again, like a plant tentatively putting out new shoots and tendrils, seeking the light. She and Heidi were still joining the sea swimmers for weekly plunges in the bracing North Sea and not only was her fitness improving with surprising rapidity, but she was enjoying the social side of the evenings too. She'd been invited to one woman, Cath's, forthcoming fiftieth birthday do, as well as bonding with another woman, Shona, when she'd admired her gorgeous linen culottes. Shona had promptly invited her to a clothes-swap evening she'd organised, with the result being that Lara had picked up a bagful of gorgeous pieces in exchange for some of her plain old cast-offs. In fact, the outfit she was wearing today – a dusty-pink crop-legged jumpsuit (yes!) with a belt around the middle – had come from that evening. Shona had also tipped her off about some amazing vintage stores in Greenpoint, Brooklyn, that Lara was definitely going to rummage through, if she had any free time here.

As well as meeting these great new women, Lara had enjoyed a few more conversations with Ollie the furniture-maker. He was really nice – friendly and interesting and easy to talk to. 'He's very handsome, isn't he?' sharp-eyed Heidi commented, noticing that the two of them had struck up a friendship. 'And single too, by the way. If that's of any interest to you.'

'But I thought Rachel—'

'She's his landlady. He rents a flat from her. Didn't I say? She's married to a lovely woman, Isla, who works at the theatre. Yeah, I did the photos for their wedding a few years ago; they're such a nice couple. Why have you turned red, Lara? Is there something you're not telling me?'

Lara had batted away the nosy questioning but all the same, the news about Ollie being single sent her into a quandary. She liked him and thought he was attractive, but did she dare take a leap and allow herself to imagine anything else happening?

As well as the swimming, she had taken another step in reviving her journalistic career. The day before they'd flown out here, she'd sat at her laptop, read through her proposal for a family advice column one last time, then attached it in a pitch email and sent it to the features editors who'd given her positive responses before. Yes, her finger had trembled a little as she clicked 'Send' each time. And no, she still hadn't told anybody that she was putting herself out there like this, not Heidi, not even Eliza, when it might come to nothing. But she'd enjoyed writing the pitch and the sample column, honing and polishing each line until it was as good as she could make it. Whatever the outcome – and she knew it was a long shot – she felt proud of what she'd achieved. Furthermore, sending the emails felt like taking a step back towards her old self, the Lara who dreamed big and had a go. The Lara who said, *Sure, why not?*

'Coming up is our next stop, near Washington Square Park, which has its famous marble arch, designed by Stanford White in the late nineteenth century,' the tour guide informed them at that point, and Lara felt her heart clench in recognition, just as Ben leaned forward with a quizzical expression.

'I think this is the nearest stop to ...' he began, then broke off, as if uncertain how to finish the sentence.

'To where we ended up that night,' Lara said for him. 'Yes. I was thinking the same.' *Sure, why not?* that voice said in her head again.

Eliza stood up as the bus pulled in to the side of the road. 'Come on, then,' she said. 'Let's have the personal tour. Show me where you two reprobates spent your final hours of freedom before my joyful conception.'

Ben was still eyeing Lara with that faint air of doubt but she nodded at him. Yes, she thought. They could do this for Eliza. Wasn't that really what the whole trip was about? 'Come on,' she said. 'I'm game if you are. In fact, I think I still owe you a beer from nineteen years ago.'

He smiled back at her, his eyes crinkling at the edges, and she realised with a little shock that when she looked into his eyes like that, she could still glimpse him there, the younger man she'd fallen for on these very streets. The man who'd laughed and held her hand, the two of them light-headed with youthful hope and attraction; the city theirs for one single night. 'I'm game,' he replied. 'I'm looking forward to seeing that tree anyway, nineteen years on.'

'The *tree*?' Lara wondered if she had misheard. She had plenty of recollections of that night but none involving a tree.

'The one you planted? From the apple pip? I'm very much hoping we'll be able to pick the fruit of your labours,' he said, straight-faced.

She laughed, delight mingling with surprise as his words registered. The apple pip! She couldn't believe he'd remembered that. 'Well, it'll be a crushing blow if we can't.'

'I'll certainly be putting in a complaint to the local authorities if it's not there,' he agreed, just as Eliza called to them, from where she was halfway down the stairs to the lower deck.

'Hurry up, then, you two!'

'That's told us,' Lara said, pulling a funny face as they followed her.

'Do you think it's you or me she gets her impatience from?' Ben asked in a low voice.

Lara spluttered. 'Oh, I couldn't possibly comment,' she replied.

Eliza eyed them questioningly as they stepped off the bus, both smiling. 'What are you two up to? Whispering behind my back, eh?' Then, before either of them could reply – perhaps she'd already decided she didn't want to know the answer – she grabbed one of Ben's hands and one of Lara's. 'Right, then, Mum and – brace yourself, I'm gonna say it – *Dad*,' she commanded, blushing furiously as Ben's face lit up in a delighted smile and he goofily punched the air. (It was actually quite sweet, Lara thought, but didn't dare comment, not least because Eliza was stumbling over her words in her attempt to get past her own self-consciousness.) 'Take me back down Memory Lane to where it all – and I'm including myself in that – began.'

Eliza was having a great trip. Even the potentially shattering prospect of finding out her A-level results in a week's time couldn't dampen her joyful mood as she and her parents (her *parents*! *Together*!) threw themselves into carrying out Ben's meticulously planned agenda. Yesterday, following the bus tour, they had explored the streets taken by Lara and Ben on their one and only date, which, bizarrely, had involved searching for a non-existent apple tree that her mum had supposedly planted all those years before. Surprise, surprise, it wasn't there (had they seriously thought otherwise?) although Lara kept saying with the air of a mystic that she liked to think someone had dug it up and taken it home to their own garden. 'I'm sure there's a tree from that pip *somewhere*.' Whatever, thought Eliza, who didn't get why the two of them were making such a big deal about the whole thing – nor why they then insisted on buying a bag of apples from a nearby deli in order to scatter further pips wherever they came across suitable planting places. 'This is our orchard legacy,' Ben said, when Eliza refused to join in.

'Mmm, yeah, sure,' she replied. 'But can you please stop being weird now before I have to disown you both?'

Afterwards, they'd taken a Circle Line cruise around Manhattan, seeing the Statue of Liberty, Brooklyn Bridge and Ellis Island. So far today, they'd walked the High Line and had lunch in Chelsea Market, and now they were at the Top of the Rock observatory, breathlessly peering down at the city below, skyscrapers glinting, the river a wide blue ribbon as it wound through the skyline. *I love it here*, Eliza kept thinking as she turned from one panorama to the next. New York had opened her eyes to a different kind of living, vitalising her with its pace and dynamism – exactly as her horoscope app had predicted that morning, in fact. *A seismic awakening takes place today*, the entry for Aries had read. *Life begins anew!*

It certainly felt that way. It felt as if life had expanded around her in every direction, her horizons infinitely broadening, as if she had been awarded glimpses into thousands of different worlds from within a tight grid of streets. All those lit windows in apartment blocks, the bars full of beautiful people, the city slickers, the panhandlers, the babel of foreign languages everywhere you went . . . so many lives, so many opportunities, so many narratives, she thought, unable to quite take in the magnitude. This was definitely life with a bright new filter; a million miles from the muted tones of her quietly elegant seaside home town. She had often felt an oddity in Scarborough, worrying that others might find her weird, not fitting in. But in a city like this, there was space for every kind of person. Quirks were definitely acceptable, differences celebrated. It was liberating!

Added to which, both Lara and Ben seemed to be having a great time as well, happy to be sharing the experience with her – and, after a slightly stilted start, with each other too. Eliza had taken to teasing her mum whenever a cyclist whizzed by – 'Careful, Mum, there's a bike in the vicinity, don't go falling over and banging your head again' – and it didn't take long for Ben to join in, the two of them amusing themselves no end by ganging up on her mercilessly. 'I didn't *fall*! I was knocked *over*! Trying to help *you*, you ungrateful baggage!' Lara protested to no avail. 'Oh, shut up,' she growled in the end, laughing along with the joke.

Eliza was trying to be discreet and allow the two of them some space in order to reconnect, but even from a distance, she could tell that they were starting to warm up to one another, with some easy-going joking and piss-taking. Could it mean ...? she wondered, hardly daring to finish her own question. Was there a chance that ...?

She mustn't get her hopes up, she reminded herself. She needed to let her parents come to the conclusion themselves that they were destined for each other. That life (and death, and missed phone calls) might have kept them apart for almost twenty years, but that it was never too late to coax smouldering embers back into a burning flame. Christ, she thought, wrinkling her nose at the poetic dalliance her thoughts had taken. She was starting to sound like lyrics from a cheesy ballad. That was quite enough of *that*.

Returning to the view before her, she lined up her phone so that she could better identify the buildings below on her map app. Ah – so that skyscraper with the cool scalloped peak was the Chrysler Building, she worked out. And beyond it was the UN headquarters, wow. And somewhere in the foreground was apparently Grand Central Station. *Wait*, she thought, narrowing her eyes. Wasn't that where her mum and dad were supposed to have met for their second date, first time around? The fateful second date of heartbreak that never actually happened?

'It's breathtaking, isn't it?' Lara said just then, coming to put an arm around her. 'The sort of view you could never get tired of. Amazing.'

280

'I know,' Eliza agreed, leaning against her as they stood there together. Being here was definitely giving her a new respect for her mum, she acknowledged. The fact that Lara had jetted across the Atlantic alone, to live in New York for four months, showed that she must have had a drive and courage Eliza could never have previously guessed at. It must have taken proper balls. Before, Lara had been merely Mum: kind, tired, practical, nagging Mum, but now that Eliza had peeked into her hinterland, she saw her from a whole other perspective.

Her eye fell back down upon the busy city streets, and a thought occurred to her in the next moment, a lightbulb flicking on in her mind. There she'd been, reading her horoscope for herself, but the same prediction applied to Lara, a fellow Aries, she realised. The seismic awakening, life beginning anew ... did that mean what Eliza hoped it meant? As her mum wandered away, she typed quickly into the search bar of her phone, her thoughts rushing excitedly. Sometimes you had to give other people a helping hand, didn't you? she told herself, fingers flying in her eagerness to organise a plan. Because if her parents were too shy to make a first move, then she certainly wasn't.

It wasn't until the elevator had taken them all the way back down to the ground – something of a relief for Lara, who'd never been brilliant with heights – that she noticed a couple of texts had come in on her phone, both from her mother.

In hospital. But don't make a fuss, read the first one. 'Oh my God,' she said, with a gulp of alarm. What on earth ... ?

Back home. Not dead. How much is it costing me to send these messages by the way? read the second, which had been sent an hour later.

'Everything all right?' asked Ben, seeing Lara standing motion-less. They were in Rockefeller Plaza where a farmer's market was in full swing, and he gently took Lara's arm and towed her to the side, so as to avoid being trampled on by a large group of tourists.

'It's my mum,' she said, speed-dialling Frances's number in the next moment. 'Mum? Are you okay?' she asked, as soon as the call was picked up.

She heard the clearing of a throat. 'Er . . . this is Harry Granger. I'm Frances's neighbour. Is that Lara?'

'Yes,' she said, startled. Hold on – Mum's *neighbour*? He of the hedge and barbecue vendetta? 'Is she okay?' she asked in the next breath.

'She's fine,' he replied. He had a lovely voice, she noticed distractedly – deep and mellow. Mind you, he'd need to be mellow living next door to Frances Spencer. 'She took a bit of a tumble – luckily I was passing so I could take her to A&E. But no damage done. Here, I'll get her for you, she's making me a coffee, apparently. Aren't I the lucky one?' He chuckled and Lara smiled, her dread ebbing away. 'Frances! Are you there?' she heard.

'I did *say* not to fuss,' her mum's first words were when she came on the line.

'Yes,' said Lara drily, 'that "I'm not dead" comment was immensely reassuring. Are you sure you're okay? What happened?' She put her thumb up to Eliza who was gazing on in concern and the three of them began drifting around the market stalls, breathing in the smells of cheese, rustic sourdough loaves and fresh fruit, Lara listening all the while to Frances's narrative. Apparently she'd tripped on a loose bit of paving on her driveway, just as her neighbour was leaving his house.

'I did *tell* Harry I was perfectly all right—' Harry, now, was it? Lara thought in amusement, 'several times over, in fact, but would he listen? Of course not. He's the most stubborn man I ever met, insisted we went to hospital. What a palaver, honestly. And I'm completely fine. Strong as an ox, you know me.'

'Nice of him, though, wasn't it?' Lara couldn't resist pressing her. 'Very neighbourly. Sounds like he really went out of his way for you.'

'Well,' Frances spluttered, 'yes, I suppose so. Anyway, what are you doing, calling me from America? This must be costing you a fortune! Go! Stop talking! Don't waste your money on me!'

'I'm not wasting my—'

'Oh – but are you having a nice time?' Frances interrupted. 'Quickly, before you go – are you okay? Eliza enjoying herself? I take it my postcard's already on its way?'

'We're having a lovely time,' Lara assured her mother. 'And I'll come round and see you when I get back. Maybe even with a present if you're good. Be nice to Harry in the meantime, won't you?'

She hung up and rolled her eyes. 'Only my mother could send a text saying "not dead" and think that was okay,' she commented to the others. 'I just hope for the sake of this poor Harry bloke that he's got the stamina to deal with her.'

Chapter Twenty-Six

Ben should have known better. Ever since he had blurted out the offer of the New York trip earlier in the summer, he had wondered if he was doing the right thing. And then, when Eliza had haltingly asked if her mum could join them, he'd felt another prickle of doubt that, whatever dad tokens he might have earned so far, he was still hopelessly out of his depth when it came to parenting a teenager. 'Every time I start to feel like I know what I'm doing, there's another curveball that takes me by surprise,' he'd sighed to Charlotte after Sunday dinner at her place the week before. She had taken to inviting him round for meals, perhaps out of guilt for the Kirsten-having-sex phone call, but maybe also because the first time he'd been there, Ben had been so patently grateful for a good meal, cooked by someone else, and an actual dinner-time conversation, she clearly considered him undernourished in more ways than one.

She'd made an amused-sounding noise. 'You don't say. Person struggles with own child on more than one occasion – shock!' He'd been washing up at the time, while she dried, and she'd elbowed him gently. 'It *is* hard, fact. But that just means you're starting to get to grips with who each of you are, if that makes sense. It was always going to be more complex than you thought, I'm afraid. Nobody teaches you this stuff; you have to keep on learning it, over and over again.'

So he was discovering. He and Eliza had been blank pages to one another initially, gradually filling with outlines and colour and descriptive words. Perhaps he'd been naïve in thinking that, having missed out on all the early years, he might be in for a comparatively easy ride. Perhaps too, he'd been blindsided by her calling him 'Dad' for the first time on their first afternoon here; as if that was some kind of enchantment that meant everything would be easier from now on. But a mere two days later, he'd come up short again on realising that not every aspect of the relationship would run as smoothly as he'd hoped. Nor was his daughter entirely blameless for this.

Despite Lara's self-professed aversion to cyclists, he and Eliza had convinced her to rent bikes together in Central Park on this particular afternoon. 'Try not to put anyone in hospital, Mum,' Eliza had advised sarcastically.

'Nor yourself,' Ben added as she stuck her tongue out.

The weather was warm and ripe but with enough of a breeze to rustle through the trees. Ben had been keen to follow the printed trail on the map he'd bought, until Eliza scoffed at his rule-keeping and said she would rather be spontaneous and discover the place for themselves. Taken aback by this small show of mutiny – had he been too rigid with his agenda thus far? – he acquiesced after the slightest of hesitations. Even though the suggested trail on the map *did* look excellent and would have taken them on an efficient, time-saving route around the park, passing all the sights worth seeing on the way.

285

Ah well. It was her trip too. And so far Ben was rather enjoying the magical mystery tour they were now taking, led by Eliza's curiosity. He wouldn't mention the fact that, according to his own surreptitious glances now and then at the map, they were pretty much following the trail anyway. He would try to relax and savour the experience rather than attempting to organise it; a habit for which Kirsten had often scolded him in the past. His shoulders sank a little as her face drifted into his head now, and he felt a wrench as he thought how much she would have loved to explore Central Park with him, under different circumstances. Had he been too rigid for *her?* Could he have tried harder to please her in their marriage, make things up to her? All those times she'd encouraged him to let go of the past and move on, and he hadn't allowed himself to be persuaded that she might have a point.

But anyway. That was then. Kirsten had moved on to this new bloke now and was almost certainly not dwelling on Ben and their relationship any more. He should try and do the same, he reminded himself. He was here, wasn't he? That was a good start. He'd finally returned to New York, and even though he'd felt the occasional twinge of anxiety at being so far from home after what had happened the last time, as far as he was aware, no family members had died in his absence. Maybe he'd defeated a curse at last.

With Eliza speeding ahead as navigator-in-chief, Ben kept to a more sedate pace alongside Lara, who apparently hadn't been on a bike for years, but was gamely giving it her best shot. After a few nervous wobbles and some steering issues, she was sitting more comfortably in the saddle now, queen-like even, and it amused him to see her confidence blossoming.

286

'Look at you, pretending you couldn't remember how to ride a bike and then cycling like an absolute pro,' he teased her. 'If I didn't know better, I might have thought you were making it all up for attention.'

She spluttered with laughter, a little breathless and pink in the cheeks. She looked young again, he realised: carefree with her hair blowing back like that, the tension gone from her face. In fact, was that a new fringe she'd had cut in? he wondered somewhat belatedly, trying not to stare. It suited her, not least because now, for the first time, he was able to see the twenty-something Lara he'd originally met animating her features. 'Okay, I admit it, I'm a former Olympic champion,' she replied. 'Just faked being rubbish for a while and slagged off amateurs so that you didn't feel intimidated by my skills.'

'As I suspected,' he said. 'Well, I appreciate your consideration. Very kind.'

They were cycling near the reservoir now and he had to keep pinching himself that they were actually there, in the place he'd seen so many times in TV shows and films, the sun sparkling off the water, a haze of summer heat fogging the buildings beyond. Ever since he'd had that first niggling worry about his heart, he'd been making an effort to pay more attention to how his body was feeling, privately checking in on himself. There had been a couple of palpitations, the occasional spot of breathlessness, but that could happen to anyone, right? And today he felt fine. More than that, actually – he felt on top of the world. 'This is great, isn't it?' he blurted out, as they skimmed past a couple taking a selfie in front of the view. 'Being here, I mean. Doing this. It's brilliant.'

Lara wobbled a little as she turned her head to smile at him. 'It's amazing,' she agreed, in that lovely, open way he'd remembered about her from their first time in the city. Guileless, she had seemed to him. Someone who wore their heart on their sleeve. He had been that way too, he thought, until real life hardened him up, dropped in a suspicious filter, turned him into a cynic. But this trip seemed to have stripped back their protective armour, along with the years. 'It was so lovely of you to invite me along,' she went on with another quick sideways glance. 'I couldn't believe you were being so generous, when Eliza told me.'

It took him a second to register exactly what she'd said. He'd invited her along? That wasn't exactly how he would have described it. 'I—' he began, his hands suddenly sweaty on the handlebars. He frowned as he tried to unpick the misunderstanding; returning to the punt on the Cam, where Eliza had asked him outright if Lara could come too. Perhaps selfishly, his instinct had been to preserve the trip for just the two of them rather than complicate matters with Lara's presence – they barely knew each other, for one thing, and the idea made him feel disloyal to Kirsten. But the point was, he hadn't invited Lara. If anything, she'd invited herself.

'What is it?' Lara asked, eyeing him uncertainly when he failed to finish his sentence. 'You've gone all stressed-looking. Is something wrong?'

'Stop a minute,' he said, because it was impossible to simultaneously pedal and think and find the right thing to say all of a sudden. They braked to a stop near a bench, his heart thumping. Had Eliza set them up deliberately? 'You said just then that I'd been generous in inviting you along,' he began, 'but Eliza straight-out asked me if *you* could come with *us*, for it to be a family trip. Something about how you'd always wanted to have a "proper family"? It wasn't my idea, I'm afraid.'

288

'What? You're kidding me.' Lara's jaw dropped. 'Seriously?'

They looked at one another for a long moment, both trying to make sense of the situation. 'She told me she felt a bit ... anxious about the trip,' Lara went on slowly. 'Apprehensive. With the best will in the world, I think she found it ... a bit much. Sorry. But ...'

'Right.' He sighed. Now he felt bad. Worse than that – clueless; the novice dad still stuck on the nursery slopes of parenting. 'I didn't realise,' he replied, with a pang for his own naïvety. 'And *I'm* sorry. I'm still learning how to do this. Clearly getting stuff wrong, too.'

She shook her head. 'Hey, don't give yourself a hard time. I'm still learning too. Every parent is. It never stops, unfortunately. And anyway,' she went on, face becoming scarlet, 'I'm the one who should be apologising – not to mention feeling hideously embarrassed too, because Eliza gave me the impression that me tagging along was all *your* idea. I wouldn't have *dreamed* of inviting myself on your trip. Absolutely not. I made that very clear to her. I said I didn't want to intrude, that this was something for the two of you.' She clapped her hands to her hot cheeks, seeming shocked that Eliza could have pulled her strings with such ease. 'She specifically said to me that you *wanted* me to come! Oh gosh, I'm so mortified. I shouldn't be here at all. I feel terrible!'

'Please don't,' he said quickly, seeing her becoming flustered. But at the same time, he felt a twist of dismay and even the faint stirrings of anger, remembering how upset Kirsten had appeared when he'd said that he was going away with Lara and Eliza; how silent she had been ever since. No more popping round picking things up. No more texts about splitting bills or other financial issues. And for it to turn out that this so-called family trip was actually founded on a misunderstanding – or worse, deceit ...

Unwittingly or not, Eliza might have permanently ruptured his marriage. He forced himself to breathe steadily. 'Don't worry. It's good that you're here. I'm—'

'Everything all right? Don't tell me you've got a stitch already, Mum?' They were interrupted by Eliza, who'd doubled back to find out why they'd come to a halt.

Ben and Lara exchanged a hurried glance that said *later*. What was done was done, after all, he thought; there was no point publicly thrashing out the situation any further, or accusing Eliza of stirring things up. All the same, he didn't like feeling as if he'd been played. He had taken everything his daughter had said to him on face value because he wanted to believe her, he wanted to think the best of her. Now he felt as if he no longer knew her as well as he'd thought.

'We're fine,' he said, noticing a nearby drinks stand. 'Just wondered if anyone else was thirsty. I'm parched. Shall we get a cold drink?'

Lara shot him a grateful look for this plausible-sounding excuse, and Eliza seemed to buy it too because she willingly wheeled her bike over with them. 'By the way,' she said, winding her long hair up in a scrunchie on her head. 'I'm having the best time ever, you guys. Genuinely – *ever*, in my whole entire life.' Her eyes glistened with emotion, her chin even wobbled a little. If Ben had had reason to question her sincerity earlier, there was no doubting it now, he thought. 'I feel so utterly happy to be here in Central actual Park, in New York actual City with you two,' she went on. 'Thank you both so, so much for everything. If we weren't all holding these bikes, I would totally be insisting on a group hug right now. And you know how I despise people who hug in public.'

Despite himself, Ben laughed at this. Whatever was going through the girl's head and however much he might suspect her tactics, he had to admit that he was glad they were all here too. It was as if events from the past had been reset, as if the three of them could begin again from this point on. 'People who hug in public are the absolute worst,' he replied deadpan, then reached over to squeeze her shoulder. 'But I'm having a great time too.'

'And me,' said Lara, bringing up the rear.

'In fact,' Eliza went on, as they reached the drinks stand, 'dinner tonight is on me, to say thank you. Yes, it is! I insist! I've got my savings from the shop, I can afford it,' she said, holding up a hand as Lara began to protest. 'Anyway, I've already arranged everything, so you can't argue. Our table is booked for eight o'clock tonight. Dress code: fancy.'

Lara put a hand to her heart. 'That's so lovely of you!' she cried. 'Are you sure? I'd have been happy with you standing us an ice cream, but ...'

'I'm sure,' Eliza said, looking pleased with herself. 'My treat.'

'Thanks, love,' Ben said, touched by the gesture. How was it that his feelings for her could swing from displeasure to huge affection in the space of a twenty-metre walk? Sometimes fatherhood was baffling. 'That sounds brilliant. Dress code fancy, eh? Thank goodness I packed my emergency crushed-velvet suit.'

The mood had changed, and Eliza and Lara now appeared to be holding back smirks as they eyed one another in response. 'I *think* he's joking,' Lara ventured.

'As long as it's not his khaki jacket and a cartoon tie, I can live with it,' Eliza said, pressing her lips together.

'Hey! Don't knock the khaki jacket,' Ben retorted. 'I'm very fond of it.'

'I noticed,' Eliza teased. 'I was starting to think it was surgically attached to you, Dad.'

'Oh, I see,' Ben said, pretending to take offence. 'It's pick-on-Ben time now, is it? Mocking a man's fashion choices . . . well, that's charming. Do I *look* like the kind of person who would wear a cartoon tie?'

'Yep,' said Eliza, giggling again. 'Got it in one.'

'Now that you mention it . . .' Lara put in.

'Do you people *want* anything from my drinks stand,' came a booming voice at that moment, 'or are you planning to just hang around catching flies and blocking me from my paying customers all day, hmm?' The three of them turned guiltily to see the aproned woman from behind the counter fold her meaty arms across her chest while maintaining a gimlet stare. Then her eyes swivelled to Ben, and she softened, batting her long fake eyelashes at him. 'By the way, honey, you look just fine to me. You ladies quit giving this poor man a hard time, do you hear me?'

Ben wasn't generally given to sentimentality or over-romanticising a situation but as he, Lara and Eliza burst out laughing then set about obediently ordering drinks and ice creams, he felt a shot of pure joy, as potent as a strong espresso, as if they were all sharing something special together. If he'd tried to put into words what had happened, he wouldn't have been able to do the moment justice, but he knew they'd felt it too: something real and golden and warm. I'm happy, he thought, as they thanked the woman and wheeled their bikes away. And whatever happens after this, we were all happy together, today. That in itself felt like a triumph.

Chapter Twenty-Seven

It wasn't until they were back at the hotel that Lara felt able to catch her breath. She was having such a lovely day! Another whirl of sightseeing and activities and moments she knew she'd remember for ever – plus the feeling that the three of them had really bonded as a unit here; that they'd shared jokes and experiences together that felt very precious. She'd been dubious about bike riding initially but it had felt surprisingly great to stretch some unused muscles, with the breeze tousling her hair, and once she'd remembered how to actually cycle (apparently you *could* forget how to ride a bike), she loved it.

Afterwards, winding their way back to the hotel, they'd witnessed a stand-up row across the street between a restaurant doorman and a very drunk businessman, largely consisting of a stream of insults, followed by a yelled warning from the exasperated doorman. 'Don't make me call security on your ass,' he'd threatened. 'Oh yeah? Well, don't make *me* call security on *your* ass!' the businessman had shouted back before toppling against a bin and falling over. Eliza had gleefully adopted this as a new catchphrase and by the time they were walking up the steps of their hotel, they were unanimously weak with giggles from its repeated use.

And yet. Try as Lara might, it was impossible to completely gloss over those awkward few minutes in Central Park where she and Ben had worked out that they must have been set up by Eliza; that Lara hadn't been invited to come along with them at all. It troubled her to realise how easily she'd fallen for the deceit; how quick she'd been to believe what her daughter said. And what must Ben have thought of her, muscling in on their trip uninvited, like some kind of grim chaperone? Had he resented her for interfering? He must have been taken aback at her cheek, at the very least, she imagined. Nevertheless, here she was in Manhattan, so either Ben had been astonishingly selfless in saying yes to Eliza when that hadn't been part of his original plan, or he'd been too intimidated by his feisty daughter to say no. (This was entirely possible. Eliza could be pretty scary sometimes when she really put her mind to it.)

Or, Heidi had chipped in, when Lara messaged to update her on the saga, *he secretly wanted you to come with them all along?! It's not like you're in Bridlington for the weekend. You're in NYC! Like he would have agreed to you being there if he hated the idea???*

Lara sighed, and poured herself another cup of tea. (Yes, naturally she'd brought a stash of Yorkshire Tea teabags with her. It had been practically the first thing in the suitcase.) She was sitting on the bed, aching feet stretched out ahead of her while Eliza showered, and her head was reeling. It was the first time all day she'd been alone, she realised, trying to unscramble her thoughts as another message from Heidi pinged in.

Does it matter, anyway? You're having a good time, right? Getting on well, just like Eliza hoped? Sounds great. By the way, we missed you at the beach last night. LOADS of people asked after you – including Ollie. Love triangle, anyone???

She'd sent a photo of a group of them waving into the camera and Lara's heart warmed as she looked from face to face. Cathy, Shona, Heidi. Ollie. Rachel. That nice guy Edward, who'd been in touch about booking driving lessons for his daughter. Peter, who volunteered for the lifeboat service, and Jane, his wife, who baked the fudgiest brownies ever. They'd all welcomed her in, made her feel such a part of something. Her eye lingered on Ollie's smile, remembering what he'd told her about his ex-wife Chrissie who must have endured a really difficult time with her phobia – and wondering how that in turn had affected Ollie and Jake. She remembered too how she'd envied Chrissie before then, imagining her to be this paragon of motherhood and berating herself that she, in comparison, had failed Eliza in so many ways. But did anyone really have the perfect family life? Even Heidi and her husband Jim went through their ups and downs. Maybe Lara had been wishing for the impossible all along. Maybe, just maybe, their own small family set-up had been good enough this whole time.

How are you? Still 'not dead'?! Hope you're feeling okay, she texted her mum, feeling a rush of fondness for Frances in the next moment. Theirs certainly wasn't a perfect – or even very conventional – mother-daughter relationship but at the same time, she wouldn't change it. (Well, maybe only a tiny bit anyway.)

'It's all yours,' Eliza said just then, emerging from the bathroom in a cloud of steam, swathed in white towels with her hair in a matching turban.

Lara hesitated before replying because her attention had been seized by the arrival of a new email on her phone – from

Our Yorkshire, a glossy monthly magazine. Probably a rejection, she told herself, but all the same, she'd fully expected any rejections to manifest as polite silences. Opening the email, heart quickening, she scanned the contents then gave a yelp. 'Oh my God!'

'What?'

The email was from someone called Bryony Foster, the magazine's features editor, and while she wasn't offering Lara her own column plus a nice big contract (shame), she had written to say that she liked Lara's style of writing, and wondered if they could meet for a coffee or chat over the phone sometime soon, to discuss other ideas?

'*What*, Mum? Stop making those squeaking noises!' cried Eliza impatiently. 'Are you happy or mad? I can't tell.'

'I'm happy!' Lara replied, reading the email aloud to her. 'Wow. I can't believe it. She likes my writing. She wants to meet me.' She jumped off the bed and hugged Eliza, wet bare shoulders and all. 'I'm so excited!'

'Wow, Mum, that *is* pretty exciting,' Eliza said, laughing as she hugged her back. 'What did you write about? Your midlife crisis?' She dodged away, her towel turban slipping over one eye as Lara grabbed a cushion from the bed and threw it at her. 'The thrills and spills of life as a driving instructor? Hey, stop!' she gurgled as a pillow followed. 'I'm kidding, I'm kidding. You're cool. You're awesome. You're definitely not having a midlife crisis.' They both grinned at each other. 'Now please have a shower and get ready for your posh dinner, and stop throwing things like a maniac. Don't make me call security on your ass.'

'Don't make *me* call security on *your*— Okay, I'm going,' Lara said, laughing too as she floated into the bathroom. Today was getting better and better, she thought, stripping off her clothes and stepping under the water.

They met downstairs in the hotel lobby an hour or so later, with Lara wearing an olive-green retro wrap dress with a hopefully-not-too-plunging neckline and a sparkly diamante hair accessory. Eliza was in a rather-too-sexy-for-Lara's-liking black bandage dress and spiky heels, although she had felt self-conscious at the last minute and added a long, shapeless black cardigan at least. Ben, meanwhile, was not wearing a crushed velvet suit at all, but a smart pair of dark jeans and a soft grey shirt printed all over with tiny silhouetted flying birds. 'Ooh,' Eliza teased, seeing him there. '*Someone's* wearing their favourite shirt.'

His eyes twinkled as he smiled at her and Lara guessed this must be a private joke of theirs. It was heart-warming how well the two of them got on, she thought as they set off. For all the upheaval it had caused, all her misgivings, she was glad that Eliza and Ben had been able to connect like this. Glad too that Eliza had become a bridge between her parents, linking them together once more. Who would have thought?

Eliza refused to reveal where she was taking them – 'What, and spoil the surprise?' – but after they had been walking a few blocks, a queasy feeling took hold of Lara that maybe she had guessed where they might be headed. Eliza wouldn't have picked *there* though, would she? It would be pretty cack-handed of her to try such a stunt, surely. Cack-handed and plain old embarrassing. Because this was not some game, this was real people's lives and . . .

They rounded the corner in the next moment and there was Grand Central Station looming before them with its vast arched windows and columns. Lara's heart skipped a beat. Oh Lord. So it was true: Eliza was taking them back to the Oyster Bar. She was really doing this?

Ben didn't seem to have twigged what was happening when she glanced over at him – he was frowning at something on his phone and seemed distracted – so Lara elbowed her daughter with a stern expression. 'Lize . . .' she muttered warningly. 'I hope this isn't what I think it is.'

'I don't know *what* you're talking about,' Eliza replied with a blithe smile that said yes, she did know full well what Lara was talking about. And yes, she was extremely pleased with herself as well.

They crossed the road and walked in through the main entrance of the station, and now of course Ben *did* realise what game was afoot because it was impossible not to notice the soaring vaulted turquoise ceiling above their heads, the twinkling chandeliers, the polished stone floor and all the hustle and bustle of a busy station terminus. Lara hadn't been back here since the evening of the failed second date and she had forgotten quite how stunningly beautiful it was. Although, beauty aside, all she could think about was how she still hadn't managed to tell him the truth about that night. Surely some things were better left unsaid?

'Ah,' said Ben, putting his phone away and gazing around. 'I see. History repeats. Or rather—'

'The present corrects,' Eliza said, thrilled at her own cunning.

Lara shot Ben an unhappy expression which she very much hoped said, *Nope, I didn't know this was coming either.* 'Listen, love, we appreciate what you're trying to do,' she began, just as Eliza stopped in the middle of the concourse, theatrically putting a hand to her head.

'Oh no, silly me,' she cried, ignoring her mum. 'I went and booked a table at the Oyster Bar for only *two*, rather than three. Whoops! No problem though: I'll grab a burger and kill some time getting a few tattoos while you two go and have a lovely time together. Look, you have to, I've already paid them a hundred dollars for your dinner,' she added quickly as both her parents started protesting. 'Let me know if it costs more and I'll pay you back, obviously.' She leaned in and gave each of them a quick parting kiss. 'The restaurant's downstairs, apparently – on the lower level, the website says. Take your time, enjoy yourselves, and I'll see you for breakfast tomorrow,' she said, already stepping backwards from them. 'Have fun!'

Lara felt like a punctured balloon with all her breath leaking out as she stood there motionless, watching Eliza stride jauntily away. 'Be careful!' she thought to yell after her. 'And you'd better be joking about the tattoos!'

'I agree with your mother!' Ben shouted in the next moment, to which Eliza merely put up a hand in a wave without turning back.

Lara and Ben looked at one another. 'I apologise wholeheartedly for my daughter,' Lara said with feeling.

'I apologise wholeheartedly for *mine*,' he replied, then elbowed her. Thankfully he looked amused rather than annoyed. 'She's only gone and played us again. Are we complete idiots, Lara? Because I'm getting the distinct impression that she's running rings around us. And making it look far too easy.'

She gave him a rueful smile. 'Agreed. I blame the parents. They must definitely be idiots to keep falling for her tricks.'

They were still hovering on the concourse with its huge departure screens updating on the wall, passengers hauling wheeled suitcases in every direction, the station's mellow golden lighting lending a sheen to the vast stone columns. Lara was about to apologise again – this was a step too far, even for meddling Eliza – when Ben shrugged and said, 'But not idiotic enough to pass up a free dinner in an iconic restaurant. Am I right?'

She hesitated, unsure. 'Are you?' she asked. 'Please don't feel you have to, just because—'

'I'd *like* to,' he said firmly. 'I would definitely have been there first time around had my dad not selfishly gone and had a heart attack that day.' They exchanged a wary smile. 'I was just congratulating myself earlier, actually, that I hadn't cursed another family member to a sudden death by me coming back to New York.'

She couldn't tell if he was joking or not. 'Were you worried about lightning striking twice?' she asked.

He nodded, looking faintly embarrassed. 'I guess in some way, I was. Rationally, I know that me coming here had nothing to do with my dad dying but . . . all the same, it kind of put me off going anywhere else. Until now. Daft, isn't it?'

'No,' she told him. 'Not at all. It must have been horrible, getting that news when you were so far away. The worst.'

He gave her a quick, grateful smile but she caught the flicker of pain in his eyes nonetheless. An event so traumatic would never leave you, she guessed. 'Anyway,' he went on, rallying. 'That was then, this is now. And we *are* dressed up, fancy as instructed,' he said. 'You look lovely, by the way. That colour really suits you.' There was an awkward pause where Lara didn't quite know how to respond, then Ben gestured towards the stairs down to the lower level. 'So, what the hell. Better late than never, I reckon. Shall we?'

'I suppose we should at least raise a glass to the infuriating person who organised all this so sneakily,' Lara said, aware that her pulse was starting to quicken. The two of them, finally making it here together after nineteen years — she couldn't quite believe it was happening. This time at least she wasn't sprinting across the concourse, but her heart still pounded as she wrestled with her feelings.

They headed towards the stairs, both falling silent. She and Ben hadn't liked each other very much when they'd met in Cambridge, but there was something about being back here in New York that had softened their previous antagonism. No, he wasn't the same handsome, funny twenty-something who'd sent her into such emotional turmoil, but nor was she the idealistic young woman she'd been then either. They'd both grown up and become different people, but as it turned out, middle-aged Ben was just as funny and surprising and — okay, yes, all right, as good-looking as his younger self. Despite everything, she really liked him. But how did he feel?

Her stomach turned over with a flurry of nerves as they went downstairs, remembering how she'd clattered down them the first time, almost tripping in her haste. How she'd arrived out of breath and frantic, gazing around in wild despair only to see no trace of him there. All of that was in the past though, she told herself firmly, trying to pull herself together. *History repeats*, Ben had said, but everything had changed so much between then and now. You couldn't rewind and replay the past, however much you might want to. Or could you?

Chapter Twenty-Eight

You had to laugh at Eliza's brazen nerve, Ben thought as they arrived at the restaurant and stood waiting to be seated. Laugh or start tearing your hair out anyway, which, for a forty-something man who'd noticed a distinct thinning up top in recent years, was not an appealing option. Honestly though, what was she like? Playing Cupid with such overt glee, secretly booking this place for them, only to vanish at the last minute, no doubt cackling all the way out of the building. Let nobody say that Eliza Spencer was not the enterprising type.

Still, there were worse places to be set up, he thought, gazing around. The beauty of the arched ceiling above them, its glossy tiles astounding in their geometry, was practically worth the visit alone. Waiters bearing trays of oysters and soft-shell crabs swept between the red-and-white-checked clothed tables as piano music tinkled in the background. The only thing that pained him was imagining Lara patiently waiting for him outside, all those years ago. It had haunted him ever since she'd told him she hadn't got his message that night – he couldn't bear to think of her standing there hopefully, checking her watch now and then, only to eventually leave, dispirited by rejection. It must have been horrible.

But they were here now at least. They'd moved on and he was determined to enjoy the evening, second time around. 'Wow,' he said, breathing in the atmosphere. 'Okay, I take everything back. *Everything.* Our kid's a genius. It's stunning, isn't it?'

'Fabulous,' said Lara, eyes wide as she took in the surroundings. She looked really pretty, he kept thinking, with her hair curled and that jewelled clip she was wearing sparkling above one ear. They both noticed she was clutching his sleeve suddenly and she withdrew her hand, looking embarrassed. 'Oops. Sorry,' she said, then added jokingly, 'I didn't dry my hands properly when I went to the ladies' earlier, didn't think you'd mind.'

He laughed out loud. 'You carry on,' he said. He'd forgotten how funny she was, he thought affectionately. 'Favourite shirt, towel, it's all one and the same really.'

A waiter came over with menus and settled them at a table in the next moment. They ordered a bottle of wine and a jug of water, then they were alone. For the first time all day, Ben wasn't quite sure what to say. They were in the most romantic place in the world, having been conned into a date, and it seemed unreal, all of a sudden, that his path and Lara's had been flung back together again, that they were sitting here, the parents of a young woman, when they barely knew one another. And yet, it could all have been so different. What if their paths had remained together? *Tell her I'll find her*, he remembered saying into that voicemail message and kicked himself once again that he could have let her slip through his fingers.

'I went to Camberwell looking for you once, you know,' he found himself blurting out. All of a sudden he wanted her to know that she had meant something to him, that their night together remained such a special memory of his.

'You did?' She seemed startled.

'Yeah. I was in London anyway, popped into The Sun to see if you were there. Just on the off-chance. This must have been a few years after we met.'

She gave a faint smile. 'I was long gone by then.'

'So I gathered.' He picked up the menu, feeling awkward. 'I imagined you must be in some other amazing place,' he confessed. 'Berlin or Madrid. Somewhere exciting. Writing for edgy magazines and planting new orchards of trees.'

'God, if only. Instead, I was a mum and housewife up north, telling myself I was happy,' she replied. 'Putting another wash on and singing nursery rhymes. Wondering what had happened to my life.'

They looked at each other for a moment, a whole unspoken conversation seeming to take place between their eyes. He glanced at the menu, aware that he was yet to read a single word of it, but then she asked, 'What would you have said? If I'd been in the pub that day when you went in?'

He put the menu back down again. 'I think I'd have said that I wished—' He ground to a halt, feeling as if he were veering into dangerous territory. Was there any point, wondering what he might have said back then? What he had wished? 'I don't know,' he admitted. 'I just wanted to see you again.'

'I wish we had,' she replied. 'Seen each other again, that is.' They exchanged another charged look and she opened her mouth as if she were about to elaborate further before closing it again. Neither of them seemed able to express themselves tonight, without Eliza there to focus on.

'Would it have worked, do you think? The two of us,' he found himself asking, just as she said, 'I had some good news today,' with a determined brightness.

She hesitated, eyes widening for a second, but the moment was broken by the waiter returning with their wine. 'Are you ready to order?' he asked, pouring them a glass each.

'Um ...' Ben still hadn't read a word of the menu. Lara hadn't even picked hers up. 'Can we have a few minutes?' he asked, taking a nervous gulp of wine. Crisp and refreshing, he had to restrain himself from knocking back the entire glass. Why had he come out with such a stupid question? Perhaps a strained silence would have been preferable after all. 'You were saying you had some good news?' he prompted Lara, when the waiter left again. Hopefully she hadn't heard his rash outpouring, he consoled himself.

'And you said something far more interesting,' she replied, raising her gaze to his. Damn it. 'I've wondered the same,' she went on after a moment. 'How it would have been, the two of us. The three of us, rather.'

'Or more,' he countered. 'We might have ended up having other children. A whole minibus full.'

She laughed. 'We might,' she said, then swirled her wine gently, twirling the stem between her fingers. 'Or we might have made each other unhappy,' she pointed out. 'We might have argued about trivial, annoying stuff, discovered we didn't have that much in common after all. We might have split up.'

'Yep,' he accepted with a shrug. 'But then again, we might have lived happily ever after. In Cambridge. Or Yorkshire. Or ... I don't know. Sydney. Maybe even here in New York.'

They were silent for a moment as myriad different lives,

homes, outcomes spooled through his head, and perhaps hers too: a ticker tape of happy family images. All the many what-might-have-beens. 'We should look at the menu,' she said, breaking the spell. 'Our poor long-suffering waiter keeps glancing over at us.'

'Sure,' he said, forcing himself to think about food options, although his thoughts kept returning to their conversation. She seemed less willing than him to consider the more positive alternative versions of reality that might have played out, he thought, but the subject had been occupying his mind increasingly since stepping off the plane. The night they'd first met had seemed so monumental to him; at the time he had been certain that she was the one. Did her reticence now mean that she was glad life had played out this way instead? Was she unconcerned that the three of them could have been a so-called 'proper family', as Eliza had put it?

They ordered some oysters to share as a starter — it seemed wrong not to — as well as their main courses, but then the diversion was over and there were no longer any menus to hide behind. 'So,' he said, 'maybe we should talk about your good news?'

She tilted her head for a moment then screwed up her face. 'I think I'd rather put the other conversation to bed first,' she replied and the words prompted him to experience an almost teenage stirring of lust at the thought of her in bed all those years ago. How he'd kissed her beautiful face and body, believing he was in love. Christ, Ben, keep it together, he ordered himself. 'Just so we know where we both stand,' she was saying. 'Shall I go first?'

He had absolutely no idea what she was going to say, he realised as he nodded, taking another gulp of wine for good measure. They'd been getting on pretty well over the last few days, definitely warming back up to one another, but now her expression was serious and thoughtful, and he wondered, with a lurch, where this might be heading.

'Okay,' she began. 'Deep breath, Lara. I'm going to be really honest because – well, because why not? We're both adults. We're good people. We can do this.'

Now he felt more apprehensive than ever. She looked so sweetly earnest that he wasn't sure he would be able to resist if she made any romantic propositions. Or was he kidding himself that such an idea was even on the cards any more? 'Agreed,' he said, feeling his pulse accelerate. He still liked her, he realised with a jolt. He really, really liked her. But what about Kirsten? How could this ever end well?

'I think,' she began slowly, 'that you're right. I think we might have been really happy together, given the chance. That night ... I had the best time with you. I felt like we completely clicked. I felt so incredibly happy. And it wasn't just the booze, was it? I woke up with you and thought ... well, this is a bit dramatic, but I thought I'd finally found the person who was right for me. That's you, in case you were wondering.'

She laughed rather self-consciously and he found that he couldn't speak for a few seconds, because his feelings seemed to be brimming almost unbearably inside him, his heart full. 'I felt the same,' he replied. And then, because an earlier comment of hers had been stinging him ever since she'd made it, he felt compelled to add, 'It really wasn't a "meaningless one-night stand" for me, you know.'

She had the grace to blush. 'Look, I only said that because ...' She wrinkled her nose. 'Well ... because I was defensive and trying to land a punch. You know I didn't really feel that way. Not at the time anyway.'

'No,' he agreed.

'So maybe, yes, we would have lasted the course. There would have been rows about housework and parenting and dramas with our kids and in-laws, the usual stuff. Sure. All of that. We don't know how well – or not – we'd have weathered the storms. And it kind of breaks my heart, you know, that we *didn't* end up having that life together, so that we could find out for definite. Especially if that life together was made up of adventures around the world, in Sydney and New York, and all those other places. Because it could have been so wonderful.' She pulled a jokey face at him but he could detect a sadness in her body language at the same time.

'I know,' he said, similarly regretful. 'If Dad hadn't been ill . . .'

'If I'd made it here to get your message . . .' she added, then snapped her mouth shut almost immediately.

He stared at her, not comprehending. He must have misheard, he thought, confused. 'Wait – *if* you'd made it here?' he echoed. 'What do you mean?'

She was blushing a deep scarlet, suddenly looking mortified. 'I . . . Well, okay, I haven't told you everything about that night,' she stammered, no longer meeting his eye.

Ben couldn't believe what he was hearing. 'Are you saying what I think you're saying?' he asked. 'Are you telling me you didn't turn up for our date either? And that's why you didn't get my message?'

Just like that, she had ruined the entire evening. Her heart thumped, her face burned with guilt. Oh my God. How had she let that slip? It was being here, drinking too fast, letting her feelings knock her off guard. 'It wasn't like that,' she protested,

308

unable to bear the sudden coldness in his expression. The hurt disbelief as the story tumbled out of her: how, on the evening she was supposed to meet him, everything had gone wrong. How her boss had kept her late that day at work, wanting a whole sheaf of last-minute revisions and how Lara had hardly been able to concentrate with panic as she'd noticed the clock hands dragging further and further past her usual leaving time. And then, how the subway train she'd finally hopped on, crammed with other passengers, stinking and hot, had slowed to a halt in a tunnel for twenty agonising minutes before eventually wheezing to the next station. There was a fatality further down the line, came an announcement, and everyone was advised to leave the station and use alternative transport as there would be a very long delay. By now, it was quarter past seven and Lara was sweating and completely flustered. Trying to flag down a taxi outside the station, she was jostled by a large aggressive man in a suit, rushing to claim it before her, who knocked her into the road, where she landed, grazing her hands and knees and fighting back the tears.

Ben seemed unmoved as she recounted this list of woes. 'Let's just get to the headline of the story,' he said. 'Did you or didn't you turn up for our date that night?'

'I did!' she cried, wishing he didn't look so unfriendly. Minutes earlier they had been fondly imagining their own bus-load of children, yet now he seemed stern and forbidding. 'But I was late,' she admitted. 'Like . . . an hour late.'

An hour and a half late, in fact, tear-streaked, tights ripped, hands still smarting from their grazes. Bursting into sobs and turning away when she arrived and saw that of course she was too late and nobody was waiting for her. Of course she had missed him. How could she have let this happen?

309

'Hang on,' Ben was saying, as if still trying to process her story. 'How come you're only telling me this tonight? After making me feel really shit, letting me believe you'd waited for me here, assuming I'd stood you up? When actually, of the two of us, *you* stood *me* up! I at least did my best to get a message to you. No wonder nobody passed it on, because I'd said to the staff here, six-thirty. She'll be waiting for me outside at six-thirty!'

Lara bowed her head, unable to argue with any of this, because he was right. 'I know,' she said miserably, wishing she'd been straight with him in the first place. Once again, she'd held back the truth and now she was having to face the consequences. Had she learned nothing? 'I did go to your hostel the next day though,' she added meekly, trying to redeem herself.

'Right, yeah, I think you said so before,' he replied, apparently unbothered. 'That must have been a waste of your time.'

'Well ...' Lara began, only to stop again when the waiter reappeared at the table, reverently setting down a plate of oysters nestled in their half shells on a bed of crushed ice, along with plump lemon wedges.

'Thank you,' she said dully. She'd completely lost her appetite by now. The waiter left once more and she braced herself to return to their awful conversation. 'Yes, I went to the hostel on the Saturday, feeling terrible,' she continued. 'When they said you'd checked out a full day earlier – before we were even due to *meet* – I was devastated.' She almost wanted to cry, remembering the shock of this discovery, how she'd stared at the gawky man behind the reception desk in complete disbelief. *Gone?* she'd repeated. *What do you mean, he's gone?* 'Because – not knowing you'd left me a message the day before, because, yes, my fault, I got there so late – I assumed it had all been a game to you. That you didn't care.'

310

He sighed and she was unable to read his expression although it looked horribly like exasperation. 'It wasn't a game to me,' he said stiffly, squeezing a half-moon of lemon on to an oyster. 'Of course I cared.'

'Well, I know that now, but—' She felt completely overwhelmed by what a mess they'd made of everything. Remembering how apologetic yet hopeful she'd felt that Saturday, heading off first thing to find the hostel where she thought he was staying; picking up a gift en route of a hilariously tacky neon pink souvenir Statue of Liberty in the hope of making him smile, determined to convince him how sorry she was for not showing. Surely he'd forgive her once she explained, wouldn't he? He'd understand that these things happened, that sometimes life threw a spanner in the works, but she would love to take him for brunch and hang out this weekend if he wanted?

Hearing from the bored-looking receptionist that he'd already left, that she'd missed him by an entire day, had been one of the worst gut-punches of her entire life. 'I've never been able to trust a man again, ever since,' she cried now, hoping to make him see just how much it had affected her.

His response was merely to shrug, as if refusing to feel bad about something that patently wasn't his fault. Fair enough. 'So what happened to my neon pink Statue of Liberty?' was all he said.

'What? Oh.' She couldn't remember. 'I probably stuffed it in the nearest bin,' she confessed, then attempted to lighten the mood by adding, 'Although if it matters all that much, I could buy you another one?'

His smile was small and not particularly warm. 'It doesn't matter,' he replied, but she knew that she'd reduced herself in his eyes by not being straight with him from the start. She knew that it *did* matter, actually, which left her feeling pretty horrible, as if she'd tarnished their friendship by omission.

'Does that mean you think I'm nasty again?' she asked in a small voice before she could stop herself.

Thankfully this time he looked at her properly, and he must have seen the anguish in her face because he shook his head. 'No,' he said. Was it wishful thinking, or was he softening a touch? 'Unless there's anything else you haven't told me?'

'No, nothing,' she said. 'I swear.' She belatedly put an oyster on her plate and sprinkled salt on it. 'I'm sorry,' she added because she knew she'd let him down. 'I was so angry with myself for being late – and I've been angry with myself all over again ever since I heard about your message. But . . .'

'Look,' he said, sounding tired, 'it's in the past now. Clearly some things are not meant to be.'

'No.' She bowed her head once more because tears were blurring her eyes. *Not meant to be?* The finality of his words seemed unbearable. 'All the same, I'm sorry that we didn't manage to find our way back to each other before now,' she blurted out. 'To find out for sure whether . . .' She couldn't finish the sentence because the regret was overwhelming her. 'Well, you know,' she ended lamely.

His lips were pressed together and she couldn't read his expression. 'I know,' he said, then changed the subject. 'Why don't you tell me your good news instead?'

She tried to pull herself together, to mask the emotional tumult she'd just experienced. 'Sure,' she said heavily. 'My good news. Well, it's not that exciting, but okay: I heard earlier that a magazine editor wants to meet me about possibly writing something for them.' Her cheeks were still hot; she so hated confrontation. *Please like me again*, she wanted to say, wishing they could return to their easy warmth of before. 'So. Da-dah. That's it.'

'Wow,' he said – and oh, thank heavens, the coldness seemed to have left his voice and he looked more normal again. Smiling, even, albeit in a slightly forced way. 'That sounds good. What will you write about?'

The tension between them eased a little as she told him her hopes and plans, and they polished off the delicious, succulent oysters between them. By the time the waiter had cleared their plates, she'd had quite enough of talking about herself though, and decided to change the subject. 'But what about you?' she asked as soon as she had the chance. 'Tell me about you and Kirsten. Is she lovely? Eliza said things had been a bit tricky; is that all sorted out now?'

Later that evening, taking off her make-up back in the hotel, Lara couldn't help wishing she'd thought of a different question to ask, rather than delving into the details of Ben's marriage – because it turned out that things were actually far from 'sorted out' on the domestic front. Eliza had said that Ben and his wife were living apart, but Lara hadn't realised that Kirsten had already moved on to someone else. She couldn't help feeling sorry for Ben, who looked doleful and wretched as he trotted out the news. It was also hard not to squirm with self-blame, for having been part of the grenade that had detonated their relationship months earlier.

Still – one humiliation had been averted, at least, because before the conversation had become knotty and difficult, she had actually been experiencing a lot of romantic feelings about Ben. When they'd been discussing their parallel lives, for instance, imagining how things could have turned out, she'd been feeling very sentimental, gazing into his eyes, her tummy full of sudden butterflies at just how lovely he was and how much she wished they could have been together. There had been a moment, even, where she'd had the strong urge to cut to the chase and lean across the table and kiss him. Thank God she hadn't, because clearly Ben was still really hung up on Kirsten. Also, hadn't he said himself that 'some things were not meant to be'? He'd probably have leapt away in horror if Lara had launched in, lips dreamily puckered.

So drenched had she been with relief to have kept her powder dry and not embarrassed herself with any kissing ambushes, that she'd ended up talking at length about how much she liked Ollie from the swimming club, so that she wouldn't look a complete saddo to Ben. *It's fine! I'm into someone else anyway!* Was that a bit pathetic? Probably, but she was still flustered by the whole late-for-the-date fiasco. After that, she'd doubled down in her attempt to get into Ben's good books once more by offering him relationship advice with Kirsten, and how he should try to win her back.

To be fair though, if anyone needed advice about how to win back a woman, she was starting to think that person was Ben. 'I reckon I might have made things worse by booking this trip,' he'd confessed. 'Because I haven't heard from her since then.'

Lara had almost screamed her horror. 'Does she know that I'm here as well? But you did tell her that you and I ... that we're just friends, right? You did make that clear to her?'

'Well ...' His face fell. 'Not exactly,' he muttered. And then it all came out about how jealous and hurt he'd been feeling, having heard about Kirsten and this mystery man – and how he'd been only too glad to hurt her right back, or at least to give her the impression that he had moved on, too. Which was understandable, Lara had to acknowledge, if also pretty childish.

'What do you think I should do?' he asked at the end of his sorry tale.

'Tell her the truth, that you still love her? Take her away on a different trip somewhere equally fabulous?' Lara suggested immediately. Gosh, but she felt *terrible* that Ben's relationship had been so badly damaged by the appearance of her and Eliza. Despite her complicated feelings for him, she had to at least try and assuage some of her guilt by helping him patch up the wounds. 'Prove that you mean all the promises you made, that you still want to make a go of your relationship? At the very least, find out who this new man is and kneecap him. Or set Eliza on him.'

Squinting into the mirror now and cursing the hotel's dim lighting, she wondered where Eliza was and when she would return. Lara had been so taken aback by the Grand Central Station set-up that she hadn't drilled down into exactly where Eliza might be heading off to in that provocative dress. A young woman, far from home – so many things could go wrong. And Eliza might think herself cool and an adult, but she wasn't half as grown-up and sophisticated as she thought. *Are you sure you don't want me to meet you? Everything okay?* she had messaged, as well as further variations on that theme. Eliza's replies had been cryptically (and frustratingly) opaque so far, with little given away. But this was a mere taster of what it would be like during the university years, Lara reminded herself. In just over a month's time, exam results permitting, Eliza could be moving into student accommodation in a city far away, and Lara wouldn't have a clue what time she'd be arriving home at night, what she might be wearing, who she was with and what she was getting up to. Maybe that was just as well, she reflected, remembering her own debauched student years. All the same, how did any parent ever sleep again without their child safely under their roof?

You've definitely got your room key, haven't you? she messaged now, as another excuse to check in with her. A rolling-eye emoji came instantly back followed by an instruction to chill out, she wasn't dead (clearly a propensity for such messages ran in the Spencer family) or locked up in a basement somewhere. Which was reassuring but only marginally. Still, she couldn't be too annoyed with Eliza, not after she'd enjoyed such a lovely evening with Ben – well, until she'd put her foot in it anyway. Had he forgiven her yet? It was hard to tell.

For the most part, though, it was a lovely, if belated, second date. He was fantastic company, a truly wonderful person. By being honest with him at last, they'd found some mutual closure, however tricky it had been to get there. And yes, she had regrets, but she wouldn't waste any more time dwelling on them, other than to acknowledge that Kirsten was a lucky woman. Let's hope, for Ben's sake, that she had realised by now precisely how much she had to lose.

Lara was just slathering her face in night cream when the door opened, and there was Eliza, looking dishevelled, with her make-up a mess and her hair tousled, but nevertheless radiating ... Well, what? Lara peered at her suspiciously. Joy? *Sex?* Or was she high?

'Gosh,' she said, intrigued. 'Are you all right?'

Eliza flung herself back on her bed, arms and legs starfishing out to the sides. 'I have had,' she began, with her usual dramatic flair, 'the *best* night. *Ever.*' She smiled blissfully up at the ceiling and Lara sniffed the air surreptitiously. Booze – yes. Smoke – yes.

'And?' she prompted. 'You can't just stop there and leave me hanging. What did you get up to?'

Eliza exhaled a great sigh of apparent contentment with the world, then seemed to come to her senses, because in the next second, she'd rolled over on to her side and was peering, slightly cross-eyed, at Lara. 'Wait, no – I completely forgot. How was your date with *Dad*?'

Lara smiled at her beloved girl-woman of a daughter. 'Oh no,' she said. 'That will have to wait. I asked you first. Tell me everything.'

Chapter Twenty-Nine

Eliza's evening hadn't started off as the greatest night of her life – in fact, once she had finished congratulating herself on the thrill and triumph of setting her parents up on a dinner date (stroke of genius, Eliza!), she'd been left to mooch around aimlessly for a while, wondering what to do for the next few hours. For the first time since she'd arrived in the city, she felt her stress levels inching upwards, now that she was on her own. A homeless man wolf-whistled her from a shadowy doorway and she walked a little faster. A hand-holding couple besotted with their own selves barged against her unseeingly and she felt disproportionately bruised by the contact. A siren wailed in the background as a couple of blokes outside a bar leered at her, and she tugged her dress down at the hem, wrapping her arms around herself and deciding that maybe she'd slope back to the hotel after all; maybe the city was too full-on for her to handle alone.

But moments later, as if some all-seeing benevolent goddess was rewarding her for getting that far, she stumbled upon a pop-up gallery in a white-painted empty store a few blocks from the station. Why not, she thought, noticing that it seemed to be full of people her age, as well as registering the 'Free Entry' sign in the window. She was all dressed up, and here, at last, was somewhere to go. If nothing else, she'd get some cool photos to put on her social media, she figured.

The artwork adorning the walls was a complete mix of styles: first she studied a clutch of moody black and white prints of old pianos and other musical instruments abandoned in unlikely places – a meadow, at a busy crossroads, in a snow drift. Next was a series of neon graffiti tags embroidered on jewel-toned pieces of velvet: aquamarine and ruby and amethyst. (Gorgeous, she thought, until she saw the hefty prices, and promptly felt faint.) Further along, in a large, clear Perspex wall box, hung an eerie collection of bracelets and necklaces which, according to the accompanying note, had been made from – was this a *joke*? – the brightly varnished bones of rodents caught by the artist's cat (no, thank you, thought Eliza with a shudder). There were also huge impressionist paintings, graphic line drawings, a series of pop-art-style collages and much more. Reading the notes for each piece, Eliza gathered that the exhibition was made up of work from the recent fine art graduates of a local university – which explained the eclecticism, she figured.

She paused, smiling, in front of three portraits of haughty-faced dogs, painted in oils with the same regal reverence as if the subjects were kings and queens, and wittily titled *(Old) Masters of None.*

'The poodle's my favourite,' said a voice behind her, and Eliza turned to see a young woman with fuchsia-pink hair, cut in a shaggy bob with an asymmetric fringe, wearing a leopard-print fake-fur jacket over a denim minidress. Pretty much the coolest person who had ever spoken to Eliza, in other words.

'Poodles are awesome,' Eliza agreed, thankful to have an opinion on the matter, if only because Saskia's dad had a black poodle who was surprisingly amenable to being taught tricks for pieces of sausage. She looked again at the painting in question, which featured a black poodle with a disapproving expression, a studded gold collar around its neck, with a chewed up red dog toy in the background nicely undercutting its pompous air. 'Curly hair and brains, what's not to love?'

'Exactly! That's what I thought,' said the pink-haired woman – or girl, really, because she couldn't have been much older than Eliza. She had tiny gold earrings in the shape of parrots and electric-blue mascara. 'My first two wishes, right there.'

'I love them,' said Eliza warmly because she'd just noticed that in the information snippet attached to the wall nearby, the photograph of the artist showed that she too had pink hair and gold parrot earrings. *Phoebe Kaminska*, she read. 'The paintings, I mean, not the dogs – although I love them too.' She cringed, hearing herself blathering on. 'So are you Phoebe?'

'That's me,' she confirmed. 'Hey, are you English?'

'How ever did you guess?' Eliza asked, mimicking the clipped tones of girls she'd come across at university open days, whose accents spoke of tennis lessons, ponies and cut glass. 'Yes, I'm Eliza,' she added, in her ordinary voice. 'Nice to meet you.'

'Good to meet you too, Eliza. How are you finding New York?'

'So you made a friend – how nice!' Lara said, having all of this recounted to her in the hotel room. She unfastened her dress and pulled it over her head, her words momentarily muffled. 'Lovely. And did you hang out together after the exhibition?'

Eliza smiled to herself, fingers pleating the bedcover and wondering how much she should say. Wondering if she should tell her mum how, shortly afterwards, when the exhibition closed up for the evening, Phoebe had invited her and a few others back to her apartment and how, sitting up on a grungy rooftop garden, they'd smoked joints and listened to music. And how, as the twilight thickened around them and a few smudgy stars poked their way through the smoggy darkness, Phoebe had caught her eye and moved over in order to sit beside her, the scent of her perfume (jasmine?) making Eliza's stomach flip right over like a tossed pancake. The words of that day's horoscope came flashing back into her head – *A seismic awakening takes place today. Life begins anew!* – as, in the next moment, Phoebe leaned towards her and gently kissed her mouth. So the prediction was for her after all, Eliza thought, feeling as if the world had stopped turning momentarily. Oh my God. Her whole body was tingling with anticipation. She was finding it hard to breathe all of a sudden.

'Is this okay?' Phoebe murmured when, soon afterwards, she led Eliza by the hand to her bedroom and proceeded to awaken her in all senses of the word. Senses Eliza didn't even know until now that she *had*.

'Yes,' Eliza whispered back, feeling as if small bright explosions were detonating around her body. *Who am I?* she had been asking herself for months – but now she knew the answer. This is who I am. This is me, right here, right now. Genes and biology were all very well, but you couldn't inherit everything. It turned out that it was the big stuff – your experiences and how you chose to deal with them – that truly moulded you into your real, pure self.

'Yeah, we hung out,' was all she said to Lara though. She'd tell her mum about this one day, for sure, but tonight, she wanted to hug it to herself for a while longer, relive those thrilling detonations in private. Go to bed feeling as if she was a real woman.

God, this city was the greatest place in the whole world, she thought drowsily, shutting her eyes with a final smile. And then, still fully dressed and without even remembering to grill Lara about her own exploits that evening, Eliza wriggled into a more comfortable position and slipped headlong into the deep, satisfied sleep of one who had just experienced a very good time.

Part Three

AUTUMN

Chapter Thirty

'Okay, you're five centimetres dilated, Alice, you're doing brilliantly,' Kirsten said, jotting down the time and measurement in her notes, and squeezing the labouring woman's hand. 'Nice deep breaths, that's it. Everything's looking great. Any word from your partner?'

'He's on his way,' Alice panted, her hair damp around her face. It was the first week of September and unseasonably warm. Even with the windows open in the birth centre, the air seemed to be laden with oppressive weight.

'Great,' said Kirsten, offering her a sip of water. Alice had come in alone half an hour ago; now thirty-eight weeks pregnant, she had stayed healthy throughout, but Kirsten knew from experience that first babies could take their time about making their grand entrance. Any support from loved ones along the way was crucial. 'Try and rest between contractions if you can. Your body knows what to do.'

There was a knock as she finished speaking, and then a man's face appeared around the door. Kirsten gasped. 'What are you—?' she began but before she could reach the end of her question, the man – *Neil* – was rushing unseeingly past her and over to Alice on the bed. 'You okay?' he asked, clasping her hand between his. She nodded, smiling, and he grabbed a tissue from the box on the small bedside table and tenderly wiped her sweaty brow. 'I only just got your message – I was over in Great Shelford, the signal was really bad,' he gabbled. 'Sorry, sweetheart. How's it going?'

'Okay,' she murmured, eyes half closed. 'I'm glad you're here.'

'Me too.' It was only then that he raised his gaze to Kirsten – Kirsten, who was valiantly trying to pull herself together before he noticed her – but when their eyes did at last meet, his own look of horror and shock was unmistakable. She registered his panicked gulp, then he blinked quickly and managed to assume a blank expression. 'Hi. I'm Neil,' he said unnecessarily. 'Alice's partner.'

'Kirsten,' she said weakly. 'Hi. Um, Alice is doing really well. Would you excuse me for a moment, please? Alice, I'll be right back.'

She somehow got herself across the floor, out of the room and a safe distance along the corridor, before she had to stop and lean against the wall, heart pounding, palms clammy against the cool plaster, her breath shallow in her lungs. She squeezed her eyes shut, trying to calm her free-falling thoughts. *Shit.* Neil was Alice's partner? Neil was with someone else, about to be a family man? Stupidly, Kirsten had had no idea, *no idea* that this was the case. Hadn't he made a point of saying to her in B&Q that first day that he was single? Or rather . . . She tried to think back, to think clearly. He'd said he didn't have a *wife*, she remembered, and gave a hollow laugh. Right. Very clever, Neil. You don't have a wife, but you do have a pregnant girlfriend and, judging by Alice's record of previous miscarriages, all of which had apparently been with the same partner, they must have been together some years. Quite a number of years. What a bastard. What an absolute bastard.

She was about to scuttle down to the staff loo for some privacy, possibly a cry, time to get her head around this unpleasant discovery, but was too late, for in the next moment, Neil emerged from the birthing room looking wild-eyed. 'Kirsten – can we talk?' he asked in a low voice.

'And say what?' she replied bitterly. 'No, we can't talk. Your labouring girlfriend needs you. Go and hold her hand, you—' She broke off, aware that she was about to call him a name, and aware too that while she was wearing her uniform and on duty, she had to remain professional at all times. Even though it felt as if something was collapsing inside her, the ground giving way beneath her feet. Her throat tightened and she knew that if she didn't get away from him soon, tears would swim up into her eyes, that she would crack and lose her composure. She had fallen for him, she realised wretchedly. She had let herself become consumed with their affair, with *him*, even though he had never promised anything, even though he'd always left her that little bit too soon each time while the bed was still warm. Having told herself that she'd only been after sex anyway, now she was left feeling completely empty. Maybe it was love she'd been yearning for, after all. How could she have been so stupid?

'I need to go,' she said abruptly, turning away. 'I won't be long. You get back to Alice.'

And then she walked away before he could stop her or say anything else, tears rolling down her face. Now what? she thought despairingly. Now what do I do?

★

'Oh, mate,' sighed Vick that evening when Kirsten recounted the story. 'So what happens now? How do you feel about everything?' The two of them were sitting out on her patio, the humid air just starting to cool as the sky darkened. Kirsten had driven straight round to her friend's house after her shift, not able to face being alone in her flat.

'I feel . . . pretty numb really,' she replied, jabbing her fork into the plate of tagliatelle Vick had made her. She kept thinking about the times Neil had dashed away from her place, having parked on double yellow lines outside. She hadn't even been worth the cost of a parking meter, then.

Through an open upstairs window came the noisy shouts and laughter of the children's bathtime taking place, and she smiled feebly at the sound of a loud, off-key pirate sea shanty, as sung by Vick's husband Sean, followed by further high-pitched gales of laughter.

'I apologise for that abomination to your ears,' Vick said drily. 'So – Neil. It's over, I take it?'

'Yeah. Definitely,' Kirsten said. 'Alice is such a lovely woman, I feel completely shit that, unknown to her, I was shagging her bloke all summer. Whoops, sorry,' she said, lowering her voice and hoping that her last few phrases hadn't carried up to the bathroom. 'Oh, and get this – they had a baby girl, perfect and gorgeous, and Alice made a joke about calling her "Kirsten" after me. You should have seen Neil's face. I've never seen a man turn so ashen with such comically lightning speed.'

'Oh God,' Vick groaned sympathetically. 'What a nightmare.'

'I know.' Kirsten forked in another mouthful of pasta, remembering to taste this one, rather than simply shovelling it down. Vick's garden was vibrant with early autumn colour – red and purple salvias blooming brightly, creamy roses sending out their scent, the lavender still open for late-calling bees – and Kirsten tried to breathe deeply and allow herself to be calmed by her surroundings. 'Thank you for this, by the way,' she said. 'I didn't know where else to go.'

'Any time,' Vick told her, then hesitated. 'So you're not thinking of going home-home, then? Back to Ben, I mean?' There was a delicate pause. 'Because it strikes me that this could be the moment to try again, maybe. Once you've got over the shock of Bastard Neil, obviously.'

Kirsten's shoulders drooped. 'I . . . don't know,' she admitted. Since his trip to New York, Ben had been back in touch, making it very clear that there was absolutely nothing going on with Lara and that he was still keen to make a go of their marriage. He'd even randomly suggested the two of them go on holiday together, which seemed a bit much, to Kirsten. Why on earth would he think that was a good idea, when they'd barely spoken for weeks? 'We've agreed to meet up on Thursday actually,' she went on. 'For a drink and a chat. I guess we need to make a decision, one way or another, about what we're going to do.'

'And do you have any idea about what you *want* to do?' Vick prompted gently. 'Because . . . you know, I don't want to oversimplify things, but Ben made one mistake, as far as I could see. One mistake in twenty years. And he did always want to be a dad. So . . .'

'I just don't know,' Kirsten said before she could go any further.

Vick's eyes were compassionate. 'Fair enough,' she said. 'But you'll give him a chance, yeah? When you see him on Thursday?'

'Yeah,' said Kirsten, quailing a little inside. 'I will. I'll hear what he has to say.'

★

Change seemed to be in the air. For Lara, certainly, who'd felt herself humming with a new do-better energy since returning from New York. It turned out she wasn't the only one.

'And so we ended up getting rather tiddly together, and do you know what? He's actually a very nice man, is Harry Granger,' Frances had told her, in astonished tones, when Lara first went round there following the trip.

'Who knew?' she replied, trying not to sound sarcastic. 'Does this mean the hedge war is now over? I see it's been trimmed at least.'

'Oh, the hedge,' Frances said airily, waving a hand as if that was the last thing on her mind. 'I did say to him, Harry, if we're going to be pals now, what are we going to do about the hedge? And do you know what he said to me in return?'

'I've got absolutely no idea, Mum,' said Lara, which was entirely true.

'He said – and pardon my language, won't you, but this was him, not me – he said, "Fuck the hedge, Frannie."'

'He didn't!' *Frannie,* Lara marvelled privately. This Harry Granger certainly moved fast.

'And I said, "I would, Harry, but do you know, it's not my type."' To Lara's astonishment, her mother gave a gurgle of laughter. (A gurgle! Lara didn't think she'd ever heard that sound coming from her mother's lips before.) 'Do you get it? Because he said—'

'I get it, Mum. Very good. I bet that made him laugh.'

'It did! We both laughed. We . . . Yes, we laughed a lot, actually. In fact, he asked me out on a date, can you believe?'

'Seriously? Like, a romantic date?' Lara could hardly process what she was hearing. She couldn't remember her mum ever going on a single date before now, in fact.

'Yes! He's taking me to Lazenbys, you know, the French place?'

'Wow. How exciting!' Look at her, wreathed in smiles, the proverbial cat with its bowl full of cream. 'Check you out, Mum. Still got it, hey?'

Since then, Frances and Harry had become something of an item, taking the air together along the prom in the afternoon, and enjoying further dinner dates, as well as Frances's initiation into his poker club (apparently she was bleeding them all dry, her and that impeccable poker face of hers). Lara and Eliza had met Harry by now and thought he was lovely – charming and sweet, but more than a match for spiky Frances – or Frannie, rather, as he called her. Was this going to become the unlikely summer of love for her mother? Who could say, any more?

Eliza, too, had blossomed recently. She'd passed her exams with the grades she needed to study at Edinburgh, and seemed to have grown in confidence over the summer. On warm evenings, when they were both home, she and Lara had taken to lying out on sunloungers, drinking made-up cocktails and telling each other all kinds of interesting things. The story about the hot girl Eliza had slept with in New York, for instance ('I *knew* there was someone!' Lara had cried), as well as what they both jokingly referred to as 'Mum's life lessons', regarding various drunken mistakes Lara had made back when she was a student herself ('If anyone dares you to drink chilli sauce, don't do it, I beg you'). And then one evening, Ben's name came up in conversation and Eliza blindsided Lara with an unexpected observation. 'By the way, did something happen with you and Dad in New York that you're not telling me about, Mum?' she asked. 'Only . . . you seemed to be really happy together one minute and then, after I set you up for dinner that night, it was like you both went back to being a bit polite and sort of pretending to like each other again.' She lifted her sunglasses to peer over at Lara, who felt herself squirm. 'Am I right?'

It took Lara a moment to reply. Had it been that obvious? She'd felt as if she and Ben had dealt with the Oyster Bar revelations pretty well, considering, but as Eliza had so astutely noted, there had been something of a strain between them in the aftermath. 'Well . . .' she began, unsure how much to say. Sod it, she decided, she was done with hiding the truth. This bad habit of hers had caused quite enough trouble for one lifetime. 'We did have a bit of an argument, yes – it was my fault, really. Because, what I hadn't told him was this . . .'

Sighing, she confessed the full story and its repercussions to her daughter. 'But in my defence, over the years, I've always thought of him as the man who checked out of his hostel and left town before we were supposed to meet that evening. The detail of me getting stuck in the office and bursting into the station ninety minutes too late . . . that didn't seem so important compared to what I thought *he'd* done.'

'Oh, Mum,' said Eliza sympathetically.

'I was so convinced that he must be a horrible person, I felt I had to protect you from him rather than try harder to find him.' Lara's voice wobbled as she regretted yet again all of the possible outcomes that had been denied the three of them. If this hadn't happened, if that hadn't happened . . . so much of her life had been built on the misplaced foundations of these moments. 'And of course, sod's law, it turns out that he's actually great, he *had* left me a message, he *did* care – but in spite of that, you and I both missed out on having him in our lives.' She bit her lip, almost too ashamed to look Eliza in the eye. 'I don't know how to forgive myself, if I'm honest.'

Eliza reached over from her sunlounger and took Lara's hand. 'Hey, don't beat yourself up, Mum,' she said. 'I would totally have done the same – I'd have been raging, just like you were, if I thought someone had bailed out on me! You don't need to forgive yourself for anything – you've been a brilliant mum, you've more than made up for him not being around. If anything, I feel sorry for *him*, missing out on having *us* in *his* life.'

There was the biggest lump in Lara's throat at this. Had any compliment ever meant so much to her? Had any words ever sounded so lovely to her ears? For a moment it was as if her heart was being squeezed as tightly as her hand; she could hardly speak for the love she felt spilling out of her for this wonderful girl who had landed on the most perfect words to say, right when she most needed to hear them. 'Thank you, darling,' she said, trying to recover herself only to fail almost immediately by choking on a sob. 'Gosh, what am I going to do without you?'

Eliza snorted. 'Well, I expect a full year of pining, for starters,' she said, then raised an eyebrow. 'But seriously, you should make a vow to stop all this self-flagellation and regret, you know. Life's too short! Besides, you're about to be free and childless for the first time in years. Stuff the regrets, you'll soon be able to do absolutely anything you want to when I'm not cramping your style. Go wild!'

Eliza was exaggerating, Lara knew, but all the same she felt she had to refute some of this. 'I'm not about to be "childless" just because you're starting university,' she pointed out. The cocktail she was drinking was perhaps stronger than she'd thought because in the next moment, sentiment took over her. 'You'll always be my girl – who, by the way, has never once cramped my style. Quite the opposite. You've added so much to my life. So much!'

Clearly this was all getting far too mushy for Eliza's liking,

333

going by her grimace. 'Okay, that's quite enough of that,' she said, letting go of Lara's hand to pick up her drink and knock back the remaining contents. Then she held the empty glass in the air with a hopeful expression. 'Although while you've still got me, you could show your appreciation by ... mixing me another of these?'

Lara laughed but got up obediently, feeling lighter, as if Eliza had unwittingly erased a layer of the guilt she had been carrying around for so long. *Hey, don't beat yourself up, Mum! I would totally have done the same.* They were alike in so many ways – hot-headed and impulsive and probably a bit too punchy for their own good. It meant a huge amount to Lara that Eliza recognised this – and had sided with her, no less. Even more humbling was that she had called Lara a brilliant mum. Goodness – the two of them had been on such a journey to reach this point! Especially as the current phase of their relationship was now drawing to a close; the pale golden dawn of a new future already glimmering on the horizon. But that was okay, she had realised. Change happened, people grew up, beloved daughters went to university and left home. The thing she'd also come to realise was that mums could change too. That she was actually quite good at making things happen for herself again. That life wasn't over just yet.

'It's all one relentless learning curve, isn't it?' Judy, her oldest student, had said to her earlier in the summer, having recently heard that her son-in-law had been diagnosed with multiple sclerosis. 'Life surprises us, sometimes harder and more shockingly than we'd like it to. We can cry and get angry, or we can make the best of things. Love each other. Be grateful for what we have and keep trying. And take our chances wherever we find them.'

Her words had resonated with Lara. Yes, accidents happened. Lives collided. Cells mutated. A person's whole world could change in the blink of an eye – a house collapsing, a sinkhole, a smiling man catching your eye in a bar. Fighting dogs could lead to conversation – and babies. A child could topple from a moving pushchair into the road or choke on a grape. Blood clots moved silently, fatally through a person's body. Beautiful old apple trees grew from single tiny pips. It was ridiculous, when you thought about it, how random everyone's existences were – all those tiny links and connections that were forged anew every single hour, every single day. What was it that glued them all together, that kept people getting out of bed each morning? Love was what it came down to, she had figured. Love and resilience and the curiosity of wondering what might happen next.

She *was* grateful though, like Judy had told her to be. Grateful for Eliza and her mum and her friends. Grateful too for Ben, and that they'd had a second chance to get to know each other again. When they had said goodbye at the airport, they'd hugged one another, so close she could catch his soap and coffee smell once more. They'd managed a cheerful goodbye, with Eliza insisting on taking a selfie of them all wearing the hideous matching baseball caps Lara had bought as souvenirs. *We make a good team*, he had written later on their three-way WhatsApp group chat when Eliza posted the photo there. For a moment, Lara thought he meant the two of them, romantically, and her heart had leapt, but of course he'd meant as a family. Which was fine too, of course. Completely and utterly fine.

Besides, Eliza had a point in reminding Lara of her impending freedom. *Stuff the regrets, you'll be able to do absolutely anything you want to! Go wild!* Lara wasn't sure exactly how 'wild' she would go once Eliza was studying in Edinburgh, but all the same, it was a liberating thought. Exciting, even …

Chapter Thirty-One

Ben had always had it drummed into him by his parents: do the right thing. Not the easy thing, necessarily, perhaps not the most exciting thing either, but the right one. 'If you ever feel yourself wavering,' his dad had said, 'pay attention to your conscience. Ask yourself if you'll be proud of your actions in ten years' time.'

Tonight he was going to do the right thing. He was meeting Kirsten for a long-awaited drink and a chat in The Empress, the pub that had once been their local back when they'd rented their first flat together just off Mill Road. 'For old time's sake,' he'd said, suggesting the venue, but now that he was pushing open the door, he found himself assaulted by a whole wave of memories, and wondered if he should have picked a place with less emotional attachment. Because the last time they'd had an evening here must have been fourteen or fifteen years ago, he worked out: when they were newly married, young and happy. It felt as if he was a different man now, as if a wide chasm had ruptured between the present and the past.

This *was* the right thing to do, wasn't it? he asked himself for the hundredth time as he walked up to the bar, casting an eye around for Kirsten. He had made those vows to her when they got married, and he had meant them. He couldn't walk away without trying to work out their differences; he owed her that much. *But,* a little voice in his head piped up, *don't you owe it to yourself to be happy, too? Which is more important?*

He gritted his teeth, wishing the little voice in his head would sod off. It was not exactly helping matters. There was no sign of Kirsten, so he ordered a pint of bitter and found a corner table, sitting down heavily, aware of the tension in his body. If this was the right thing to do, then why wasn't he feeling more buoyant, more positive? He felt instead like a condemned man, awaiting sentence.

The situation might have seemed less complicated, he thought, if he hadn't just spent such a great time with Lara and Eliza the month before, even with all the emotion and regret the trip had stirred up. He'd have felt clearer-sighted, less muddled. Because the following week, when Eliza and Lara video-called to tell him the jubilant news that Eliza had received the grades she'd hoped for in her exams, and had got into Edinburgh University, all he could think about was how much he wished he could be with them at that moment, to celebrate together. Lara had called separately a week later with details of Eliza's accommodation and moving date, before asking, tentatively, if he wanted to come up, so they could drop her off together. It was no exaggeration to say that he'd felt undiluted joy at the thought, that he couldn't wait to see them both again. He was due to fly up to Edinburgh in just over a week's time and felt a renewed rush of happiness whenever the thought crossed his mind. Was it soppy to confess that he'd missed them both since their New York adventure? Well, he had. And deep down he had the distinct feeling that perhaps he'd missed them a little too much, considering he was meant to be trying really hard to save his marriage.

'You've got to do what feels right for *you*,' Charlotte had said to him when he'd dropped in on her the night before. He'd gone over there ostensibly to lend her his wallpaper steamer, but he'd ended up staying for a chat and pouring out his dilemma. Ever since he'd laid the law down with his sisters over the business of the missed phone calls, they had all been much less demanding, he'd noticed – and, as a bonus, more solicitous too, as to how *he* was feeling, if *he* needed anything. They and his mum had been wonderful about welcoming Eliza into the family with open arms – making a huge effort to include her in everything, individually texting her and sending her little gifts when they heard about her exam results and (of course) falling over themselves to recount all sorts of dreadful stories about his youth to her. He wasn't sure who'd enjoyed the latter most, but it was certainly a bonding experience for niece, aunts and grandmother alike, cackling over Ben's bad haircuts and misdemeanours, with photographic evidence keenly proffered whenever possible. Aside from these incrimination attempts, Charlotte, in particular, had proved brilliant to talk to throughout the whole saga: wise, non-judgemental and always willing to listen.

As he was about to leave that evening, she'd hovered on the doorstep as if reluctant to let him go. 'Listen, I know you're the most loyal person in the world,' she'd said. 'But Ben, promise me you won't sacrifice your own happiness by leaving yourself out of the equation. People do grow apart in marriages, and it's often not anyone's fault – just life. If you think you'd be happier with Lara, then—'

Ben had been startled. Where was this coming from? 'I didn't even *say* anything about Lara,' he'd protested. 'Not like that anyway.'

'You didn't have to,' she said, leaning against the door jamb. 'It's written all over your face whenever you've spoken about being in New York with her. You haven't looked so animated in years, Ben. You like her, don't you?'

He'd felt hot around the collar, even though the evening was the first cool, properly autumnal one of the year. 'Well, yes, but . . .'

'So then don't go making any offers to Kirsten that you might regret,' she said. 'Think of it this way – you've got years left to live, hopefully. Decades. Who would you rather spend the rest of your life with, Kirsten or Lara?'

'I . . . I . . .' he stuttered, mind churning. 'Charlotte, no, it's not as simple as that.'

'Isn't it?'

'No! Lara likes someone else anyway. Some hunky swimmer she's met. Me and her – it's not on the cards,' he said, suddenly feeling a burst of dislike for the bloke she had mentioned. He couldn't even remember what she'd said about him now but his imagination was unhelpfully conjuring up a muscled god of a bloke with a six-pack and biceps like boulders. The sort of brainless lunk who challenged other men at arm-wrestling only to practically dislocate their opponent's shoulder with a single powerful slam.

'Whatever you say, Ben,' Charlotte had replied, eyebrow arched before finally letting him off the hook and saying goodnight, leaving him to frown all the way home.

Yeah, well, he thought now. Charlotte could think what she liked but 'simple' was not a word that could be applied to this particular situation. Lara had made it clear she wasn't interested, even suggesting how he might rekindle the flame with Kirsten, but should he be embarking on a reconciliation with Kirsten at all, if he was floundering amidst such uncertain feelings? What was he going to do?

'Hi,' he heard just then and looked up to see her there beside him, looking tired but pretty in a flowered shirt and dark jeans, her blonde hair loose around her shoulders. 'Are you all right for a drink?'

'I'm fine, thanks,' he said, trying to read her expression. Nope. Impossible. He found himself disloyally thinking of Lara's open face, how he'd come to know vividly from those few days in New York if she was happy or sad, annoyed or tired, from a single glance. He'd seen her looking awkward and furtive too, as she'd made her confession to him in the Oyster Bar – and yes, he'd felt annoyed with her at the time for misleading him for so long. But then, out of the blue last week, a parcel had arrived with a Scarborough postmark, and he'd opened it and burst out laughing on finding a neon pink Statue of Liberty souvenir that she must have ordered specially. *Better late than never*, she'd written in a card. *Can you forgive me for being a twat?* Although tonight was about Kirsten, not Lara, he reminded himself, smiling quickly at his wife before she headed to the bar.

'So,' he began when she returned. 'Thanks for coming. I thought it would be good to talk about what we both want, going forward.' He stopped, wishing he hadn't said 'going forward' as if he were some kind of management consultant, then hurried on before he lost momentum. 'You know how I feel – that I'd like to give our marriage another try.' *Like to? Or feel obliged to?* asked the annoying little voice in his head. 'But if you don't want to, then I won't keep badgering you,' he went on. 'Because I know – or rather, I hear – you've been seeing someone else, so ...'

340

She flinched and it was all the confirmation he needed. His voice shook because, despite everything, the thought of it upset him. 'So you might already have moved on from me,' he continued, trying to sound as if he was cool about the idea. 'In which case, you know, that's ... understandable. I get it.'

She sipped her red wine before replying and his agitation grew. 'I was seeing someone else,' she said quietly, not quite meeting his eye. 'But it's over now. It was nothing significant.'

'Okay,' he said, allowing her words to settle. So if that relationship was over, then ... ? 'And how do you feel now?' he ventured after a short, uneasy silence. 'About me. About us. Is there any future, do you think?'

She gazed at him full in the face, looking troubled. 'Oh Ben,' she said sorrowfully, and his heart twisted because even now, he only wanted her to be happy. 'I wish I could give you a confident yes, about us because I still think you're a wonderful human being. And what I'm going to say has got nothing to do with you having a daughter or ... any of that stuff.' She put her hand on his, her long fingers cool and soft. 'But I feel as if we've sort of reached the end of the road. Of our road, as a couple, I mean. Don't you? I've done a lot of thinking and wonder if maybe I need a new start, somewhere different. My parents are getting older and I'd like to see them more often so ...'

'You're going to move away?' he asked, startled. He hadn't expected Kirsten to fall straight back into his arms, when she'd so far resisted his attempts to win her over, but he hadn't anticipated her thoughts being quite so unambivalent. So *final*-sounding.

'My lease on the flat is up in six weeks,' she said. 'I'm going to think about it a bit more, but yes, my gut feeling is that a move would be the right thing. Someplace near my parents, away from Cambridge. Mark myself a new dot on the map.' She gave him a small smile that didn't make it all the way to her eyes. 'It seems as good a time as any.'

He breathed out slowly, trying to take this in, hardly able to imagine Cambridge – and his life – without Kirsten there. 'God,' he said, passing a hand through his hair. 'Well ... good for you, I suppose,' he managed to say. My marriage seems to be over, he thought dazedly, his heart thumping. My wife – my ex-wife – is leaving town, and me in the process. It's really and truly over. The possibility had been there all along but now that she was making it real, he felt poleaxed.

And yet ... as the words began to sink in, he felt a simulta-neous lack of surprise. A year ago, he'd have been devastated to be having this conversation, completely unmoored with shock. But there was a part of him that knew, deep down, that she had analysed the situation correctly. In fact, if anything, she'd had the courage to set them both free. 'I think you're right,' he said, his voice thick with feeling. This was all happening so quickly – and it all felt so huge. 'I've been hoping this whole time that there might still be a chance but ...'

'I'm sorry,' she said, when he broke off. 'I did love being married to you for a long time, Ben. You know that, don't you? You're such a good person. A wonderful husband. I really loved you, with all my heart, for years and years and years. I'm just ...' Her lip wobbled. 'I'm sorry I couldn't give you what you wanted. I'm sorry we didn't have a child together.'

His throat was tight. His heart cracked at the vulnerability in her eyes. She had always been the strong one throughout their fertility trials while he'd been the person who fell apart. Maybe that hadn't been entirely due to her staunchness, he thought now, but a coping mechanism in its own right. 'But you *did* give me what I wanted,' he told her, desperate to offer comfort. 'You were there for me when I needed you after Dad died, during the hardest year of my entire life. And we're okay now, aren't we? We got by.'

She nodded without speaking, lips pressed tight together. He tried again. 'Kirsten, you don't have to apologise for anything. None of it. This wasn't about you giving me a child, or not. You gave so much of yourself to the *idea* of us being parents; you were the one who had to undergo all of the gruelling IVF stuff. It was horrific for you sometimes, I know. And you did that – for me, and for us – to try to make everything good for us. So thank you. Thank you for doing that.' He wiped his eyes with the back of his hand, emotion getting the better of him. 'Sorry. This all feels so ... so big. And so sad.' He tried to pull himself together. 'But I've got no regrets, whatsoever, about our marriage. And we'll still be friends, won't we? We can still keep in touch?'

'Of course we will,' she replied. Her voice was gentler than he remembered it being for months, as if sorrow had softened her hard edges. 'We'll always keep in touch.'

A raucous round of 'Happy Birthday' started up from a table across the room and Ben and Kirsten smiled ruefully at one another, silently acknowledging the clash in different atmospheres. His thoughts whirled as he tried to orient himself within this strange new no-man's-land of being officially single for the first time in nearly two decades. He had set out this evening wanting to do the right thing in terms of their relationship – and yet in a strange sort of way, maybe Kirsten had pre-empted him with the *real* right thing for them both. The bravest thing of all.

They finished their drinks but there didn't seem to be much

else to say other than practical matters: what they should do with the house (would he have to buy her out?) and furniture, closing down their joint bank account and wading through paperwork; the mundane unpicking of two lives that had been tightly woven together. And then that was it, the evening over as well as their marriage. He walked her to her car, his head swimming with everything. My life is falling apart, he kept thinking. My wife doesn't love me any more.

His heart was still racing as they said goodbye and parted ways and then, as he headed back to where he'd chained up his bike, he suddenly felt a crushing sensation inside his chest. It was hard to breathe. He leaned against a wall to steady himself, gulping for air, but he couldn't drag enough oxygen into his lungs. He clutched at his heart, black spots dancing before his eyes. Oh God. This was really happening. He thought about the palpitations he'd been having, the occasional breathlessness. He remembered Eliza asking him about heart disease within the family. All the warning signs had been there and yet—

'Ben! Are you all right?' Kirsten had caught up with him, her car window lowered as she peered out. 'Ben?'

He couldn't answer. He couldn't breathe. His phone started ringing in his jacket pocket but his limbs wouldn't move to retrieve it. The world before him was breaking up into a mosaic of images, memories, blizzarding in his vision. Sitting cross-legged on the shiny floor of his primary school hall, a scab on one bare knee. His sister Sophie being born and him poking her resentfully through the bars of the cot when nobody else was looking. A hot day in Kelvingrove Park, a can of Tennent's in his hand. A peanut flying through the air into a beautiful young woman's mouth. A white carnation buttonhole against a charcoal grey jacket. Eliza's shy smile as she gave him his Great Dad badge. And a glossy brown apple pip, shaped like a teardrop, on the end of a finger before being pushed down into warm, summer-baked earth.

He was choking. He was gasping for air. What an irony that he was going to die just like his dad, when he of all people should have known that the human heart could be so fallible. That life could change in a single moment. Why had he assumed he'd be protected from the swoops and falls of fortune?

The street swam before him, the streetlights becoming soft, blurring yellow balls of light as his body crumpled and fell to the ground. Kirsten was there to catch him just in time, and he had a moment of regret for everything that he was going to lose, everything he hadn't done. He tried to say sorry, he wanted to say goodbye, but it was too late because then the lights flickered out in his head, and he was gone.

Chapter Thirty-Two

Lara was on the beach, her hair wet, a plastic cup of wine in hand, buzzing with the glow that followed an energetic swim in the cool September sea, along with the sugar rush of her post-exercise brownie. She felt *great*, she marvelled; maybe even confident enough to ask Ollie if he wanted to go for a drink sometime. Didn't she owe it to herself to take the plunge in more ways than one?

Judy had said to her the other day that people should seize a moment whenever one presented itself, and Lara agreed. You could hang around for ever hoping someone would take a chance on you – or you could switch roles, take a deep breath and do something about it yourself. The strange thing was, this feeling had been dawning on her the whole summer: that she *was* worthy of love, that she *did* have love to give. That maybe, like her mother, she wasn't done with romance quite yet after all.

But it wasn't until she had taken another emboldening glug of wine and began walking towards Ollie that she realised, with a sudden start, that the word 'romance' did not instinctively conjure up images of Ollie's face, the two of them holding hands or kissing. Instead, it brought to mind laughing with Ben in Central Park; the ache of longing she'd felt as they'd discussed their parallel lives together in the Oyster Bar; him wearing his so-called favourite shirt and smiling into her eyes. How comfortable she'd felt with him that first morning together in her tiny apartment, the way he had kissed her bare shoulder and she'd seemed to melt inside. And actually, now that she stopped to think, it was *Ben* who had caused her to feel worthy of love again, Ben who'd reminded her she had value. It had been Ben all along. She remembered how she'd laughed at the photo he'd texted her, of the horrible Statue of Liberty souvenir in pride of place on his (otherwise extremely tasteful) mantelpiece, how the knowledge that he'd forgiven her had brought an overwhelming sense of relief. It hit her then like a lightning bolt, as if the truth had been under her nose the whole time: that of *course* she was still in love with him. What was she thinking, going to chat up Ollie, when it was Ben she had the truest feelings for? She loved *Ben*!

Standing there on the sand, reeling with her own discovery, she tipped the rest of her drink down her throat then made a snap decision: she was going to tell him. It was the only possible thing to do. On the off-chance that he might feel the same way, she was just going to tell him, get it out there. Why not? Life was short, as Eliza had said the other evening – and Lara and Ben had wasted so much time already. She felt the strong urge to let him know exactly how she felt, and to hell with the consequences. Now! She couldn't wait another minute!

Before she could change her mind, she dialled his number, phrases jumbling excitedly in her head. *Hello, guess what, I've always loved you.* No, that was ridiculous, she thought, as his phone started ringing. Way too much. *Hi, this might be a bit sudden but I'm mad about you. Always have been. Should have trusted my instincts from the start.* His phone was still ringing, which was lucky, frankly, because this line sounded even madder than the first. She would just have to improvise when he answered. Go with the flow. *If* he answered, that was. Why wasn't he answering? Come on, Ben, pick up before I lose my bottle, she thought, agonised. But then the call went to voicemail and her boldness promptly evaporated. She might be something of a loose cannon, full of feelings (and wine), but even Lara drew the line at making impulsive declarations of love into someone's voicemail service.

The anti-climax was almost enough to make her laugh – because wasn't that typical of their luck so far? Missed chance after missed chance – and here was yet another hurdle in their way with his bloody voicemail message! She shook her head in frustration, adrenalin slowly draining away. Maybe it was a sign that she shouldn't rush headlong into this particular conversation. She'd probably only have regretted such rashness tomorrow anyway. She was due to see him next week in Edinburgh and it could have been *really* awkward. Perhaps she should wait and see how things were when they met again, gauge the vibe and *then* make her declaration. It was surely better to throw yourself at a person when with them, anyway, so that you could start kissing them immediately if they felt the same way. Or, of course, if it all went wrong, she'd be able to blame it on the emotion of the occasion, she figured, and run off to drown her sorrows in the nearest whisky bar.

'Everything all right?' Heidi asked just then. 'You've got a weird look on your face. Come and try one of Jane's blondies, they're amazing.'

Lara put Ben out of her mind as best as possible for the rest of the evening but the awareness of her newly acknowledged feelings for him continued to pulse beneath the surface of everything she said, everything she did. Even through the extreme delight of Jane's amazing blondies. *I do love him. I miss him. I just want to be with him. Is it too late for us to be together? We got on so well in New York. He made me feel so happy. I love the way he laughs. Should I have tried to kiss him after all?*

'Are you sure you're okay?' Heidi asked again, frowning at her. 'You seem quiet all of a sudden. Worrying about Eliza going to uni next week?'

'Something like that,' Lara mumbled, avoiding eye contact. The revelation she'd experienced seemed too precious, too pure to drop into casual conversation on a beach; she needed to speak to Ben first before she told another person about her feelings. Oh, what the hell, forget waiting for Edinburgh, it was impossible to be restrained when she felt this way. She'd try him again, she decided impulsively, because she couldn't concentrate on a single other thing right now. 'Just going to make a quick call,' she added, walking a safe distance away and hitting redial.

This time – thank goodness! – she got through after a couple of rings. 'Hi!' she said joyfully, breaking into a smile at the prospect of hearing his voice. I love you, she thought with giddy hysteria. Guess what? I love you!

'Lara? This is Kirsten,' she heard to her surprise, though. 'Um. Hi. Ben's actually ... I'm at the hospital with him.'

'Oh my God,' Lara said, her breath catching in her throat. He's dead, she thought with sudden conviction. I'm too late and he's dead. Why hadn't she acted sooner while she still had the chance? Why hadn't she launched herself at him in New York as she'd wanted to? 'What's happened? Is he ... ?' She could hardly ask the question because she was so sure she already knew the answer. 'Is he all right?'

'He's having some tests,' Kirsten said. 'We were out at the pub and he collapsed. He's been having some palpitations, apparently, and—'

Lara had tears in her eyes. No, she thought. No, not another heart attack ruining everything. I refuse to let this happen again! 'Oh God,' she gulped a second time.

'. . . And so he's being checked out,' Kirsten went on as Lara clutched her own heart in turmoil. 'Hold on, he's saying something.' Her voice became indistinct as if she'd moved her phone away. 'Yes, it's Lara. What? Seriously?' Lara heard. Then Kirsten was back. 'Um . . . he said to tell you he's "not dead",' she said. 'Which is kind of blunt, if you ask me, not to mention melo-dramatic, but—'

Lara didn't know whether to laugh or cry. 'Tell him that's not funny,' she said, a sob in her throat. *Not dead*. She had never been so glad to hear a stupid joke in her life. 'That's not funny at all.'

He phoned her himself the next morning, during a break in her lesson schedule. He'd stayed in hospital overnight for obser-vation, but assured her that he was fine and that, following an ECG and a series of blood tests, the doctors didn't think there was anything seriously wrong with his heart. 'They put the pal-pitations down to stress,' he explained. 'And my blood pressure's on the high side, apparently. It's been a bit of a year, I suppose. "Just a massive panic attack" one of the consultants said, but there was no "just" about it at the time, it was horrible. I thought I was dying. My life flashed before my eyes and everything.'

'Oh Ben,' Lara said, feeling sick at the thought. What a relief it was to hear him sounding so normal though. 'When Kirsten said last night you were at the hospital, I had this awful feeling that ... well, that the worst had happened. You scared me.'

'I'm fine, honestly,' he told her. 'Hopefully I can go home soon; I need to hang on for the all-clear from the docs but then I can get out of here. My sister Annie's going to pick me up.'

'Well, please look after yourself,' she replied, still too worked up to be reassured that easily. 'You're important to us. To me.' And then, just as she was on the verge of blurting out her feelings to him, something occurred to her. Something that she would have registered sooner, had she not been so worried. *We were out at the pub*, Kirsten had said to her yesterday. Should Lara be reading anything into this? 'Um. So ... you and Kirsten were out together last night?' she asked tentatively.

'Yeah, we went to the pub. We had a really good talk for the first time in ages, actually. Sorted everything out,' he said, which took the wind right out of her sails.

'Oh,' she said, immediately swallowing back whatever spontaneous declaration she might have made. 'Great,' she managed to squeak, her throat completely dry.

'She was brilliant last night, too. Thank God she was there. It feels like everything's going to be okay now,' he said, before adding, 'Ah, the doctor's here. I'd better go. Talk to you soon, yeah?'

'Yeah,' she said heavily. 'Talk to you soon.' *Oh. Right.* So she had missed her chance again. That was that, then. End of. It was lucky she had a driving lesson to get to in ten minutes otherwise she might have sat with her head against the steering wheel and cried her eyes out. Instead, she took a deep breath, started the engine and drove off. At least she hadn't made a fool of herself, she thought grimly. At least she still had her dignity, if nothing else.

★

A week later, and there was a whole new drama to keep her occupied: the journey up to Edinburgh where Eliza's university life awaited her. Lara was still struggling to come to terms with the fact that this was really happening: that her daughter's bedroom back at home was now empty and stripped of its posters, clothes, make-up and shoes. That the world had turned once more and nothing would be the same again. Life was coming at her hard and fast this week, that was for sure. Ben was flying up from London and meeting them there, and she had just about got over the tumult of feelings she'd weathered since that night on the beach and his hospital experience. She'd learned a valuable lesson though: from now on, she would keep her cool and keep her distance. No more wearing her heart on her sleeve.

Eliza had been allocated a room in a shared flat in a modern, purpose-built block not far from Holyrood Abbey, and they arrived to find the place swarming with nervous-looking students and their parents. Well − Lara had initially assumed they were parents anyway, but if this year had taught her anything, it was that families came in all shapes and sizes and that presuming anything about other people's lives was a mistake. Just look at the three of them, for instance. Nobody would guess their particular story, on seeing them − and no doubt there were other unusual set-ups here today too. She thought of Ollie, due to take Jake to Bangor University the following weekend alone. She thought of Judy, who had recently passed her driving test, and was now able to pop easily between her house and her daughter's in Pickering, to step in for granny duty while her son-in-law received treatment. And she thought too of Romilly, the quiet, thoughtful twenty-year-old who had passed out at the wheel of Lara's car two years ago, weak and starving, in the grip of an eating disorder. Lara had been delighted when Romilly had recently started lessons again, having made a good recovery: her skin clear, hair shiny, a new determination visible in her body language. And yet the bad times left their scars – you could still see the watchfulness in her mum's expression as she waved her daughter goodbye at the start of each lesson. But this was Lara's point really: every family had their share of happiness and agony, their wounds and their blessings. The perfect family simply did not exist. Amen, sister, she thought wryly, as she spotted Ben, the third member of their own unconventional set-up, across the car park, and waved.

Despite her intentions of composure, Lara couldn't stop herself from running over and hugging him, so relieved was she to see him striding towards them from the cab, looking completely healthy and well. 'Are you all right? Still feeling okay?' she asked in concern, withdrawing and giving him a searching look. 'Please don't feel you have to carry in any of Eliza's boxes if it's going to be too much for you, by the way.'

'Hello to you too,' he said, sounding amused. 'And there's no need to give me that face – I've been getting it all week from my sisters and mum, fussing about me, expecting me to collapse on the spot again. I'm fine, okay? Solid as a rock. Boxes, schmoxes. Hi, darling,' he said, as Eliza joined them. 'All set?'

Once they'd picked up her key from the accommodation office and Eliza had signed various documents, they each lugged a box up to her new bedroom: a bland, magnolia-painted rectangle with a desk, chair and bed. 'Home, sweet home,' Ben joked as they stood there in the echoing empty space. Lara was glad for him all over again then – admittedly partly because Eliza had brought a *lot* of stuff with her that would have to be carted in, but also because his calm, affable presence was so effective in quieting the emotional maelstrom within her.

'Let's make it homely,' she was able to say in a cheering way. 'Do you want to make a start unpacking, Lize? Your dad and I will bring up the rest of your stuff.'

It was so strange, being in this place that was to become Eliza's new home. To make up the bed for her, and help her hang clothes in the small, cheap-looking wardrobe, and to loiter at a tactful distance while Eliza met her first couple of flatmates in the shared kitchen and they introduced themselves. Within a few weeks – days, probably, hours even – these flatmates would become friends, confidantes, drinking buddies; they'd have danced together in sweaty freshers club nights, explored the university buildings and tracked down lecture halls in their small, wide-eyed pack. They'd have cooked terrible first meals and, if Eliza was anything to go by, completely forgotten to wash up afterwards. Lucky them, to be young and carefree, with so many adventures and discoveries awaiting them.

Despite the constant sensation that time was running between her fingers as the deadline of separation approached, Lara kept her brave face pretty well fixed in place. Friendly smiles to the other parents but no embarrassing attempts at conversation, as she'd promised Eliza. Absolutely no tears or dramatic emotional displays. But soon afterwards, when she and Ben took Eliza for a late lunch in a nearby café, Lara realised that she was sitting there looking at the menu without being able to decipher a single word. And then it came rearing up inside her: a huge, engulfing sadness that something was unmistakably over. That her little girl – now a smart, confident young woman – had flown the nest and that everything was about to change for ever.

'Mum? Do you know what you want to eat yet?' Eliza asked, and Lara's response was to drop the menu, put her face in her hands and burst into floods of tears. 'Oh, Mum!'

So much for not being an embarrassment. It took several minutes and a whole handful of napkins before Lara was able to control her sobs long enough to apologise for the spectacle she was making of herself. 'Don't worry,' Eliza said, with all the wisdom of someone who had their own new address and door key, 'we fully expected you to have a meltdown. In fact, we both thought you would have gone way earlier than this. I was starting to think there was something wrong with your tear ducts.'

'Don't make us call security on your ass,' warned Ben.

Not sure whether to laugh or keep crying, Lara excused herself from the table, sorted out her splotchy mascara in the loos and gave herself a stern pep talk. Come on. Eliza's big day. Don't make it harder for her by weeping through it.

She managed to pull herself together, admittedly helped by the woman who came into the loos just then and commented admiringly on the gorgeous shirt dress Lara was wearing that day, black with a golden palm-leaf print, which always made her feel a million dollars. Back at the table, they enjoyed a jolly lunch, with Ben producing a beautifully wrapped bracelet for Eliza at the end of it, as well as one of his map prints he'd made specially for her, with Edinburgh, Scarborough and Cambridge picked out in teal, indigo and scarlet. That almost set Lara off again but she dug her fingernails into her palms, gritted her teeth and breathed deeply until the feeling passed. (*Well done, Lara. Amazing work.*)

At last, despite having dragged out lunch as long as possible, it was time to say goodbye. Newly independent Eliza didn't want them to walk her back to her accommodation block so they hugged each other at the end of the road. They were all due to go their separate ways soon afterwards: Lara was staying in a city centre hotel that night (she'd had the foresight to predict she'd be too overwrought and shattered to face the four-and-a-half-hour drive home), while Ben was booked on an evening flight down to London. As the three of them embraced in a small emotional human triangle on the corner of the street, it took all Lara's resolve not to burst out in torrents of weeping again.

'Take care, lovely,' she said instead, with a gulp. 'I'll ring you tomorrow to find out how it's going, okay? I'm going to miss you so much, darling. But I love you and I'm so proud of you and I know you're about to have the most brilliant time here.'

'Let us know if you need anything, won't you?' Ben added. 'Anything at all, day or night. We've got your back.'

'Thanks,' Eliza said, looking rather choked herself now that they'd arrived at this point. 'Send me loads of photos of Bruce, won't you? Every day?'

'Of course I will,' said Lara, making a mental note to remind her mum that she was meant to be feeding the cat in her absence. If Frances could tear herself away from Harry long enough, that was.

Talking of tearing oneself away . . . 'Right,' Lara went on, aware that if she didn't forcibly separate herself from her girl soon, she was in serious danger of never letting go. 'Love you. Have a fab first night and look after yourself. You're very precious to me.'

'All right, all right,' Eliza said. Now she was rolling her eyes and they were back on familiar territory. 'Talk to you soon. Bye, Mum. Bye, Dad.' And then she was walking away, backwards at first so that she could wave and blow kisses to them but then pivoting smartly on one foot, one hand in the air, and no longer looking back.

356

Lara stood there for a moment, feeling as if all of the breath had crashed out of her body before Ben put a comforting hand on her arm. 'She seemed really happy, didn't she?' he said.

'I know,' Lara croaked, taking refuge in the thought. It was true that in recent weeks, she'd noticed her daughter walking a little taller, appearing more at ease with herself, as if she'd got the world sussed. She swallowed hard, trying to buck herself up, then gestured at the nearest coffee bar, suggesting that they go for a quick drink before Ben had to head out to the airport. Anything to delay the moment when she'd be alone in a hotel room and bawling into the pillow, she figured.

'Coffee? We can do better than that,' Ben replied. 'Come on! This is a big day. Let's have a proper drink. Something celebratory, somewhere posh. Don't you think? I'm not in any rush to sit around at Edinburgh Airport for hours on end.'

As if the city had gifted it to them, they went on to find the perfect place: a sedate old wine bar near the station, with dark purple walls and soft lighting, and comfortable, tweed-covered armchairs arranged in intimate clusters. Lara hadn't realised quite how on edge she had been until they walked in and she heard the low melodic tone of Nina Simone from the speakers; it was only then that she felt her pulse slow to a normal rate for the first time all day. 'Oh yes,' she said gratefully. 'This was a very good idea. If ever I needed a drink . . .'

'Agreed,' he said, eyeing the wine list. 'Do you know what? I'm thinking today calls for champagne. Is that disgustingly extravagant for three o'clock in the afternoon?'

Lara smiled, because this was an infinitely more uplifting suggestion than the melancholy coffee she had originally anticipated. 'Yes, it *is* disgustingly extravagant – especially at that price,' she replied, 'but what the hell, I'm with you. It's not every day your only child leaves home. Let's extravagance ourselves silly.'

Leaning back in her chair now while Ben waited at the bar, she watched through the window as a train pulled out of the station, thinking about all the comings and goings that occurred to and from a busy city like this. All the new arrivals pouring in today, so many different narratives that would bed into the place, twisting together and apart in random patterns; Eliza just one of them, a single cog in the elaborate, complex machinery that was Edinburgh life. This would become her city in time: her story bound in with these historic old streets winding up to the castle, the blackened sandstone buildings with their gothic spires, rows of squat chimney pots and leaded windows. She would learn to recognise the secret passages and doorways, dance under spinning glitter balls in basement nightclubs, discover favourite new pubs and the best place for a hangover fry-up; she'd take oh-so many windswept selfies up on Arthur's Seat . . .

'Cheers,' Ben said at that moment, having reappeared with two glasses of brimming fizz. 'So how are you anyway? How's everything been since New York?'

'Cheers,' Lara replied, clinking her glass against his. It took her a second to redirect her attention inwards for a change, having focussed it thus far into one intense Eliza-beamed spotlight. 'Well,' she began, considering the question as she took a sip. Delicious. 'Quite good, actually. And a lot better now I'm here, with this in my hand, too.'

She started telling him about her meeting with the *Our Yorkshire* features editor a few weeks ago, and how she'd successfully pitched an idea about Yorkshire artists and craftspeople.

'Wow!' he cried, on hearing that her subsequent piece about

358

the stained-glass artist from Ripon had been accepted, along with a request for two further follow-ups. 'Woohoo, Lara! That's brilliant.'

She laughed to see him cheering out loud in this sedate wine bar, giving an air-punch for good measure. His obvious pleasure for her made her feel so good. When was the last time anyone had *cheered* for her with such unbridled enthusiasm?

'I'd have ordered a bottle if I'd known there would be so much celebrating for us to do,' he added, looking at his half-empty glass. 'This is going down far too easily. What do you say, shall we make an afternoon of it?'

'Definitely! I'd love that,' she replied, her mood having swung the pendulum from grief to exuberance with what seemed like indecent haste. 'Although ... are you meant to be keeping an eye on your booze intake or anything, after your hospital visit? And what time is your flight?'

'Not till seven,' he said, checking his watch. 'And the booze thing is fine. Honestly, Lara, I'm really okay. Bit of a scare at the time but I'm glad to have been checked out. And to be "not dead".'

Lara gave him an exasperated look. 'Seriously, Ben, if you're going to start taking catchphrases from my *mother*, as a thing, then I'm not sure we can be friends any more. And also—' She hesitated then ploughed on. 'I meant it when I said you scared me. I don't know what I'd have done if – if things had been worse. I don't think I could bear it, if that was the end of our story.'

He nodded, looking more sober now. 'I know what you mean. Without wanting to sound a total doom-monger, I've had a few dreams where ... well, it's like an alternative reality, where I die on the pavement: my heart stops and my life flashes before my eyes again. All these ... images, the same ones every time. I'm back being a kid at school, and a student in Glasgow, and it's my wedding day.' A funny look crossed his face. 'You're there, throwing a peanut into your mouth and nearly choking to death—'

'That sodding peanut!' she groaned. 'Couldn't your subconscious come up with something more flattering?'

'And Eliza, and ... Look, things could have been a lot worse. But they weren't. And it's *not* the end of our story. And for that reason alone, let me order us a bottle. Because life's good. Also because, sod it, sometimes you have to live in the moment and celebrate that. Right?'

She put up her hands in mock defeat. 'I hear you.'

'Good,' he said, signalling to a passing waiter. 'That's settled, then.'

People probably assumed the two of them were a couple, Lara thought to herself, smiling as she caught the eye of a woman her own age in a stylish magenta wool coat. Tourists, or perhaps visiting for a romantic weekend to celebrate a birthday or anniversary. She glanced back at Ben, who was ordering more champagne, and felt a further rush of affection that they were here together today. She'd already lost him once, nineteen years ago. The last week had brought it home to her that she wasn't ready to lose him again so soon. Even if she had to share him with Kirsten, she could live with that, as long as he was still in her life in some way.

'How about you?' she asked, as the waiter left the table. 'How's work going, are you braced for the Christmas rush?'

He started telling her about the sets of new cards he was having printed, and the calendars he'd designed for the upcoming year,

360

and then he hesitated a moment, looking self-conscious, before adding, 'Now that Kirsten's moving away, we're probably going to sell the house, so it makes sense to clear out all the—'

She had to interrupt because she felt as if she must have missed something crucial. 'Wait, what? You're moving away?' she asked in surprise. 'Where are you going?'

'*Kirsten's* moving,' he replied, which only added to her confusion. 'Somewhere nearer her parents – they're in Northants.' He looked down at the table for a moment then went on. 'Kirsten and I . . . we've split up actually,' he said. 'That was why we were together, the night I had my scare; she'd just dumped me in the pub.'

Lara's mouth fell open. This didn't make sense. 'I thought you said everything was okay? That you'd sorted it all out?'

'Yeah, we did. In a splitting-up way, I meant. Sorry, I obviously wasn't very clear—'

Her heart gave a gigantic thump. 'You *were* still in hospital, I suppose,' she said, trying to ground herself, keep herself in check. 'Gosh. Are you all right? Do you think that's what caused you to collapse?'

'No,' he said quickly. 'Or maybe it was the tipping point, I don't know. I'd been having palpitations every now and then for months beforehand but kept telling myself it was nothing. Anyway, yeah, it's all over. She's applying for jobs in Northants and will live with her parents initially, then we'll put the house on the market, probably in the New Year, so . . .' He spread his hands wide, as if he didn't know how to end the sentence. Maybe it was too painful for him to finish.

'Oh Ben, I'm sorry,' Lara said, feeling awkward.

He paused again, fiddling with his glass to position it carefully in the corner of the table, before raising his gaze to hers once more. 'Well ... that's the strange thing,' he replied. 'Kirsten and I ... we've spent so long apart in the last few months that nothing feels immediately different. And in some ways, you know ...' Another pause. This was clearly really difficult for him, Lara thought sympathetically.

'In some ways,' he went on, 'she was probably right to make the call. I don't know that my reasons for wanting to get back together were necessarily the best ones.'

Lara bit her lip, not certain that she understood what he meant. 'Right,' she said carefully.

'Weirdly, once I'd got used to the idea that our marriage was over, I even felt ... well, liberated, if that doesn't sound too awful,' he confessed. 'I'd been so set on doing the right thing and sticking by her that I hadn't properly considered if that was what I truly wanted.'

'Right,' said Lara again. What *did* he want, then? 'And so, on balance, you're okay?' she asked, gazing at him intently. 'I know it'll take time to get over a relationship like that, of course, but ...'

'I'm okay,' he confirmed. 'I'm actually surprisingly okay, yeah. It's sad but it's not terrible. I think we can both be amicable and move on.' He smiled at her. 'Really – stop looking so worried, Lara. I'm fine. These things happen. In hindsight, we'd been more like friends than husband and wife anyway, for a long time. It's hard to see that when you're in the midst of it though.'

She wasn't quite sure what to say because she was trying very hard not to get her hopes up. Trying very hard to squash down a spiral of excitement about what this might mean, eventually, for her. That was selfish, wasn't it? Really selfish. 'Good,' she replied, then could have kicked herself. 'It's good that you're fine, I mean, not good that you've split up,' she amended hastily. She clutched at her face in embarrassment but he was grinning now, topping up their glasses. 'Argh. You know what I mean.'

'I do, don't worry,' he said. 'Thank you. And now it's your turn to be grilled. What happened with that bloke you liked from swimming, then? Have you swept him off his feet yet? Is he now the luckiest man in Scarborough?'

He was teasing, obviously, but all the same, Lara felt a blush spread across her face. She'd forgotten she'd blabbed about Ollie to him, in a misguided fit of bravado the month before. 'Not exactly,' she replied, thinking about that evening on the beach: how everything had fallen startlingly into place. But now, surely, was not the time to be making that sort of announcement to Ben, she reminded herself. Not when she had vowed to keep her cool. 'I sort of changed my mind on that front,' she admitted cagily.

'How come?'

Oh God. Why did he have to ask *that*? 'Well . . .' She stalled, trying to come up with something plausible without revealing her true feelings. 'Because I don't think there's any point in rushing,' she said eventually. 'Do you know what I mean? I don't want to throw myself at the first nice new man I've met, just for the sake of it – there needs to be more than that. Don't you think? I need to feel certain that there's a spark, at the very least.'

'Ah,' he said sagely. 'But how do you know when there's a spark? Genuine question.'

She sipped her drink. 'Well,' she said, as the bubbles fizzed in her mouth. 'I think you just know, don't you?'

They looked at one another and she felt a charge between them. Was he feeling it too? 'I mean,' she went on, with a sudden rush of boldness, 'you must have felt it that night, back when we got together. There was definitely a spark then for me.'

'Oh, me too,' he said. 'A massive spark. Practically a rocket.'

That same look was exchanged, loaded and intense. Lara felt as if her skin was prickling. Perhaps they were both tipsier than they thought. She was a lightweight at the best of times, let alone when it came to drinking in the afternoon. Rein it in, Lara, she ordered herself. Keep that runaway heart in check. 'I'm surprised we weren't both electrocuted,' she joked, trying to lighten the mood, just as he leaned closer and asked, 'Have you ever felt a spark like that since?'

Her mouth closed with a snap.

'Second genuine question,' he said. 'Be honest.'

The intimacy of the moment caught her off guard. Had she? 'Um. Not really,' she admitted. 'Although . . .' She risked a glance at him, wondering how far she should go. He'd said 'be honest' but dared she tell him the full truth? Because now, as in New York, she was aware of the connection that buzzed between them, that pulled her magnetically back towards him once again. But he was reeling from his marriage break-up – and was meant to be curbing his stress levels, besides. He was definitely not in a good place for any kind of emotional scene she might lay on him. The timing was way off, she reminded herself.

Then again though, had their timing ever been perfect? When she thought Ben might be seriously ill, one of her first thoughts was how much she'd regretted not kissing him in the Oyster Bar, after all. Shouldn't she follow Judy's advice and take this chance, in this moment?

'Say it,' he urged, his voice low.

'That night in the Oyster Bar,' she began apprehensively. Even now, she wondered if she was going to ruin their blossoming new friendship by revealing her inappropriate feelings. But they were there, still burning inside her, and becoming impossible to ignore.

'Yes,' he prompted.

'I felt a spark then,' she replied. 'Between us. Did you?'

He nodded, looking her straight in the eye, and she realised she was holding her breath. 'Yes,' he said. 'I did.'

'Until I went and ruined everything, that is,' she blundered on, embarrassed. 'Sorry again about that, by the way.'

'Hey,' he said, spreading his palms wide. 'Water under the bridge now. In fact, if anything, I think it's quite funny that, after all that, neither of us made it there on time to meet the other. And I've got my beautiful Statue of Liberty ornament at last, haven't I? How can I possibly complain?' He looked down at the table for a moment as if gearing up for something. 'Anyway, I should apologise too. Because the message I left at the Oyster Bar was that I would find you again. That I'd been called back home and I was really sorry for not being there, but that I would find you.' His mouth twisted with regret. 'But for whatever reason, I didn't. So I went back on my word, is what I'm saying. We're as bad as each other. Does that mean we're quits?'

She nodded, feeling so much love for him she could hardly speak for a moment. 'We're quits,' she agreed and held out a hand, which he shook, their eyes meeting as their fingers briefly entwined. There it was again: that spark, impossible to ignore. This is it, she told herself. She had to tell him how she felt right now, because if she didn't, she'd always be wondering what might have happened. And she was so sick of wondering what might have happened, frankly. 'Seeing as we're putting everything out on the table today,' she said, taking a deep breath, 'the truth is, there was another reason why I never asked Ollie out for a drink. It's because – despite everything – it turns out I still have feelings for you, Ben. I'm in love with you.' There was a moment of awkward silence, save for the surely very loud thudding of her heart, and then she raised her fist, self-consciously. 'Damn you,' she joked.

A nerve-racking few seconds passed. 'In that case, damn you right back, because I feel exactly the same,' he told her quietly. 'I am wildly, ridiculously in love with you, too.'

They stared at one another, taking it in. 'Are you sure?' she asked, suspicious to the last. Because it couldn't be that straightforward, could it? After so many dead-ends and false starts between them, she still didn't know if she could trust that anything real and pure and shining could emerge from the rubble of all that had gone before. 'You *have* just split up with Kirsten, remember,' she felt compelled to point out. 'Please don't go and say anything you don't mean on the rebound.'

'I'm sure,' he said. 'I'm really sure. This is not a rebound reflex. I've tried to deny it and I've tried to block out those feelings, but I can't keep pretending they're not there. They are.' He scrubbed at his face, looking awkward, then went on, as if needing to convince her of his sincerity. 'Because even though we live in completely different parts of the country and have only ever spent a handful of days together in nineteen years, I find myself thinking about you all the time.' He gazed into her eyes with such earnestness, she felt a shiver run down her back. 'All the time, Lara. The way you make me laugh. Your beautiful, expressive face. The way you can't bear being bossed around by anyone, even a satnav or a coffee tin. Your bravery. Even your bolshiness. And I want to be with you. To get to know everything about you. To spend days and days and days together. If you want that too.'

Lara had the most enormous lump in her throat. She was acutely aware that so many decisions and reactions and turns had brought them to this precise moment, in this Edinburgh bar. And then she thought of all the other Laras existing in parallel universes to her – the Lara who hadn't been quite brave enough to go to New York for the internship, the Lara who might have been bereaved when her tiny daughter was knocked over by a car, the Lara who'd hit her head too hard in Cambridge and never fully recovered, the Lara who'd fallen in love with Ben all over again, only to lose him in a tragic fatal heart attack.

'I want that too,' she managed to squeak. Thank God she was *this* Lara, she thought, who was looking at Ben with astonishment and delight. Who was laughing a strange, tearful sort of laugh just as he was, who was rising from her chair in unison with him, the two of them throwing their arms around one another and holding on tight. Tighter. And somehow that single embrace seemed to contain everything: love and joy and passion, as well as a deep, deep certainty that this was right. That this was true and real.

'Don't get your flight,' she blurted out into the warm space of his neck, desperate for their togetherness not to end yet, nor any time soon. 'Why don't you stay tonight too? With me?'

'I thought you'd never ask,' he replied, his voice low in her ear, his hand reaching up into her hair. And then, in the next moment, they had found each other's lips and were standing there, kissing like a pair of lovestruck teenagers. Kissing all the breath from one another, as if nothing else mattered.

'Well,' she said, giddily, as they eventually drew apart. 'First kiss in New York, second one in Edinburgh – say what you like about us, but I think that's a pretty classy start, don't you?'

His eyes were soft and shiny; her heart fluttered just to look into them. 'That's definitely a high bar we've set ourselves,' he agreed. 'But I'm willing to put in the effort. Although I'm hoping our next kiss will be in Edinburgh, now that we're here. And the one after that too,' he said. They sat down again, holding hands as if neither of them could bear to be fully separated. 'And ... well, quite a lot more, actually. If that's okay with you?'

Lara couldn't stop smiling. 'Hmm, let me think about that ... *Yes*, a million times yes,' she replied. 'But right now – I don't want to be presumptuous so early on in our relationship – but what do you say about us getting out of this place, and heading over to my hotel?'

'I say that's the best idea you've had all day,' he replied.

And, as it turned out, he was right.

Epilogue
An Ending and a Beginning

Winter

It was late February in the Yorkshire Dales and snow lay across the hills in thick gleaming blankets. Michael Moffatt, area manager for White Rose Estate Agents, had his heated seat turned up to max as he drove back to the office in Skipton, still thinking about the couple he'd just shown around Wharfe Cottage. Aged thirty-eight, with twenty years' experience under his belt, and the winner of not one but two regional awards for sales success, Michael prided himself on sizing up customers at a glance and almost always being right. But the two he'd met that afternoon hadn't been like any other couple he'd come across before.

Downsizers, he'd assumed initially on meeting them outside the cottage. He'd heard them mention a daughter at university and wanting a place that wasn't too far from where she'd grown up, and guessed that they'd be selling an old family house that was too big for them these days. But no. Not that simple. They were a very unusual pair with, as it turned out, some extremely

369

unusual priorities. Most clients looking for a new house tended to focus their search on a certain area. Not these two – they'd apparently considered places in Northumberland, Newcastle, York and Chester, before checking out the Yorkshire Dales. They had driven past the cottage purely by chance, they said, and decided to call the office and ask to take a look. Michael had frowned to himself on hearing this, hoping that he wasn't dealing with a couple of time-wasters. You got them sometimes, especially at this time of year when people didn't seem to have anything better to do. 'Can I ask where you'll be working?' he inquired smoothly. 'In case we have other properties that might be of interest to you?'

They could work anywhere, they told him airily. She was currently a driving instructor in Scarborough but was passing her business on to some young man called Tyrone who'd recently qualified as an instructor, because she'd landed a freelance writing gig instead. He, meanwhile, was a graphic designer with a successful online business who'd been running a shop in Cambridge for years, but had just appointed a manager to take over the day-to-day care of it. (Michael had tried not to look too confused at all of this information. His geography wasn't brilliant, admittedly, but considering they had a daughter together, the two of them seemed to live an awfully long way apart.)

That wasn't all. They seemed to like the house very much – the garden was perfect for Bruce, apparently (another child? A guinea pig?) while the man was excited about the cycling possibilities the Dales offered him. There was a room that Eliza could have (the daughter, Michael guessed) as well as a generous-sized spare bedroom that would be great for – well, Michael couldn't remember all the names now, but there seemed to be a lot of people that Lara and Ben anticipated would be visiting them. Frances and Harry, Heidi and Jim, Gwen, Charlotte, Annie, Sophie ... He'd tuned out after a while to be honest, because other people's social lives were not that interesting. Whatever – you're popular, we get it, there was no need to go on about it.

After looking the cottage over, Michael had a strong sense that the two of them were pretty keen on the property, neither of them bothering with the poker faces that buyers usually tried to assume. 'This could be such an adventure for us,' the woman said once they were back in the living room, running a hand along the thick oak mantelpiece.

'We could build a workshop, get a dog, keep some chickens,' the man agreed enthusiastically. 'It's got potential, right? Anything could happen.'

The funny thing, Michael later told his colleagues back at the office, was that he almost forgot to give them the full tour of the grounds at all. In his experience, buyers were generally more bothered about the houses than the area surrounding them, and preferred to knock on walls with a knowledgeable air and go around quibbling about curtains and light fittings than anything beyond the exterior of the property. And yet, as soon as he said the words, 'Oh, yes, and the last thing to show you is the orchard,' these two had swung round to stare at him, open-mouthed, and then looked at each other, their faces suddenly radiant. 'You'd think I'd just told them there was a swimming pool and gym out there, rather than a few rows of craggy old apple trees,' he chuckled as he recounted the moment later on at his desk. But no – they were laughing and hugging each other and saying, 'It's a sign! This is it!' and stuff like that, all because of an orchard at the bottom of the garden.

Some people, honestly. There's nowt so queer as folk,

Michael's mother was fond of saying – and she was right, because frankly, what were these two on? Although even to a jaded cynic like Michael, it was clear that the pair of them seemed really happy about something.

It takes all sorts, he'd told himself, shaking his head in bemusement as he'd followed them out there into the pale winter sunshine. And, looking on the bright side, he had a feeling that he was going to make a good sale today, at least – which would make *him* pretty happy too. Funny how things worked out that way sometimes, wasn't it? As if everything was falling perfectly into place - exactly as it was meant to be.

Acknowledgements

I've always loved writing (and reading!) stories about characters who take a chance and make a new start ... and having written *Anything Could Happen*, I decided to take a leaf out of my own book. Moving to a new publisher felt simultaneously exciting and nerve-racking – but I could not be happier to have joined the mighty Quercus Books, and have been thrilled by their enthusiasm and creativity from the very first moment. Many thanks are due to Cassie Browne, my wonderful new editor, who has worked tirelessly on this novel through draft after draft (after draft!) Cassie, I so appreciate the care and attention you have given to each and every line, your many smart, insightful suggestions for improvement and your overall championing of this book – here's to many more together, I hope. Thanks also to Kat Burdon and Sharona Selby for fantastic editorial support and the best copy-edit any of my books has ever had – I'm so grateful. Thanks to Milly Reid and Bethan Ferguson whose publicity and marketing ideas wowed me from the get-go, and to the rest of the team too – Jon Butler, Dave Murphy, Izzy Smith, Micaela Alcaino, Abbi-Jean Reid, Amy Knight and Frances Doyle. It's a huge pleasure to get to know and work with so many talented people.

Rewinding further back in time ... I owe the most enormous

thank you to my agent, Lizzy Kremer, who helped greatly with early drafts of this book with many, many phone calls and notes, before going on to steer me brilliantly through the process of finding a new publisher. Lizzy, you played an absolute blinder, as ever – thanks a million for your advice, good humour and ambition for me. Thanks also to the wider team of superstars at David Higham – Maddalena Cavaciuti, Kaynat Begum, Margaux Vialleron, Alice Howe, Emma Jamison, Sam Norman, Lucy Talbot, Imogen Bovill and Johanna Clarke for your hard work, and for getting my books out there around the world. You're all fantastic at what you do.

Thanks to my friends and family who, as ever, put up with my mid-draft wails of 'I can't do this', 'I'm not sure I can finish this one' and 'Maybe I should get a proper job instead now?' with their usual mixture of patience and kindness (with only occasional bouts of eye-rolling or sarcasm). Special love and lurid cocktails to Kate Tilley and Hayley Bangs – how about making our next trip one to New York?! Big kisses to the Swans and other author friends for solidarity, gossip and the best lunches. Thank you to Chief Inspector Jason Kew for policing advice! (It goes without saying that any mistakes are my own.)

Thanks so much to all my readers for making me laugh, cheering me on and for the many kind messages you've sent me over the years. I'm so happy to have your support and appreciate it more than you'll ever know. If this is the first time you've picked up one of my books – thank you! I really hope you enjoyed it.

Finally, last but never least, all the love in the world to Martin, Hannah, Tom and Holly. I'm so lucky to have you in my life. Thank you.

Discover more from *Sunday Times* bestselling author

Lucy Diamond

Visit www.lucydiamond.co.uk for:

About Lucy

★

FAQs for Aspiring Writers

★

And to contact Lucy

To sign up to Lucy's newsletter
scan the QR code here:

Follow Lucy on social media:

@LDiamondAuthor

@LucyDiamondAuthor

@lucydiamondwrites